The Girl at the Gate

To Colleen —

God bless!

Rita [illegible]

2022

OTHER BOOKS AND AUDIOBOOKS

BY ANITA STANSFIELD

First Love and Forever
First Love, Second Chances
When Forever Comes
For Love Alone
The Three Gifts of Christmas
Towers of Brierley
Where the Heart Leads
When Hearts Meet
Someone to Hold
Reflections: A Collection of Personal Essays
Gables of Legacy, Six Volumes
A Timeless Waltz
A Time to Dance
Dancing in the Light
A Dance to Remember
The Barrington Family Saga, Four Volumes
Emma: Woman of Faith
The Jayson Wolfe Story, Five Volumes
The Dickens Inn Series, Five Volumes
Shadows of Brierley Series, Four Volumes
Passage on the Titanic
The Wishing Garden
The Garden Path
Legally and Lawfully Yours
Now and Always Yours
Heir of Brownlie Manor
The Color of Love
Lily of the Manor
Love and Loss at Whitmore Manor
The Stars above Northumberland
The Heart of Thornewell
The Lady of Astoria Abbey
The Empty Manger
The House of Stone and Ivy
The Emerald Heart of Courtenay
The Angel of Grey Garden
Home to Sommersby
The Heiress of All Things Beautiful
The Heart of Hampton House
The Dowry of Lady Eliza
Secrets of Stonebridge
Magic of Starlight
The Girl at the Gate

a
regency
romance

The Girl at the Gate

ANITA
STANSFIELD

Covenant Communications, Inc.

Cover image: *Woman with Umbrella and Ornate Gate* © Mark Owen, Arcangel

Published by Covenant Communications, Inc.
American Fork, Utah

Printed in Mexico.
First Printing: January 2022

30 29 28 27 26 25 24 23 22   10 9 8 7 6 5 4 3 2 1

ISBN 978-1-52442-066-6

Prologue

London, England—1794

Theodore Weatherby hurried from the north wing of his enormous home to the south wing where his parents' rooms were located. With each step, he mentally reviewed his determination to get their permission—and the necessary money—to travel to Liverpool with his three closest friends, who also came from families who were wealthy enough that such a venture would cause no financial strain whatsoever. A few days earlier, the four of them had made plans to ease their boredom by visiting an uncle of one of the young men—a man who would be happy to let them stay in his luxurious home but would care nothing about the hours they kept or the activities in which they engaged. Theo knew that his friends were also seeking permission and funding from *their* parents this evening, and they all hoped to be able to pursue this adventure with their parents' full support. But Theo knew well enough that whether his parents approved would have a great deal to do with whatever mood might be upon them. He doubted his mother would care one way or the other, and even if she did, she could never convince her husband to heed her opinion; he was far too stubborn and arrogant to have his thinking influenced by a woman. It was highly unlikely that he would find both of his parents in the same room at the same time; he knew that well enough—even though their rooms were all located in the same vicinity. Theo's hope was to get his father's permission and then simply inform his mother of his intentions.

There had been times when Theo's father had wholeheartedly supported him in traveling with one or more of his friends, knowing they would be accompanied by servants who would diligently keep an eye on them. But there had been other times when his father had adamantly told Theo he could *not* go gallivanting about so frivolously, as if the very request had been, in and of itself, a crime. Theo had no idea what manner of mood he might find his father in, but he was determined to remind him that he was no longer a child and was certainly old enough to make his own decisions. At the age of fifteen, Theo was now slightly taller than his father and needing to shave his face every day; he was regularly mistaken by others as being much older than his years. Since he considered himself far wiser and more intelligent than the average young man—and even most of the adults he knew—he had complete confidence in his ability to manage the decisions about his life on his own. The only problem was that the amount of money he was allotted monthly for his personal recreation was not enough to cover such a large scheme as traveling to Liverpool and indulging in the social opportunities available there.

By the time Theo turned down the hallway where his parents' rooms were located, he felt confident and excited, convincing himself that a positive attitude would sway his father's opinion in Theo's favor, no matter what kind of mood he might be in. But Theo stopped abruptly, and his heart sank to the bottom of his stomach when he heard raised voices arguing in tones so cruel and demeaning that he felt a harsh shudder move through his entire body.

Theo sighed and leaned his back against the wall not far from the door of his father's bedroom. He knew his parents slept in separate rooms, which wasn't at all unusual. However, he also knew that it was not particularly unusual that every time he'd found both in the same bedroom or sitting room, they were arguing. The fact that they were arguing *now* made it clear that this was not a good time to approach either one of them about his plans and his subsequent need for his father's financial contribution to those plans. He knew he should just walk away and allow the argument to continue; he'd learned many years earlier that even begging his parents to be kind to each other was a fruitless endeavor. It was best for him to just keep his distance—especially since listening to them talk to each other like that always upset him deeply. He'd been trying for years to stop caring about the continual, ugly discord between his parents, but it still disturbed him so thoroughly that he already knew he would have difficulty sleeping tonight simply because of what he'd already overheard, and he wasn't even close enough to clearly understand all they were saying.

When certain accusing words floated clearly to Theo's ears, his discomfort immediately exploded into anger, and without a moment's thought or hesitation he burst into the room without so much as knocking to warn his parents of his approach. For only a second, it occurred to him that one or both of them might not have been properly dressed for their son's intrusion, but he was relieved to see that his mother was wearing one of her many elaborate dressing gowns over a nightgown, which was her typical mode of dress all day every day—because she never left this part of the house. Her face appeared tight and sour, and her brown hair was hanging wild around her shoulders. Theo knew immediately that her bad mood was likely a result of the heated argument taking place between his parents.

Theo's father looked younger than his years. David Weatherby was tall and well built, with sleek dark hair that he kept styled meticulously; a hair out of place would be an affront to David's vanity. But Theo knew that David's strong desire to socialize with the most elite people in London was his greatest motivator in always wearing the finest clothing to be had; it was important for him to maintain an appearance and personality that would make him appealing company. Clearly, Theo's parents were highly incompatible in this regard, but he couldn't understand why that would be sufficient cause for such volatile wrangling. And it made him angry.

"Knocking would be appropriate, son," David said, clearly not pleased by Theo's interruption.

Theo ignored his father's reprimand, considering that his intrusion was warranted, given the situation. His eyes went to the partially packed luggage on his father's bed, and the reason for the argument became clear. He'd intended to just tell them to stop yelling with the hope of calming them both down to some degree, but his thoughts now went in an entirely different direction.

"You're leaving . . . again?" Theo asked his father, looking at him eye-to-eye, given their similar height.

"I have business in France," David stated without apology. "It's not your place to question what I'm doing or why."

"Must there always be such terrible shouting over every little thing?" Theo countered, reverting to his original intentions for barging in.

"He's going off with that Richard Peyton again," Dorothea said to Theo, as if he might understand what that meant or be able to do something about it. Theo had heard the name spoken several times in the context of being his father's new friend, but until now Theo had never had any reason to believe that this Richard Peyton was any cause for concern.

When Theo just stared at his mother in confusion, she turned again toward her husband and lifted a harsh finger. "He's a terrible influence on you, David; I know he is! He sought you out because of your wealth, and he's taking sore advantage of you! You know it, and I know it! I'm begging you not to go.

Whatever it is the two of you are up to this time, I fear it will be your undoing. And what will become of us if you end up in prison?"

Prison? Theo wanted to shout but kept silent. Were his mother's concerns warranted? Or was she exaggerating? The only thing Theo could judge for certain was that his father looked discreetly guilty, which let Theo know that there was at least some degree of merit to his mother's concerns. And if that was the case, Theo felt a tiny glimpse of a different perspective regarding his parents. If his father were involved in unlawful activities, then perhaps that could be the source of his mother's cynicism and depression. He felt a moment of compassion for her, but his thoughts quickly went back to the more pressing matter at hand. His father was leaving, and his mother was concerned for reasons that frightened Theo.

David sighed and looked at his wife as if she'd completely lost her mind; Theo knew that look well. David's gaze alone could silence anyone attempting to convince him that he was wrong. "I assure you that we are simply going to take care of some business in France. It's nothing. I'll be back before you know it."

"Which often turns into weeks," Dorothea said, echoing Theo's own thoughts, "or even months."

"And I have no control over how long it will take," David said. He then turned to Theo and said, "Is there something you want, son? Or did you just feel the need to intrude upon our conversation?"

Theo wanted to say that calling their confrontation a conversation was like calling a blizzard a light snow flurry. He knew he couldn't bring up his original reason for coming here—not now. And the thought made him angry. These problems between his parents had ruined his own plans more times than he could count.

Attempting to explain but also avoid what would only add fuel to the present disaster, Theo simply said, "I wanted to ask you something, but it can wait."

"We'll talk when I return, then," David said with a measure of civility. "You mind yourself while I'm away; you're the man of the house while I'm gone."

Theo nodded, thinking snidely that he could hardly be the man of the house when he had no power over anyone or anything—and he certainly didn't have enough money to follow through on the plans that had him feeling excited about something for the first time in months.

"Run along and let your mother and I finish our conversation," David added, and again Theo wanted to correct the definition of the word *conversation*.

But Theo just hurried out of the room, closing the door behind him, then running back to his own rooms, wanting to put as much distance as possible between himself and the ugliness that existed between his parents.

A few days after David Weatherby had left for France, Theo was deeply dismayed over the knowledge that his friends all had their parents' permission and had been given plenty of money for their excursion to Liverpool, and they intended to leave two days later. The more Theo thought about not being able to go with them, the angrier he became—until he finally arrived at a decision that left him feeling quite pleased with himself. And he felt certain that his parents with their extremely poor parenting skills likely deserved such behavior from their son. He felt completely entitled to take some money from his father's safe—since he knew where David kept the combination written down. He left a note for his mother, admitting to his theft and explaining his plans—but not so specific that he could be found and brought home—and reassured her that he would be safe and would return in two weeks' time.

The following morning, he was off with his friends before the sun had even come up, proud of himself for having accomplished such a ploy, and thrilled with the adventure that lay before him. And he simply didn't care what his parents might think or how they might feel. He couldn't recall much evidence that either of them had ever cared much about his own thoughts and feelings. He reasoned that he might or might not apologize when he got home, and if he had consequences to face, he would face them; it would be worth it. For now, he put thoughts of his home and parents away, determined to enjoy every moment of getting away from London and enjoying new experiences he desperately craved.

Theo's time in Liverpool was everything he had hoped for and more, even though he felt certain that he and his friends had participated in activities his parents would never have approved of; nothing too scandalous or inappropriate, but things they would surely consider less than desirable for a boy of fifteen. He sneaked into the house upon his return, knowing that supper was over, and his parents would likely be in their separate sitting rooms—unless his father hadn't yet returned from France. He hoped that would be the case, certain his mother would be less angry with him; or perhaps it was more accurate to say that her anger would be easier to ignore. Or perhaps she wouldn't even care; that had certainly been the case more times than he could count.

Regardless of what her possible response might be, Theo was aware that there were servants who knew he had come home, and he had to see his mother before word came to her ears of his return before he had a chance to tell her himself.

Theo approached the door to his mother's sitting room and found it open, but he could hear a man's voice that he didn't recognize speaking from inside. As Theo stepped into the frame of the door, he could see that his mother's countenance was more grave and stonelike than he'd ever imagined possible. His younger sister Lilith was sitting near their mother, her expression much the same. He shared the same dark hair as his sister, but beyond that they bore little resemblance to each other—a fact that was enhanced by her fragile health and extreme shyness, which made her hesitant to associate with people who were not a part of the family. When Theo realized there were other people in the room, he wondered why Lilith would not have left. It wasn't that Lilith had any aversion to the butler, the housekeeper, or their aunt, but he couldn't recall ever having seen her remain in any room when there were more than one or two other people present. And Theo's heart sank like a rock when he saw that the man speaking was his father's solicitor—who spoke directly toward Dorothea but in a way that implied he wanted everyone to hear what he had to say. It was evident Theo had missed important news, and he wished that he'd arrived just a few minutes earlier.

"Mr. Peyton and his wife were also lost," the solicitor said. "They left behind a young daughter—a child—who is with her grandparents."

"I see," Dorothea said without changing her expression.

"Lost?" Theo echoed, turning everyone's attention toward him. A quick glance revealed that all eyes were pinned on him, and he felt equally conspicuous and fearful. "What do you mean?"

"Theodore," the solicitor said as he stood to face him. Theo's mother and sister didn't move or change their expressions. His aunt's face showed a glimmer of compassion; the housekeeper and butler looked at the floor. "We were all hoping you would return soon."

"What's happened?" Theo asked, trying not to betray the panic he felt.

"The ship on which your father was sailing across the channel met with some terrible weather," this man said, and Theo wished he could remember the solicitor's name. "It sank, and there were no survivors." Theo sucked in a sharp breath and couldn't let it out as the explanation continued. "We had believed your father sailed several days earlier than this ship's departure, so it took time to gather the correct information, but now we know he was on this particular ship."

Theo dropped into the nearest empty chair and tried to catch his breath as a thousand memories and heaps of regret assaulted him all at once. And yet all he could feel was anger. He didn't understand why, and he didn't know what to do about it, but he'd never felt so angry in his life. Angry with his mother for being so difficult, his father for getting involved in dubious business matters that necessitated such travel, and this Mr. Peyton for dragging his father into whatever this particular endeavor might have been. And Theo felt angry with himself, recalling that his last encounter with his father had been filled with contention. Now David Weatherby was dead and gone, and Theo instinctively wanted someone or something to blame. He couldn't be angry with the happenstance of foul weather, so his mind went immediately to Richard Peyton—this supposed friend of his father's—who had lured him into this endeavor that had taken him away from home. What had his mother said prior to David leaving? *He's a terrible influence on you, David; I know he is! He sought you out because of your wealth, and he's taking sore advantage of you!* Despite knowing that this Mr. Peyton had also perished along with his father, Theo knew he could never forgive this man for taking David Weatherby away from them. For all his father's imperfections, Theo loved him—and now he was gone. Life as he knew it had fallen out from under him, and he wondered if he would ever recover.

Chapter One
HIDDEN LETTERS

1808

Vivian Peyton reluctantly hung the *Closed* sign in the window of her grandfather's cobbler's shop and let out a weighted sigh as she surveyed the rain drizzling incessantly down the windows. The sky had hung dark and heavy all day, and even the night sky felt far darker than usual; the rain hadn't ceased for even a minute since the previous evening. Vivian wanted to blame the lack of business on the rain—which could be partly true—but she knew the full truth had far more to do with the fact that one of the best cobblers in the area had become too ill to do the fine work he'd once done; hence, people were taking their business elsewhere. Vivian was proficient at running the shop, keeping track of the books, ordering supplies, and handling customers. But she regretted not having had her grandfather teach her the actual skills of the trade while he'd been younger and healthy enough to do so. Now, the rain and the darkness perfectly empathized with her mood as she locked the outside door before she doused the lamps and took hold of the knob on the door that divided the shop from the small living quarters she shared with the man who had helped raise her.

Hesitant to leave the shop, as if there might be some miraculous possibility of one last customer in desperate need of new shoes—or even to have old ones repaired—Vivian waited a few long moments before turning the doorknob so that she could leave the shop behind for the night with the hope that tomorrow would bring an excessive number of new shoppers. Vivian locked the door behind her and turned her attention to her grandfather, Samuel Peyton, who was dozing as usual in the worn, overstuffed chair located especially close to the fireplace, since he was always cold. Samuel had a blanket around his shoulders and another over his lap, exactly as Vivian had left him when she'd last checked on him an hour or so earlier. The cup in which she'd given him some hot tea sat empty on the little table beside him, next to the book he'd been reading, along with the spectacles he needed in order to read. For a long moment Vivian just watched her grandfather sleep, trying to imagine how vibrant and productive he'd been before this mysterious illness had overtaken him. His hairline had continually receded as he'd aged, but the silver hair that grew back from it was thick and soft; she knew this well from the many times she'd helped wash and comb his hair. He was handsome for a man of his age, and she often admired his youthful countenance, which had only diminished slightly with his growing weariness.

Vivian allowed herself another long moment to wonder and worry, even though she knew he wouldn't want her doing either. But she worried almost constantly about the reasons for his declining health and the financial impact it was having on their lives. Not wanting to burden him with such things, Vivian pushed away every negative thought and looked forward to a nice, quiet evening.

Vivian stoked up the fire to raise the temperature in the room, which roused Samuel from his little nap. She'd learned long ago that it was impossible to do such a task without making some noise, but then her grandfather had warned her a great many times not to ever return from the shop or anywhere else without waking him since he never wanted to miss any opportunity to see her.

"Ah," Samuel said, lifting his head slowly, "there's my one true joy."

It's what he often called Vivian, but she never grew tired of hearing such tender words from the person she loved more than any other in the world. Despite the isolated life they lived—relying almost wholly on each other for companionship—Vivian felt deeply blessed to have been raised by such a kind and tender man, and to know that his ongoing love and affection for her was genuine and everlasting.

"And there is *mine*," Vivian said, pressing a kiss to his balding forehead after she'd set down the fire poker and brushed her hands on her apron. "Is there anything I can get for you before I set to work on supper?"

"No, but thank you, precious." Samuel sighed. "I wish I had the strength to help you with supper. I'm no good to anyone anymore."

"I'll not have you saying such things," Vivian said, squatting down beside her grandfather. "Your love sustains me, Grandpapa. What purpose would I have without you in my life? I must feed myself anyway, now, mustn't I? It's no more work to cook for two than it is for one. Besides, there's plenty of soup left from last night's supper and it has kept plenty cold in this weather. I'll just heat it up, and there are some leftover scones as well that I can warm in the skillet." She kissed his brow again and stood up, putting her hands on her hips. "It'll not take long, then we can sit here by the fire and you might show your appreciation for your supper by telling me more stories of your early years. You know how I love them."

"I'll have to consider that a fair trade," Samuel said, smiling up at her, "since there's naught else I can do to help."

While Vivian built a fire in the kitchen stove so she could heat the food, she felt especially annoyed by a perpetual dripping from the ceiling into a pot she'd placed strategically on the floor to catch the water. The pot had been there for months now, since they never knew when it might rain, and the drip was inevitable. On days when the rain was heavy, Vivian was accustomed to emptying the pot regularly, and on rainy nights she always left towels all around the pot in case it overflowed, hoping it would be sufficient to keep her from having to contend with excessive amounts of water running over the kitchen floor.

With the fire gaining momentum, Vivian washed her hands and pressed a straying lock of nearly black hair back from her eyes with her forearm before she dried her hands on her apron by pressing them down over her well-rounded hips. Putting the soup and scones on the stove to heat, Vivian wished there were some way to force the same old circle of thoughts from going round and round in her mind. Her grandfather's declining health had been declared a mystery by the doctor, beyond the explanation that he was simply getting older and needed to stop working so hard and get more rest. And yet the more he rested, the weaker and more feeble he became. Samuel had always been frugal and had set aside money for times such as this, but Vivian knew well enough that with the months he'd been unable to do more than the most minimal work, their reserves were almost gone. She'd been careful with the money in every possible way—which had made it last much longer than it might have—but now the rent on their little shop and home combined was almost due without enough money to pay it. And Vivian knew well enough that their landlord was neither patient nor forgiving when it came to his monthly collections.

Vivian knew she needed to speak with her grandfather about the reality of the situation that was closing in on them, but she kept putting it off day after day, not wanting to worry him or have him feel guilty for his health challenges over which he had no control. While she stirred the soup and flipped the scones over in the skillet to heat both sides, Vivian convinced herself that this difficult conversation could wait another day. Tonight, she just wanted to enjoy a simple meal by the fire with her grandfather and hear him tell her the stories of his life. He was truly a grand storyteller and could make the simplest tales sound magical and exciting—not because he exaggerated or embellished the truth, but simply because he had a talent for making the ordinary seem grand; his ability to recall intricate details always made Vivian feel as if she were right there in the past with him, experiencing all the sights and sounds and smells of his life's adventures.

Of course, Samuel's greatest adventure was the way he'd met and fallen in love with Vivian's grandmother Edna, and how he'd wooed and courted her amidst many challenges in both their lives. But love had triumphed, and they'd finally married and lived happily together for nearly forty years until her death from a sudden illness. Vivian remembered her grandmother well, since she had been the mother figure in Vivian's life following the strange and unexpected accident that had taken the lives of both Vivian's parents. Samuel and Edna had been devastated when they'd lost their only son, and they'd grown to love Vivian's mother like their own daughter. But over the years they had told Vivian hundreds of times that she was a rare and precious gift that God had given to them as a source of continual joy and beauty that had helped compensate for the terrible loss they'd experienced. Vivian barely remembered her parents, and there were times when she couldn't be certain if what she saw in her mind were real memories, or simply images her brain had created from the stories she'd been told about her mother and father. She knew very little about them except that her father had also worked as a cobbler, having learned the trade from *his* father; and even after her parents had married, they had all lived together in the tiny house behind the cobbler's shop.

As always, Samuel was excessively grateful for Vivian's efforts in providing him with a tasty and satisfying meal. But Vivian noticed as he ate carefully from the little table she had placed in front of him where his food had been laid, that it was taking more and more deliberate effort for him to eat, which made it difficult for him to share any of his stories with her while they shared a meal. Once they were finished eating and Vivian had cleaned up the kitchen for the night—and again emptied the pot of water that caught the rain dripping through the ceiling—she stoked up the fire again in the tiny parlor where her grandfather was still sitting before she sat down herself and encouraged him to tell her a story. Vivian doubted there was anything he could tell her that she hadn't heard many times before, but she loved watching his eyes brighten as he spoke of the good life he'd lived. Despite the many challenges and losses in his life, he'd always maintained a positive attitude and frequently expressed his gratitude to God for all the countless ways he'd been blessed. But tonight, Samuel just seemed especially tired, or perhaps sad—likely a combination of both. Vivian knew him well enough to know that he didn't want to complain, but perhaps he couldn't think of anything to say that didn't *sound* like complaining when he felt so miserable and subsequently frustrated with his inability to be productive.

Attempting to get Samuel to talk about something—anything—that might distract him from his misery—and in turn distract Vivian from her own worries—she pleaded lightly, "Come now, Grandpapa. Surely there's something you could tell me that I can think about while I'm falling asleep."

"I'm afraid my old brain is feeling very tired, my dear," he said. "Perhaps you could get the box out from the bottom of my wardrobe; maybe that might spark some memories."

Vivian knew well enough the box he was talking about and quickly said, "You've told me a thousand times never to peek in that box; you told me it held secrets from your past that were yours and yours alone." She thought of what else he'd said, and reminded him as if he might have forgotten, "You said that even Grandmama didn't know what was in that box!"

Samuel chuckled. "I was teasing on that count. Your grandmother knew everything about my life before I met her, and she knew about everything in that box. But I suppose I believe there are some things that happened in my life that a child might not understand." He reached his hand toward hers and she took it, squeezing gently. "But you're not a child anymore; almost twenty years old, now. And I might soon be dead, and you'd be rummaging through my belongings anyway."

"Don't say such things!" she said and shuddered; she couldn't bear even the idea of losing him.

Samuel chuckled as if he'd truly just been teasing; Vivian hoped and prayed he wasn't having any premonitions about his impending death.

"Go and get that box," Samuel said. "Let's have a look inside, shall we?"

"If you're sure," Vivian said, and Samuel nodded with a sparkle in his eye and a hint of a smile that implied he was pleased with the idea of finally sharing its contents with her.

Vivian went into one of the two small bedrooms of their living quarters and opened the doors of her grandfather's wardrobe. She paused a long moment to lovingly stroke her grandmother's clothes hanging there which hadn't been bothered since she'd passed away more than six years earlier. After indulging in fond memories of Edna for more than a minute, Vivian knelt and immediately saw the simple wooden box she'd often looked at curiously; but upon her grandfather's strict instructions, she had never so much as lifted the latch that kept the lid tightly closed.

Vivian slid the box out, blew the dust off the top, and took it with her back to the parlor, setting it on her grandfather's lap before she added a little more wood to the fire and sat back down. She was surprised when he handed the box to her, saying with a hint of mischief in his voice, "Why don't you have a look. Perhaps something of interest will catch your eye."

"Very well," Vivian said and unfastened the latch, which took some effort; it obviously hadn't been opened in an exceptionally long time. She then lifted the lid, aware that her heart was pounding. Considering all the delight she'd gotten over the years from her grandfather's stories, she wondered what clues he might have hidden away, like treasure maps leading to stories she'd not yet heard.

Vivian didn't know what she'd expected to see—perhaps a variety of little keepsakes and trinkets—but she was certainly surprised to see nothing but a stack of letters with a tattered and frayed ribbon tied around them to hold them altogether.

"They're from my first love," Samuel said before Vivian fully perceived what she was looking at. "And yes, your grandmother read them all; she knew all about Estelle—Esty I called her. She also knew that the love Esty and I shared never would have been permitted to blossom, and we were both grateful that things worked out the way they did. I loved your grandmother more than I could ever adequately express, Vivian." He took her hand and squeezed. "So don't you be wondering about that." His eyes took on a distant look, and a faint smile touched his lips. "Still," his voice was heavy with nostalgia, "Estelle was indeed my first love, and I *did* love her—and she loved me. It just wasn't meant to be."

"I never knew," Vivian said.

"Because we never told you," Samuel said, sounding more alert than he had in quite some time. "There was no reason for you to know; as I said, there are some things that are difficult for a child to understand. But now you're old enough to know that some people have more than one love in their lifetime, and Estelle certainly left a deep impression on me; she made me a better man—that's for certain."

"How did you meet her?" Vivian asked.

Samuel chuckled in a way Vivian hadn't heard in a long while, which made her laugh with delight. "I was a cobbler—like my father before me and my son after me—and Estelle had the finest and most varied collection of shoes in the city." He chuckled again as if he found the statement—or perhaps the truth of it—hilarious. Vivian considered the possible underlying message of such a statement and the clue it might offer regarding the situation. If Estelle was a woman who could own many fine and varied pairs of shoes, then she would have been wealthy, and of course it was practically unheard of for a wealthy young woman to marry a poor cobbler. Was that the reason her grandfather and Estelle had not ended up together?

Vivian forced her mind to stop speculating and turned her attention back to her grandfather to hear what he had to say. Samuel's eyes revealed that his mind had drifted back a great many years as he sighed and hesitated to speak so long that Vivian felt hard-pressed to not intrude upon his memories with her impatience to hear about them. He finally said, "She came into the shop with her mother; they were looking for a very particular type of shoes—something that would perfectly match a gown they had just ordered for some grand social event or another. She certainly attended a great many such events."

Vivian took this in as added evidence to her theory, but she remained eagerly silent, waiting for her grandfather to continue.

"It was raining rather heavily that day," Samuel said, "and I'll never forget the sound of the rain growing louder as they opened the door, combined with their giggling as they hurried inside and had some trouble maneuvering their umbrellas. They behaved more like sisters than mother and daughter; their close relationship was immediately apparent. But the moment I saw Estelle I felt something change inside of me; I could never put it into words. To this day I still cannot find words to describe how I felt when I saw her; perhaps the way she looked at me had something to do with it, since it seemed she had been immediately afflicted with the same problem when she saw *me*. She told me as much later."

"So, the two of you fell in love the moment you laid eyes on each other," Vivian said, hearing a lilt in her own voice that reminded her of a much younger version of herself, caught up in the telling of a fairy tale.

Samuel chuckled softly. "I don't know that what we felt that first day could be called love; we didn't know each other well enough to be in love—but we certainly felt intrigued with one another. And I'm certain Estelle's mother noticed; how could she not when we were both tripping over our words and making fools of ourselves simply trying to exchange simple conversation? But Mrs. Weatherby was discreet and polite and pretended not to notice, I think." Samuel sighed. "So, I helped Estelle choose the materials for the new pair of shoes she wanted, and we looked at the drawings of designs for a ridiculously long time. I think she saw the style she wanted right away but was purposely trying to lengthen her time in the shop. Her mother finally hurried her along, and the shop felt more dismal once Estelle had left. But I looked forward to her return when she would pick up her order; she needed to come personally, of course, so she could try them on and make certain the fit was perfect. I'll never forget the simple delight I felt when I measured her feet, and my anticipation of helping her try the shoes on once they were completed."

Samuel sighed again and leaned his head back on the chair, closing his eyes in a way that indicated he was getting tired. "My father still ran the shop back then, but I'd reached a point in my training where I had mastered my craft; I occasionally sought his guidance, but I knew I could create the perfect shoes for Estelle. I thought of her every moment I was making them, anticipating her return with such excitement that it seemed I had a swarm of butterflies in my stomach every waking moment for days. When she finally came back, she was even more beautiful than I'd remembered, and by the way she looked at me I knew she'd been thinking of me as much as I'd been thinking of her. Mrs. Weatherby was a kind woman and very polite—not snobbish toward me as many people of her class would be toward a simple cobbler. I learned later that she was a woman who believed that people should marry for love, but her husband—Estelle's father—had quite different views. The man held no title of any kind; he'd simply inherited a great deal of wealth and they were a part of very prestigious social circles here in town."

Samuel's expression grew sad—or perhaps extremely weary—or both. "I'm very tired all of a sudden," he said, much to Vivian's disappointment. "We'll have to finish this story tomorrow."

"But . . ." Vivian struggled to come up with the words that might convince her grandfather to keep talking, "you must at least tell me if she liked the shoes you made."

"Oh, she did!" Samuel said with a seeming final burst of enthusiasm. "The fit was perfect, and she told me they were as comfortable as they were beautiful, and they were exactly what she'd wanted." He moved to the edge of his seat with an indication that he intended to stand, which was always a slow and difficult process. "I suppose that's why she kept coming back to our shop every time she wanted a new pair of shoes—and that was a rather frequent occurrence, I'm glad to say."

Samuel stood carefully, saying, "I'll tell you more tomorrow, my dear."

"Are you all right?" Vivian asked, standing as well but not getting too close; she had become fully aware that he preferred to do all that he possibly could on his own, and despite having become very weak he was still capable of walking the distance from his chair in the parlor to his bedroom, and he was able to see to his own personal needs. The house was small enough that Vivian knew she could hear him call if he needed help, and she'd assured him far too many times that she was capable and willing to do anything for him that he might need; there was no need for embarrassment between them when it came to the practical matters of life. He'd assured her just as many times that he wasn't at all ashamed or embarrassed to ask for her help if he needed it, but he wanted to care for himself for as long as it was possible. And Vivian couldn't blame him; still, she worried about him. And once he'd gone into his room and closed the door, her mind was snapped away from the romantic tale he'd been telling her and she began to worry about a great many things, none of which she could do anything about.

Vivian had trouble sleeping that night, which had become a common problem of late. But instead of allowing herself to stew and fret over problems she couldn't solve, she indulged in imagining the love story between her grandfather and Estelle Weatherby that had taken place before he'd met and married Vivian's grandmother. Vivian was glad to know that Edna had known all about Estelle; she didn't believe that such secrets should be kept between a husband and wife. If Edna were still alive, Vivian wondered if her grandfather would speak so openly to Vivian about his first love, but since Edna had been gone from their lives for some years now, it didn't feel as awkward or strange to Vivian to think about her grandfather and Estelle as it might have seemed otherwise.

While Vivian believed she could likely guess the gist of the remainder of the story between Samuel and Estelle, she longed to hear the details from her grandfather's own version of his memories. Vivian felt sorely tempted to read the letters he had left in the parlor, but she would never do so without her grandfather's permission. They were personal, to be sure, and none of Vivian's business. Still, she longed to know every detail of how love had blossomed between a simple cobbler and a wealthy young woman who loved fine shoes. But of course, this story didn't have a happy ending. The happy ending had been between Samuel and Edna who had shared more than forty years of their lives together. And even though Edna was gone now, they had parted with a deep and abiding love between them, and they had given Vivian a good life. And while she hoped and prayed that her grandfather lived a good many more years, Vivian believed that when the time came for him to leave this world, Edna would be waiting for him and they would be together again in a place far better than this world. *That* was a happy ending in Vivian's opinion. The happiest. Still, she couldn't stop thinking about Estelle and wondering about the rest of the story she shared with Samuel Peyton.

Vivian was glad to awaken and realize that she had finally been able to sleep; given the busy day she had before her, she certainly needed her rest. It didn't take much effort to watch over the store when customers were few if any; nevertheless, she had to remain alert during the regular hours of business and always be listening for the bell over the shop door to ring. And of course, she had to prepare meals for herself and her grandfather, keep the house tidy, and today it would be necessary to launder some clothes and linens. Thankfully, the rain had stopped, and the sun was out, which meant she could hang the laundry on the ropes stretched across the tiny yard behind the house, instead of hanging them on twine which she often had to string across the parlor and kitchen to dry their wet clothing.

Vivian hurried to freshen up and get ready for her day, wishing her overly curly hair was more easily managed with the pins that were meant to hold it respectfully in place. She checked on her grandfather and found him sitting on the edge of his bed, looking more tired than when he'd gone into his room the previous evening. He assured her that he was fine, and he didn't need anything, so she left him to take care of himself. She hurried to build a fire in the parlor where Samuel would inevitably go to get warm, and another in the stove in the kitchen where she would quickly warm up from working near the heat it radiated. The April air was much warmer than the winter temperatures they had recently left behind—especially with the sun shining—but spring was still chilly, and Vivian knew that Samuel often felt cold no matter the temperature outside.

While a pot of porridge was simmering, Vivian took a careful inventory of the food in the larder and was glad to note that there was sufficient for at least another week. She still had some money in a tin that would help, but it wasn't enough to make the rent which would be due in less than two weeks. Stirring the porridge as it thickened Vivian told herself she needed to summon her courage and have a frank conversation with Samuel about their financial situation. He would not be happy with her for keeping *any* secrets from him, but most especially when it came to household or business matters that affected them both. But oh! How she dreaded the way she knew it would inevitably dampen his spirits when he already felt so helpless and unproductive. When a person was accustomed to remaining busy and working hard, being reduced to such a state was especially difficult. And Vivian didn't want to add to her grandfather's burdens. She desperately wished that she had a skill—any skill—that could provide a source of income. She had considered the possibility of looking for work elsewhere and simply closing the cobbler's shop. She was particularly good at cleaning and knew there were many grand houses in London where multiple maids were employed. She also had a fair amount of skill in the kitchen. She could never be considered experienced enough to cook for wealthy people, but she could certainly assist. Settling her mind more firmly on a plan of seeking out employment rather than spending her days minding an empty shop, Vivian felt a little better about having a conversation with her grandfather. If she had a plan, she could offer him hope rather than despair, and the idea lightened her mood. If she could *do* something about this problem, she would certainly feel better about herself. And although she didn't want to leave Samuel on his own for hours every day, she knew he *could* take care of himself, especially if she planned ahead and left him with easy access to everything he needed.

Vivian took a bowl of porridge and a glass of milk to the little table beside her grandfather's chair where he was sitting once again with one blanket around his shoulders and another over his lap.

"Oh, thank you, child," he said gratefully, but Vivian noted a sadness in his eyes that hadn't been there the night before.

"You're very welcome," she said and went back to the kitchen to get her own food so they could eat together. Ever since Samuel had decided he preferred eating by the fire, the little dining table in the kitchen had gone unused—at least for eating. Vivian wanted to share meals with her grandfather, and they both enjoyed being able to visit while they ate. But Vivian noticed as soon as she got settled that Samuel was severely glum and especially quiet.

"Is something wrong, Grandpapa?" she asked.

"No, no. I'm fine, dear. No need to worry." He sounded convincing but his expression contradicted his words.

Trying to sound chipper and enthusiastic, Vivian said, "I've been waiting for you to tell me the rest of the story about Estelle. Did you—"

"Her father forbade us to marry," Samuel interrupted. "I'm afraid there's nothing more to tell."

Vivian was taken off guard and stunned into silence when she couldn't think of anything to say in response. She wasn't surprised at all by this conclusion to their story, given what she had already known. What surprised her was the fact that Samuel had been cheerful and perhaps even somewhat animated when he'd spoken of Estelle the previous evening, and now he appeared sadder than she had likely seen him since the weeks following Edna's death. Even the deterioration of his health had not reduced him to such obvious gloom.

Vivian made a few more futile attempts at conversation and finally gave up. They shared breakfast in taut silence, and Vivian certainly couldn't bring herself to broach the subject of their financial situation when his mood was already so grim.

While Vivian put the kitchen in order, setting aside the leftover porridge for tomorrow, she couldn't help wondering what had happened to Estelle. Had she been able to marry someone who had made her as happy as Edna had made Samuel? Vivian hoped so, and she felt certain her grandfather hoped so too.

Wanting to get the laundry outside to dry as quickly as possible so it could soak up the sun through the warmest hours of the day, Vivian hurried to put water on the stove to heat and pulled out the large tubs she used for washing and rinsing. It was her least favorite task in running a household, and she was glad when everything that had needed cleaning was hanging on the lines in the yard, and the tubs had been cleaned and put away. She spent the remainder of the day doing extra tasks around the house: sweeping, wiping away every possible speck of dust, and doing some extra scrubbing in the kitchen—all the while listening for the bell in the shop that would ring if a potential customer entered. But the bell remained silent. While she tidied and cleaned, Vivian's mind began wandering through a myriad of thoughts that were equal portions of her intrigue regarding the story of her grandfather and the mysterious Estelle, and her worries regarding their financial situation.

Vivian's only distraction from these thoughts was a sudden pang of missing her friend Betsy. They'd met at church a few years earlier after Betsy had come to London from the country looking for work. At the time, she'd recently been hired as a maid in a large, fine home owned by a baronet, and she was pleased to have work that included having her own room in the servants' dormitories of the house, all her meals each day, as well as a salary sufficient to meet her personal needs.

As Vivian and Betsy had gotten to know each other better, Vivian learned that Betsy had come from a very wealthy and titled family herself. But her father had gambled away their fortune and then taken his own life, leaving his children to fend for themselves. Vivian felt a great deal of compassion for Betsy's situation, but she'd admired this young woman's determination to provide for herself and not allow the past to ruin her prospects for the future.

All had been well until other servants in the household had somehow learned through the gossip grapevine about Betsy's aristocratic background. It seemed there had been a kind of unspoken law within the house that separated those in service from people like Betsy who had been born into privilege.

From that time forward, Betsy had been ostracized and ridiculed by *everyone* in the household, and she had shed many tears while sharing with Vivian how hurt and alone she felt in her situation. And since she lived under the same roof where she worked, there was no getting away from the cruel ostracism. She had attempted to find work in a different household but had quickly learned that the gossip regarding her unique situation had been passed from the servants of one household to another, since many of them attended the same church congregation, or they socialized at the same pubs or through mutual connections. When Betsy had been unable to find a different job, and persecution related to her present employment had become unbearable, she had become deeply troubled over the situation. And then Betsy had been physically assaulted on a dark street, beaten so badly that she had feared the two men responsible would kill her. Betsy knew without any doubt that their attack had been related to her personal situation because they'd said so over and over in crude terms while they'd been beating her. Afterward, she'd barely been able to get herself to the cobbler's shop where Vivian had been able to care for her while she healed. However, seeing the evidence of Betsy's suffering day after day had driven home to Vivian the unalterable truth that it simply wasn't wise for social classes to interact in such a way. It certainly wasn't Betsy's fault; she had been desperate and had done what she'd needed to do. But the outcome made it abundantly clear that some people could never tolerate interaction with people from different stations in life. Once Betsy had recovered, she'd left London, knowing that she could never remain in the city and be happy or safe. And she certainly wasn't the same young woman whom Vivian had come to know years earlier.

Vivian had been heartbroken over the departure of her dear friend who was the only woman she'd been close to once she'd become an adult. Betsy had sent a few letters—enough to let Vivian know she had found work—but they were vague regarding any details, and there had been no information about her location that would allow Vivian to write back to her. It was as if Betsy had wanted to completely put her life in London behind her—traumatized as she was by what had happened—and even though her friendship with Vivian had been gratifying, it had still been a part of her experiences in the city. Thus—unfortunately—it too had to be severed.

Vivian sighed deeply to recall how difficult it had been to accept that she'd lost Betsy's friendship over such senseless reasons. And it was truly ironic and tragic that while those from the upper classes in society looked down on those less privileged, it seemed to work in reverse as well. Vivian's heart ached for all that Betsy had endured. Enough time had passed that she'd become accustomed to Betsy's absence, but she still missed her friend and prayed that all was well with her, wherever she might be.

Vivian forced her mind back to the present and focused on the necessary tasks at hand. Soon after she'd shared lunch with her grandfather and he had dozed off in his chair, it occurred to Vivian that tomorrow she should spend the day searching out employment. She would leave enough food prepared for her grandfather so that he could manage on his own, and she would set out right after breakfast, visiting as many fine houses as she could before she needed to return home and prepare supper. Perhaps thinking of Betsy had provided the incentive for the idea that she could find work in such a household, and she certainly didn't have the problem that had caused difficulties and trauma for Betsy.

Having a plan in place strengthened her confidence for telling her grandfather the truth about how bad their circumstances had become, and the moment he was finished eating the shepherd's pie she'd made for their supper, Vivian took a deep breath and just hurried to blurt out a memorized recitation of their present situation—including all she had done to try and be as frugal as possible, as well as her plan to find work.

Samuel listened with a growing expression of sadness, and there were many moments of terrible silence after she'd finished before he asked simply, "Has it really come to this?"

"It's really not so bad, Grandpapa," she said, sounding convincingly positive. "You've worked hard for a great many years and you've surely earned the privilege of taking it easy. We're very blessed that you're not so ill you can't take care of yourself for the most part, and I think it could very well be good for me to have the opportunity to meet new people and have new experiences." While that last part terrified her, Vivian believed that might be the very reason such a step was necessary. She'd lived a life that was far too sheltered here with her grandparents—and only her grandfather since Edna had passed. Beyond attending church and an occasional social with those same people, Vivian had hardly enjoyed any kind of social experience beyond her interaction with the shop customers. But that had trickled down to nothing of late, and she'd only gone to church about half the time since her grandfather had become too ill to attend with her.

Samuel looked off into the distance, clearly lost in deep thought, and Vivian allowed him some time to absorb everything she'd just told him. He finally reached for her hand, and tears glistened in his eyes. "Such a precious, hardworking girl you are," he said. "I'm certain you wouldn't have come to this decision without a great deal of pondering . . . and likely a lot of praying as well."

"That's true," she said gently.

"I'm not happy about this, my dear. It's *me* who should be taking care of *you*. But I suppose this is the nature of life and I need to be careful not to get caught up in my pride; I need to be gracious and simply appreciate that I've been blessed with such a dear girl in my life."

"It is I who am blessed," Vivian said, squeezing his hand as she pressed a kiss to his cheek.

Nothing more was said about the matter, but neither was anything else said about his history with Estelle. Vivian couldn't coax him into telling her any more about his first love, even though her curiosity felt almost painful. But Samuel just said he wasn't in the mood to talk, and Vivian wanted to cry as she took in how sad he looked. She honored his wish to avoid conversation and put the kitchen in order, wanting to be able to leave the following morning as early as possible. When she'd finished, Vivian was surprised to find Samuel sitting on the edge of his bed, even though it was still a while yet until the time when he usually retired. The door was partially closed, and she quietly peeked around it to see that her grandfather was reading one of the letters that had been in the box. The ribbon that had tied them together was on the bed beside him, along with the other letters. Vivian initially felt glad to know that he would allow himself to revisit his past, then she realized he had tears trickling down his face. She gasped unexpectedly and was glad to note that he hadn't heard her.

Vivian crept away to begin getting ready for bed. She laid out her best clothes for the next day and retrieved a small satchel from the bottom of her wardrobe. It was barely large enough for her to store some scones that she could wrap in a small towel. She didn't want to have to buy food while she was away from home, and she wanted to take advantage of the entire day to attempt finding a place within walking distance that might hire her in any possible capacity. She was willing to do the most menial tasks if only to provide a living for herself and her grandfather.

Vivian stole silently back to her grandfather's room to check on him and realized he was behind the curtain in the corner of the room that afforded him privacy for personal matters. He was likely getting himself ready for bed. Seeing the letters on his bed, an idea rushed into her mind with a sudden force, as if it had come on a harsh burst of wind that had blown into her face. Vivian tiptoed into the room in her stockinged feet and picked up one of the letters, her heart pounding as she realized that the information she needed to carry out her idea was there. The street and house number were written in an elegant script beneath the name *Estelle Weatherby*.

Feeling almost lightheaded, Vivian hurried to find a pencil and some paper. She found a pencil quickly enough but was dismayed when she couldn't find any paper. She knew there was some in the shop, but if she unlocked the door to go in there, she knew Samuel would hear her. She needed to be silent, and she needed to hurry. Desperate and bursting with anxiety, Vivian grabbed a book—one of three novels they owned that had belonged to Edna—and hurried back into Samuel's room, glad to hear evidence from behind the curtain that he was changing into his nightclothes. Vivian hurriedly opened the back cover of the novel and wrote on the blank page located there the information she needed that might help her find Estelle. She carefully put everything back exactly as it had been and barely managed to get out of the room before she heard her grandfather shuffling toward his bed.

Vivian went back to her room and stuffed the novel into the satchel she planned to take with her the following day. Impulsively she held the satchel against her heart, considering whether this was actually a good idea. Estelle had likely married many years ago and would have left the home she'd been living in when she'd been exchanging letters with Samuel Peyton. She could be deceased, or she could simply want no contact with Samuel or his nosy granddaughter. Vivian felt terrified over the very thought of even attempting to find Estelle, but at the same time the idea was so intense and consuming that she wondered if she would ever be able to find peace with herself if she didn't at least try. She had to at least try. She had to!

Chapter Two
ESTELLE

Vivian slept poorly but managed to get *some* rest. She was glad to awaken to a sunny day, not wanting to wander the streets of London while the hem of her dress got wet and muddy, nor did she want to be burdened with carrying an umbrella. Wanting to look her best while seeking employment, she knew a lack of rain and wind would be to her advantage; therefore, the lovely weather seemed a good omen.

With breakfast over and the kitchen tidied, Vivian took a tray to her grandfather with a good supply of buttered scones beneath a towel to keep them from drying out. "I'm afraid there's no variety," Vivian apologized, "but it will keep you from going hungry while I'm out."

"Your scones always taste good," he said with an encouraging smile. "I'll be fine; don't you worry about me." He took her hand and squeezed it. "I hope and pray the day goes well."

"Thank you," she said and kissed his brow. "I'll be back before dark."

Samuel nodded as if he appreciated knowing that; he'd never liked having her out after the sun had gone down.

Vivian went to her room and pinned a black velvet hat (which was nearly the color of her hair) into place on top of her head. The hat had belonged to Edna, and it was the only woman's hat in the house that looked somewhat respectable, although it didn't take too much inspection to see that it had seen better years. Since it was more appropriate for Vivian to wear a hat as opposed to going without, she simply sighed at her reflection and decided it would have to do.

Vivian went out through the shop door and locked it behind her, tucking the key into her satchel along with the scones she'd wrapped in a little towel, and the novel where she'd scribbled the location of Estelle's home—the home where she'd lived more than forty years ago, anyway. Vivian could only hope that someone there might have some information to give her that might help her find out where Estelle was now. While Vivian walked toward a much more affluent residential area of London, she imagined being able to write Estelle a letter in which she might explain how much it would mean for Samuel to simply receive word from her after all these years; Vivian felt certain he would be overjoyed to know that she was well and happy, and Vivian hoped that would be the case.

Since Vivian wasn't well acquainted with most of the enormous city in which she lived, she asked a man who sold newspapers for directions to the street where Estelle had once lived. He was kind, and Vivian was surprised to realize that it wasn't as far away as she had feared. Of course, Estelle had once visited Samuel's cobbler's shop regularly, but Vivian knew she would have likely traveled by carriage—and yet it made sense that the family would do their shopping in an area not terribly far from their residence. It would still be a lengthy walk for Vivian, but not as far as it could have been.

Vivian worked her way toward Estelle's home, both dreading and anticipating her arrival there—and not at all certain what she might do or say. It would be inappropriate for someone of her social station to come calling at the front door. Wouldn't it? Did that mean she should go to the back where the servants entered and speak to someone there? Or perhaps she would be wise to simply let go of this crazy scheme and not make any attempt to acquire current information on Estelle's whereabouts.

Thankfully, Vivian had a long time to think about it since she stopped at several fine houses along the way where she *did* go to the servants' entrance at the back, inquiring whether there was any employment available. At five of these houses, she was rudely told that there was no work to be had. Vivian was told at two other locations that a position for a maid was available, but she would need to speak with the housekeeper and that required an appointment. And those she spoke to were kind enough to offer her a much-needed glass of water. She scheduled appointments two hours apart the following day and was glad to be given a note at each house with the time and location written there so she wouldn't forget.

Vivian ate her scones while she walked between houses, not wanting to waste any time. Each visit had taken a great deal of courage, and she felt some satisfaction with having overcome her fears, and in knowing that she had two possibilities for getting hired. Of course, it was always a possibility that those interviews could go badly, and she would need to keep searching, but that was surely the nature of finding work. She just prayed that she could find work before their situation became desperate.

All the fear Vivian had felt throughout the day didn't compare to the terror rising inside of her as she approached the house where Estelle Weatherby had once lived. An artfully crafted iron fence stood between the house and the street, with a gate that opened not far from the front door. Vivian stood in front of the gate, wondering if anyone related to Estelle even lived here after all these years. And she couldn't decide whether to go around to the back and talk to someone who worked here, or to just go through the gate and use the enormous, elaborate knocker she could see on the door. Her heart was pounding so hard she feared it might do her physical harm if she didn't hurry up and decide. The third option was to just turn around and go home. And perhaps that would be best. She felt relatively certain her grandfather would *not* be happy with her if he knew where she was and what she intended to do.

"May I help you?" a deep voice asked, startling Vivian so badly that she literally jumped back a step from the gate, and a small sound erupted involuntarily from her mouth; it was more of a scream than a gasp.

Vivian took a moment to examine the man standing in front of her, starting with the intensity of his brown eyes and the scowl on his face, accentuated by the excessive arch of one eyebrow. His hair was nearly as dark as her own, with a crease in it that circled his head, surely a result of the hat he was holding in his gloved hands. A quick glance from head to toe showed Vivian that everything about him was proper and meticulous. He wore a thin beard that had clearly been shaped with a razor to frame his perfectly proportioned features. His attire was opulent and pristine—from the muffler around his throat to the brocade coat, the fine breeches, and *very* expensive shoes. Vivian knew quality shoes when she saw them. Staring at him for a couple of seconds felt longer when he nodded as if to repeat his question.

"Who are you?" she demanded, knowing it sounded rude, but she was still trying to recover from the fright he'd given her. She'd already been contending with a pounding heart due to the decision she'd been trying to make, and now she felt decidedly lightheaded and had to concentrate extremely hard on keeping herself upright.

"The only answer to that question you need to know is that I live here," he said, motioning toward the house with his hat. "And you are standing in front of the gate through which I must enter in order to go inside."

"Oh," was all she could manage to say.

"And *why*," he countered, "may I ask, are *you* standing in front of my gate?"

Vivian forced herself to focus on the moment and at least try and accomplish what she'd come here to do—despite the many reasons she had to feel intimidated by this man. She drew back her shoulders, lifted her chin, and cleared her throat as if doing so might remove any obstruction to her words coming out into the open.

"I don't know whether you can help me," she began, courageously ignoring the heightened pounding of her heart, "but I'm trying to find some information on a woman who lived here more than forty years ago. If she's still living, I very much need to get a message to her and—"

"Who exactly is this woman?" he asked, his voice deepening with skepticism.

"I don't know if she married and moved away . . . or whether her family remained in this home or not . . . or if she would still even be alive today or—"

"My family has lived in this house for generations," he said with an indignance that implied she should have clearly known and understood this simply through some form of metaphysical means.

Vivian's excitement over this revelation made it easier to overlook his arrogance, and she found it easier to work toward achieving her goal. "Then you would know of Estelle Weatherby—or Weatherby was her surname more than forty years ago. That's all I know."

The man's eyes narrowed on her, as if he might be attempting to discern if she had criminal intentions. "And how," he asked, "are you familiar with this woman—based on information more than forty years old, when you are—I would guess—approximately half that age?"

Vivian found it progressively easier to ignore his cynical attitude and remain focused on her objective. "She and my grandfather were . . . friends. I recently became aware of letters she'd written to him and—"

"Friends?" he interrupted with increased skepticism in his voice as his eyes roved down to her feet and back up to her face—and the meaning in his gaze was clear. The evidence of her lowly station in life—in contrast to his own wealth and status—made him highly doubtful that any kind of friendship could have ever existed between her grandfather and Estelle. But again, Vivian ignored his attitude and pressed on.

"Yes, friends," she insisted firmly, not wanting to tread anywhere near the information that they had shared a romantic affection for each other; this man would *surely* find that even more absurd than the possibility of their having shared a friendship. "My grandfather is a cobbler and Miss Weatherby had a great penchant for shoes. She made many visits to the cobbler's shop where I live now with my grandfather. As I said, I recently became aware of some letters she had written to him, and I have no motive except perhaps the possibility that she might be willing to simply post a brief note to him that might lift his spirits, given that his health is not good. There; that is why I'm here. My name is Vivian Peyton in case you're wondering. And my grandfather is Samuel Peyton of Peyton's Cobbler Shop."

Vivian saw this man's expression betray a kind of surprise, while his eyes sparked with what seemed to be anger, although she surely didn't know him well enough to know how that could possibly be the case. He remained silent for several grueling moments while he seemed to consider all he'd heard before deciding whether he should believe Vivian to be telling the truth—and whether he should help her or send her away. He finally sighed as if he'd reached a conclusion and said with some hesitancy, "My name is Theodore Weatherby, and Estelle Weatherby is my aunt."

"You know her?" Vivian blurted with such excitement that she knew her response was far from dignified—or even coherent.

"Quite well," he stated with obvious reluctance and another sigh. However, his eyes now showed some hint of curiosity, and she wondered if he might be willing to help her if only to satisfy his own reasons for wondering why his aunt might have once shared a friendship with a poor cobbler. At the same time, Vivian could almost imagine that he might have preferred to deny his relationship with his aunt but knew Estelle wouldn't be pleased if he did. He sighed yet again and added, "She never married, and she lives here with myself and my mother and sister." Vivian drew in a harsh breath of excitement and relief. Estelle was here! Right here! In the house on the other side of the fence by which they were standing! Vivian couldn't believe it! She felt dismayed to think that Estelle had never married, and she knew her grandfather would feel the same. Like Vivian, he would have wanted Estelle to live a full and complete life. Still, Vivian had found her. She only had to contend with the woman's nephew who had appointed himself a sentry on his aunt's behalf.

Theodore Weatherby hurried on as if he didn't want to give Vivian any further opportunity to speak. "I will give my aunt your message. If she truly was friends with your grandfather and he still lives in the same place, then she will know where to send a letter if she chooses to do so. Good day, Miss Peyton." He put his hat back on and tapped it firmly onto his head, nodding slightly as if he were a king dismissing a lowly serf.

"Do you promise?" she asked, not certain if he could be trusted.

"I assure you I am a man of my word," he said, as if her even thinking otherwise was a great affront.

"I'm not to know that, now, am I?" She made no effort to soften the fact that she was questioning his integrity. "I know absolutely nothing about you. How do I know that you'll actually give my message to your aunt?"

"Because," he said, sounding impatient, "I am a man of my word, and I promise you that I will tell her."

"Perhaps I could see her and tell her myself," Vivian said, knowing she was being presumptuous but not caring, considering the possibility that Estelle might never know she'd been here.

"Given the fact that I have no idea if my aunt even remembers your grandfather, or if she would have any desire to send any communication to him, I must insist that you allow me to give her your message and we will let *her* decide what to do from there." His expression made it clear that he highly doubted Estelle would even care, but Vivian had to concede that it would indeed be improper for her to press the matter any further. She thought about the situation long enough to come up with the idea that if Estelle sent no communication within a few weeks, Vivian could write Estelle a letter. She certainly wasn't giving up simply because this man was asking her to trust him.

"Very well," Vivian said. "I will take you at your word, Mr. Weatherby." She was glad her grandfather had told her that Estelle's father had not held any kind of title, which meant that the man she was speaking to would not have inherited one; therefore, she didn't have to address him as anything more formal than *mister*. She resisted the urge to demand more evidence of his integrity and simply added, "Thank you for your time. Give your aunt my regards."

"Indeed," was all he said before he opened the gate and stepped through it. Vivian winced at the sound of the gate closing and watched Theodore Weatherby disappear through the door that sported the elaborate knocker. She winced again when it slammed shut, and she reluctantly turned away to walk home, glancing at the sun in the sky to reassure herself that she had plenty of time to get there before dark as she'd promised her grandfather.

Theodore was met in the foyer by a footman who took his hat, gloves, muffler, and coat, while he asked politely, "Did you have a pleasant walk, sir?"

Theo considered how his walk had just ended with such an unpleasant encounter at the gate and simply replied, "The weather is lovely for this time of year."

"It is, indeed, sir," the footman said.

"Do you know where my aunt is at the moment?" Theo asked, having no idea of this young man's name, even though they encountered each other every day.

"I saw her a short while ago in the window upstairs," the footman said.

"Thank you," Theo said and hurried up the staircase, knowing exactly where to go. It was his aunt's favorite place within the walls of this massive house.

The stairs emerged onto the glimmering polished marble floor of a hallway that went both directions into the north and south wings of the house. Directly in front of Theo was an enormous grouping of windows that looked out over the large and pristine fenced-in gardens behind the house where he had grown up, mostly in the care of his aunt and his mother—although he could honestly say that it was his aunt who had taken more of a vested interest in his life. Still, he loved both these women and he was grateful for all the love and concern they had offered him throughout his childhood and youth, and into adulthood. The contributions his father had made to his upbringing earlier in his life were something he didn't care to think about.

Theo went around the end of the banister and walked toward the front of the house, pressing his hand along the balcony railing over which he could look and see the foyer below and the grand staircase he'd just ascended. The late-afternoon sun shone brightly through the west-facing windows in front of him that mirrored those at the back of the house—except that those in front of him were built in a half-circle where an elegant carpet of dark blue and rich gold covered the floor. There was ample space for the small sofa strategically placed for a perfect view out onto the street below, as well as the overstuffed chair that faced the sofa, and the small table between them that was perfect for enjoying tea in this very spot—which Estelle often did, along with whoever might care to join her. He'd been purposefully determined to return home in time for tea and wasn't surprised to find his aunt lounging comfortably on the sofa, reading from a book she had tilted toward the sunlight. Her slippers were on the floor and her feet were tucked up beneath her skirt, which was typical for her.

"Hello, Aunt," he said as he approached, and she looked up from her book, her countenance showing so much happiness to see him that he might think they'd been separated for weeks or months, when in truth they'd shared lunch not so many hours earlier. Her silvery blonde hair was styled to perfection as always—except when he might see her early in the morning or late in the evening when it would be hanging in a long braid down her back. Her face was remarkably unwrinkled for a woman her age, which Theo had observed mostly from comparing his aunt's appearance to that of his mother, whose face was filled with deep wrinkles. He suspected that the main reason for the difference was hereditary, and since the two women were not related by blood, they would not share that tendency. Although Theo believed that the matter also likely had something to do with the differences of attitude in these two women. His mother was certainly not a bad person and he loved her dearly, but she tended to worry and to be somewhat pessimistic, which meant she was often scowling. Estelle, on the other hand, was inherently cheerful and positive, even though her life had not turned out at all the way she had hoped or expected.

"Hello, my sweet Theo," Estelle replied. "Did you enjoy your walk?"

"I did," he said, sitting in the big, comfortable chair that faced her. He'd spent so much time in this chair, visiting with his aunt, that it felt as if the padding and fabric had become well acquainted with him, offering an especially comfortable respite.

"And who was that young lady you were speaking with outside the gate?" she asked, taking him by surprise until he realized that she could easily see the front gate from where she was seated.

Theo would not have broken his promise to Vivian Peyton to pass her message along to Estelle—even if he might have preferred to avoid it—but now he didn't have the option of procrastinating the conversation. He resisted the temptation to inform his aunt that the woman he'd spoken to by the gate could never be classified as a *lady*. Her gender had nothing to do with the reality of her upbringing, which Estelle would soon realize once she had all the facts.

"She was looking for *you*," Theo said, and Estelle's eyes widened as her voice took on a surprised lilt. She then took Theo completely off guard when she asked, "Then why didn't you invite her in?"

Theo tried not to sound defensive even though he certainly felt the need to defend himself. "Because, Aunt, I have no idea who she is or if her reasons for wanting to see you have any validity whatsoever. I promised her I would pass along her message, and I'm doing that now."

"Very well," she said, setting her book aside and motioning impatiently with her hand. "What did she say?"

Theo sighed and forced himself past his own reluctance to convey the message. "She was standing at the gate when I arrived home, looking as if she were trying to decide whether or not to come to the door."

"Yes, I noticed that," Estelle said.

"Of course, that would have been highly inappropriate," Theo declared.

"Why?" Estelle asked as if she had no idea what he might be talking about.

"Why?" he echoed, astonished by her attitude. "Because she was clearly not suitable to be calling in such a manner. She should have gone to the back door and—"

"I love you dearly, Theo," Estelle said, and Theo knew well enough that this phrase often preceded some form of gentle criticism. She was never unkind, but she did consider it her duty as his deceased father's sister to help guide him in life. "However," she went on, confirming his suspicion, "you certainly inherited some attitudes from your father, to be sure. He was a good man in many ways, as we both know, but he held to opinions that were a little too much like *our* father to suit me. Bless them."

"And how is that?" Theo asked, knowing he wouldn't like the answer. Estelle always used the word *bless* in connection with gentle criticism as well, or perhaps when she simply felt the need to state her lack of agreement with someone else's opinion or behavior.

"People have no power over the circumstances into which they arrive in this world, Theo. The servants use the back entrance because they work here. A young lady making a social call should come to the front door."

"I love you dearly, Aunt," Theo said with a hint of facetious sarcasm and a little wink, not wanting her to be offended, although they were well accustomed to being completely honest with each other about their opinions on any matter, and they had a long-standing agreement to never take offense simply because they might disagree. "But this young *woman* was clearly not someone who should be paying a social call on someone such as yourself."

"Why?" Estelle snapped. "Because she's poor? Do you think I wouldn't invite a poor woman in through the front door if she had reason to speak with me?"

"I'm certain *you* would," Theo said. "And I think it's good that *I* happened upon her before that occurred, since you might sometimes need a gentleman to intercede on your behalf and determine what's right and proper—and safe."

Estelle laughed softly. "Do you think her intention was to put me in some kind of danger?" she asked and laughed again. "Because she's *poor*?"

Theo sighed impatiently. "Might we spare the disagreement and get to the point?"

"Excellent idea," Estelle said. "Why did she want to see me? I couldn't see her face very well, but she's a pretty girl, and she seemed sweet."

Theo was briefly distracted by his recollection of just how pretty this young woman was. Even while he'd been talking to her, he'd been aware of the contrast of her very dark hair and a complexion that was much like porcelain. Her features were lovely, and he couldn't deny that she had a certain grace about her that was not typical for women of her social station.

Estelle gently cleared her throat as if she knew his mind was wandering, which brought him abruptly back to the present conversation. "How can you possibly know if someone is *sweet* simply by looking at them?" Theo asked.

"To the point?" she reminded him.

"Of course," he said and cleared *his* throat to force back his frustration over their dramatically different opinions on the matter of social status. They had so much in common regarding most of their views of the world that he hated it when they disagreed on anything. But Estelle had never been one to be intimidated, or to succumb to another's opinion simply to avoid contention. "She said she was looking for an Estelle Weatherby who had lived here over forty years ago."

"What?" Estelle asked breathlessly; this was clearly not what she'd expected. "Why?"

"She said that she recently came across some letters—or something like that—from you to her grandfather . . ." Theo had no trouble recalling the grandfather's name, but he felt an aversion to speaking it for reasons he didn't want dredged up; and surely it had to be a coincidence. "He was a cobbler and—"

"Samuel Peyton," Estelle said in a hushed whisper, solving the problem of Theo not wanting to say the name; but he was a little unnerved with the way Estelle's hand went unwittingly to her heart, and her eyes took on a distant glow.

"Yes, that's right," he said, solely for the purpose of breaking the silence that persisted while Estelle's mind seemed many miles away—or perhaps decades.

Estelle abruptly returned to the present and gave Theo a penetrating stare. "What else did she say? Tell me everything!"

Once again Theo was taken aback. He knew Estelle to be typically cheerful and positive, but he couldn't recall *ever* seeing her so enthused about *anything*. "Um . . ." he muttered with the hope of being able to recall what the young woman had said; he now wished that he'd paid better attention. He never would have imagined that his conversation with her would be so important to Estelle. "I believe she said that . . . her grandfather's health was failing and—"

"Oh, no!" Estelle exclaimed with absolute devastation. Theo would have believed from her tone of voice and expression that this man had been a part of her everyday life for the last forty years, rather than someone she'd not had any contact with in all that time. "Did she say why?"

"No, Aunt," Theo said, trying to maintain a practical outlook on the matter; one of them had to. He didn't understand Estelle's reaction, but he felt relatively certain nothing good could come from her bizarre emotional response. "She only said that she'd recently come across some letters you'd written to him many years ago, and she was hoping you might be willing to post a note to him that might lift his spirits."

"Oh, my!" Estelle muttered, still seeming far more emotionally committed to this situation than he ever would have expected. "Was there anything else?" she asked eagerly, as if any little bit of information he might give her would be an enormous gift.

"Not that I recall," he said, not wanting to admit to how unsavory his conversation had been with this young woman. And he couldn't shake the distinct discomfort he felt from having heard the name *Peyton*. Again, he told himself that it surely had to be a coincidence. "Oh," he recalled, "she said that you and her grandfather had become acquainted because he's a cobbler and you had a penchant for shoes. I can't deny that this made it clear that she *was* talking about you."

Estelle giggled; *giggled*, like a besotted schoolgirl. Theo wondered where his dignified and pragmatic aunt had disappeared to in the last few minutes.

"So," he said firmly, hoping to conclude this conversation by honoring Vivian Peyton's request and being done with it, "you can write a note to your old friend this evening and I'll see that it's delivered tomorrow, and that will be that."

"Nonsense!" Estelle countered. "I will be paying a visit to Mr. Peyton tomorrow morning so that I can see and speak with my old friend and find out for myself what it is that's ailing him."

"You cannot!" Theo protested.

"And why not?" Estelle questioned vehemently. "I'm a grown woman with access to a carriage and a driver and footman who will accompany me. Do you think that Twig and Cooper would let anything bad happen to me while I'm in their care?"

"No," he had to admit, knowing these men were trustworthy employees of many years who had a deep regard for Estelle; still, he didn't like this at all even if he couldn't find the words to explain his feelings. "But . . . I'm just not certain it's a good idea. Is a letter to your friend not sufficient, Aunt? Do you really need to—"

"What?" she interrupted, sounding downright indignant. "Go to a part of the city where I once went with my mother quite frequently to visit a great many shops? Visit an old friend because . . ." she made a rolling motion with her hand as if to encourage him to finish the sentence. When he didn't, she added, "Because he's poor! That's why you don't want me to go, and the very notion is ridiculous. I love you dearly, Theo," she continued; there was that phrase again, alerting him to an inevitable declaration of an opinion that she knew he wouldn't like. "Nevertheless, it might serve you well to remember that I'm old enough to be your mother, and since my father passed, I've not once allowed anyone—man or woman—to intimidate me into doing or not doing anything once I've made my mind up to it. You should know that well enough. I'm going to visit Mr. Peyton in the morning; you are welcome to accompany me if you think I need a protector or chaperone." She made a scoffing sound as if the very idea were ridiculous, but she was giving him the option of going with her, for which he was grateful because he had intended to insist on accompanying her anyway; this just made it unnecessary for him to introduce the idea.

"Thank you, I would love to meet Mr. Peyton." Theo knew his aunt couldn't have missed the sarcasm in his voice, and he sincerely regretted that it had been so obvious. With the hope of softening their disagreement, he added more gently, "And I *do* want to make certain you're all right. I'm happy to go anywhere with you if it will help keep you safe."

"Your concern is appreciated, Theo," she said, sounding more like herself, "and I'm glad to have you come along, but I can assure you there is no need to fear for my safety. Come with me to meet Mr. Peyton if you like, but I expect you to be kind and respectful."

Theo swallowed carefully, not wanting her to accuse him once again of being too much like his father—even though he knew it was true. "I promise," he said.

"Good," she said triumphantly. "We'll leave right after breakfast."

"Very well," he agreed resignedly, being careful not to let on to how deeply he was dreading this excursion. The simple fact of having to encounter Miss Vivian Peyton again didn't help.

As if Estelle had read his mind, she asked, "And speaking of being kind and respectful, why did you not call a carriage to take Miss Peyton home?"

Theo was astonished by the question and let out a brash scoffing sound before he could think to hold it back. Estelle's brow creased with disapproval over his attitude, and he hurried to consider a suitable answer to her question. "The weather is fine and there were still a good two hours of daylight left when she departed. She had clearly walked here with no difficulty; I'm certain she could find her way home with no assistance from me."

"Hmm," Estelle drawled thoughtfully before she added, "and if it had been an elegantly dressed lady from a well-established family you would have tripped over yourself to make certain she was given proper means to get safely home."

"You give me very little credit, Aunt," he said in his defense, even though he couldn't deny she'd ignited a smoldering regret inside him that made him wish he *had* called for a carriage to deliver Miss Peyton to her home. "Sometimes I think you believe me to be a heartless scoundrel."

"You are by no means a scoundrel, Theo," she said firmly, and he was glad to hear reassurance that she knew this to be true; he sincerely endeavored to live his life with integrity. "And you are certainly not heartless," she added and leaned forward, putting her feet on the floor as she took both his hands into hers. "Nevertheless, I know there is something cold inside of you that I don't completely understand, and it tends to make you hold to attitudes that could easily be hurtful to others—if not yourself."

Theo didn't think too deeply about what she'd just said; it was far from the first time she'd alluded to such a thing, and he'd always managed to push it away, considering it to be based mostly in the musings of an overly analytical old woman. Wanting only to steer away from any such introspection, he simply said, "I promise to be kind and respectful to your friend."

"And his family," she added adamantly, and he wondered if she had been able to tell from her view of the front gate that he'd been arguing with Samuel Peyton's granddaughter.

"And his family," he repeated.

"Thank you," she said and let go of his hands to resume her comfortable position on the sofa just before a maid approached with everything they needed to enjoy a fine tea. Theo was deeply grateful for the interruption, and extremely glad to be able to maneuver the conversation with his aunt into trivial everyday matters that were more typical of their regular interactions. She said nothing more about her old friend or their pending visit, but Theo knew she was thinking about it. There was a dreaminess in her eyes that was completely unlike her, and Theo simply didn't know what to make of it. He desperately wanted to ask if there was any connection to Samuel Peyton and the man with the same surname who had been responsible for his father's death. But he couldn't bring himself to even say the words. If there was a connection, he wasn't certain he wanted to know. And either way, he simply didn't want to talk about it. All of that was far in the past, even if most of the time it didn't feel that way.

Vivian returned home to find her grandfather dozing in his usual chair, which was better than finding him anxious or unsettled over her absence. She quietly began preparing a vegetable soup for their supper, wishing she had even a little bit of meat to give it more flavor. But she convinced herself it would be tasty enough and focused on her gratitude that they had plenty of food to fill their stomachs.

Recounting the events of the day, she felt good about her efforts at finding work since they had resulted in appointments for two interviews the following day. She avoided thinking about how nervous she felt about those appointments and instead imagined that at least one of them would result in a job that could solve a great many problems for her and her grandfather.

Her mind went reluctantly to her encounter with Theodore Weatherby. She was pleased to have found Estelle, but not at all pleased with trusting the woman's arrogant nephew with delivering what she considered to be an extremely important message. He obviously hadn't agreed with the level of importance, which made Vivian doubt that even if he kept his promise, he might well do so in a careless manner that might not give Estelle the opportunity to realize how important it could be for Samuel to just hear from her. Vivian's deepest hope was that Estelle would simply make the effort to write a brief note to Samuel and have it posted; the sooner the better so that Vivian could put the matter to rest and stop worrying about it. She didn't know why this had come to feel so important to her, but it did, which meant she would never be able to free her mind from the matter until something came of it—hopefully, something that would lift her grandfather's spirits rather than contribute to his sadness.

Samuel was pleased to hear about Vivian's day while they shared supper near the fire. Of course, Vivian omitted any mention of going to the home of Estelle Weatherby, along with her unsavory encounter with Estelle's nephew. Vivian just hoped there wouldn't be any kind of negative repercussions from what she'd done; she couldn't imagine such a thing, but still she hoped.

After Vivian had finished putting the kitchen in order, she once again found her grandfather sitting on his bed reading Estelle's letters. He had a blanket around his shoulders and over his lap as he often did, but Vivian doubted he felt truly warm when there was no fire burning in his room. Wanting to conserve wood and coal, they only lit fires at night in the bedrooms during the coldest winter months. Otherwise, they only used those rooms for sleeping and made use of a great many blankets. With the doors open to the parlor where the most effective fireplace in the house emitted a great deal of heat, they managed well enough. But Vivian wondered why her grandfather hadn't stayed by the fire to read the letters; he seemed to want more privacy but at the same time had left his door ajar, which implied that he didn't care if she knew he was reading them. Then again, he didn't *look* as if he felt cold; perhaps reading the letters of his first love had made him more oblivious to discomfort than usual. The idea strengthened Vivian's resolve that she'd done the right thing in finding Estelle's home and passing along a message with her nephew. She just hoped once again that the message had been properly repeated to Estelle.

Vivian fell asleep quickly and slept more deeply than she had in quite some time. Perhaps the very fact that she'd actively gone out looking for a job gave her less reason to worry about their situation. All that walking had also worn her out. She also no longer had to dread having a difficult conversation with her grandfather, and she was glad that she'd summoned the courage to at least try and get a message to Estelle. The matter was out of her hands—at least for now.

Vivian rose feeling rested and hurried to the kitchen to heat some water for both herself and her grandfather to use to wash up. She also filled the tea kettle and put it on the stove as well. A short while later, both Vivian and Samuel were cleaned up and dressed and sitting by the fire in the parlor, each with a cup of tea while they waited for the leftover porridge to warm up on the stove. They said little to each other while they ate their breakfast except that Vivian reminded her grandfather that she had two appointments for interviews later in the day, and she would probably leave by the middle of the morning to check in at a few other houses, wanting to have other options in case her interviews didn't go well.

Vivian was nearly finished cleaning up the kitchen when a noise startled her. It had been such a long time since she'd heard the bell above the shop door—except when she was going in or out of the door herself—that she'd almost forgotten how it sounded from a distance.

"Oh, my," she muttered to herself and wiped her hands on her apron to dry them.

"Is that the shop?" she heard her grandfather call.

"Yes," Vivian said on her way to the open door between the shop and the house, "I'll take care of it."

Vivian's heart was beating quickly as she entered the shop, even though she knew that any single customer would never change the fate of this cobbler's shop and what it meant to her and especially her grandfather. She entered to see a fine, elderly lady with a slim figure who was about the same height as Vivian, which was a little shorter than the average woman. The lady's face glowed with a kind smile, outshining the evidence of her wealth and station that showed keenly in everything from her confident posture to the meticulous detail of her stylish dress of narrow blue and silver stripes, her matching hat, and the coordinating shoes, the tips of which could be seen peeking out from beneath her skirt. Sometimes Vivian almost found her habit of noticing people's shoes to be annoying and quickly looked back at this lady's face.

"Good morning," Vivian said. "How may I help you?"

"I should like to ask you the same," the lady said, her smile widening just as the door behind her closed, once again ringing the bell, and Vivian realized that the elderly lady hadn't arrived alone. A man stepped forward to stand beside her, and Vivian took in her breath so sharply that she feared she might start coughing.

Vivian managed to clear her throat and breathe deeply enough to acknowledge him by saying politely, "Theodore Weatherby. We meet again."

"Miss Peyton," he said, bowing slightly before he motioned toward the lady at his side at the very moment the reality began to fully sink in, and Vivian's heart began thudding painfully hard. "My aunt, Estelle Weatherby."

"Estelle!" Vivian muttered breathlessly, feeling her own eyes widen and her skin turn hot. She immediately realized the lack of propriety in how she'd just addressed this lady, a fact that was reiterated by Theodore's severely arched eyebrow. "I mean . . . Miss Weatherby," Vivian quickly corrected. She couldn't believe it! In all her hopes of what might result from her attempts to find Estelle Weatherby, she had certainly not imagined this! But Estelle was standing here in the shop, and Vivian needed to gather her wits so that she didn't make a complete and utter fool of herself.

"It's such a great pleasure to meet you, Miss Weatherby," Vivian said, dipping into a slight curtsy. "You are so kind to come."

"Oh, my dear," Miss Weatherby said, taking a step toward Vivian with outstretched hands that Vivian had no choice but to take, "you must call me Estelle. You must! And you are Vivian. Is that correct?"

"Yes," Vivian said and had to force herself to take a deep breath. Ignoring the scowl on Theodore Weatherby's face, she tried to accept the fact that she had just become on a first-name basis with Estelle—her grandfather's beloved Estelle.

Chapter Three
THE REUNION

Vivian froze, suddenly overcome with an inability to move, or speak; she simply wasn't certain what should happen next, given that she'd never been in any such situation, nor had she even imagined this as a possibility. She was deeply relieved when Estelle broke the awkward silence.

"I was so pleased when Theo relayed your message to me," Estelle said. "After my father had made it impossible for me to ever see Samuel again . . ." Vivian noticed Theodore's eyes widening in astonishment at this declaration; he'd obviously never heard anything of this story. But then, Vivian herself had only heard it recently. Estelle continued, ". . . I heard nothing from him for many months until a note that came by way of one of my maids telling me that he was going to be married and he wished for me all the happiness that *he* had found. I believe her name was Edna."

"That's right," Vivian said, realizing Estelle had to be very invested in her affection for Samuel if she recalled such details. "My grandmother. She passed more than six years ago."

"I'm so sorry, my dear," Estelle said, squeezing Vivian's hands which she still held to rather tightly.

"Thank you," Vivian said, warmed by this woman's sincere compassion. "Time does make loss easier—or at least you become accustomed to the absence. But of course, we still miss her."

"Indeed," Estelle said with a firm nod of her head that added emphasis to her agreement with Vivian's statement. "And was he?" she asked, and Vivian felt confused by the question until Estelle clarified what she meant. "Happy? Were he and Edna happy together?"

"Very," Vivian said, knowing she needed to be completely honest, even if the matter was a sensitive one to this woman who had once loved Samuel but had been unable to marry him. "They were very happy together."

Estelle smiled warmly. "I'm so very, very glad to know that" she said. "I've wondered, and I've hoped. The Samuel I knew was such a good man in every way, and he deserved every happiness. When it became evident that I could not give him that happiness, I could only hope that he found it elsewhere."

Vivian wanted to ask Estelle if she had been happy all these years, but she couldn't bring herself to do it. Not only would the question seem potentially impertinent coming from a woman of her station, but the fact that Estelle had never married bore an implication that Vivian didn't feel inclined to approach.

When Vivian became once again strangled by an inability to know what to say, Estelle said, "I assume he's here. I was hoping to see him . . . as opposed to just sending a note."

"Oh, he is!" Vivian said, then felt a sudden panic that pushed its way into the words that spewed out of her mouth. "Forgive me, but . . . I didn't tell him that I'd tried to find you; I didn't want him to be disappointed if I *couldn't* find you, and . . . so he has no idea that . . . and well . . ." Vivian considered a fact that she didn't want to voice, but she felt it was necessary. "Our home is very humble, and . . . of course if he'd known you were coming, he would have dressed more appropriately to receive company; as it is, he's only—"

"Oh, my dear," Estelle said with a kind, brief laugh, "you mustn't worry about such things. I did not come to make any assessment of your home, nor to expect any special treatment; I didn't forewarn you of my visit because I did not want any fuss made; nevertheless, I would very much love to see Samuel if—"

"Of course," Vivian interrupted with sudden enthusiasm. Estelle's reassurances had put her at ease, and she could only feel excited about the surprise her grandfather was about to get. "Just . . . give me a moment to . . . make certain he's . . . comfortable . . . and to warn him that he has a visitor."

"We'll wait right here," Estelle said. "Take as long as you need."

Vivian smiled appreciatively at Estelle and quickly glanced at Theodore, noting that he was clearly not pleased with his aunt's offer to wait as long as necessary. Or perhaps he was just displeased over this situation in its entirety. Vivian suspected it was more the latter, perhaps compounded by the former.

Vivian slipped her hands out of Estelle's and hurried through the open door that divided the shop from the house. She was glad that she generally kept the house tidy, and that she'd done a good dusting recently. She found her grandfather dozing, which was extremely common, but his lack of snoring let her know that he wasn't sleeping deeply. It took only a light touch on his shoulder to snap him back to consciousness, and he lifted his face curiously toward her, likely expecting her to tell him that she was going out or that she had made him some tea.

"Is everything all right?" Samuel asked when Vivian hesitated to speak, wishing she'd gathered the correct words before she'd awakened him.

"Yes," she said, unable to keep from smiling. "You have a visitor, Grandpapa; someone who has come to surprise you."

Samuel's eyes widened with skeptical curiosity. She could imagine him assessing the possible people who might visit him, and he likely couldn't think of anyone who might be considered a surprise.

Vivian sat down so that she could look at him more directly. She took his hand, inhaled deeply, and hurried to admit, "Grandpapa, I did a little investigating while I was out yesterday, and . . . I hope you won't be unhappy with me, but . . . I found Estelle, and . . . she's here. She wants to see you."

Vivian heard her grandfather draw in a sharp breath as his eyes widened further. After grueling moments of silence while she waited fearfully to know whether he was pleased or unhappy, he finally let out his breath along with the hushed response, "What? How?" He took another sharp breath. "She's really here?"

"Yes, Grandpapa," Vivian said, relieved that he seemed pleased and surprised, but not the least bit upset with her. "She's come with her nephew. Is it all right if I invite them in? They're waiting in the shop."

"Oh, my," Samuel muttered and pressed his hands down over the front of the worn and comfortable clothes he wore, clearly questioning whether he looked presentable.

"It doesn't matter," Vivian reassured him. "She came to see *you*, not what you're wearing."

Samuel nodded with appreciation in his eyes, but he did remove the blanket from around his shoulders and quickly handed it to Vivian who stood and hurried to fold it and place it over the back of the nearby sofa before she looked closely again at her grandfather. "Are you ready? Do you need anything before I invite her in?"

"No, I'm fine," he said with a nervous tremor in his voice, but he nodded stoutly and smiled, clearly pleased. "I'm counting the seconds."

Vivian smiled at him and hurried back into the shop, removing her apron on the way which she left in the kitchen before she entered the shop to find Theodore looking bored while he fiddled with his hat, and Estelle examining the variety of shoes on display. "Oh, they're lovely!" Estelle said with a quick glance toward Vivian.

"Thank you," she said. "Or rather . . . thank you on behalf of my grandfather. I help with the business side of things, but I know nothing of how to craft shoes; I've often wished he would have taught me."

Vivian couldn't help noticing the wave of shock and perhaps disapproval that passed over Theodore's face from her comment. Was it the fact that she had admitted to assisting with business matters that he disapproved of, or her implication that she might have worked as a cobbler if circumstances had given her that opportunity? But Vivian turned her attention fully to Estelle, not caring a whit about the opinions of Theodore Weatherby.

"The house is small," Vivian said to Estelle without feeling any need to apologize for that fact. "If you prefer to speak with my grandfather privately, we can remain here in the shop or—"

"Oh, no need for that," Estelle said. "We have no great secrets that need to be kept, I can assure you." Vivian was more relieved than she could say, given her deep curiosity over this love story from the past that had come to light. She didn't want to miss a single word of what Estelle and Samuel discussed, even if admitting to the fact might classify her as being particularly nosy.

"Please come inside and make yourselves at home," Vivian said, motioning toward both Theodore and Estelle with her hand, but keeping her eyes focused on Estelle, a woman for whom she had already gained a deep fondness. She could certainly understand why her grandfather had once loved this woman—perhaps in some way he still did. From the serene smile and hint of nervousness on Estelle's face, Vivian wondered if Estelle still felt some form of love for Samuel, even after all these years. The fact that they'd not once seen each other or communicated since before Samuel and Edna had married showed a great deal of integrity on both their parts, and Vivian knew for a fact from a lifetime of observation that Samuel and Edna had loved each other very much and had shared a good life. Samuel certainly hadn't been holding back anything of himself—that was evident in Vivian's memories of how happy a woman her grandmother had been, and how Samuel had doted on her and clearly adored her, which he proved each day with the way he treated her in every way, large and small.

However, Edna had now been gone from this world for several years, and Estelle had never found that kind of happiness in her life. Vivian reproached herself for indulging in the possibility that this might have a fairy-tale ending for the two of them; just the idea of them being friends again warmed Vivian's heart, and she hoped this would be the first of many visits, rather than happening just this once.

Vivian led the way and heard the footfalls of Estelle and Theodore following her through the door and into the little parlor. Vivian motioned for Estelle to take the chair where Vivian usually sat, since it was comfortable and close to the chair Samuel occupied. Vivian saw Estelle hesitate a moment, take a deep breath and move tentatively to the chair where she sat close to its edge, keeping her back straight while she looked toward Samuel who was staring at her with wonder in his eyes. Vivian felt close to tears as she observed the reunion, but she choked back her emotion, aware that Theodore Weatherby was standing near her side, also observing. A quick glance at his expression made it clear that his emotional reaction to the situation was entirely different from Vivian's; he strongly disapproved, and in fact, Vivian could go so far as to say that his countenance betrayed disdain, perhaps even disgust. Oh, how she loathed this man! How could he possibly share a close relationship with the lovely and kind Estelle Weatherby?

"Can it really be possible?" Samuel said, his voice an incredulous whisper as his moist eyes took in the lovely visage of his first love.

"I assure you I am not a hallucination," Estelle said with a small laugh as she reached out her hand and Samuel quickly took hold of it. Vivian became caught up in observing the tender moment, noting that their hands were trembling slightly as they exchanged a slight squeeze of their fingers before Samuel lifted Estelle's hand to his lips and kissed it in a gentlemanly manner.

Vivian's ethereal engagement in the tenderness of the scene was disrupted by the sound of a loud, disgusted sigh erupting from the arrogant Theodore Weatherby who was standing beside her.

"Would you like to sit down?" Vivian asked him quietly, not wanting to disrupt what was taking place between Samuel and Estelle. "Some tea, perhaps?"

"No . . . thank you," Theodore said, "I would prefer to stand."

Vivian could well imagine that he either considered their sofa unsuitable to support his fine clothing, or else he very much hoped this would not take long and he could quickly be on his way with his aunt. Since Estelle's back was mostly turned to her nephew and she was clearly ignoring anything except Samuel, Vivian suspected that Estelle intended to stay as long as she chose, no matter how impatient Theodore might become. Vivian wondered if Theodore might be wary of drinking tea from a kitchen such as the one in this lowly house, as if it might not be safe for consumption.

Vivian once again ignored him and focused her attention on Estelle and her grandfather just as she heard Estelle say, "Before anything else is said between us, I want you to know that I never felt anything but happiness on your behalf when I learned you had found someone with whom to share your life, and your sweet granddaughter has told me that Edna was a fine woman."

"She was, yes," Samuel said, "and we had a good life. I *did* love her, Esty—and I always will—but that doesn't mean I ever forgot you. I always wondered . . . hoped . . . that you found your own happiness."

"I've had a good life," Estelle said, then laughed softly, "not that I consider it anywhere nearly over. There are some things that didn't turn out as I'd hoped; nevertheless, I have much that is good in my life; much to be thankful for."

"I'm very glad to hear it," Samuel said, and Vivian saw him smile. They gazed at each other in silence for a long moment before they both laughed at the same time, then Samuel added, "I cannot believe you're actually here. I never would have dreamed. And you've hardly changed a bit."

"Now, that's not true," Estelle said, laughing again. "I think we can be honest with each other about anything, especially the fact that more than forty years have passed, and those years have certainly had a great impact on both of us."

"Still," Samuel said with a distinct sparkle in his eyes, "you are as lovely as ever."

"You're too kind," Estelle said, looking down as if she might be able to hide the blush that rose in her cheeks. In that moment, she almost looked decades younger, mildly flustered by a compliment from a sweetheart.

Vivian sat quietly on the sofa, doing her best to ignore Theodore who continued to stand, although he'd begun to quietly pace a small area on the opposite side of the room from where Samuel and Estelle were sitting. Vivian wondered if she should offer Estelle and her grandfather some tea, even though Theodore had refused. But she didn't want to interrupt their conversation—at least not yet.

For nearly an hour Samuel and Estelle talked and laughed as they shared stories that had occurred in their lives during their long separation, and they also talked about memories of times they'd spent together when they'd been secretly in love, knowing that Estelle's father would disapprove. Vivian knew there were many details to this story she didn't know, but she hoped with time she would be able to get her grandfather to fill in the missing pieces of the puzzle.

Theodore finally gave up on his incessant pacing and sat on the sofa—as far from Vivian as he possibly could. She scooted over a little to widen the distance between them, hoping he picked up on the implication that she had no more desire to sit near him than he did to sit by her.

When there was finally a bit of a lull in the conversation between Estelle and Samuel, Vivian hurried to take advantage of the opportunity to stand up and move closer to them as she said, "May I offer you some tea? I had the kettle on the stove before you came. It wouldn't take long to—"

"That would be lovely, my dear," Estelle said. "Thank you." Her acceptance of Vivian's offer implied that she intended to extend her visit, which provoked a loud, impatient sigh from Theodore. Vivian expected Estelle to ignore him as she had done so far, but she turned toward him and said in a voice that was firmly kind, "If you recall correctly, Theo, I told you that you didn't need to accompany me; that I would be quite safe. You're welcome to walk home, if you like; the distance isn't terribly far, and I know you love a brisk walk." She smiled as if she'd told him his favorite dessert would be served after supper.

"Take your time," Theo said, motioning with his hand for her to continue with her visit. "I'm perfectly fine."

"I'm glad to hear it," Estelle said in a way that implied any further evidence of impatience from him would prompt her to order him to leave. Vivian liked Estelle more with every minute they spent in the same room.

The only disadvantage to preparing tea was that Vivian couldn't hear what Samuel and Estelle were saying, but she knew it was ridiculous to think that she could—or should—hear every bit of their conversation. She stoked the fire in the stove so the kettle would heat up after sitting for more than an hour. While the water worked its way toward boiling so the tea could steep properly, Vivian prepared a tea tray with some scones and butter and jam, using the finest dishes they owned, which she knew would still look paltry in contrast to those Estelle and Theo would be accustomed to.

Vivian served tea to her grandfather and their guests with all the proper decorum her grandmother had taught her. Vivian could still hear Edna saying—as she had many times: '*We may be a simple cobbler's family, but that doesn't mean we can't have proper manners and adopt some refinement in the way we do things.*' Estelle graciously accepted a cup of tea and a scone, which was set aside on a tiny plate on the little table between her and Samuel. Vivian's grandfather thanked Vivian for her efforts as he accepted the same. Theo refused Vivian's offer of refreshment; he did so politely, but Vivian couldn't brush off the feeling that he simply didn't want to eat or drink anything that had come from such humble surroundings.

Vivian once again did her best to ignore him as she poured herself a cup of tea and resumed her place on the sofa. She realized that Samuel and Estelle were sitting with their heads closer together and they were speaking in softer

voices, as if they didn't want every little thing they said to be overheard. Vivian certainly understood, despite her overwhelming curiosity. She was surprised to realize from the few words she caught here and there that her grandfather was talking very humbly and openly to Estelle about the issues of his health. Vivian knew him to be a man who preferred to keep personal matters to himself, and she also knew he hated the vulnerability and lack of productivity that his fatigue and weakness had brought into his life. Vivian felt certain it was nothing but a good thing for him to be able to talk about it with someone who was his peer—as opposed to his granddaughter for whom he felt responsible.

Shortly after Vivian had finished her tea and set the cup and saucer aside, she noticed Samuel glancing discreetly toward where she and Theo were sitting, and she knew him well enough to know that however subtle his expression might have been, he was wishing that he and Estelle did not have observers. He hadn't seemed to mind until now, which made Vivian wonder if he wanted to speak with Estelle about matters which he considered more private—things to do with the romance they'd once shared, perhaps. Either way, she felt prone to honor the hint she'd just received from her grandfather and immediately popped to her feet, saying to Theo with a firm voice like that which she'd heard Estelle use with him, "We should give them some privacy. Come with me."

She ordered rather than requested and was glad when he stood and followed her back into the shop where Vivian sat down and was glad that Theo did the same on a chair across the room, rather than resuming his pacing.

After many minutes had passed, Vivian began to wonder if she should go and get a book to read so she could pass the time without being so aware of Theodore Weatherby in the room. But she remained indecisive about just sitting there patiently as opposed to crossing the parlor to get a book, which would disturb Samuel and Estelle.

Vivian was surprised when Theo suddenly broke the silence with what seemed an attempt to make casual conversation. "So . . ." he motioned with his hand to indicate the shop in which they were sitting, ". . . what do we do if a customer comes while we are sitting here and—"

"No need to worry," she said, forcing her own voice to remain kind and respectful since his question had not held any hint of the disdain she'd felt from him previously. "We've not had a single customer in weeks. My grandfather's inability to work quickly became common knowledge in the area, and people have taken their business elsewhere."

"Oh, I see," he said, sounding genuinely sympathetic to the problem. "I'm very sorry for your troubles, Miss Peyton."

"Thank you," she said kindly even though the comment bristled her. She didn't sense any kind of condescension from him, but she had to resist the urge to tell him that he had no idea how difficult life could be when unexpected health problems could equate to potentially being without a home to live in or food to eat. Vivian pushed away any hint of defensiveness on her part and stated with confidence, "We'll soon have the problem solved once I'm able to acquire a position."

"You're going into service in order to care for your grandfather?" he asked, still not sounding condescending—simply curious.

"Yes," she said. "He's given me a good life and always made certain I had everything I needed. I'm only too happy to now repay the favor; that's the way it's meant to be with life moving on."

"I suppose it is," he said in a noncommittal tone.

Before either of them could make any further comment, they heard Estelle's footsteps approaching. The sound of her shoes on the floor sounded entirely different from the way Samuel shuffled as he walked. Vivian and Theo both stood before Estelle appeared in the open doorway of the shop, wearing a pleasant smile as if she'd just enjoyed an audience at the palace.

Looking directly at Vivian, Estelle said, "Your grandfather is worn out, I believe, and needs to rest. But I've promised him I will return soon for another visit. I'll send word ahead next time so that I don't interrupt your routine."

"You are welcome *any* time," Vivian said. "We will gladly adjust our routine for your visits."

"You are such a kind, dear girl," Estelle said, once again taking hold of both of Vivian's hands. "He's so blessed to have you, and I'm so glad to know that he has someone so kind and competent caring for him."

Vivian could only smile and nod slightly in response to her compliment, mostly because it had sparked an unexpected temptation to cry. She was then surprised to see Estelle take a seat, as if she had some matter of unfinished business that needed to be completed before she left. A quick glance toward Theo let Vivian know that he too was surprised, although he didn't sit back down.

Estelle patted the chair next to herself to indicate that Vivian should sit beside her, which she did. "Now," Estelle said, taking Vivian's hand, "I don't want you to feel any discomfort from what I'm about to say."

"Very well," Vivian replied, not knowing *how* she might feel since she had no idea concerning Estelle's intentions.

"Your grandfather has told me that you are looking for work," Estelle said, and immediately turned a firm glare toward her nephew as she held up a

finger with her free hand, silently making it clear that she didn't want to hear any opinion he might have on this subject. Turning back to Vivian, Estelle continued. "Your grandfather didn't tell me this with any hint of asking for my help; he was simply talking candidly about the situation. I'm certain that you are capable of finding work and putting yourself to it fully without any help from me. Nevertheless, I would like to offer you a position in my home. There's always something to be done in a house so ridiculously large."

"Oh," was all Vivian could manage to say, due to becoming suddenly breathless.

"Don't worry about those other appointments you have later today," Estelle said. "Just come to the servants' entrance at half-past two and ask to speak with Mrs. Thatcher. She will be more than happy to visit with you and provide suitable employment. I'll make certain of it."

While Vivian was trying to think of a way to appropriately protest, certain she should not take advantage of Estelle's affection for her grandfather in this way, Estelle raised a finger toward Vivian just as she had done toward Theo a moment ago. "I won't hear any argument, my dear. Let me just say that your grandfather offered me a great many kindnesses at a time in my life when I very much needed kindness. To repay him in this minuscule way is nothing but a pleasure." She stood, which prompted a relieved sigh from her nephew; he might as well have come right out and declared that he was overjoyed to finally be leaving this place.

"It's been such a great pleasure to meet you, my dear," Estelle said to Vivian, "and visiting with your grandfather is likely the best thing that's happened to me in years."

"The sentiment is mutual," Vivian said, "and I'm certain my grandfather would agree."

"I'm certain we will see each other again soon," Estelle said and moved toward the front door. Vivian couldn't miss the smile and wink she tossed toward Theo as she added, "And now that my nephew knows I am perfectly safe here, I doubt he'll feel the need to chaperone me in the future." She laughed softly to conclude the statement, which made Vivian realize that despite Estelle making it clear that she was Theo's elder who expected his respect, they also shared a mutual fondness that enabled her to tease him; Vivian wondered then if some of their prior interaction had at least partially been in jest. The idea fascinated Vivian and sparked her curiosity, but they were on their way out the door.

"Thank you so much for coming," Vivian said before they exchanged formal farewells, and Vivian stood in the open doorway as Theo helped his

aunt step into a grand carriage that had been waiting outside all this time. He nodded politely toward Vivian before he disappeared into the carriage himself and they were quickly off. Vivian waited until the carriage turned a corner and she could no longer see it before she went back inside to find her grandfather dozing. But she could have sworn he had a smile on his face.

Vivian felt suddenly overcome with exhaustion after the unexpected visit of Estelle and her nephew. Everything about Estelle left a warm glow in her absence, as if a pleasant breeze had wafted through the house, leaving behind the fragrance of fresh flowers and spring rain. Vivian wanted to just sit back and close her eyes to indulge in the memory of every detail of Estelle's visit and the joy she had brought into their living space with her natural kindness and compassion. In contrast, Vivian felt a strange exhaustion in recalling the presence of Estelle's nephew. Her interactions with him—even just having to sit with him in strained silence—all felt as if they had taken great effort. Vivian had never been one to care what other people thought of her, and yet she absolutely felt as if Theodore Weatherby had been in a constant state of assessing her and everything about her life, all of which he had judged to be unsuitable. She would have loved to hear the conversation between Estelle and Theo during their brief carriage ride home, certain that Theo would have expressed his disdain for her involvement with the cobbler and his granddaughter, while Estelle would have stood her ground with quiet dignity, neatly putting her nephew in his place.

Vivian became so lost in her musings regarding the delightful surprise visit of her grandfather's dear friend that it took her off guard to suddenly recall that Estelle had offered her a job. While Vivian would have preferred for her relationship with Estelle to remain comprised of the older lady's occasional visits to her home, she couldn't help feeling deeply grateful for Estelle's offer and the compassion with which it had been delivered. Still, Vivian hoped that her work wouldn't require her to ever actually cross paths with Estelle *or* Theo. She preferred to never see the arrogant Theo again, despite the hint of evidence she'd gleaned while they'd been alone in the shop together that he *was* capable of being polite. On the other hand, Vivian hoped to see Estelle a great deal in the future, because she hoped that her visits to Samuel might become a regular occurrence. But while Vivian was working in Estelle's home, she would prefer to never see her. Having known more than one woman—besides her friend Betsy—from her congregation at church who worked in service at a big house, Vivian knew that being hired meant starting at the bottom of the household hierarchy, doing the most menial of chores, and remaining invisible to the family for whom they worked—never being in the same room at the same time, but rather cleaning or serving when they would be elsewhere. And there were always tedious tasks to be performed in the kitchen and laundry where members of the family would never go. If Vivian could earn a wage sufficient to meet the needs of herself and her grandfather, she would be only too pleased to be one of those invisible servants, and to only see Estelle here in her own home. Betsy's terrible experience came to mind in a way that made Vivian wonder if it would be wise to take employment in a household where she had a connection to the lady of the house. If the other servants ever discovered this, she felt certain it could cause a great deal of trouble. However, Vivian sincerely believed that she *could* remain invisible and keep their connection a secret, and she suspected that the household of Estelle Weatherby would likely be a place where employment was far more favorable than it might be in other households.

Realizing it was past the usual time for lunch, Vivian heated up some leftover soup and buttered some thick slices of bread. She woke her grandfather before it was ready so that he could freshen up first. By the time he'd returned to his chair by the fire that Vivian had stoked up, she had their lunch set out.

As soon as Samuel had offered the usual brief blessing on the food, Vivian said, "Your visit seemed to go well. Did you enjoy yourself?"

"Oh, very much!" Samuel said with enthusiasm and a dreamy sparkle in his eyes. He then looked right at Vivian and added with a mock scowl, "I never would have thought you could get up to such mischief at your age."

"But you can't tell me you aren't glad that I found her," she stated with confidence and a smile.

"So very glad," Samuel said with a contented sigh. "I never thought I'd see her again, and I certainly never imagined that we could just have such a visit as old friends, with no need to hide the way we once felt about each other."

"She seemed very pleased to see you," Vivian commented between bites, allowing herself time to chew properly and swallow.

"Not as pleased as I was to see *her*," Samuel said with a little chuckle. He then scowled slightly and added, "I'm not certain what to make of her nephew; he reminds me a little of her father. He seemed rather disapproving, but I doubt there's much he can do about it since she's his senior."

"He does come across as rather arrogant," Vivian said. "It was him I spoke to when I found the house."

Vivian went on to repeat what had happened now that her search for Estelle was no longer a secret. Samuel found the story amusing, especially given the fact that it had turned out well.

Vivian heard the clock chime and glanced at it, letting out an alarmed gasp. "Oh, my goodness!" she muttered. "We started lunch later than usual and we've been visiting, and . . . oh, I must hurry!"

"That's right," Samuel said. "You have those two appointments for interviews."

Vivian felt a little astonished to realize that he had no idea Estelle had offered her a job. But of course, Vivian had to tell him. "Actually . . ." she drawled, "no. I have an appointment at half past two to meet with Estelle's housekeeper. She's offered me work, Grandpapa, so there's no need to go to the other appointments; still, I mustn't be late."

"I see," Samuel said, and Vivian had no idea how he felt about the matter, but she didn't have time to talk about it now. She left him to finish his lunch and took her own dishes to the kitchen before she hurried to make herself presentable, wearing the same dress, shoes, and hat that she'd worn the previous day. She had no other options for clothing that was suitable to wear in public. The thought passed through her mind that it would be nice to earn enough money to be able to buy something new for herself and for her grandfather, that her wages might be sufficient to meet their needs and give them a little bit of surplus for such luxuries. But Vivian hurried to push that thought away; right now, she was simply grateful at the prospect of having employment that *would* meet their needs.

Vivian checked on Samuel to make sure he had all he needed before she set out, walking at a brisk pace to be certain she wasn't late. She estimated the distance between her own home and Estelle's to be more than a mile, perhaps closer to a mile and a half. It wasn't a difficult distance for her to walk, by any means, although she didn't want to think about the inevitable cold and stormy days when she would need to walk this path from her home to work and back. She'd spent her entire life living and working under the same roof; this would be an adjustment, but her gratitude far outweighed any of her concerns.

Vivian was grateful for the watch she'd inherited from her grandmother, which was pinned to the front of her dress. She lifted it every few minutes to check the time, wishing the glass face was a little less scratched so she could see the position of the hands without needing to move the watch around to find the correct angle to see them accurately. At this pace, she estimated that she would arrive with a few minutes to catch her breath and gather her courage before embarking on this new adventure, hopefully with enough dignity that it wouldn't be snuffed out by her nervousness. Again, she hoped to not cross paths with Estelle or her nephew; not today, not ever—at least not within the walls of the enormous, grand house where they resided.

Vivian walked slowly down the drive situated to one side of the house where she felt certain several wheeled vehicles traversed back and forth between the city streets and the carriage house and stables that she could see in distance. She purposely took in deep breaths and blew them out slowly as she walked at a comfortable pace, checking her watch frequently with the intention of knocking on the door at exactly half past two. When she turned the corner around the back of the house, she caught sight of an enormous garden with scattered trees and a vast variety of shrubberies and flowers that were just coming to life with spring. She'd never seen anything so beautiful and had to take a moment to just try to comprehend that such a lovely place had been created. She was startled back to the present and feared that her goal of arriving punctually might have been delayed, but her watch let her know that she was perfectly on time as she knocked on the door that was clearly the servants' entrance. She nodded toward three onlookers—two women and one man—who were visiting casually, likely taking a break from their work—and they nodded in return. A grouping of chairs was situated beneath an awning that also covered a great many crates that appeared to be filled with vegetables and other supplies for the kitchen. The three onlookers seemed curious but not unfriendly, and Vivian hoped she would not meet with any animosity from those with whom she would be working. She noticed the uniforms they wore and wondered if she would be required to do the same; that would solve the problem of the fact that her clothing was of little variety and barely presentable. And she certainly didn't want to wear her best dress—the one she had on now—to be cleaning and scrubbing or whatever they might have her do.

Vivian took a deep breath and knocked again, but one of the nearby women said kindly, "Oh, just go on in. Everyone's either too busy to answer the door, or they just don't hear it. I think Mrs. Thatcher's expecting you."

Vivian was a little startled to think that everyone had been made aware that a potential new maid was arriving today. But she warded off her nervousness and embarrassment by laughing softly and saying, "Thank you. I don't think I've ever been gossiped about before."

They all laughed comfortably. "No need for concern there," the man said. "Just information we were given; no gossip."

Vivian nodded, and the other woman said, "Good luck. I hope she takes you on; I think we could all use just a little less work."

"Not that we're worked to death or anything," the man said. "It's just nice to spread the work out a little."

"Of course," Vivian said. "Thank you. I'd be awfully glad to have the job . . . and be able to help." She nodded toward them and went inside, not wanting to be late.

Once inside, Vivian immediately became aware of pleasant aromas and a great deal of noise and bustle coming from what was obviously the kitchen, the door to which was just ahead of her on the left. She debated going to the kitchen to ask for directions, then noticed an open door on the opposite side of the hall and she went there first, peeking in to see a robust woman of about forty years with gray streaks in her brown hair that was tightly knotted at the back of her head. Her focus was entirely on some papers on the desk in front of her, but Vivian felt relatively certain this had to be Mrs. Thatcher; she would never know if she didn't ask.

Vivian knocked lightly on the open door, and the woman's head popped up curiously.

"I'm looking for Mrs. Thatcher," Vivian said.

"And you've found her," the housekeeper said, coming to her feet. She smiled and her countenance was kind—much to Vivian's relief. "You must be Miss Peyton; Miss Weatherby told me you would be coming."

"Vivian," she corrected, preferring less formality as she stepped forward and offered her hand in greeting.

Mrs. Thatcher shook her hand briefly, then motioned toward the door. "Would you mind closing that so we can visit privately?" Vivian did so and the housekeeper added, "Please sit down; make yourself comfortable. Would you like some tea?"

"I'm fine for now, thank you," Vivian said, "but if you wish to have some yourself don't let me keep you from—"

"Perhaps when we've finished talking, we'll have some," Mrs. Thatcher said and leaned back in her chair, relaxing her hands in her lap.

"Now," the housekeeper said as if she were about to declare something extremely important, "Miss Weatherby has given me the highest recommendation of your character and your willingness to work. I assume you will not give me any reason to contradict such high praise."

"I will certainly try my best," Vivian said. "Miss Weatherby is far too kind."

"She is the kindest of ladies," Mrs. Thatcher said. "Those of us who are privileged enough to work in her home are aware of how very blessed we are. I'm told you have no experience with household service, but you have practical experience that will be useful here; hiring someone without certain prerequisites is not always the case."

"Then I feel very blessed as well," Vivian said, wondering then if her hope of getting work in such a household would have failed due to lack of experience if not for Estelle's intervention. Feeling the need to respond to the other part of Mrs. Thatcher's comment, she added, "I do indeed have practical experience. Even though I've not actually worked in service, I've cared for the home I share with my grandfather completely on my own for years. I'm capable of doing whatever you might need done, and I'm glad to help wherever I'm needed; I'm certainly not above doing the most menial tasks. I'm simply grateful for the work."

"And that's exactly what I like to hear," Mrs. Thatcher said and smiled again, giving Vivian the hope that this was going to work out, and it might not be such a difficult transition in her life after all.

Chapter Four
CHANGE

Vivian visited with Mrs. Thatcher for more than an hour and felt completely relaxed. Their conversation was a pleasant mixture of explaining how the household functioned and the work that would be expected of Vivian. When the housekeeper told Vivian the monthly wage she would be receiving Vivian couldn't help but be pleased. It would be enough to comfortably cover their basic expenses. There wouldn't be enough for any luxuries or indulgences, but neither she nor her grandfather depended upon such things, and she knew they would both be incredibly grateful to have their needs met.

The two women also shared a congenial, personal exchange, getting better acquainted with each other. Mrs. Thatcher was genuinely interested in Vivian's life and the reasons why she currently needed work. Vivian explained the situation regarding her grandfather, being careful not to offer any information that might inadvertently betray Samuel's connection to Estelle. In turn, Vivian learned that Mrs. Thatcher had grown up in an orphanage and had been collected from there by a man who took orphans into his home to have them trained in service so they could work and provide for themselves. She admitted that certain aspects of her life had been difficult, but she found great satisfaction in the way she had worked her way up the ladder to the position she held now, which she enjoyed very much. "At least most of the time," she said with a wink. "Of course, there are always challenges."

"I'm certain!" Vivian said.

She then learned that Mrs. Thatcher had never been married; the missus was a title that came with her position, which Vivian found somewhat strange. It was as if this woman had been declared married to the house. But Mrs. Thatcher seemed happy and fulfilled, and Vivian was relieved beyond words to know she would be working for and reporting to such a kind and forthright woman.

When Mrs. Thatcher asked Vivian if she had any questions, and Vivian honestly couldn't think of one—given that the housekeeper had explained everything in precise detail—Mrs. Thatcher left the room for a moment and returned to announce that tea would be brought for them to share and they could visit a little longer. Vivian felt certain that once she began working here at the very bottom of the ladder she would not be invited into the housekeeper's office for tea; therefore, she was determined to enjoy this experience while it lasted. She wondered where Estelle might be and what she might be doing, but immediately forced the thought away with the reminder that she would do well to not wonder about Estelle at all while she was here at work. She only hoped that Estelle might occasionally visit her grandfather at times when Vivian wasn't working so that she could enjoy the company of this kind and gracious woman.

Vivian enjoyed the lovely tea more than she dared admit without sounding like a fool. She'd never tasted such fine biscuits and little cakes and delicate sandwiches. In fact, she'd never imagined that such elegant food existed. And the tea itself was divine! She thought of Estelle drinking the tea that Vivian had prepared and realized how gracious she had been, considering the quality she was accustomed to. Vivian even felt a little less miffed with Theo for declining the tea and scones she'd offered him. She couldn't blame either of them for living a life where their tastes had always been accustomed to such fineness.

Vivian enjoyed more conversation with Mrs. Thatcher while they shared tea and the delicious fare with which it had been served. When they were finished, the housekeeper seemed to reluctantly recall that she had many responsibilities to which she must see. She thanked Vivian for a lovely visit and concluded with the simple declaration, "I will see you in the morning, Vivian, and we'll have your uniforms ready for you when you arrive. Meet me here, and I will help get you started."

"Thank you," Vivian said. "Thank you so much for everything." She nodded at the smiling housekeeper and echoed, "I will see you in the morning," before she hurried out of the office and out of the house, where she paused to take in the view of the magnificent gardens and breathe in the spring air, feeling a burden lifted that she'd been carrying ever since she'd realized that her grandfather would no longer be able to work and their resources were slowly diminishing.

Vivian enjoyed her walk home, slowing her pace to a comfortable stroll since she had plenty of time before sundown, and the lack of weight on her shoulders invited her to pay more attention to her surroundings and simply enjoy the world around her. She noticed a variety of satisfying aromas coming from the bakeries and pubs and food vendors that she passed, and she made a couple of stops to purchase a few things to improve their menus at home, having the confidence that doing so would not consume money she couldn't replace. Children playing in the street made her laugh right along with them as she observed their antics and recalled playing much the same way near the cobbler's shop during her own childhood.

The closer Vivian got to her home, the more people she saw who she knew. She'd never ceased her efforts to be cordial and polite in her greetings to others, but she hadn't realized until today that she'd been putting a great deal of effort into doing so, whereas today it seemed easy and even delightful to exchange hellos and how-do-you-dos to those she encountered. Vivian wondered if people might have noticed the change in her over recent months as she'd descended into a state of worry and discouragement. And now those feelings had been replaced by hope and gratification, knowing she would be given the opportunity to work for a fair wage and see that all was well for her and for the man who had raised her and had always kept her safe and cared for, and had made her feel especially loved.

Vivian returned home to find her grandfather in his usual chair, but he was reading rather than resting. He looked up and greeted her with a smile as she entered the parlor, removing the pin from her hat that had kept it connected to the mound of hair on top of her head.

"How are you?" Vivian asked Samuel.

"I'm well enough," he said, which Vivian knew to mean that he couldn't find a particular complaint—or he didn't *want* to complain—but he very much wanted to feel more like his normal self and be able to return to the busy life he'd always lived. "And you?" he asked. "You look happy. I assume it went well."

"Oh, it did!" Vivian said and sat down, repeating in detail how the experience had played out, including her own feelings about every facet of what had happened and all that had been discussed.

When Vivian admitted that she hoped to never cross paths with Estelle or her nephew while at work, Samuel seemed surprised. "But why?" he asked. "I know her nephew has not been very cordial, but Estelle is—"

"I like Estelle *very* much," Vivian said, "but I'll be working in her home, doing the most menial tasks. I prefer to share any conversation with her *here* when she comes to visit; I assume she'll come to visit."

"She said she would." Samuel couldn't hold back a smile.

"But I would never want to be seen by other members of the staff as being shown any preference from her, and . . . well . . . I think it would just be awkward, so . . . I'm grateful for the job, but I'd like to keep a clear division between these two aspects of our life."

"I think I understand," Samuel said. "Does this have anything to do with what happened to Betsy?" he asked with concern.

"I can't deny that it makes me somewhat wary," Vivian admitted, feeling a vague shudder go through her, glad that Samuel hadn't noticed. "I'd simply prefer to be known by my fellow workers as just another maid with no connection whatsoever to the family we work for."

Samuel nodded and began, "When you—"

He was interrupted by a loud knocking at the outside shop door. Since Vivian had locked it when she'd come in—knowing there wouldn't be any customers—no one would have been able to enter. Certain she'd been right about that conclusion, she wondered who could possibly be knocking, and was surprised to open the door and see a pleasant-looking man with extremely curly blond hair. He wasn't particularly tall, but he exuded an aura of strength. In one hand he held his hat, and in the other a very distinctive-looking bag. *Was he a doctor?*

"Miss Peyton?" he asked.

"Yes," she said.

"My name is Dr. Muller. I've come to check on your grandfather and see how he's feeling."

"But . . ." Vivian protested, thinking of how much a doctor's visit might cost, and knowing they couldn't afford it, "we didn't—"

"Miss Estelle Weatherby has sent me," he said with a smile, "and there's no cost to you or her." He winked in a way that made his eyes almost twinkle. "Shall we just say I owe her a few favors; she's been very kind to me."

"I'm not at all surprised to hear *that*," Vivian said, gladly opening the door more widely for him to enter. For months she'd wanted the opinion of a different doctor regarding Samuel's health, but it simply hadn't been financially possible. She wanted to protest the generosity of both Estelle and this doctor, but she felt only gratitude for such a miraculous visit.

"Please come in." Vivian stepped aside and motioned with her arm. The doctor entered and closed the door. "My grandfather is in here."

Vivian led the way to the parlor and found her grandfather looking expectantly curious; perhaps he was hoping it had been Estelle at the door.

"A kind doctor has come to visit you," she said with calm confidence and a smile that she hoped would convince her grandfather to graciously cooperate rather than protest.

"But how . . ." he began but couldn't seem to come up with the words.

"I'm Dr. Muller," their visitor said and stepped forward, holding out his hand, which Samuel took, and they exchanged a hearty handshake. "Miss Estelle Weatherby has asked me to check in on you, but I assure you her motives are only based in concern for a good friend; that's what she told me. And she's not paying me for my visit since I owe her a few favors, and I'm only too glad to come and meet someone she's spoken of so highly."

"Oh, I see," Samuel said and motioned to the chair where Vivian generally sat.

The doctor sat down and put his bag on the floor beside him. Vivian sat on the sofa, deeply curious about how Dr. Muller might assess the changes in her grandfather's health, and unable to keep from hoping that he might have some answers—or even a remedy—for what ailed Samuel.

"Now," Dr. Muller said, "tell me about what happened when you first began to feel ill. I understand it was several months ago, but I'd wager you remember. Don't leave out any detail you can recall; even the smallest thing might give me a hint as to what the problem might be."

Vivian listened attentively as her grandfather described his initial illness when he'd had a sore throat accompanied by aching all over his body. He and Vivian had agreed that it was likely one of those common illnesses that came and went, and Vivian had been careful in the way her grandmother had taught her to not get too close to her grandfather, to thoroughly clean everything that he used, and to frequently wash her hands. Edna had been singularly wise and perhaps even brilliant when it came to such things, and Vivian trusted her advice. She had seen many instances throughout her life of how one person in the household might become ill, but others did not contract the same illness if they carefully followed Edna's regimen. Vivian inserted herself into the conversation to explain this to the doctor and he seemed pleased, stating that he agreed with Edna's theories and he had seen much evidence of the same thing.

Samuel then told the doctor how his initial symptoms had included terrible fatigue and weakness, and his concern that when the other symptoms had disappeared, the fatigue and weakness had remained, leaving him deeply frustrated with his inability to do much of anything except rest. And those symptoms had continued to this day.

"Are you able to see to your personal needs?" the doctor asked.

"Yes," Samuel said, "but I'm terribly slow at it and the effort takes a lot out of me, if that makes sense."

"It does indeed," the doctor said. "And I understand your granddaughter sees that you're properly cared for. She prepares your meals?"

"Yes," Samuel said with pride in his voice, "she's a wonderful girl; I don't know what I'd do without her. She makes certain everything is taken care of, and she's a fine cook."

"I'm glad to hear it," Dr. Muller smiled. "And how is your appetite? You look a little thin. Have you always been this way, or are you eating less?"

Vivian answered when Samuel hesitated. "He's always had a lean build, although I do believe he's lost weight. He eats his meals fairly well, but not with the appetite he once had."

"I see," the doctor said. "So . . . let me see if I understand correctly. You initially felt the symptoms of what might have been perhaps some kind of mild influenza or a cold, although those symptoms lasted longer than normal."

"That's right," Samuel said.

"But even after those symptoms had disappeared, you were left with this debilitating fatigue and weakness that has not relented, even after all these months. And so, you are still incapable of exerting much energy in any respect."

"That's right," Samuel said again.

The doctor turned to Vivian and asked, "Would you agree with that assessment? Is there anything you've observed that you'd like to add?"

"I agree," she said, "and I believe that summarizes the situation."

"I understand you consulted a doctor about this."

"Yes," Samuel said.

"And what," the doctor continued, "if I may ask, was his assessment? His diagnosis might be helpful in determining my own evaluation."

Samuel looked at Vivian. "I can't recall exactly what he said. Do you remember?"

"I do," Vivian said, appreciating the way Dr. Muller looked directly at her and showed a genuine interest in her opinions and the information she might offer; the doctor they'd consulted before—who was the only doctor they'd ever dealt with—had mostly ignored Vivian except to give her orders about how she needed to take good care of her grandfather, implying that she'd not done so previously, which had felt insulting. "He said very little except that my grandfather was getting on in years and this was just one of those things that sometimes happens to the elderly."

Dr. Muller seemed surprised and was quick to say to Samuel, "You're not so very old, sir. I'm not certain what's happening but I do have an idea I'd like to address. Whether or not I'm right, I heartily disagree with such a diagnosis. The deterioration of the body that comes with old age comes on much more slowly and generally with other symptoms beyond fatigue and weakness. The fact that this followed an illness is a big clue to the problem." The doctor leaned his forearms on his thighs so that he could look at Samuel more closely. "I might be wrong in what I'm thinking the problem is, and I'm never afraid to admit that I don't always have the answers; sometimes there are simply no answers to be had. There is so much we don't know about what ails the human body. But I wonder if you would be willing to experiment with me to assess whether I might be right. If the experiment fails, we haven't lost anything, but if it works, I believe there's a good chance we can get you feeling better. What do you think?"

"I'm willing to try anything that might help," Samuel said eagerly, and Vivian noted that her own heartbeat had quickened over the very possibility that her grandfather's condition could be improved. Oh, what a miracle that would be! Now that she had a job that could support their financial needs, she wasn't concerned about Samuel being able to return to his work, but if he could simply do more and feel better, she knew he would be so much happier.

"Wonderful!" the doctor said as he sat up straight and clasped his hands together abruptly in a gesture of excitement, as if he'd already gained a great personal investment in Samuel's health. Vivian really liked this man, and from her grandfather's expression she surmised that he did as well.

"Now," Dr. Muller went on, "it's my belief that you contracted an illness that I've seen many times through the years, although it generally manifests in younger people. It lasts much longer than the usual cold or influenza, and its symptoms are generally milder—except for the overwhelming fatigue. The thing about this level of fatigue is that it naturally makes a person do little but sleep. And when a person is further along in years, it doesn't take as much for a sedentary lifestyle to settle in more deeply, making it more difficult to get back to normal. The body quickly becomes accustomed to the need for excessive rest and it's not so easy to recover. And the more the physical body remains sedentary, the weaker and less mobile a person can become. Your symptoms are real and valid, Mr. Peyton, but I believe we can slowly eliminate them."

"Truly?" Samuel asked, a glisten of moisture in his eyes. Vivian completely understood and felt the sting of tears in her own eyes.

"Truly," the doctor said, "so this is what I want you to do. Each day I would like you to increase your activity just a tiny bit. When you get on your feet for any reason, take an extra turn around the room before you sit back down. Increase this just a little each day. Now," he lifted a finger in caution, "if you become acutely aware of your heart beating, or you have any difficulty breathing, these symptoms could be an indication that we *are* dealing with a more serious, very real condition, and we will reassess. A little bit of mild breathlessness when you're exerting effort your body's not accustomed to is normal, and if that happens, just sit down, and catch your breath. But if it's anything beyond very mild and doesn't calm down within a few minutes I want to know about it. Does this make sense to you, Mr. Peyton?"

"It does, yes," Samuel said eagerly. "I can certainly do what you're suggesting."

"Good!" the doctor said enthusiastically, then turned again to look at Vivian. "Are you here at home with him?"

"I work during the days," she said, "but I'm here in the morning and evening."

Dr. Muller nodded, then looked at Samuel. "Until we can know whether your efforts cause any negative reactions, I don't want you exerting any extra energy unless your granddaughter is here in the house with you. That way she can send for me if there's a problem. If our experiment goes well, then you can slowly increase your activity even when she's not here with you. Are we in agreement?"

"Yes, indeed!" Samuel declared at the same time Vivian said, "Oh, yes!" She could hardly believe what she was hearing. They had just taken the word of the other doctor who had simply seemed to shrug it all off, chalking it up to Samuel's advancing years and implying that he would never have any chance for improvement. But everything Dr. Muller had just told them made perfect sense, and Vivian felt some real hope that her grandfather could indeed improve. Oh, how she prayed that their hopes would not be in vain!

Theodore enjoyed a lengthy visit with his mother and sister before he went to the library and attempted to make himself comfortable to enjoy a small amount of brandy while he relaxed with a book before going to bed. When he found himself reading the same page over and over, he finally slammed the book down beside him and let out a harsh scoffing sound even though there was no one in the room to hear it. He felt completely infuriated with himself over the simple fact that ever since he'd met the perplexing Vivian Peyton, he'd hardly been able to stop thinking about her. For no apparent reason, she appeared in his mind far too often, provoking a strange quivering in his stomach that he found annoying if not entirely discomfiting. According to all logic and reason, he didn't even like the woman. And they certainly had nothing in common. Yet he couldn't concentrate on *anything* without having her intrude upon his thoughts like a fly that wouldn't stop buzzing around his head.

Theo gave up on trying to read and left the library, seeking out a *different* distraction. He hurried with pleasant anticipation to his aunt's sitting room, once again surprised with how he never grew tired of her company, and he felt deeply grateful to know that she would always be there for him. He didn't know how he would have ever managed without Estelle.

Theo knocked lightly on the door and heard her call for him to enter.

"Hello," Theo said, peering around the door as he opened it.

"Oh, hello!" she said with an enthusiastic smile when she saw him; that smile alone always made him feel loved. How could he not when she was so genuinely pleased to see him, just as he was to see her? He couldn't think of any other person in the world who might remotely feel the same way. His mother and sister were always pleased to see him, but they lacked the exuberance over his visits that he always received from Estelle.

"Come and sit down," she added, setting aside the book in her hands. He closed the door and took a chair while she added, "The book is boring, anyway. I'm so glad you came." Before Theo could begin any kind of pleasant, benign conversation that might distract him, Estelle furrowed her brow and added, "Something's troubling you."

"Why would you think that?" he asked feigning some attempt at innocence, feeling as he often did that she could practically see into his soul.

"I know you better than anyone," she insisted. "You know you can talk to me and I would never betray your confidence."

"I *do* know that," he said.

"In fact, I suspect the very reason you're here is that you're debating whether you *should* talk to me about something."

Theo sighed, feeling as if he'd been caught making mischief and he either had to confess the truth or come up with a lie. And he believed in being completely truthful; Estelle had taught him the value of honesty, with the example of some real-life situations that had driven home the point of how important it was to maintain integrity.

"Out with it," Estelle ordered, although she had an uncanny way of giving orders while maintaining an attitude of kindness and compassion.

"Well," he began and cleared his throat as if it were necessary to clear the way for difficult words to come out of his mouth, "the thing is . . ." he sighed and cleared his throat again, "I . . . seem to be having trouble with . . . well . . . I can't stop thinking about . . . someone . . . and this has never happened to me before, and yet . . . the situation is ludicrous, and . . ."

"It's Vivian, isn't it," she stated firmly with a mischievous smile.

"How do you do that?" he demanded, unable to hide the truth when she was so thoroughly perceptive.

"It was just a hunch based on my observations," she said. "I saw the way the two of you interacted at the front gate . . . and at the cobbler's shop."

"We could barely tolerate each other!" Theo pointed out.

Estelle's smile broadened. "Which is exactly how the seeds of love sometimes begin to grow."

"Love?" he repeated the word as if it were profane.

"Yes, my dear," Estelle said and slid over on the couch so she could lean forward and put her hand over his where it rested on the arm of the chair. "She's a wonderful young woman. Is it so strange that you might feel some attraction toward her? Some affection?"

"It's ridiculous and impossible," Theo insisted. "We come from completely different worlds and—"

"Like Samuel and me?" she countered. "If I *could* have married him all those years ago, I would have. My mother would have supported such a decision. We are all human beings, Theo. There are no social barriers when it comes to the people we love."

Love? Marriage? Theo felt so fidgety he might as well have had three or four pesky flies buzzing around his head. "Could we talk about something else?" he asked.

Estelle leaned back on the sofa and relaxed, but her expression implied that she knew this would not be their last conversation about Vivian.

"If you wish," she said then hurried to add, "Vivian *will* be working here in the house. She begins tomorrow."

"What?" Theo exclaimed, wishing he'd not let on to how astonished and perhaps upset he felt over such a prospect. "Why?"

"She needed work due to Samuel's health making it impossible for *him* to work. You already know this; you were there when I talked to her about it."

Theo couldn't deny the truth of this, but he felt embarrassed to realize he'd completely forgotten. With all the time he'd spent thinking about her, he'd entirely pushed away the possibility of her working here, perhaps because he felt so thoroughly uncomfortable with the idea.

"I discussed the situation with Mrs. Thatcher," Estelle continued, "and it's all arranged."

"But . . ." Theo wanted to tell his aunt that he had no desire to come upon Vivian anywhere in the house.

Once again Estelle proved her ability to practically read minds. "Don't worry. She's not going to be serving our meals or anything like that. You won't even know she's here."

Theo wished that might be true, but he could already feel the reality settling in that just knowing Vivian was working in the house would surely make it more difficult for him to stop thinking about her. But he kept that thought to himself. He wanted to ask Estelle if Vivian and Samuel were any relation to the Richard Peyton who had lured his father into a scheme that had led him to his death. But Theo couldn't bring himself to even put a voice to his suspicions. A part of him didn't want to know, and he certainly didn't want to talk about it.

"Might we indulge in some kind of conversation that has nothing to do with Vivian Peyton?" Theo asked.

"Very well," Estelle said. "Tell me all the gossip from the gentlemen's club. You were there this afternoon, were you not?"

"I was," he said, keeping to himself that spending time at such a place was becoming less and less appealing. But he knew Estelle enjoyed hearing the social news of London, so he did his best to remember anything he might have overheard, hating the way his thoughts kept flitting to Vivian, wondering what she might be doing now.

As soon as the doctor left, Samuel was anxious to immediately stand up and begin the experiment of moving about just a little more than usual with the hope that he might be able to rebuild his strength. Vivian walked around the parlor with him, close enough to take hold of his arm if he showed the need for any support but allowing him to do this on his own if possible. They circled the little parlor twice before Samuel admitted he was feeling weak—but he said it with a smile, as if this little bit of effort helped him feel better about himself. Vivian couldn't resist hugging him tightly before he sat back down, declaring proudly, "I certainly didn't feel any of those things the doctor said might be a problem; I'm glad of that."

"So am I," Vivian said and went to the kitchen to prepare some supper. She peeled, sliced, and fried some potatoes, mixed with just a little bit of sausage she'd diced into small pieces to add flavor. While the potatoes and sausage cooked, she set some sliced carrots simmering in another pot. Vivian wondered if having a job, combined with the hope the doctor had given them, made the meal she was preparing seem more appetizing, or if she was simply very hungry. Likely both, she concluded, as she turned to take her grandfather's food to the parlor, only to find him sitting at the little table in the kitchen where they had once eaten all their meals. He'd brought along his blankets, which he likely needed more than ever, given the distance of the table from the fire, but he had a smile on his face as he announced, "This is a nice change."

"Yes, it is," Vivian replied and hurried to set their supper out on the table.

"I wonder," Samuel said, "if I am feeling the cold more acutely because I don't move around enough."

"It's possible," Vivian said, thinking that it made sense.

"Do you really think," Samuel continued, "that there could be such a simple solution to all this?"

Vivian reached across the table to squeeze her grandfather's hand. "We can't be certain yet, but it sounds encouraging, and we'll keep hoping."

Samuel smiled. "And with any luck, you won't need to keep working for long once I've gotten back to work myself and—"

"Grandpapa," Vivian said earnestly, "let's take this slowly . . . one step at a time. I don't mind working; I really don't. I think it will be good for me to broaden my options and perspective. If and when you might be able to begin working again, perhaps you should do so at a more leisurely pace. It's all right to slow down and enjoy life more; you've earned it. And I suspect you'll need to set aside time to visit with Estelle."

Vivian choked back a giggle when her grandfather blushed visibly and lowered his head, attempting to hide the undeniable delight he felt over such a possibility. "I suppose we'll see about that," he said and resumed eating, shifting the conversation as he complimented Vivian on the tastiness of their supper.

Samuel returned to his chair by the fire and dozed off while Vivian tidied the kitchen. When it was time for her grandfather to go to his room to get ready for bed, he took two more turns around the parlor first and had no difficulty except—as he'd said earlier—feeling weak by the time he made it to his bed where he sat to rest before changing into his nightclothes.

After Vivian had made certain Samuel had everything he'd need, and she'd gotten ready for bed herself, she climbed beneath the covers and stared toward the ceiling, reviewing all that had happened today that could potentially change their lives a great deal. She felt some nervousness about beginning her job, simply because she wasn't certain what to expect. Despite all the effort Mrs. Thatcher had put into explaining Vivian's duties and the household rules, Vivian knew she still couldn't anticipate what the job would really be like; she would have to engage herself in the work and mingle with the other members of the staff to truly experience the reality of her new situation. She was grateful beyond words to know that the housekeeper was so kind and helpful, which would surely make everything easier. And Vivian still hoped and prayed to be able to completely avoid Estelle and her nephew, no matter what tasks she might be assigned. She was caught off guard completely when unbidden thoughts of Theodore Weatherby provoked a tingling down her back, which she surmised was simply because he made her nervous; he tended to be more than a little intimidating. She truly hoped she never crossed paths with him again.

Vivian shifted her thoughts to the doctor's unexpected visit and his beliefs regarding her grandfather's health. Oh, how she prayed that he was right! And perhaps she and her grandfather had needed this experience to adjust their priorities and their perspective regarding certain facets of their lives. Vivian genuinely believed that even if Samuel returned to his full measure of health and could resume his work full time, he was at an age where he should at least partially retire from working so hard for so many long hours each week. And she also believed it truly would be good for her to have a life beyond the confines of this house and the cobbler's shop. It would be fulfilling to earn her own wage and be able to help support the household in which she lived. Even if her grandfather were able to bring in just a little money each month by making and repairing shoes, they could easily enjoy a comfortable life and want for nothing.

Vivian was glad when the pleasant imagery of such hopes lulled her to sleep, knowing she would need to be well rested for her first day on the job.

Vivian was disappointed to wake up and find it raining. She was grateful to own an umbrella that was in reasonably good condition; otherwise, she would arrive at work looking dreadful. Wanting everything to go smoothly despite the rain, she hurried to get ready for the day, prepare breakfast, and make certain her grandfather had everything he needed. While she was nearby and busy with her tasks, he walked the circumference of the parlor a couple of times, seeming determined and hopeful regarding the doctor's theory. But the doctor had told him to only engage in his extra exercise when Vivian was in the house; therefore, Samuel wanted to be certain he completed this new routine before she left for the day.

Vivian had timed her walk to the Weatherby home the previous day so she could estimate exactly when she needed to leave to arrive a few minutes early. She didn't feel particularly nervous until she'd left her home and was walking through the rain that pattered onto the top of her umbrella and created puddles that she had to be careful to avoid. When Vivian arrived and went into the servants' entrance, she once again heard and smelled the evidence of a great deal of important activity taking place in the kitchen. She noticed a long row of hooks on the wall with shelves stretching the same distance. There were coats hanging there, and hats and gloves on the shelves where a few umbrellas were leaning. Vivian did the obvious and hung up her coat after she'd leaned her wet umbrella next to the others. For a moment she thought there should have been more of these things, then she recalled that many of those who worked here lived in servants' dormitories located within the house, which meant they wouldn't have needed to go outside at all to get to work.

Seeing no one that she might ask for instructions, Vivian went to the open door of Mrs. Thatcher's office and was glad to see the housekeeper seated behind her desk. Only then did she recall that Mrs. Thatcher had told her to come to the office when she arrived.

Vivian knocked on the open door and Mrs. Thatcher looked up from her work before she smiled and stood, taking a quick glance at the clock. "A little early," she said. "Very good." Walking around the desk she added, "From estimating your size, I've had two uniforms prepared for you; of course, two are necessary so that you can alternate between them, giving you the opportunity to keep them clean and pressed. Your appearance must be pristine at all times, even if you might never encounter a member of the family; still, one never knows." Vivian didn't like the sound of that, but she certainly liked knowing she would have *two* uniforms, so that she *could* keep them clean and pressed.

"Now," Mrs. Thatcher said, picking up the folded uniforms from the corner of her desk and setting them into Vivian's hands. "Since you won't be living in the servants' dormitories you would normally put on your uniform before leaving home. Today you can use my sitting room to change." She motioned toward a door. "I'll stay here to guard the door and give you privacy while you get ready. There is a mirror and some hairpins you can use to pin your cap in place, and you can leave your things in there for today until you go home. Now, hurry and get yourself dressed. There's work to be done."

"Yes, ma'am," Vivian said and hurried to follow Mrs. Thatcher's instructions.

Vivian was pleased to find that the black dress was a reasonably good fit, as was the crisp white apron that went over it. Once she had pinned the cap into place, Vivian quickly surveyed her reflection and liked what she saw. She felt a sense of belonging without having yet done a single task. Knowing that Mrs. Thatcher was waiting for her, she neatly folded her clothes and put them with the other uniform on a chair in a corner that looked as if it didn't get used much.

Mrs. Thatcher expressed approval when she saw Vivian in the uniform, then she took her on a brief tour of the ground floor of the house, explaining that every member of the family was in the habit of eating breakfast in their rooms, which gave the staff more time to prepare the parlors and drawing room for when they might be needed throughout the day. Following the tour, Vivian was assigned the task of removing the ashes from each fireplace and then laying kindling and wood on every grate so that a fire could be easily lit in each room should it be needed. She was then required to sweep away any evidence that she'd been there and finish with a polishing rag to be certain every hearth was perfectly clean. Vivian was given everything she needed to do her work, all of which had been put into a box with a handle that she could easily carry with one hand, while she carried a bucket for the ashes with the other.

Vivian felt completely confident with such a task since she'd done the same at home thousands of times. And she was only slightly nervous about the need to hurry so that she would be long finished before anyone in the family came to any of the rooms in which she'd been assigned to work. Mrs. Thatcher knew that Estelle had recommended her for this job, but she couldn't begin to understand how passionately Vivian felt about never seeing Estelle while working in her home. And even more so, Vivian hoped to never see Theodore Weatherby—anywhere. The potential humiliation made her shudder.

Vivian was pleased to finish her task quickly since it was evident a fire hadn't been lit in most of these rooms and there was no need for her to do anything at all. After following instructions on where to dump the ashes and where to store the equipment she'd used, Vivian was taken to the kitchen and told to simply do whatever the cook asked of her. She had trouble catching her breath when she first entered the room; never had she imagined a kitchen so large, and so many people stirring and chopping and bustling about very busily. In truth there were only four people there, but they were all so fully engaged in their work that initially it had appeared to Vivian like a small army. Mrs. O'Neill, the cook, spoke with an Irish accent that coincided with her name. She was shorter than Vivian, which was *quite* short, and she seemed pleased to have an extra pair of hands to help. Mrs. O'Neill's plump figure implied that she enjoyed her work—and her wares—and Vivian felt certain that if she herself spent her days cooking fine meals and rich desserts, she would likely end up looking the same way. The cook was polite as she exchanged greetings with Vivian and told her to start scrubbing some dirty pots from the previous night's dinner, but she wasn't as warm and amiable as Mrs. Thatcher; Vivian doubted most people would be and told herself that at least the cook wasn't grumpy and harsh.

Vivian found satisfaction in efficiently washing, rinsing, and drying the stack of dirty pans that had been left next to the large sinks. This too was a task she'd learned to do well from overseeing the kitchen at home—even if she only cooked and cleaned for herself and her grandfather. But Edna had taught her well during the years she'd been alive and had needed Vivian's assistance.

The remainder of the day was filled with a variety of tasks in different parts of the house, and thankfully the maids' cleaning schedules had been carefully mapped out so that they would not be seen by the family. Vivian enjoyed lunch and tea in the servants' dining hall; Mrs. Thatcher had told her that meals were included with the job, but Vivian hadn't anticipated the fact that the servants ate much of the same food that was being prepared for the family, and she'd never tasted anything so fine in her life. By the end of the day, she was tired but felt satisfied with the work she'd done and the overall kindness of the people who were now her fellow employees.

When Vivian went to collect her clothes to take them home, it occurred to her that it was still raining, and she doubted she could get them home without having them arrive soaking wet. But Mrs. Thatcher had anticipated the problem and provided a large canvas bag with handles.

"We use these for carrying the large purchases of a great many things needed for such a household," Mrs. Thatcher explained. "We have more than we need; you may keep that one to carry your things back and forth to work."

"Thank you very much," Vivian said with enthusiasm. It had become more evident throughout the day that most of the servants lived here in the dormitories that were located on the top floor of the house. While Vivian had no desire to live under the same roof as her employers, she definitely saw disadvantages to living elsewhere. But one of those problems had just been solved with this bag that was large enough for Vivian to transport anything she might need on any given day.

"You're very welcome," Mrs. Thatcher said. "You've done well today; I'm certain this will work out fine."

"Thank you," Vivian said again.

"And stop in the kitchen before you leave. Mrs. O'Neill wants a word with you."

Vivian nodded and crossed the hall to the kitchen, wondering if the cook might have some issues regarding her work. But Mrs. O'Neill smiled at Vivian when she saw her enter the kitchen.

"Take these," the cook said, motioning toward two covered dishes that were used to keep food fresh and warm until it was served. Before Vivian could ask any questions that might help clear up her confusion, Mrs. O'Neill added, "Meals are meant to be a benefit for all who work here. Since you leave before supper, you should take some home, so you don't have to cook after a long day's work." She nodded at the dishes. "There's enough there for your grandfather; since you don't eat breakfast here, I believe that works out fair enough."

"Oh, that's so kind!" Vivian declared since the thought of having to cook after she walked home was something she'd been dreading. She also couldn't help but think that whatever was in those dishes would be far finer than anything Vivian might be capable of cooking, given her limited skills and the minimal variety of food available at the house.

"Not at all," Mrs. O'Neill said. "You're not the only one who enjoys this benefit; it's just the way we do things. Bring the dishes back clean and plan on picking up your supper here after each day that you work."

"Thank you!" Vivian said and carefully put the dishes into the bag Mrs. Thatcher had given her, understanding even more why it was so large. She put the dishes on the bottom and replaced her clothing on top of them to avoid having the fabric become wrinkled or soiled if the dishes leaked. "And thank you for being so kind."

"You're a good worker," Mrs. O'Neill said, then turned away to get back to work.

Vivian stopped near the door to put on her coat and get her umbrella before she headed out into the rain for the walk home. She wasn't surprised to find that it was dark outside already, but she was glad to know that the streets between the Weatherby house and her own home were busy and generally well-lit from the light emitting through windows, and from the lamps that flanked many doorways. Vivian looked forward to telling her grandfather all about her day while they enjoyed a delicious meal by the fire. And she smiled to think of how he would be looking forward to having her there so he could walk his laps around the parlor. All in all, Vivian felt happier and more at peace than she'd felt in a long time. There was ample reason to feel hope for a better future for both herself and her grandfather, and she silently thanked God for having Estelle Weatherby bring so many blessings into their lives.

Vivian enjoyed her evening with Samuel. He was in good spirits, since Estelle had visited him that afternoon. He said nothing of what they'd talked about, but he did say they'd shared a great deal of laughter and that he hadn't laughed so much in years. How could Vivian not be thrilled to hear him give such a report, even though she was disappointed over not being able to see Estelle herself? But this would likely become the pattern going forward. If Estelle wanted to visit Samuel, it was more likely to be during the day, and that was when Vivian would be working—five days a week and every other Sunday.

Vivian felt the physical strain of a long day's work that was different from what she was accustomed to, but the emotional satisfaction overpowered her physical discomfort, and she knew that her body would quickly adjust to the changes. The meal that had come from the Weatherby house was delicious and satisfying, and Vivian's gratitude deepened over not having to cook supper on the days that she worked, which allowed her to just put her feet up and relax while she visited with her grandfather, and even while he walked around the parlor, already able to stay on his feet longer than he had the day before without feeling any alarming effects. They both felt hopeful that the doctor's theory was correct, and that Samuel would continue to improve.

Vivian decided that she would do any necessary housework and laundry on her day off and only do what was essential on the days she worked. Her grandfather completely agreed and enthusiastically declared that once he gained a little more strength, he would be able to help with some of the housework and ease Vivian's responsibilities. Vivian didn't mind at all doing the housework; but seeing the evidence of her grandfather's enthusiasm at the prospect of being able to help prompted her to simply say, "We will manage fine either way, but that sounds like a great goal to work toward."

The only work Vivian did before turning in for the night was to clean the dishes that needed to be returned to Mrs. O'Neill the following day. She then made certain Samuel had all he needed before she laid out her uniform and got ready for bed, grateful beyond words for the changes that had taken place in their lives and the hope of a better future for them.

Chapter Five

THE DISTINGUISHED THEODORE WEATHERBY

While Theo enjoyed breakfast in his sitting room, looking out over the gardens which he could see clearly from the window in front of him, he felt a strange—but recently familiar and all-too-common—sensation overcome him at the realization that Vivian Peyton was now working in this house. He wondered why he couldn't force himself to stop thinking about her and reprimanded himself for what seemed the thousandth time for trying to pretend that he'd not thought about her a great deal since the day he'd met her. He would never admit to anyone—not even Estelle—that one of his greatest motivations for accompanying her on her first visit to the cobbler's shop was his desire to see Vivian again and perhaps gauge whether the feelings he'd been left with following their first encounter held any merit. He'd been pleasantly surprised to find her quite amiable, and ever since that day he'd felt fascinated with her in ways he didn't want to admit—even to himself. Their different stations in life were an obvious impediment to even considering the possibility of getting to know her better, and yet Estelle seemed quite taken with Vivian's grandfather, so how did that theory hold much weight, exactly? If he followed his aunt's example, as opposed to that of his parents, having such feelings for Vivian was not something that should be measured by any standard of wealth or social standing, and yet he found himself somewhat strangled by the habit of believing otherwise. He regretted having allowed even a hint of his thoughts to be discovered by Estelle, but then he doubted he could keep any secret from her for long.

Theo had tried extremely hard *not* to think of Vivian—but without much success. And now—only a few days after having met her at the front gate of his home—she was employed here and there was the possibility of happening upon her at any given moment anywhere in the house. Except that he knew such a likelihood was improbable, if not impossible. As he found himself unexpectedly wondering what it might be like to kiss her, he made a scoffing noise that was a futile attempt to scold himself for such a ridiculous idea and concluded that it was *particularly good* that he would never cross paths with her again. Now, he just had to find a way to get her out of his head.

Nevertheless, as time passed—and despite all his efforts to find any possible distraction—he only found himself thinking about Vivian more and more. She was there in his head each time he went to sleep, and still there when he awoke. And hardly a minute or two passed during any given day when he didn't wonder where she might be, how she was doing, and what it might be like if he was ever able to see her again. He considered whether he should figure out when and where she might be working so that he could come upon her and perhaps pretend he'd done so innocently, but he firmly decided that was not a good idea for more reasons than he could count. Theo determined that if there was truly any merit to his growing obsession with Vivian, fate would surely bring them together again, and he would do well to just do his best to think about something else.

Checking in on his mother and sister seemed a good course for distraction, and he found them lounging in his mother's sitting room, both looking lovely while they each busied themselves with some needlework.

"Oh, hello," Dorothea said, and Theo bent over to kiss her cheek. "How nice to see you!"

"You always say that," Theo said and bent down to kiss Lilith as well, exchanging a warm smile with her.

"Because it's true," Theo's mother said as Theo sat down in his usual chair. He noted that Lilith looked well today—at least as far as it was possible for her to do so; her health was fragile, but there were days when she did much better than others and today seemed to be one of those days. Her medical condition was a great mystery to every one of more than a dozen doctors who had been consulted; therefore, Lilith simply needed to take her life at a slow pace and be gentle with herself. And that's exactly what she did. Thankfully, Dorothea had always preferred avoiding social situations and venturing out; it was simply her personality to enjoy her privacy. This made Theo's mother and sister excellent companions for each other, although he checked in on them nearly every day. Sometimes he only stayed for a few minutes, and other times they shared tea or had a lengthy visit.

"What are you up to?" Dorothea asked.

"Nothing of importance," Theo said. He wanted to talk to his mother about all the thoughts he'd had rolling around in his head, but he preferred to try and simply enjoy this distraction as he settled in to talk about whatever might be on the minds of these women he loved so dearly.

Over the following weeks, spring began easing toward summer with warmer days. Vivian had quickly become comfortable with her routine, and there was truly little she didn't like about working in the Weatherby home—and that just consisted of certain tasks which no one in the house wanted to do, but she was among the maids who were required to take their turn at completing the most menial labor.

Vivian's body had become accustomed to walking back and forth to work, as well as the amount of time she needed to be on her feet, or bent over laundry tubs, or kneeling by fireplaces, or scrubbing floors. In fact, Vivian felt sure that the regular walking and variety of labor had made her healthier and stronger—just as it had done for her grandfather. They had both been amazed at how Dr. Muller's advice had worked, and with his weekly visits, Samuel had been pleased beyond words to show the good doctor his progress. The doctor finally declared that his services were no longer needed, but he invited them to contact him if a need ever arose.

With Samuel's increased strength, he had begun sweeping floors, dusting furniture, and cleaning the dirty dishes. He was not only insistent that from now on he would take responsibility for these things but expressed satisfaction in simply being able to contribute to the work in the house in some small way. His happiness in feeling needed this way warmed Vivian, and she couldn't deny being grateful for having to do less around the house. Samuel hadn't expressed any interest in getting back to work in the shop, and in fact had said that perhaps it was indeed all right for him and Vivian to reverse the roles of their lives, and he could take over most of the chores at home while she provided the income necessary to pay their rent and purchase food and other necessities. Vivian considered the possibility that if the cobbler's shop was no longer of any use to them, perhaps they should find a different place to live, where the rent might be less. But Samuel had lived there for so many decades that she hesitated to bring up the idea. Perhaps with the passing of more time while the shop just gathered dust, he might be more open to the possibility. Or perhaps a day might come when he'd feel drawn to working there again, even if it involved fewer hours a week than he'd been doing previously—provided they could regain some of the customers they'd lost.

Vivian enjoyed being able to attend church every other Sunday when she had the day off work. Her grandfather insisted that he didn't feel ready to go out with her just yet, but he anticipated that he soon would. And Vivian felt less guilty leaving him at home since he could get around more and feel less discouraged.

Samuel's spirits were greatly uplifted, not only because of his improving health but also very much due to Estelle's regular visits. She had established a schedule of visiting Samuel three days a week, coming late in the morning and bringing with her a hamper of lunch that had been prepared by Mrs. O'Neill for the two of them. Samuel delightfully referred to the now-established ritual as their picnics, even though they didn't leave the house. Vivian was relatively certain that no one who worked in the Weatherby home—except for Mrs. Thatcher—had any idea of Vivian's connection to Estelle Weatherby, and that was exactly how she wanted it. Vivian knew that Mrs. O'Neill had no idea that the picnics she prepared for Estelle to take out were to be shared with Vivian's grandfather; in fact, she doubted that Mrs. Thatcher even knew of the connection. Vivian was grateful for her own anonymity in the house, and even more thankful for how thoroughly happy her grandfather had become. Her only disappointment was that Estelle's visits were most often on days that Vivian was working, which meant she didn't have the opportunity to see this woman she liked so much and who had blessed their lives so abundantly.

Then a day came when Estelle informed Samuel that she needed to change her schedule of the days she visited. She gave no explanation, but she began visiting on Vivian's day off, bringing enough food for three in her picnic hamper. Vivian enjoyed Estelle's visits so much that they absolutely became the highlight of her week. The three of them always ate together and visited comfortably before and after their meal; then Vivian would withdraw from the parlor and give Estelle and Samuel some time to talk privately without her intrusion. Still, she was indescribably glad for the opportunity to get to know Estelle better, and the older woman said many times that she felt the same about Vivian. Estelle only grew more and more admirable in Vivian's eyes, and she knew Samuel felt the same. Even though Estelle had never married, she was anything but bitter and resentful about any facet of her life. She lived in a continual attitude of humility and thankfulness for all that she'd been blessed with, and she seemed perpetually happy—always spreading that happiness each time she came through the door of their humble home.

Vivian gradually learned—both from hearing the servants talk at work, and from things Estelle said—about the other members of the family living in the Weatherby home. Theo's mother—and Estelle's sister-in-law, Dorothea—was generally viewed as a somewhat mysterious woman simply because none of the servants had ever actually shared any conversation with her during the times they were assisting or serving her in any way. She mostly kept to her rooms and rarely left the house, even to go out into the gardens behind the house, which were surrounded by a high fence and perfectly private. Estelle's always-kind version was that Dorothea had been terribly devastated by her husband's tragic death—an event that everyone knew had occurred, but no one seemed to know exactly how; or if they did, they didn't talk about it. The inability of Theo's mother to come to terms with her husband's death—even after a great many years—was something that had apparently amplified her tendency to keep to herself, which had always been a part of Dorothea's personality. And it was the consensus of the household that Theo's sister Lilith was very much like their mother, although Lilith had always been afflicted with poor health, and her fragility made her even more prone to remaining in her own rooms and never encountering the outside world. From what Vivian had heard, mother and daughter kept each other company but preferred to avoid any other company except for Estelle and Theo, with whom they were already entirely comfortable. Both Estelle and Theo checked in on Dorothea and Lilith every day, but the servants all knew that they only occasionally shared a meal or tea. Vivian just hoped to never have to encounter either of them, just as she hoped to never see Theo or Estelle while at work. She considered the situation regarding Theo's mother and sister to be strange, and said so to Estelle, who agreed entirely.

"Which is one of a great many reasons," Estelle said, "that I'm so grateful for Theo. He and I have a great deal in common and we always enjoy stimulating conversation with the meals we share, and he makes certain I'm never lonely."

The comment surprised Vivian, considering her own encounters with Theo, but she cautioned herself against being judgmental; in truth, she hardly knew the man. She was even more surprised when thinking of him provoked a strange fluttering in her stomach, but she forced her thoughts to the conversation she was sharing with Estelle and chose not to think about Theo at all.

Thankfully, Estelle was quick to continue. "If I had to depend on Dorothea and Lilith for company, I'd be doomed—bless them." Estelle went on as if talking about her family with Samuel and Vivian was entirely natural. "Of course, Theo has his own life—his friends and habits—and it would be silly of an old woman like me to expect him to be on hand all the time. Which is why," she reached for Samuel's hand to squeeze it, winking at Vivian before she smiled at Samuel, "I'm so very glad to be able to come here and enjoy *your* friendship."

"No more glad than I am," Samuel said.

"Nor I," Vivian agreed with enthusiasm, pleased that Estelle seemed to be done talking about Theo's fine qualities. Estelle's visit continued much as it normally did, with no more mention of her family.

Occasionally when Estelle visited, she would ask Vivian about her job and how it was going. Vivian told her honestly that all was well; people were kind, the work was satisfying, and the wage was fair. Estelle seemed pleased and reported that Mrs. Thatcher had told her more than once how impressed she was with Vivian's work, and that she had made a positive contribution to the household. This couldn't help but make Vivian feel good about herself and her situation at the Weatherby home, but she was glad that Estelle didn't bring it up often. She preferred to keep these facets of her life clearly separate and to see her relationship with Estelle only as it related to their mutual affection for Samuel, rather than the fact that Estelle was her employer.

Quite by accident one day in the servants' dining hall, Vivian overheard a conversation among a handful of maids and groomsmen regarding how difficult it must have been for Theo to not have inherited his father's wealth, even though he was the only man left in the family. Vivian listened curiously while she pretended to be reading until it was time for her to return to work. Apparently, it was common knowledge that Estelle's father had left behind a very unusual will which had given the house and all his wealth to his daughter rather than to his son, due to a serious dispute *between* father and son. Apparently, the unusual will was made more feasible by the fact that Theo's father had not inherited any kind of title; the inheritance was only a matter of his wealth. When Estelle's brother had died tragically, the entire fortune had fallen to her rather than Theo. Upon Estelle's death, Theo would inherit; but until then she was entirely in control of the Weatherby fortune. It was the unanimous opinion of the servants that they could never work for a more kind and fair individual than Estelle Weatherby, although it was also agreed upon that if Theo were in charge, nothing would be any different. After that, Vivian found herself occasionally wondering what kind of situation had prompted Estelle's father to make such a drastic stipulation in his will, especially when it was highly unusual for a woman to inherit anything when there was a living male relative. But gradually she put her curiosity to rest, realizing that she was grateful to have favorable employment in this house, and equally grateful for the personal visits of Estelle to her own home. And nothing else mattered.

By the middle of summer, Samuel's health was mostly back to normal. Through his own determination he'd continued to improve at a steady pace, and little by little he completely took over the household chores. He kept everything tidy and even asked Vivian to teach him how to launder their clothing and linens. He had a little experience, since he'd always been a supportive husband, and there had been times when Edna hadn't been well enough to do everything without some assistance. But that had been years ago, and he now wanted to take over that task fully to relieve Vivian of that burden.

Samuel believed that leaving most of the cooking to Vivian was better, since he lacked confidence in his abilities in the kitchen beyond the skill of making a decent pot of porridge. But they generally had porridge for breakfast on the days that Vivian worked, or scones or bread with butter and jam. With Vivian's wages, she could now afford to purchase a few goods from a bakery she passed on her walk home from work, which meant she no longer had to put time and energy into baking and cleaning up the big mess it always made. On Vivian's days off—except for the meal that Estelle always brought to share with them—Vivian and Samuel would work together in the kitchen, and they always prepared a much finer meal on the Sundays when Vivian was at home.

As the hot days of summer began easing toward autumn, Vivian was pleased to examine her life and find how pleased she was with its established routine. She mostly enjoyed her work as well as her walks back and forth from the Weatherby house. She'd gained a comfortable camaraderie with her fellow workers for the most part, although there were a handful of the men who had never spoken a word to her. But she just assumed they were the type who had no desire to socialize with every maid in the household.

Vivian's grandfather had become a striking contrast to the man he'd been earlier in the year—weak, and tired, and generally discouraged and unhappy. He was now cheerful and sincerely enjoyed his responsibilities of keeping the house in order. Samuel and Estelle had become the best of friends, and Vivian couldn't help but notice how their eyes seemed to sparkle when they'd sometimes just get lost for a moment gazing at each other. Vivian was more pleased every day that she'd acted on the strong feelings she'd had about finding Estelle and wondered what their lives might be like if she hadn't. It was a thought she couldn't even bear to consider.

As Samuel got steadily stronger and more at ease with accomplishing his tasks, he began to feel a little bored sometimes and took it upon himself to give the shop a thorough cleaning. With everything in pristine condition, he made a sign that he hung in the window, which advertised that the shop was open for business, and that shoe repairs could be done at a special rate. Only a small number of customers responded, but it was enough to give Samuel something to do that he was exceptionally good at, and he enjoyed being able to visit with customers as they came and went. And his efforts gave them a little more income that they could save for an emergency or use for extras when they were needed.

Vivian loved autumn and enjoyed seeing the leaves changing colors, but that also meant that her walks back and forth to work began to necessitate that she bundle up more, and the rainfall that was common in London became a great deal chillier. She didn't want to think about making this walk in the cold of winter, but she was grateful to own adequate winter clothing and knew that she would manage.

Vivian was glad to come through the door of the Weatherby house and leave the rain and brisk air behind. The warmth of the kitchen stoves and ovens always permeated into this section of hallway, and she soaked it in while she collapsed her umbrella and removed her coat and gloves, putting them all away in their suitable places where they would wait for the end of her workday.

Vivian went directly to the roster that was always hanging near the kitchen door where the daily assignments for the maids such as herself were posted. She was glad to see that today she would be cleaning the fireplaces and preparing them for fires to be easily lit when needed. The disadvantage was that the rooms would be cold; on the other hand, Vivian would be working alone rather than listening to the continual chatter among her colleagues in the kitchen and laundry. Today, Vivian preferred to be in the stillness of empty rooms, and she hurried to retrieve the tools she would need before beginning her usual regimen of starting with the drawing room which had *two* fireplaces, given the size of the room, and moving on through a handful of parlors, and a breakfast room that no one ever used, which meant there was little to do except wipe away any dust that had accumulated around the fireplace. There was a study that she knew Theodore used to see to his estate business, since she'd learned that he oversaw all such things, while his aunt oversaw the running of the household. But thankfully, a different maid attended to the fire in that room since the eldest—in fact *only*—male in the house was known to begin his work there early in the morning, which was before Vivian even arrived. She also knew that other maids saw to the fires in the bedrooms upstairs, since they too needed to be stoked up early in the morning. Vivian was pleased with this arrangement, given her strong desire to avoid any encounter with Estelle or Theodore, which strengthened her resolve that she would never want to live in the dormitories—despite there being certain advantages—because then she would surely be assigned occasionally to tasks that would more likely force her to interact with the family. She was pleased that she'd been instructed to leave the fireplace in the study to someone else, and Vivian instead concluded her work in the library with the goal of being finished with all the rooms on the ground floor before she enjoyed lunch in the servants' dining hall with some of her fellow workers.

Vivian loved the magnificent library, and it seemed a reward for her hard work to go there last. She'd been told the room was rarely used and Vivian wondered why. Since a fire was rarely lit in this room—which also had two fireplaces—her work there never took long, but she always allowed herself a little time to admire the row of long narrow windows, flanked by rich, dark-green draperies that coordinated with the different shades of green and gold that were present in every element of the decor. Two long sofas and many comfortable chairs were covered in a lovely brocade fabric in those same colors, and the enormous rug that covered most of the floor had obviously been custom-made to go with the furniture. The mantels and tables held some elegant ceramic figures that had been chosen to accentuate the colors in the room. The overall effect of the room, with its endless shelves of books covering the entirety of its two longest walls, which faced each other, always took Vivian's breath away, and each time she came here she just had to take a moment to absorb the beauty, which somehow had a soothing effect upon her.

Allowing herself only a minute for her personal respite, Vivian set to work polishing the hearth and making certain everything was in order with the first of the two fireplaces, which was quick and easy since it hadn't been used in a long time. Satisfied that it was as it should be, Vivian came to her feet just before she heard someone enter the room. Her heart quickened as she hoped it might just be Mrs. Thatcher or one of the other maids coming to call her away to do something elsewhere. But a quick glance toward the door let her know that Theodore Weatherby had just come into the library. She turned her face away, hoping to slip out of the room before he recognized her.

Vivian felt some relief when he said, "Carry on; don't mind me. I've just come to quickly get a book."

Vivian believed it would be appropriate to respond verbally, but she was afraid he'd recognize her voice. She bent down to retrieve the ash bucket and the box of cleaning supplies, thinking she would come back later to check the other fireplace. As she stood, looking toward the door through which she needed to exit, she found Theodore standing there, looking directly at her.

"It's you," he said in a toneless voice that gave her no indication of whether he might be disgusted or pleased; she couldn't imagine the latter being true. But there was no doubting that he was completely surprised to find her there; in fact, he looked somewhat shocked and disarmed.

"Yes, it's me," she said and found his gaze unnerving. "I'm finished here for now. I'll leave you to—"

"There's no need to rush off," he said as she stepped toward the door. But he remained standing in the direct path between her and the only means of exiting the room.

Vivian swallowed hard and cleared her throat, determined to face him with dignity even though her heart was pounding. "I've been instructed to avoid encountering any members of the family, so I'll just—"

"Miss Peyton," he said in a mildly scolding tone, "we both know that we share a connection beyond your working here. Might we not share a moment of cordial conversation before you leave?"

She fought back the temptation to snap at him that she wondered if he was capable of cordial conversation, but she couldn't deny that he'd been cordial toward her when they'd sat in the shop together while Estelle and Samuel had been visiting in the parlor.

"And what might we possibly have to say to each other?" she asked, eyeing the open doorway as if she might somehow be able to bolt past him to safety—although she didn't want to consider the possibility that a tiny part of her was glad to see him, and perhaps it was safety from her own feelings that she was seeking.

"I understand my aunt is very much enjoying her regular visits with your grandfather," he said as if it were a direct answer to her question. She was surprised when he added, "I've never seen her happier. Mind you, she's never one to be gloomy or indulge in feeling sorry for herself, but still . . . it's evident your grandfather's friendship has brightened her life."

Vivian swallowed her animosity and replied politely, "My grandfather has also benefitted a great deal from their friendship. He enjoys her visits very much."

Vivian hoped that might be the end of this encounter and he would allow her to leave, but instead he stepped toward her, and she felt a little panicked. "I've been hoping I might see you, but you've been in the house for months and I've not once crossed your path. Today must be my lucky day."

Vivian suddenly found that what she was holding had suddenly become very heavy, which she suspected was mostly due to a strange weakness overtaking her as she focused all her efforts into figuring out how to manage this encounter. She set down the box and the bucket at her sides and put her hands on her hips, as if doing so might help her feel stronger. She didn't want to tell him how glad she was that they *hadn't* crossed paths, and how much effort she'd put into making certain it didn't happen—partly because she'd been instructed to avoid him and his family, but even more so because she had absolutely no desire to interact with this man who had made no effort to hide his arrogance or disdain toward her on their previous encounters. What he'd just said was an indication that he'd come to see the good in Estelle and Samuel having found each other again, but it didn't mean he'd changed his mind about the contempt he felt toward *her*—a fact which he'd made inescapably clear in the past. His brief moments of being cordial were greatly overshadowed by his arrogance.

"I can't imagine," Vivian said, forcing herself to remain polite and respectful, "what more we would have to say to each other than what's already been said. I'm extremely glad that you approve of your aunt's friendship with my grandfather, but beyond that, you and I have absolutely nothing in common and therefore no reason I can think of to attempt making any kind of conversation when I should be working, and you should allow me to do so."

He smiled, which took her by surprise—mostly because she'd never seen him do so. She was taken off guard by her sudden fascination with his countenance as she was reminded—in the absence of his scowl—that he was quite handsome. The thought made her heartbeat quicken even more until she realized he'd taken another couple of steps toward her, which made her heart threaten to beat right out of her chest. She didn't feel afraid of him, but for no reason she could think of, she suddenly felt distinctly uncomfortable.

"Vivian," he said, his voice slightly husky, and she gasped when he placed a hand to the side of her face.

"What are you doing?" she demanded but felt too frozen to move.

"I keep thinking about you . . . and I don't understand why," he said, his eyes showing a sincerity that seemed to contradict what she believed to be happening. "I was hoping if I could just see you . . . talk to you . . . that perhaps I could figure it out."

"Well . . ." she struggled to find the right words—or any words—that might be an appropriate response, ". . . I work here; this is . . . not where . . . or how . . . we should be . . ."

He interrupted her stammering by saying, "That's true. I *do* know where you live. It would likely be more proper if I called on you to discuss such a thing."

Vivian wanted to scream: *'That's not what I meant!'* The last thing she wanted was to have Theo come to her home so they could share an awkward conversation *there*.

"I've never met anyone like you," he said, and Vivian gasped again, convincing herself that he probably said the same thing to any and every maid with whom he might have the opportunity to flirt and take advantage of. She'd never heard any talk of his being that kind of man, but that didn't necessarily mean it wasn't true. His voice softened, and he moved a little closer. "There is truly no other woman like you in all the world; I'm convinced of it."

While Vivian was desperately trying to think of a way to reprimand him for such behavior, her astonishment exploded with the realization that he was kissing her. For a moment she found herself caught up in the pleasant sensation of his lips against hers and the way it provoked a quivering in her stomach. For a moment she wanted to believe his intentions were sincere and there might be some hope of a future between them. But it took only a moment longer for her to realize she was being a fool—a colossal fool—for even allowing this to happen. He was toying with her; there could be no other possible explanation, given the vastly different lives they led and what she knew about his views on such things.

Vivian took an abrupt step backward, which put a harsh end to their kiss, and without even thinking about it, she slapped him hard, not even realizing what she had done until she heard him let out a sharp groan at the same moment that he put a hand over his wounded cheek. He looked at her with confused eyes while she struggled to find the words to tell him how rude and cruel and presumptuous his behavior had been. The words eluded her, but she figured her slap had given him the message she wanted to convey. With no further explanation, she picked up her things and rushed from the room and down the hall and around a corner where she could be alone without the risk of being found. Feeling suddenly weak, she set down her cleaning equipment and leaned against the wall, sliding her back downward until she was sitting on the floor where she clapped a hand over her mouth to keep her need to sob from being overheard. She reviewed what had happened while she wept, despite knowing absolutely that she hadn't felt in danger or threatened in any way. What she had felt—and still felt now—was mostly confused. There was something about the way he'd looked at her after she'd slapped him that made her deeply regret having done so. What was it? She thought and thought while she managed to calm down, then she gasped still again when it came to her. Betrayed! He'd looked betrayed. And disappointed. And confused. Was it even remotely possible that his attention to her had been based in sincerity? No! She couldn't believe it! And yet . . . he'd looked so . . . *betrayed.*

Vivian finally came to her senses and forced away all the thoughts of her strange encounter with Theodore. Even though she knew she should check the other fireplace in the library, she felt relatively certain that it didn't require any attention that anyone would notice, and she was terrified to even think of going back there on the chance that Theo might be taking a good, long time to find the book he'd come searching for.

Vivian hurried to the kitchen after disposing of the ashes and properly taking care of all her cleaning equipment. After Vivian had washed her hands thoroughly, the cook put her to work chopping onions that were to be added to some extravagant dish being prepared for this evening's meal. Unable to keep her mind away from the encounter in the library and surprised by the way tears kept threatening each time she thought of Theo's reaction to her slapping him, she was glad to be chopping onions, which allowed her to let her tears fall without needing to explain their presence to anyone who might notice.

The remainder of the day crawled by far too slowly for Vivian. She became increasingly agitated while she tried to mentally make sense of what had happened between her and Theo; and at the same time, she feared he might seek her out again to try and explain his actions. And she simply didn't want to see him under any circumstances.

When it was finally time to go home, Vivian was grateful as always for the supper that Mrs. O'Neill sent home with her so that she didn't have to dread cooking this evening after a long day that had been far more draining than usual. It was as if those few minutes in the library with Theo had taken away hours' worth of strength and energy. She was glad the rain had stopped, which made it easier to navigate her way home, and once she arrived Vivian assumed a proper façade as she greeted her grandfather and told him her day had been fine and nothing out of the ordinary had occurred. It was only when she finally got into bed at the end of the day that Vivian allowed her mind to fully revisit what had happened and how it had made her feel. She realized now that she had slapped Theo partly because she'd been so startled by his kiss, but mostly because she'd assumed his motives had been less than gentlemanly. But what if she'd been wrong? She'd assumed that everything he'd said had been the kind of words a philandering cad would use over and over on any vulnerable woman to whom he might be temporarily attracted. But what if he'd been sincere? After far too much analyzing and pondering, Vivian finally decided that Theodore Weatherby *was* a cad, and slapping him had been completely justified. It was the only way she could make peace with herself enough to drift off to sleep.

Theo was so overcome with shock from Vivian's harsh response to his kiss that it wasn't until she'd fled the room that the possibility of how his behavior must have appeared to her washed over him. He sank onto the nearest sofa, pressing his hands into his hair and groaning with humiliation. He'd spent so much time thinking about Vivian Peyton and sharing imaginary conversations with her, and yes, he'd even imagined kissing her more times than he could count. When he'd finally come face-to-face with her, he'd simply acted without even thinking, completely forgetting that she had absolutely no idea how much she'd come to consume his mind—entirely against his own will. And now he'd made a complete and utter fool of himself in the worst possible way. He couldn't begin to imagine what Vivian might think of him now; actually, he *could*, and her impressions of his character were surely anything but respectable. He'd been hoping for many weeks that their paths would cross, and now he wasn't certain if he ever wanted to see her again. Except that he did! He wanted to be able to apologize, to explain, and to have the opportunity to get to know her better. But he'd been given an opportunity and he'd handled it all wrong; all things considered he couldn't have handled it worse. And now he wondered if she would ever give him the chance to explain himself. As utterly mortified as he felt, Theo found it impossible to even move from the sofa in the library until he became thoroughly exhausted from punishing himself for being such a fool.

Vivian awoke the next morning with a distinct dread about spending the day working under the same roof where Theo Weatherby lived. Their encounter in the library was still echoing through her mind, her most prominent memories being the betrayal in his expression after she'd slapped him, and the completely unexpected kiss he'd given her. What concerned Vivian most was the quiet thrill she felt each time she recalled that kiss. And if she'd concluded that Theo's motive for kissing her had been less than admirable, what did that say about her own reaction each time she thought about it?

Trying to clear her mind of anything and everything to do with Theodore Weatherby, Vivian went about her usual routine and was soon on her way to work, using her umbrella to ward off a gloomy drizzle that perfectly reflected her mood. Once at the house, she quickly got to work, disappointed to realize that her hopes and prayers that she would not encounter Theo were making her think about him continually.

Vivian was cleaning around a fireplace in one of the parlors when she heard the door open, and her heart began to pound. Oh, how she prayed that it was one of the maids sent by Mrs. Thatcher to request her assistance elsewhere! But a quick glance in the direction of the door showed her that Theo was standing nearby, his hands behind his back, his expression somewhat sheepish.

Vivian shot to her feet and brushed her hands on her apron even though she knew they weren't dirty because the fireplace hadn't been used since it was last cleaned.

"What do you want?" she blurted, wishing it hadn't sounded so harsh and defensive. Despite what had happened between them, she preferred that he believe she'd been completely unaffected.

"Miss Peyton," he said respectfully, nodding his head slightly, "I owe you the deepest and most sincere of apologies."

Vivian was taken completely off guard. First of all, she realized that she had likely expected him to avoid her as much as she had wished to avoid him. And secondly, the last thing she had anticipated was an apology. She was so stunned that she couldn't think of a single word to say in response.

"While there is no excuse for such deplorable behavior, I ask that you give me a moment to explain. I confess that you have left a very favorable impression on me, and in the months since we last saw each other I have thought about you a great deal. I'm embarrassed to admit that when I unexpectedly saw you yesterday, I inanely leapt past the reality that you and I had never shared all the conversations that I had hoped we might one day share, and I simply acted on an entirely inappropriate impulse and . . . well . . . I don't need to explain further . . . except to say that . . . your response was absolutely warranted. I want you to know that I bear you no ill will, and I doubt that I could ever apologize sufficiently for behaving in a manner so ungentlemanly."

When he'd finished what it seemed he'd come to say, a taut moment of silence followed, during which Vivian realized he was likely expecting her to offer a response. But she was still far too stunned to know what to say. It would have been polite to simply accept his apology, but before she could form the words he said, "Thank you for hearing me out. I wish you good day, Miss Peyton." He nodded again and quickly left the room, quietly closing the door behind him.

Vivian suddenly felt a little weak and sat down on the floor in front of the fireplace, wondering what on earth she was to make of the distinguished Theodore Weatherby now. Despite knowing she should be returning to her assigned tasks, she found herself incapable of moving until she mentally reviewed everything he'd just said—and the fact that he had sought her out in order to speak his piece. She wondered how many parlors he'd gone to before he'd found the right one. Then his words echoed in her mind in time with the sudden pounding of her heart that seemed to have awakened to the reality that she'd just shared yet another strange encounter with Theo.

She'd left a favorable impression on him? He'd had the hope of sharing many conversations? "Good heavens!" Vivian muttered breathlessly. And then there was the irrefutable issue at the center of all this madness, the very reason for his seeking her out to apologize. *He had kissed her!* Vivian had never been kissed before, but she was certainly aware that it was considered inappropriate to share a kiss until . . . well . . . she had to think about it. She couldn't recall ever being taught a specific time in a relationship, but it surely had to be well into a proper courtship, perhaps even after an official betrothal. His apology was certainly warranted, given how he'd kissed her so unexpectedly when they hardly knew each other. And yet, his confessions had carried with them a certain humble tenderness that warmed Vivian, making it possible to recall his kiss with more tenderness, which only resulted in her heart beating even faster along with a strange quivering that seemed to rush from her toes to the top of her head and back again.

"Oh, good heavens!" she muttered again and forced herself to get back to work, wondering if she'd seen the last of Theo. Of course, it was possible that she might cross his path here in the house, or perhaps given the growing friendship of her grandfather and his aunt, they might encounter each other due to the mutual connection. But Vivian wondered if his apology was an admission that the consideration of any personal relationship between them had been a mistake, or if he might be harboring some hope of a fresh beginning between them that was more appropriate. Vivian quickly determined that the latter was preposterous. Still, as she went about her work throughout the remainder of the day, and returned home as usual, she doubted that a minute passed without recalling the undeniable and delightful reality that Theodore Weatherby had kissed her.

Chapter Six
THE TRAITOR

With the passing of weeks, Vivian didn't encounter Theo at all, which cemented her conclusion that he had figured out that any further pursuit of sharing those conversations he'd admitted to hoping for was ludicrous. And Vivian felt certain he was right. Over time, it had become easier to not think about him—or perhaps it was more accurate to say that she'd stopped feeling fluttery inside each time she did. Whatever the truth might be, Vivian put the matter behind her and tried as always to focus on all the positive aspects of her life—which wasn't difficult whenever she stopped to think about how difficult life had been for both her and her grandfather not so long ago.

On a particularly cold and rainy Sunday, Vivian walked home from church. Her umbrella was not doing her much good, given that the wind kept whipping it away from protecting her head. Vivian finally gave up and collapsed the umbrella, holding it in her arms as she kept her head down and hurried home as quickly as she could manage, imagining how good the warmth of the fire in the parlor would feel after she'd changed into dry clothes.

Vivian was startled to approach her home and see Estelle's carriage in front of the cobbler's shop. She knew that the two men who drove and watched out for her would be waiting comfortably inside the carriage with blankets, books to read, and their own hamper of food. Estelle had explained this arrangement on one of her earliest visits. But Vivian wondered why Estelle would visit on a Sunday; she couldn't recall her ever having done so before.

Vivian breathed a sigh of relief to finally enter the shop and get out of the rain, but she hated knowing how thoroughly drenched she was—which meant she surely looked like a stray cat—and she had no choice but to encounter Estelle whose voice she could hear through the open door that led into the parlor.

Vivian took a deep breath and hurried into the house, speaking before anyone else could.

"What a lovely surprise!" she said to Estelle. "I'm afraid the weather has gotten the better of me. I'm going to change into dry clothes and—"

"Oh, of course, my dear," Estelle said. "Take all the time you need. I don't want you fussing over me just because I decided to impose myself upon you today."

"I'd say be quick about it," Samuel said. "We don't want you catching a chill."

"I'll hurry," Vivian said and moved as quickly as possible into her bedroom where she closed the door and leaned against it a long moment to catch her breath. While she got out of her wet clothing, draping everything over chairs and the foot of her bed so they would dry out, Vivian felt pleased that Estelle knew she was welcome to come and visit any time she chose, since Samuel was always delighted by her company. Vivian too enjoyed Estelle's company, although the passing of time had left Vivian feeling more and more on the outside of their relationship. Estelle was always polite and kind toward Vivian and tried to include her in their conversations, since she was sincerely interested in Vivian's thoughts and opinions on any given topic. And Vivian always tried to balance the time she spent visiting with them and allowing them the privacy to visit without her sitting there during their conversation.

Vivian put on dry clothes and lit the fire in her room so that she could warm up a bit before joining the others; it would also give her wet clothes a better chance to dry out. She felt grateful as always that her grandfather had Estelle's company, but this was her Sunday off—one of two days a month when Vivian and Samuel worked together to prepare a nice meal they could share together. Now Vivian would have to set to work in the kitchen on her own to prepare potatoes, parsnips, and onions that she would add to the small cut of lamb she'd put in the oven to roast before she'd gone to church.

Feeling a little disappointed, Vivian started toward the kitchen to get to work, calculating how many vegetables she should prepare to make the minimal amount of meat go further so they could invite Estelle to stay and have Sunday dinner with them. Vivian had never served Estelle anything but tea and scones, but she doubted the woman had come for her unexpected visit with the usual hamper of food.

Before Vivian made it to the kitchen, she heard Estelle say, "Come and sit with us for a few minutes, my dear."

Vivian did so, taking her usual seat on the sofa where she could clearly see Estelle and her grandfather; she noticed they were holding hands. It was far from the first time she'd observed such a thing, but she also noted a glance they exchanged that seemed to imply their affection for each other had become more serious. Checking their expressions, Vivian felt certain Estelle's irregular visit and the need for them to talk held a deeper implication, and she felt her heart quickening.

Vivian barely had a moment to wonder before her grandfather said, "Estelle and I are going to be married."

Vivian wished she hadn't gasped quite so loudly, and she also wished that she might have been able to speak before the silence became filled with the awkward expectation of her response. "That's . . . wonderful!" Vivian finally said, managing an enthusiastic voice and a convincing smile that completely contradicted how she felt and the myriad of thoughts swirling around in her mind. This truly *was* wonderful for her grandfather. Who would have dreamed that he could find such happiness again at this time of his life? "I'm so very happy for the both of you!" Vivian added firmly and meant it, even though her thoughts were caught up in the logistical aspects of this situation. Of course, this meant that Samuel would move into Estelle's home; it could never be the other way around. Estelle could give her grandfather a good and comfortable life, and Vivian knew there was no element of unnecessary pride between them that might complicate the situation of a man with no money or worldly possessions becoming the husband of a very wealthy woman. Vivian felt confident that they would work everything out very nicely.

But what of Vivian? Would she now live alone behind an unused cobbler's shop while she worked in the grand house where her grandfather would be living? She didn't even have to think about it to know that taking advantage of this situation for her own benefit was out of the question. After working in the Weatherby house for months and finding a comfortable place among the other servants, she could never suddenly become a part of the family for whom those people worked. She felt respected by these people—at least the ones who had spoken to her enough that they'd been able to get to know each other—and she respected them in return. She would never want to do anything to damage the comfortable acceptance she'd found among them and felt certain she would never find the same advantages working elsewhere. And she didn't even want to consider how Theodore Weatherby would respond to such a prospect! Despite their strange encounters and the implication that he had felt an inexplicable attraction toward Vivian, she still couldn't believe that he would approve of his aunt's decision. But Estelle choosing to marry and bring a husband into the household was something she would need to work out with her nephew and anyone else who might be affected. And regardless of anything else, Vivian could never—ever—be a part of this situation. Perhaps if she'd anticipated the possibility of Estelle and Samuel marrying she never would have agreed to work in the Weatherby home, but it was probably better that she did; the issue of her working there would be much easier to explain to Estelle and Samuel than trying to tell them that she absolutely abhorred the very idea of living under the same roof with Estelle's nephew; she couldn't begin to guess how Theo might feel about that, but she never intended to find out. The very idea left her hard-pressed not to shudder visibly without fully understanding why.

"Now listen, my dear," Estelle said, looking intently at Vivian, "I can see that you're concerned about such drastic changes even though you're trying awfully hard to hide your concerns and be happy for us." Vivian felt wholly unnerved by the way Estelle had been able to read her thoughts so clearly, which resulted in the sudden overwhelming urge to cry. While she was fighting desperately to hold back her tears, Estelle added firmly, "Of course, this means that you and I will be family. As my husband's granddaughter, you will be my granddaughter as well. The two of you will come to live with me and we will have many grand adventures. We can go on holidays together and . . . well . . ." Estelle let out a delighted laugh. "We can do whatever we want." Estelle reached for Vivian's hand and squeezed it. "You mustn't worry about a thing. It will be an adjustment, I know, but I promise you that everything will be all right."

Vivian swallowed hard and gave up on attempting to hold back tears that were too strong to fight. As they escaped, she admitted honestly to Estelle, "Your kindness and generosity mean more than I can say." Vivian sniffled. "Forgive me for crying, but—"

"You must never apologize for tears, my dear girl," Estelle insisted. "Please . . . just tell us what you're feeling."

Vivian wasn't surprised by the growing concern on her grandfather's face, but she forced herself not to look at him, fearing her tears would erupt into sobbing if she weren't careful. Encouraged by Estelle's insistence, Vivian coughed and sniffled again and forced herself to just say what she knew had to be said sooner or later. "I am grateful for the happiness you've brought into my grandfather's life; I truly am. I'm so glad to know that the two of you will be able to spend the rest of your lives together, and that he will be cared for in the best possible way. But Estelle—dear, sweet Estelle—I simply cannot live in your home as a supposed member of your family after working there and—"

"What nonsense!" Estelle insisted, but Vivian ignored her and pressed on.

"It would simply be far too awkward. I could perhaps find work elsewhere; and perhaps I should regardless. But I could never expect the people I've worked with to start waiting on me and—"

"They would understand," Estelle said firmly. "And if any of them don't, that is no concern of ours. They work for *me* and—"

"But it's so complicated," Vivian declared, "and I'm not certain how your nephew would feel about—"

"I don't care a whit what Theo thinks about any of this," Estelle said, her vehemence rising. "I will never answer to any man except my husband! I was relieved of that necessity when my father finally left this earth. And I'm sad to say that after all the ways he had controlled and manipulated my life, I felt little—if any—sorrow at his death. But then, he never gave me the tiniest bit of love or affection, so what was there for me to miss? I'm wavering from the point, however. My dear Vivian, Theo has nothing to do with this."

"He does," Vivian insisted. "He's your nephew! Will he not be at the same dining table, and walking the same halls, and—"

"Vivian, my precious girl," Estelle interrupted in a voice that was soft and calm, "we mustn't upset ourselves so much over this when we have time to work out the details and we will make certain to talk everything through with everyone involved." Vivian thought of Dorothea and Lilith—Theo's mother and sister whom Vivian had never laid eyes on—and wondered if they would even notice Estelle bringing a husband into the house when they rarely left their rooms; but that was no concern of Vivian's. Estelle continued, "I understand that it will be an adjustment for you—both of you—but I promise you I will do everything in my power to make certain you are both comfortable and happy in my home. I can assure you that nothing in the world would bring me more happiness than to make the both of you a part of my family."

Vivian thought about that for a long moment and realized she wasn't even the tiniest bit convinced that she could step into the life that Estelle was offering. Overcome with another rush of emotion, Vivian stood abruptly and said, "You are perfectly kind and thoughtful as always, Estelle. Clearly, I have a great deal to think about, but that does not negate my happiness for the two of you in any way. Please excuse me."

Vivian hurried to her room and closed the door, wishing desperately that she could leave the house and go for a walk, but that was impossible in this weather. She also wished her bedroom weren't right next to the parlor, which made it necessary for her to remain extremely quiet so as not to be heard. As the inevitable torrent of tears overcame her completely, she hurried to climb into her bed and pressed her face into the pillow to muffle the sound of her crying.

Vivian hadn't realized she'd dozed off until she heard the closing of the front door of the shop, which awakened her. Listening carefully, she heard no sound of conversation between her grandfather and Estelle, and she felt fairly certain that Estelle had left. She knew her grandfather would be wanting to talk to her, and she also knew there were dinner preparations waiting to be completed in the kitchen. But she felt so weighed down by the complications that had been thrust upon her that she doubted her ability to even get out of bed. She certainly didn't want to. Remaining here beneath the covers for the remainder of the day felt preferable, even if that meant having nothing to eat. At the moment, she didn't have much of an appetite, anyway.

A light knocking on the bedroom door startled Vivian and she sat up in bed, knowing it was her grandfather. Hoping she didn't look as if she'd cried herself to sleep, she called, "Come in."

Samuel opened the door slowly and peered in. "I'd ask if you're all right, my dear, but I know you're not. I'm just not sure what to do about it."

Vivian forced a convincing smile. "Forgive me if I responded badly," she said. "I was just so . . . surprised. I'm so incredibly happy for you, Grandpapa; truly. I would never want my own feelings or opinions to stand in the way of your happiness."

"May I come in?" he asked.

"Of course," she said, and he sat on the edge of the bed, taking her hand into his, reminding her of the countless times he had done so throughout her life when she had been upset or struggling.

"Now that you've had a little while to adjust to the news, I would like you to start over and tell me how you're feeling and what your concerns might be." As if he'd read her mind he added, "Dinner can wait a little, and I just emptied the pot that catches our regular drip of rainwater."

Vivian gave him a wan smile and let go of his hand so she could adjust her pillows against the headboard and lean back against them before she sighed heavily and told her grandfather in more detail her feelings about how uncomfortable and awkward it would be for her to become a part of the Weatherby family. She explained that she had become friendly with many of the servants there, and at the very least well-acquainted with most of the others. She admitted that she didn't believe anyone there—even the housekeeper—knew that the man Estelle went to visit regularly was her grandfather, and she didn't want to be seen as being favored simply because of that connection.

Samuel listened thoughtfully before he responded, "I can understand why that would be a difficult adjustment for you. I certainly can't begin to imagine how my life will change by moving into Estelle's home with her and having people wait on me; it's not the way I've lived; and if I had my choice, it wouldn't be the way I'd want our marriage to be. But that's the reality of Estelle's life, and we love each other. I'm too old to waste time with letting my pride stand in the way of sharing my life with her, however large an adjustment it might be. When we were younger, it was her intention to leave her home and move into the cobbler's shop with me when we were married. She was willing to leave all her wealth and comforts behind for me. I can certainly leave behind my pride and discomfort for her. In fact, I will be making legal arrangements to ensure that none of her wealth will come to me." He sighed and once again took hold of Vivian's hand. "But you're a grown woman, and I can't force you to make such dramatic changes in your life—I wouldn't want to. I can't deny that I'd prefer to have you living there with us; I'd want to see you as much as possible and have you enjoy a good life with us. And I hate the thought of you needing to work to provide for yourself when Estelle has so generously offered to open her home to us. I know it's all very strange; I only ask that you give the matter more thought. Even though we'll be getting married within the month, you can take as long as you need to make a decision."

"Thank you for understanding," Vivian said, even though she believed he *didn't* fully understand. But he was always respectful of her feelings.

They agreed to talk again in a few days, then they went to the kitchen to work together on preparing a fine meal they could share. Vivian was glad that he didn't bring up the topic again at all throughout the remainder of the day, even though she suspected he likely wanted very much to talk about the enormous changes coming in his life—and his obvious happiness regarding those changes. Vivian just wished she could find a place in her own mind where she could comfortably be filled with perfect happiness for her grandfather and at the same time feel overwhelmingly sad for herself. Her own life was about to change dramatically. She just couldn't imagine exactly what those changes would entail when it was impossible to foresee the outcome of any possible choice. Samuel had made a wonderful choice for his own future; now it was up to Vivian to choose what the future would be like for herself.

Vivian didn't sleep well at all that night, but she was still ready to leave for work on time and was glad that her grandfather didn't say anything during breakfast about the new quandary they were facing. She didn't even want to think about it. But truthfully, she couldn't force herself to think of anything else.

While Vivian walked to the Weatherby house beneath an overcast sky, she at least felt grateful it wasn't raining. She was so overwhelmed with the burden of her thoughts and the uncertainty of her future that she doubted being able to even contend with an umbrella. Attempting to approach the problem from a purely logical view, Vivian concluded that it would be ridiculous for her to continue living behind the cobbler's shop when her grandfather no longer lived there. She didn't need that much space for herself, and she certainly didn't need to rent a shop that wasn't being used. To let go of the shop and its attached house would mean no longer needing to pay rent on the place, and Vivian felt confident she could rent a room in a boardinghouse for a great deal less money each month. She knew that such rooms didn't have any personal kitchen facilities, but she had the privilege of being able to eat at the Weatherby house on the days she worked. And paying less rent meant she could purchase meals for herself when necessary, and there were certainly a great many options for that on the busy streets of London. If she could find a room to rent that was closer to where she worked, she would also have the advantage of not having to walk so far back and forth. Of course, she felt certain Estelle and her grandfather would strongly disapprove of such a decision. They wanted her to move into the Weatherby house as a member of the family and be waited upon and taken care of by the very people with whom she'd become friendly and well-acquainted. And she just couldn't imagine such a possibility without cringing and shuddering. The very idea felt humiliating and completely inappropriate. She thought of the plight of her dear friend Betsy—the tears she'd cried and the terrible persecution she'd had to endure, which had eventually driven her away from London. The very thought of possibly bringing such experiences upon herself was simply unthinkable. While it felt impossible to imagine that any of the other employees would be so offended by her change in status that they would violently assault her, she couldn't say for certain that she knew all of them well enough to be assured that something akin to that *wouldn't* happen. And the very idea was utterly terrifying!

Even if Vivian could have talked herself into not caring what the servants might think of her place in this strange situation, and if she could somehow overcome the fear of meeting a fate like that of Betsy, the very idea of living as if she were a member of the same family as Theodore Weatherby made her literally nauseous. Every encounter she'd had with him had been strange and confusing. The thought of sharing meals at the same table and lounging in the same parlors made her cringe and shudder even more.

Of course, Vivian knew there was the option of living in the servants' dormitories beneath the same roof where she worked. Most of the staff lived in those rooms; she'd helped clean them and had visited with other maids in their rooms, so she knew they were fine and comfortable. To some it might seem the perfect solution. She wouldn't have to pay *any* rent and she wouldn't need to walk back and forth to work at all. But to Vivian, the very thought of living and working under the same roof just didn't feel right. She could never put her reasons into words, which meant that she would never be able to explain her reasoning to Estelle or her grandfather or anyone else. She only knew that it wasn't a comfortable option for her. She could acknowledge that perhaps Betsy's experience was contributing to her discomfort, although she knew there were other factors as well. Whatever the reasons, it simply didn't feel right. The best solution was to find a room at a boardinghouse, and she determined that on Wednesday when she had a day off, she would begin searching for her new home. Just as when she'd finally made the decision to find work to solve the financial challenges she and her grandfather had been facing, Vivian felt better for simply having made a plan for moving forward.

Vivian arrived at the Weatherby house, doing her best to keep her mind focused on that plan—rather than thinking about how difficult the forthcoming changes in her life would be. Not living with her grandfather would be a brutal adjustment; nevertheless, every other possible option felt exceedingly more difficult. They would devise a method for being able to visit without others knowing their connection, and with time they would adjust.

Vivian had barely hung up her coat when one of the maids approached and told her that Mrs. Thatcher wished to speak with her immediately.

"Thank you," Vivian said and smoothed her apron as if that might ease the sudden pounding of her heart. As she hurried to the housekeeper's office, she told herself that this was surely nothing more than being given instructions regarding a specific task that needed special attention. It had certainly happened before.

Vivian took a deep breath and knocked on the open door of the office. Mrs. Thatcher looked up from where she was studying a ledger on her desk and smiled. "Good morning, Vivian," she said brightly.

"Good morning," Vivian said. "You asked to see me?"

"Yes," Mrs. Thatcher said, "Miss Weatherby asked to speak with you as soon as you arrived. She'll be in her sitting room. You know where that is?"

"Yes," Vivian said, her heart pounding so hard now that she feared it might leap right out of her throat. She'd certainly worked in this house long enough to know where to find Estelle's sitting room, but she wanted to hotly protest being told to go there now. She felt like a thief who had been found out and would now surely face inevitable consequences. She wondered then if Mrs. Thatcher knew about the connection between Vivian and her employer's fiancé. She had to assume the housekeeper had been informed of Miss Weatherby's intention to marry. But Vivian certainly wasn't going to say anything to give herself away when she still had the hope of remaining incognito.

"Run along then," Mrs. Thatcher said, turning her attention back to her ledger as if her instructions were nothing unusual. Vivian hoped that was genuinely how she viewed the situation.

"Thank you," Vivian said as she always did in response to any of the housekeeper's instructions. She then hurried up the back stairs, so filled with anxiety she had to remain conscious of each breath filling her lungs and then leaving them so that she didn't become lightheaded before she even arrived at her destination.

Vivian paused a short distance from Estelle's sitting room to take in a few deep breaths and blow them out slowly to calm herself. She willed her heartbeat to slow down and her stomach to stop smoldering, but neither of them heeded her commands.

Realizing she was as ready as she would ever be and that she needed to be punctual, Vivian pressed forward and found the sitting-room door open, giving her a perfect view of Estelle sitting on a sofa near the windows, with her feet curled up at her side. She was absorbed in a book and Vivian couldn't help but think how lovely she looked—almost like a painting. Knowing that Estelle was every bit as beautiful in her heart and mind as she was in appearance made the scene even more enchanting, but Vivian forced her musings aside and knocked on the open door.

Estelle looked up and smiled when she saw Vivian. "Oh, there you are, my dear!" She put her feet on the floor and eased them into the slippers she'd left there. "Do come in! Close the door and sit beside me. We have much to talk about."

Vivian couldn't help feeling nervous, but she was dismayed to realize that Estelle had picked up on it when she added, "There's no need to be concerned, child. Mrs. Thatcher knows you won't be expected." Vivian tried to smile, wishing she could explain that this was something that only increased her nervousness. She knew how the staff was well aware of all the happenings in the house, and if word got around that Vivian had been visiting privately with Miss Weatherby, she wondered if her ability to blend in comfortably with the rest of the staff would ever be the same.

Vivian did as she was told and closed the door, moving to the sofa where she sat down. Estelle immediately took her hand.

"We need to talk," Estelle said immediately. "Woman to woman. I wasn't at all surprised that our news upset you yesterday; I'd been worried about that very thing, because I know that you and your grandfather share a close relationship, and this will certainly bring a great many changes into both your lives. Samuel too is concerned about you, but men just don't see things the same way, do they? Since I'm soon to become something of a grandmother to you, I want us to be able to talk about our struggles and difficulties—and this is certainly a good place to start. So, please . . . tell me what you're feeling, child. Talk to me about your concerns."

Vivian was stunned into silence, given the fact that she had not anticipated such a conversation. But it only took a few seconds for her to realize that she *should* have anticipated it; Estelle was not the kind of woman to be oblivious to the feelings of those around her, and Vivian had not responded well to the news she'd been given when they'd last seen each other.

Vivian admitted honestly, "I . . . don't know what to say; don't know . . . where to even begin."

"You must feel incredibly overwhelmed, then," Estelle guessed accurately.

"Yes," Vivian said, glad to note that her heartbeat was slowing down. Estelle's genuine kindness certainly had a way of easing her anxiousness.

"I would guess that you're wondering what the future might be like for you now, when you have probably always assumed that things would forever remain the same between you and your grandfather."

"Yes, I suppose so," Vivian said. She couldn't deny that the statement was accurate, even if it didn't encompass her most prominent thoughts.

"And what about when *you* marry, my dear?" Estelle asked. "Would your grandfather not be left on his own when that happens?"

Vivian was surprised by the question; it was something she'd not thought about in a long time, although she didn't want to admit to Estelle that she'd all but given up on the possibility of marriage for herself. Instead, she focused on giving her an answer that she'd once believed in. "I always just assumed that my new husband would move in with us, or that I would take my grandfather with me wherever I might live with my new husband. Truthfully, since my grandmother's passing, I've simply never imagined living my life without him." Vivian took a deep breath and hurried to add, "This doesn't mean that I'm not genuinely happy for the both of you. Just because I never imagined my grandfather finding love again—getting married again—doesn't mean that I would want it any other way. It's wonderful! I mean that, Miss Weatherby! I do!"

"And why on earth are you being so formal with me when you have always called me Estelle since our first meeting?"

Vivian glanced down, feeling mildly embarrassed as she admitted, "I suppose that . . . I've always mentally kept my life here in your home . . . where I work for you . . . separate from our social visits which have always taken place at *my* home."

"I understand why you might feel uncomfortable, my dear, when you are dividing your life between two hugely different worlds. But you and I are alone here, and I prefer that you call me Estelle. We are as good as family, child. And now that your grandfather and I are to be married, there will no longer be any need for your life to feel divided. Your place will be here with us now, and—"

"No!" Vivian interrupted, wishing it hadn't come out sounding so harsh. But she simply couldn't hold back the truth of her feelings another moment. "I can't! I just can't!"

"I don't understand," Estelle said, looking sincerely confused. But rather than making assumptions or becoming defensive as most people might, Estelle tightened her hold on Vivian's hand and said kindly, "Please tell me what you're feeling, my dear. Talk to me. You are clearly terribly upset, and I want to understand. I can't help you if I don't know what's troubling you."

Vivian gave herself a few long moments to consider the best way to respond. She trusted Estelle, and even if this woman whose life's experiences had been so much different from her own could never understand, Vivian still knew that Estelle would be compassionate—even if they disagreed.

Trying to broach the topic from a positive aspect, Vivian began, "I could never adequately express my gratitude to you for employing me in your home. I've felt acceptance from others who work here, and from what I've heard of working conditions in other homes, I know—as the others do—that we are very blessed to be employed by someone as kind and generous as you are. I've found a comfortable place here; my life is good. It simply feels as if . . ." Vivian paused and drew back her shoulders while she filled her lungs with sustaining air as she approached the difficult part. "I just don't feel comfortable with the idea of being served and cared for by the people with whom I've worked. What right do I have to be elevated to such a position? My life and circumstances are no different than anyone else who works in your home, Estelle. How can I live in this home, encountering these people at every turn, knowing that I came here only as a great kindness from you to begin with? It just doesn't feel right to me. I don't know if you can understand; perhaps it sounds silly to you. I don't think my grandfather agrees at all, but that's how I feel."

Estelle was quietly thoughtful for a long moment before she responded. "Your feelings are entirely valid, my dear. And whether anyone agrees with them or not does not change that fact. Of course, you are a grown woman, and you need to make your own choices about how you live your life. I wish that I'd possessed your courage to speak my views when I was your age; my life might have turned out very differently."

"But it all turned out the way it was meant to, didn't it?" Vivian asked, voicing a thought that had occurred to her many times as she'd pondered the situation between Estelle and her grandfather. "I would not be who I am if Edna had not been my grandmother, and—"

"You're absolutely right," Estelle insisted. "I've debated the matter a great deal, if you must know. I daresay I believe that life is more a result of our choices rather than any kind of fate or destiny, although I must add that I also believe God guides our lives and we should certainly be paying attention to the paths He offers. No one can say how all our lives might have turned out if I'd run away from home and married Samuel all those years ago. There's really no point in wondering about such things. All we have power over is the present, and right now I'm choosing to marry your grandfather so that we can make the most of the life that we have left. *You* need to make the choices that are best for you. Still, I want you to know my opinion on the matter, and I would like you to promise me that you will consider what I have to say. And then I will support you completely in whatever choice you make."

"Very well," Vivian said. How could she possibly refuse such a reasonable request?

"While I understand that it could be a difficult transition for you to go from working in this house to being a member of the family, I don't believe the other members of the staff would be as unsupportive as you think they might be. But perhaps there are facets to your concerns that I simply don't understand from my perspective, and I can accept that. I want you to consider, however, the difficulty for your grandfather if you choose to separate yourself from him in this way. In essence, it would be as if you are asking him to make a choice between sharing his life with me as opposed to sharing his life with you." Vivian wanted to protest; it sounded terrible when she put it like that. But Estelle quickly moved on. "I don't believe that's your intention, but I believe that's how it would feel for him. Still, he knows you want him to be happy. And you must remember that he wants *you* to be happy; as do I. Now, if you choose to—"

Vivian and Estelle both let out a startled gasp when the door flew open as if a terrible storm had invaded the sitting room.

"Please tell me the gossip I just heard is *not* true!" Theo bellowed, clearly angry, his eyes riveted to his aunt's until they shifted—then widened—in a combination of horror and embarrassment as he realized that Vivian was sitting beside Estelle, their hands still clasped.

Despite Vivian's own embarrassment and horror over this sudden intrusion—with her being an unintended witness—she was appalled with herself for the way her heart quickened just seeing Theo. She had no doubt that this response was due only to the fact that she found him so thoroughly attractive. But then her stomach also fluttered, briefly letting her forget that he was furious and that the gossip to which he referred *had* to be about Estelle's intention to marry Samuel. To make matters worse for Vivian, she just had to recall how it had felt when he'd kissed her. Feeling her face go warm, she looked away, not wanting him to see her blush, which also gave her the advantage of appearing to ignore his intrusion.

Through the breadth of seconds that passed while Vivian wondered what Estelle and Theo might say to each other next, it occurred to her that she not only needed to take advantage of the opportunity to escape this uncomfortable conversation with Estelle, but it would be inappropriate for her to expect to stay when aunt and nephew clearly needed to speak privately.

"I should go," Vivian said and stood, taking a step toward the door as she said over her shoulder to Estelle, "We can talk more at another time and—"

"I would prefer that you stay," Estelle said in a firm voice that was difficult to argue with. "Please sit down, dear. There's nothing Theo has to say that you shouldn't hear."

Vivian took her seat again and folded her hands on her lap, looking at the floor, suddenly hating this situation more than she could possibly say—as if she could say *anything* amid a potential argument between Estelle and Theo. It felt as if she were already a part of their family, whether she chose to be or not.

"Are you certain about that?" Theo asked Estelle and slammed the door in a way that implied that if Vivian wasn't leaving, he didn't want it left open and risk being overheard. The way he lowered his voice to an angry whisper made it evident he had something to say that he wouldn't want to become a part of the household gossip. "Are you truly certain that you want her to know?" Theo continued. "Ever since she showed up at our front gate, I've wondered if it was only a coincidence, but it isn't, is it? I've kept my thoughts to myself, figuring it didn't really matter considering your friendship with Samuel and having Vivian work in the house. But it most certainly *does* matter if you're intending to make them a part of the family!"

Vivian had no idea what he was talking about, but Estelle replied firmly, "No, it's not a coincidence, and I wondered if you would even remember the name. Nevertheless, I can assure you it has *nothing* to do with either Samuel or Vivian, and—"

"How can you say that, given what we know about her *father*, and the fact that—"

"What?" Vivian interrupted with a breathy gasp. "What does any of this have to do with my father?"

"Should you tell her, or should I?" Theo asked Estelle, his voice edged with sarcasm, as if Vivian were not present. His blatant anger and the evidence that he knew some terrible secret about Vivian's father made every bit of admiration she'd felt for him disappear instantly. Her every nerve became suddenly alert and on edge, as if she were about to be attacked by a wild animal and her very life was in danger. The seconds that passed seemed eternal while she waited for Estelle to answer Theo's question, wondering frantically and desperately why Theo would be so upset about something to do with her father. Vivian's memories of her parents were vague, but they were tender and sweet; she felt ill over the very idea that Theo had the power to shatter all the goodness she believed about her father.

Estelle finally spoke, saying calmly to Theo, "I don't believe we should be discussing *anything* when you are so angry. Why don't you *sit* down and *calm* down," she added, as if it were an order. Theo hesitated, then huffed into a chair across from them, but he was clearly anything but calm. Vivian noted how he purposely looked away from her or his aunt, and she saw the muscles in his face twitch as if he were suppressing so much anger he might be on the verge of exploding.

"Now," Estelle said, looking at Theo even though he wasn't looking at her, "why don't you start at the beginning, Theodore, and tell me why you're so upset."

Vivian fought back the temptation to protest. She didn't want to start at the beginning. She wanted to know why her father had something to do with the source of Theo's anger. But Vivian swallowed hard and clasped her hands together more tightly, forcing herself to remain silent.

Theo finally turned to look at his aunt, his eyes ablaze with fury. "I just heard from my valet that you're intending to marry Samuel. He assumed that I already knew. I should have known before the servants, don't you think?"

"It was my intention to speak with you as soon as I'd completed my business with Vivian," Estelle said, entirely unruffled by the anger sparking in the room.

"I would have thought you'd have spoken with me *before* you even made such plans—especially under the circumstances."

Estelle's voice betrayed only a hint of anger as she responded to her nephew. "I don't need your permission or anyone else's regarding the decisions I make about my own life. Samuel and I discussed the matter thoroughly, and it is only the two of us who have the right to be involved in such a decision."

"And yet Vivian knew," Theo snapped, tossing a sharp gesture toward her without so much as giving her a glance.

"Yes, we told Vivian yesterday because it is her life that will be most affected by our marriage." Estelle's voice held no hint of apology. "She has a great deal more to contend with than you could ever comprehend, growing up as privileged as you have."

"I fail to see the significance of *that*," Theo said.

"Are you angry because I'm marrying Samuel, or because of the choices of people who have been dead for years? Surely you realize those choices have nothing to do with any of us still living."

"I heartily disagree," Theo said and shot Vivian a brief, harsh glare that she believed might have disintegrated her entirely if he'd looked at her for more than a second. "Vivian was a child. Clearly, she is innocent of anything that happened. But Samuel raised the man who destroyed my father's life and eventually led him to his death and—"

"What?" Vivian gasped with shock and pressed a hand over her pounding heart. "What on earth are you talking about? How could you possibly believe that—"

"It's a fact, Miss Peyton," Theo said, now glaring at her directly, but her own shock somehow made it easier for her to glare right back. "The initial connection between my aunt and your grandfather somehow led to a connection between your father and mine many years later. Your father cheated and swindled and manipulated my father to gain access to his wealth, and indeed drew him into a scheme that was taking them to France where your mother's wealthy parents resided, all with the intent to swindle *them* out of as much money as they possibly could. I'm certain you knew your parents died when that ship crossing the channel sank, but you likely didn't know that my father perished on that same ship, and it was because of *your* father that he was there. Otherwise, he would be alive today."

Vivian couldn't speak; she could barely breathe. The implications were too horrible to even consider. Every good memory of her father was shattered instantly, and any tiny hope she might have had of finding a place among her grandfather's new family had become completely irrelevant. And she couldn't begin to understand any of the reasons from what little she had just heard. She had so many unanswered questions that she couldn't imagine how she might even begin to uncover the truth.

"There is a great deal of speculation and assumption in what you just said," Estelle countered, and Theo snapped his gaze toward her. "Given the fact that neither your father nor Vivian's ever told anyone about their plans—and they are both long dead—we don't know exactly what happened and—"

"I know enough," Theo insisted. "I know that you're marrying a man who raised a traitor; he betrayed his family and destroyed ours. I tolerated your friendship with him because I could see that it was important to you, but . . . *marrying him*? You can't! You simply can't!"

"I can and I will," Estelle said. "One day you might actually grow up enough to realize that a parent rarely if ever has any control over the choices of their children—especially when they become adults. Samuel is not to blame for his son's choices, and I am not to blame for those of my brother."

"I didn't even imply that you were!" Theo insisted.

"It's impossible for you to cast blame in one direction without tossing it in the other," Estelle declared. "We don't know what happened, Theodore, and we will not speak of it again. This has nothing to do with Vivian *or* Samuel. You are entitled to your opinions, certainly, but I would hope you'd be happy for us. We'll all be living under the same roof, and I expect you to treat Samuel and Vivian with the respect they deserve. And perhaps once you've calmed down you will consider the possibility that your anger over matters you don't understand might be less important than my finally having a chance to share what is left of my life with the man I love. I do hope you'll be at the wedding. Either way, I will see you at lunch."

Theo glared at his aunt while Vivian could almost literally *feel* all the disparaging words he was barely managing to hold back. He made a sharp scoffing sound as he launched himself out of his chair and left the room, slamming the door behind him.

Chapter Seven
REGRET AND REMORSE

Vivian winced at the slamming of the door, and before she even realized she wanted to cry she felt tears trickling down her face. As she hurried to wipe them away, she could only be glad that Theo had left the room before she'd started crying.

"Oh, my dear," Estelle murmured with perfect compassion as she handed Vivian a delicate lace handkerchief. Vivian was briefly distracted by the fact that she'd never held a handkerchief that was so fine and soft. She dabbed her cheeks with it to interrupt the ongoing flow of silent tears as Estelle added, "Theo was at a difficult age . . . a difficult season of his life . . . when he lost his father. I've always wondered if his perception of the experience was somewhat . . . skewed. You mustn't take anything he said too seriously. You mustn't."

"Is it true?" Vivian asked, looking directly at this woman she'd grown to love and admire so dearly. "Whether or not anyone knows the details . . . is it true that my father and . . . your brother . . . were involved in some kind of unsavory business? That your brother was on the same ship as my parents when it sank in the channel? Is it true?"

"That much is true, yes," Estelle said gently. "But it was an awfully long time ago, my dear, and it simply doesn't matter anymore. The past is in the past. We need to look to the future and move forward as a new family . . . together . . . and . . ."

"Together?" Vivian snapped. "How could it ever be possible for me to consider myself a part of the same family as Theo? His feelings on the matter were inescapably clear, Estelle." Vivian shot to her feet, overcome with a sudden need to get out of this room and be alone—somewhere, anywhere but here. "I am grateful for your kindness," she hurried to say, wanting her feelings made clear, and not certain if she would ever have another opportunity to voice them. "And I'm extremely glad that you and my grandfather have found each other again . . . that you can make each other so happy. But you mustn't worry about me. I can take care of myself, and I will. I would like to remain employed here, if that's all right with you, and—"

"Of course it's all right," Estelle said, looking astonished and perhaps desperate.

Vivian wiped her tears again with Estelle's handkerchief, wondering what more she could say before she burst into uncontrollable sobbing—as if she didn't already have more than enough reasons to feel utterly mortified. "We'll just leave it at that, then." Vivian curtsied quickly. "Thank you for your kindness."

Vivian hurried toward the door, ignoring Estelle's protest. "Please stay and talk to me, my dear. You mustn't leave like this and . . ."

Once the door was open, Vivian ran, and Estelle's voice faded. She wanted to just get busy with her assigned tasks for the day. But she knew she couldn't go anywhere near where the other servants were gathered until she was able to regain her composure, and she doubted that would be possible until she was able to vent a fair amount of the tears threatening to explode. Realizing she was still holding Estelle's handkerchief, she knew she could discreetly slip it into her room after it had been laundered. For now, she was glad to have it as she pressed it hard over her mouth while she ran, hoping to hold back the threatening storm.

Vivian hurried to a section of the house that was rarely used; it was difficult to comprehend the need for several guest rooms, but apparently there were times when grand socials might be held in such a house and traveling guests would need to stay the night—or longer. But no such social had occurred in the time that Vivian had been working in the house, and she knew she could sneak into one of the unused rooms and have some privacy. Once inside with the door closed behind her, Vivian took in the eerie way that all the furnishings were covered with white fabric to protect them from dust. She crossed the room and sat on the floor in the corner farthest from the door. Only then did she allow herself to cry. She cried for all her fears regarding the forthcoming changes in her life, for confusion over what she'd just learned about her father, and for a great deal of sorrow connected to all of it.

Vivian lost track of the time while she wept, not caring if she was missed downstairs, or even if Estelle might be unhappy with her for running off like that. And she certainly didn't care what Theo might be doing or what he was thinking about all of this. Thinking of Theo only made her angry, most likely because *he* had been so angry, rather than approaching a sensitive topic with . . . well, some sensitivity. More than ever, she hoped to never encounter him again, and she found some solace in her certainty that he felt the same way, which meant he would go to great lengths to avoid her.

Vivian was most concerned about her grandfather. She wondered how much he knew about whatever unsavory business his son—her father—had been involved in prior to his death, and that of Vivian's mother. She felt a strange heartache to consider how all of this must have affected him—and Edna—when it had been taking place so many years ago. Thinking of Samuel left Vivian feeling certain that he would not be happy if she made any decision except to live with him in one of the many available rooms at the Weatherby house. But Vivian simply couldn't do it. She loved her grandfather dearly, and she would never allow him to have any doubt in that regard, but she could never live in this house—not as a member of the family, and not even as a servant. She needed a place to go at night that was her own; she needed a distinct separation from her life here and her own identity that had nothing to do with anything or anyone else—not even Samuel. She sincerely wanted to continue working here; she liked and appreciated the situation greatly. And she would remain here doing her work quietly and invisibly as long as it didn't cause any difficulties for herself or her grandfather. She could only hope that it wouldn't.

Vivian finally felt as if she could return to her work and maintain her composure. She tucked Estelle's very wet handkerchief into the pocket of her apron and checked her appearance in a mirror that was hanging on the wall. The light was too dim to be able to tell if her face showed evidence of all the tears she'd shed, but she patted her cheeks firmly with the hope of evening out any possibility of redness in her skin before she hurried downstairs to Mrs. Thatcher's office to find out what tasks the housekeeper wanted her to complete. A sudden rumbling of her stomach let Vivian know that it was likely lunchtime. Perhaps it had passed, and she'd missed it. She glanced at the watch pinned to her apron but there was not sufficient light in the hallway to see it. So, she just hurried on.

Once Vivian arrived in the hallway near the kitchen, she could hear evidence that the staff was eating lunch. Despite feeling hungry, she wanted to speak with Mrs. Thatcher first and went to the housekeeper's office before she realized that of course Mrs. Thatcher would be eating lunch with the rest of the staff. Entering the servants' dining hall, Vivian hoped she wouldn't draw too much attention to herself by arriving late, but Mrs. Thatcher came to her feet immediately.

"Oh, there you are," the housekeeper said. "Come with me for a moment."

When they were both in the hallway, Mrs. Thatcher said in a kind, quiet voice, "Miss Weatherby informed me that you're not feeling well." Vivian was taken off guard and wondered if the housekeeper had any idea of her connection to their employer's fiancé. But she refused to ask because she could only hope that *no one* knew the connection. "She gave me strict instructions to send you home to get some rest, and if we don't see you tomorrow that will be fine. If you need more time after that, just send word. Now, Mrs. O'Neill's packed up some food for you to take home and it's on the worktable in the kitchen. You must be hungry. Should I call for a carriage to take you home? If you're not well, then—"

"No, no," Vivian said, overcome but relieved to have some time to become accustomed to all the turmoil she was feeling before returning to work. "I'll be fine. Thank you so much."

The housekeeper nodded and returned to the dining hall. Vivian found the food that had been prepared for her and her grandfather and packed it into her canvas bag as usual before she put on her coat and left the Weatherby house to walk home, wondering how it would feel when the home she'd always known would no longer be a place where she could go, and leaving work would mean leaving her grandfather behind. Fresh tears stung her eyes at the thought, and she forced them back, too exhausted to even consider allowing herself to cry anymore.

By the time Vivian arrived home, she had firmly decided not to bring up the subject of her father and his possible scandalous behavior. She preferred to just ignore it—at least for now. If Samuel brought it up, she would take that on when it happened. She also didn't want to talk about his forthcoming wedding, the enormous changes that would occur in both their lives, and his deep desire to have her live in the same house with him. She was prepared to tell him that she simply wasn't feeling well, and she only wanted to have a little bit to eat and then take a nap. But she found Samuel napping in his bed, snoring softly in a way that made it clear he hadn't heard her come in. Of course, he wouldn't have been expecting her at this time of day.

Vivian ate some of the food sent by Mrs. O'Neill. As always, it tasted good, but Vivian's appetite had diminished despite the hunger she'd been feeling. She put the remainder of the food in the larder where it would stay cool before she left a note in the kitchen for her grandfather, then she went to her own room and closed the door. After removing her shoes, she crawled into bed, wishing she could remain there indefinitely, and extremely grateful that she'd been given this time away from work. Once again, she appreciated Estelle's insight, even though a part of her never wanted to have to face the woman again.

Theo had lunch brought to his sitting room since he wasn't at all in the mood to share a meal with his aunt until he'd had some time to cool down. Not long after he'd finished eating, he wasn't at all surprised when Estelle entered his sitting room without knocking and closed the door behind her, but he didn't feel at all prepared to face her obvious wrath. The dark expression clouding her face, her rigid stance, and the sharpness in her eyes were all evidence that she was probably more displeased with him than she had ever been. He couldn't recall *ever* seeing her in such a foul mood. And now that he'd calmed down to some degree and had given himself a little time to consider how he'd behaved a short while ago in *her* sitting room, he couldn't deny that her displeasure was justified. He also knew that this conversation would go much more smoothly if he just got straight to the most important point.

"I owe you an apology," he said, setting aside the newspaper he'd been reading.

"You most certainly do," she said, her voice sharp. "But until I'm assured that you understand exactly what it is you're apologizing for, I don't feel inclined to accept it."

Theo turned to look out the window and heaved a sigh that seemed to come all the way up from his toes. Estelle sat in a chair across from him but remained at the edge of her seat as if she might want to be prepared to stand up quickly and either get out of the room or grab hold of his shirt collar the way she had often done throughout his childhood when he'd been guilty of mischief and she'd wanted to make certain he was paying attention to what she had to say.

"I didn't know Vivian would be there with you," he said, still looking out the window. "In my defense, I did suggest that she leave the room; it was you who insisted she stay."

"I cannot dispute the fact that Vivian needs to know the truth about her father," Estelle said, a keen edge still vividly present in her voice. "The news was inevitably bound to come to her ears eventually, and I had intended to tell her myself; I wanted to be able to help soften the blow for her. As it turns out, the difficult news of her father's less-than-admirable choices could not have possibly been delivered with any more insensitivity or disregard for her feelings. I had believed that despite your obvious anger when you entered the room, you would have had the decency to communicate the situation to her like a gentleman, not some kind of enraged heathen."

"Enraged heathen?" Theo echoed, looking at his aunt in astonishment. "That is a gross exaggeration, don't you think?"

"No, I do not," she insisted firmly. "When you allow yourself to review the conversation, I'd like you to consider how everything you said—and the way you said it—must have come across to *her*. She had no idea her father was involved in anything unsavory; she was a child when her parents died. Whatever did or did not happen has *nothing* to do with her, and it has *nothing* to do with Samuel. Just so you know, Samuel wept when he spoke to me about how hard he tried to convince his son to live his life with integrity and not to get caught up in things that could bring about terrible consequences. I had similar conversations with my brother. We both experienced the same kind of helplessness in having no power whatsoever to convince our loved ones to make different choices. No one could have predicted the terrible accident that took their lives. But Theo, the trauma you experienced when you lost your father so unexpectedly has *nothing* to do with Samuel and his granddaughter. And while you might think you know what happened and why, hear the wisdom of an old woman who has many times been confronted with the reality that things are most often not what they appear to be. *Whatever* may or may not have happened, the truth has gone to the grave with your father and Vivian's parents. And we need to let go of our grief, our sorrow, our anger, and move forward. Do you understand what I'm saying, young man?"

Theo swallowed hard and cleared his throat. "I hear what you're saying, Aunt." He wanted to add that he respectfully disagreed with certain points, but he couldn't find sufficient words to defend what he felt; he only knew that he felt extremely uncomfortable with the entire matter. Instead, he admitted, "It's true that this has nothing to do with Vivian, and I sincerely regret the things I said to her, and the way I said them."

"That's a start," Estelle said sternly. "I accept your apology on that count, but you absolutely owe *her* an apology as well."

"Oh, surely that is not necessary!" Theo protested, wishing he hadn't sounded something like a spoiled schoolboy.

"It is most absolutely necessary!" Estelle insisted. "She is the granddaughter of the man I'm going to marry, and I will not begin my new life with Samuel with such an issue left unresolved between you and Vivian. You are precious to me, Theo, just as Vivian is to Samuel. This simply won't do. Promise me that you will seek her out and apologize to her, or we can conclude this conversation right now."

Theo sighed loudly and deeply, then he did it again. The very thought of having to face Vivian and humbly express regret for what he'd said made him cringe. But it only took him a long moment to realize that his hesitance was completely rooted in his own embarrassment. He *should* have been more sensitive and respectful about how he spoke of the circumstances regarding Vivian's father. His own anger over the situation had not diminished throughout the years since he'd lost his own father, but that didn't give him the right to take his anger out on Vivian. And he knew it. He'd been raised to be a gentleman, and regardless of Vivian's social station, he never should have spoken to her that way. Everything else aside, the reality was that he still found it difficult not to think about Vivian a great deal, and he was often haunted by how it had felt to kiss her—and subsequently enduring the humiliation and sting of her slap. Clearly, she brought out the worst in him for reasons that were far too complicated to admit aloud.

Theo sighed yet again and reluctantly declared, "Very well. I will apologize to Vivian; I can see that you're right about the way I handled the situation. And I promise you that I will be sincere and behave like a gentleman."

"Excellent," Estelle declared triumphantly. "Now, let me make this point absolutely clear so that there will be no question regarding the matter from here forward: what happened between your father and Vivian's father is separate and irrelevant to the love that Samuel and I share, and we will not speak of it further. It's in the past, and we will leave it there. I want Vivian to feel completely welcome in our home; and completely comfortable. And since you're the one who has so overtly offended her, I'm counting on you to help make certain that such is the case."

"Oh, I see," Theo countered. "You not only want me to apologize, but you also want me to clear away any obstruction on the path to her coming to live here with her grandfather."

"Exactly," Estelle said, smiling with increased triumph in her voice. Then her expression softened along with her voice as she asked with sincerity, "Is there a reason—beyond what we've already discussed and put to rest—that you are not comfortable with having Vivian live here?"

Theo felt immediate guilt as the recollection of Vivian slapping him once again appeared in his mind. He then became lost for a long moment in the memory of the remarkable and magical kiss they had shared preceding the slap. He'd felt Vivian respond to his kiss, and he'd genuinely believed that she would be receptive to his affection. But he'd handled all of that as badly as he'd handled the conversation earlier in Estelle's sitting room. It seemed he had a great deal to learn about appropriately expressing himself when it came to sensitive matters.

When Theo didn't respond, Estelle asked, "Do you disapprove of my marrying Samuel and bringing him into our home? Your opinion will not change my mind, but I'd still like to know how you feel."

Theo wanted to tell her that he didn't like the idea at all. But he sincerely didn't know if his own feelings were based in his beliefs about the responsibility Samuel's son bore in his own father's death, or if he just didn't want their family situation to change. He'd already gradually felt himself losing a degree of the closeness he'd once shared with his aunt. She'd spent a great deal of time with Samuel throughout the months since they'd become reconnected. And when Theo *had* spent time with Estelle, he had steered the conversation away from talking about Samuel, even though he'd known that doing so wasn't fair to her; if it were the other way around, he certainly would have wanted to be able to talk comfortably with his aunt about someone important in his life. Right now, Theo quite simply just felt overwhelmed with so many confusing emotions that he hardly knew what so say. He cleared his throat if only to let her know that he truly intended to speak, and to give himself a few more seconds to consider what he should say.

"I completely respect your love for Samuel—and his for you—and I would never do anything to stand in the way of your happiness. I suppose I don't want things to change, but I recognize that this is an incredibly positive change for you, and I'm certain that with time we will all adjust. I promise you that I will be respectful and appropriate—to Samuel *and* to Vivian—even though I realize you might have good cause to doubt such a promise. I know I can be . . . hot-tempered and . . . difficult. And I know I need to do better at controlling that; I have you to thank for guiding me through my upbringing, Estelle; otherwise, I fear I would be entirely controlled by my own anger and selfishness and I would have become a terrible person."

"Nonsense," Estelle insisted gently. "You're a good man with a good heart, Theodore. Although I do believe there is something smoldering inside of you that sometimes rises and causes you to speak in anger before you think. I believe it was festering there even before your father died, but the timing and circumstances of his death seemed to solidify something deeply troubling. I don't fully understand it, Theo, but I think that *you* should figure out the source of your anger. I recall well that you were in a difficult stage when we lost your father. It's not at all unusual for young people in their teen years to go through stages of trying to figure themselves out . . . and how the world works . . . and how they fit into it. There was nothing abnormal or strange about that for you, except that I believe you may have felt especially frustrated by your parents' behavior toward you; they were never terribly attentive to you or Lilith. I've wondered if the strong discord between them was so consuming that neither of them felt they had the energy to deal with children, which was entirely unfair to you and your sister. Following your father's death, your mother became less agitated and less prone to being angry, even though she still preferred to remain mostly secluded. But if I recall correctly, I had a feeling that you'd become aware of their customary neglect in a way that very much troubled you, and then . . . I think the timing of your father's death somehow . . . well . . ."

"Left me stuck at the age of fifteen?" he guessed when she couldn't seem to find the words—or she didn't want to say them for fear of offending him. "And so, I've been behaving like a rebellious youth ever since?"

"You do not behave like a rebellious youth," Estelle said, "except for an occasional outburst of anger or arrogance. But since you put it that way . . . I suppose it's possible that on some level you might very well be stuck at the age you were when your father died. It's something for you to think about, I suppose. And you know that if you ever need to talk, I am here for you."

"Yes, Aunt," he admitted humbly. "Thank you." He indulged in another deep sigh and prodded himself to bring up something that had been bothering him ever since he'd heard the news earlier today that Estelle and Samuel would be married. If he didn't bring it up now, he would surely regret it, and he certainly didn't want the issue to smolder inside of him until it burst out in one of his famous bouts of anger.

"There is something I want to discuss regarding your plans to be married, and I ask that you hear me out and not be offended. I feel it's a valid concern despite your belief that Samuel is a good man; and if you believe that, then I do, as well. I trust your judgment, Estelle, and I know you are not a fool, by any means. Nevertheless, this affects me and the entire family, and I must address it."

"Very well," she said. "I'd like to guess and then you may correct me if I'm wrong." Theo motioned with his hand for her to continue. "I would venture to say that you're concerned about the legal aspects of the financial situation, because as long as I'm living, the entire estate is legally mine, but once I marry, everything that's mine will belong to my husband—therefore everything that *you* would inherit from me would become more complicated."

Theo couldn't deny that she'd hit directly upon the truth. "Yes, that's my concern. I'm not implying that he has any unsavory motives, Estelle, although . . ."

"Although, given the character of his son and its impact on our family, you can't be certain," Estelle stated with confidence, and Theo couldn't speak since she'd stated his exact thoughts. Sometimes he hated how thoroughly perceptive she was, except he couldn't help but be grateful in that moment to not have to speak his true concerns.

"Well," Estelle said, lifting her chin slightly, "you can breathe easy, Theo. Within minutes of when Samuel and I agreed that we intended to get married, he insisted that we have a legal document drawn up that would clearly state an exception to this law in our case. He will have no legal rights to anything that belongs to me. He has graciously and humbly accepted my sincere and wholehearted offer to bring him into my home and see that all of his needs are met; I'm certain you can understand why that might be difficult for a man who has always worked to provide for himself and his family."

"Yes," Theo said with a combination of humility and astonishment. His respect for Samuel had just increased dramatically; and his concerns had completely dissipated.

"We simply want to share our lives," Estelle said. "I am blessed with this enormous house and a fortune I could never spend in three lifetimes. I want Samuel to enjoy those blessings with me. That's all there is to it, Theo. Now," she rose to her feet, "you make certain you apologize to Vivian at the first opportunity. I told Mrs. Thatcher she wasn't feeling well since she was terribly upset after what happened, so she's gone home for the rest of the day, and she's been given tomorrow off work, as well. Just so you know, you won't find her in the house. Let me know when you've had the chance to speak with her; I'd very much like to hear how it goes."

Estelle smiled and winked at him as if nothing of their conversations today had been dramatic and life-altering. She bent over to kiss his brow before she left the room, saying over her shoulder, "I will see you at tea in the hall."

With the closing of the door, Theo immediately felt immersed in a confused frustration so overwhelming he felt hard-pressed to not grab a nearby porcelain vase and throw it. He forced himself to breathe deeply to control the anger that Estelle had pointed out was his problem. And she was right. Why was she always so blasted right? If he were to examine his heart with complete honesty, Theo couldn't deny that he'd struggled with being quick to respond with anger to any frustration long before Vivian Peyton had shown up at the front gate in search of Estelle. He'd been disarmed by Estelle's desire to visit Samuel Peyton, even though he'd not been certain at the time if this man was any relation to the Peyton who had lured his father into illegal and dangerous schemes—and to his death. But it had taken little effort to find out for certain their familial connection. It had required great discipline to not even bring up the matter with Estelle, and he'd convinced himself that it simply didn't matter. Estelle and Samuel were friends, and even though Vivian was working in the house, Mrs. Thatcher was sharp regarding those she supervised, and he had dismissed that issue as having nothing to do with him—even though it had bothered him a great deal. And then the news of Estelle's plans to marry Samuel had brought out everything he'd been working so hard to suppress. He absolutely felt much better knowing that Samuel would legally have no right to any of Estelle's financial assets. For Theo, it was more the principle of the matter than the money itself, although there was no questioning the number of people they were responsible for; the employment of every member of the staff relied on the family always having sufficient funds to support them and their families. But Samuel clearly had no selfish motives for marrying Estelle, and Theo felt some relief. He wished that he could simply trust Samuel the way Estelle did, but Theo couldn't deny that he had trouble trusting anyone except Estelle. But that was it: he *did* trust Estelle, and she was certainly no fool. If she trusted Samuel and Vivian, then he needed to do the same, even if he didn't agree with her decisions to make them a part of the family.

Thinking of Vivian took Theo's mind to the promise he'd made that he would apologize to her. He took out his pocket watch to look at the time and realized that if he left right now, he could go to the cobbler's shop, make his apologies and be done with it and get back in time for tea. Otherwise, the need to fulfill this promise to Estelle would continue to hover over him like a dark cloud until it was completed. Better to just do it now and have it over. He could only hope that she wouldn't be too hard on him for his behavior toward her earlier, even though she had every right to be.

Vivian came suddenly awake from the sound of someone knocking on the front door of the shop. She'd left it locked as had become her habit, unless she or her grandfather were available to help the rare customer who might come through the door. But she'd left the door between the shop and the house open so that she *could* hear if someone knocked on the outside door. Having just been jolted out of a pleasant and much-needed nap, she was regretting that decision.

For a moment, Vivian was tempted to ignore the knocking, but if it had awakened her grandfather, he would be much slower in being able to get to the door, and he would be unhappy about having missed a potential customer. Even if they no longer needed the money, he needed the satisfaction of being available to help those who desired his services.

Vivian didn't even try to put slippers on her feet, glad to know that the length of her dress would cover her stockinged feet. She'd removed her apron and cap before crawling into bed, but she was still wearing the black dress that was a part of the maid's uniform required for her job. She glanced quickly in the mirror and attempted to smooth her hair, hoping her face didn't look too much as if she'd just awakened, then she hurried to answer the door, prepared to amiably greet the person likely in need of having shoes repaired, despite their having inadvertently interrupted her nap.

Vivian unlocked the door and pulled it open with a forced smile on her face which melted away immediately when she was met—not with a customer, but instead with Theodore Weatherby. He was the *last* person on the planet she wanted to see and wondered what in the world he was doing here.

Without any greeting, Vivian said, "If you've come to further degrade me regarding my father's supposed bad choices in life, then you might as well leave because I'm not willing to engage in any further discussion on that topic."

"I assure you that is not the purpose of my visit," he said, sounding far kinder and more humble than he had earlier when he'd been so angry. "You look very tired," he observed, then added with alarm, "I didn't wake you, did I? If I did, I'm terribly sorry and—"

"I *am* tired," she declared, not caring much about being polite with this man when he had been anything *but* polite toward her. "I had a very trying morning. Thank you for noticing." She stated the last with an edge of sarcasm that was by no means subtle, and she hoped he noticed *that* as well. "As a matter of fact, you *did* wake me, Mr. Weatherby. But I'm awake now, so you might as well state your business and be done with it. If you've come to speak with my grandfather and attempt to talk him out of marrying your aunt, I'm afraid I will find it necessary to intervene. If you've come to speak with *me,* do so and get it over with. I can't begin to tell you how thoroughly I am *not* in the mood to have *any* conversation with you right now, or perhaps ever."

Vivian felt a little surprised over the intensity of her own harsh language directed at this man. She'd never spoken to anyone with such disdain, but she felt legitimately angry over the things he'd said to her earlier, and the way he'd said them.

"I've come to speak with *you*, Miss Peyton," he said, turning his hat in circles with his hands. "May I come in?"

Vivian had to think about that; she preferred to have this conversation with him standing on the other side of the door so that she could close it if he descended into any kind of rudeness or arrogance. But she certainly didn't want anything they said to each other to be overheard by passers-by.

"Very well," she said and moved aside for him to enter. After she closed the door, Vivian impulsively closed the door between the shop and the house, not wanting her grandfather to overhear anything they might say to each other—especially if it drifted again into the territory of how wronged Theo felt by Vivian's father.

Vivian *didn't* invite him to sit down, but her omission became mildly embarrassing when he asked, "May I?" while motioning to a chair.

"Make yourself comfortable," she said and sat down herself, thinking that she didn't want him to be comfortable at all. She wanted him to say what he'd come to say and leave as quickly as possible.

"I won't take much of your time." Theo sighed, and Vivian noticed that he appeared highly uncomfortable.

Vivian considered his possible reasons for being here and ventured to guess, "I would wager that you're here because Estelle insisted." He glanced down quickly but not before she saw the abashed truth in his eyes.

"Yes," he said, lifting his eyes to meet hers, his countenance now showing nothing but courage and determination, "Estelle insisted that I come and apologize to you. I can admit to behaving foolishly at times, Miss Peyton. I confess that I've always struggled with being impatient and having a temper that often makes me say things that would be better kept to myself. Honoring Estelle's wish that I speak with you does not mean that I don't agree with her; I *do* owe you an apology. I did *not* expect you to be in the room with her, and when she insisted that you stay, I should have bridled my words more carefully. I behaved terribly and said things that shouldn't have been said."

Vivian thoughtfully took in his words and measured them before she responded. "Your apology is appreciated, Mr. Weatherby; nevertheless, I would like to point out my belief that the very definition of integrity would be that a person speaks and behaves in the same way, no matter who might hear or observe. If you are the kind of man who would talk about me and my grandfather that way when we are not present, should I trust that you would *ever* be kind and respectful about us in our absence? Ever? The information you revealed about my father was shocking, to say the least. I've not yet had the opportunity to speak with my grandfather about what he knows concerning the situation, but I can assure you it's a conversation I'm dreading very much. You don't know my grandfather—or me for that matter—very well, but I can assure you that if he had knowledge of any kind of unethical behavior his son might have been involved in, he would have done everything in his power to turn such behavior around. Do you think it's right for my grandfather to be punished for the possible sins of his son? Do you honestly believe that any of what may or may not have happened all those years ago is relevant to my grandfather and your aunt sharing a future that has the potential to bring them both a great deal of happiness?"

Theo didn't answer; he only stared at her, his face expressionless, leaving her with no idea what he might be thinking. Vivian suddenly hated this entire situation and decided to put an end to it. She stood abruptly, which prompted him to do the same, his expression now filled with alarm and confusion.

"I thank you for your apology, Mr. Weatherby, but respectfully I do not accept it. I'm not one to hold grudges, and I absolutely believe in the power of forgiveness. I *forgive* you for your insensitivity and selfishness, but I do *not* trust you, nor am I likely to *ever* trust you. It's my intention to graciously stand aside and allow my grandfather to make these changes in his life, and I wish him and Estelle every possible happiness. But I will continue my life as it is, and I have no intention of ever being involved in anything that might even put you and me in the same room at the same time. I will visit my grandfather privately and do my best to avoid ever crossing paths with you again. You may assure your aunt that you kept your promise to her and apologized, and you don't have to tell her anything else. You can rest assured that *I* certainly won't be speaking to her about this conversation. Now, I ask you to leave. I'm very tired."

Vivian held his gaze while he seemed flustered, not knowing what to say or do. She motioned toward the door, hoping to snap him out of what appeared to be some sort of daze. Theo nodded slightly and hurried out without speaking any parting words. The moment the door closed, Vivian sank weakly back into her chair. She immediately knew that while she'd claimed to have forgiven him, she would need to put some continued effort into making that forgiveness complete. Right now, she felt so overcome with anger and frustration she wanted to follow him out the door and yell terrible things at him, even though she knew that would only make her the worst kind of hypocrite. And then there was the reality that made her feel even more hypocritical. How could she be so angry with him, so disappointed in him, and still find herself recalling fondly how it had felt when he'd kissed her? She thought about that moment far too much, and time had not diminished the sweetness of the memory. And she hated him for it! How dare he toy with her affection in such a way, and then behave so atrociously that she hoped to never see him again?

Such thoughts only heightened her anger and she forced them away as she stood up to lock the outside door. Then she went into the parlor, closing the door between the shop and the house. If anyone else should come knocking—or Theo had the nerve to return—she hoped not to be able to hear it. She wondered if her grandfather was awake; she was both dreading the conversation she needed to have with him and wanting to have it over and done. She sighed as she recalled leaving for work this morning, believing that today would be like any other day. That moment felt as if it had happened days ago; no wonder she felt exhausted!

Vivian stoked up the fire in the parlor and added more wood, not even bothering to see if her grandfather was still sleeping before she plopped into her usual chair in front of the fire, unable to comprehend how thoroughly messy and complicated her life had become. But for the sake of her grandfather's happiness, she needed to press forward with dignity and courage and remember that she was indeed completely capable of taking care of herself. If circumstances made it impossible to continue working at the Weatherby house, she would find work elsewhere, and she would find another place to live. There was sadness in the very idea of such decisions, but there was also a defined peace. She had the power to take charge of her own life, and she would take on whatever happened and find her way. With that knowledge cemented in her mind, she felt more capable of facing her grandfather, even if she dreaded her need to speak with him about a great many things that would be difficult for several reasons. But they loved each other, and they could surely get through anything. She could only hope and pray that getting through the forthcoming changes would not be too difficult for either of them.

Theo arrived early at the appointed place where tea would be served at the front end of the upstairs hall. He was glad to not find Estelle there reading while she waited for tea, mostly because he needed a few minutes to just try and make sense of all that had happened since this day began, and why it had all added up to leave him feeling more glum and confused and dismal than he'd likely felt since news had come of his father's death many years ago. He wasn't at all happy about Estelle marrying Samuel. However, he felt a deep relief in knowing that Samuel would legally have no right to Estelle's wealth, which helped him believe that Samuel sincerely loved Estelle and his intentions were only for the two of them to be happy. Still, Theo didn't like the idea of this man moving into their home and completely changing Estelle's life—which included his own relationship with his aunt. Such an idea was purely selfish, and he knew it, but that was how he felt.

Far, far worse was the enigmatic situation regarding the duplicitous son of Estelle's fiancé. He could not argue with the reasoning that it was in the past, and that no one living knew exactly what had occurred between Vivian's father and his own. Still, Theo knew enough to be certain that Samuel's son had been unethical and lacking in integrity, and it was their involvement in a shady scheme that had put them in a place where they had lost their lives. He felt compassion for Vivian having lost her parents at such a young age and knew she was entirely innocent of any wrongdoing. But thoughts of Vivian made him groan and hang his head, after which he immediately looked around to be certain no one was nearby who might have overheard such a reaction to his own thinking. His behavior toward her this morning in Estelle's sitting room had been deplorable; he could see that more and more as the passing of time continued to improve his perspective. And his attempts to apologize had gone more badly than he ever could have imagined. Her words kept circling around in his mind like a haunting melody. She could forgive him, but she could never trust him. Was he really so contemptible? Trying to answer himself honestly, he had to admit that he believed he was a fairly decent human being and that his heart was generally good. But he also had to admit that his behavior very often did not reflect such characteristics, and he could understand why Vivian would not only be hesitant to trust him, but strongly inclined to dislike him. When he considered his deepest, most private feelings for Vivian—feelings he would never dare admit aloud after how badly he'd handled trying to declare them before—he just wanted to sink into the floor and disappear.

Theo was relieved to hear Estelle approaching and looked toward her, sharing a familiar smile that put him more at ease despite the difficult conversations they'd had today. The moment she was seated, he hurried to say, "Before you ask, I went to the cobbler's shop and apologized to Miss Peyton."

"Well done, my boy," Estelle said. "And how did it go?"

"As well as could be expected, I suppose," he said even though he'd certainly hoped it would have gone much better. "She accepted my apology, but it's evident she's not very happy with me; and I can't say that I blame her."

"Understandable," Estelle said, never one to hold back her thoughts, even though Theo would have preferred to have her soothe his own bruised confidence. And Estelle knew nothing of the way that Theo had done such a poor job of trying to let Vivian know that he'd become very attracted to her—an experience that had ended with an unforgettable and much-deserved slap on the face. Thinking about it seemed to bring up a fresh, tangible sting on his skin.

When Theo couldn't think of anything else to say on the matter—and hoped that Estelle wouldn't ask any specific questions about his conversation with Vivian—he was relieved when his aunt broke the silence. "I do hope I can convince her to live here with us. I don't think Samuel will be genuinely happy if she doesn't—at least until she herself marries, when of course she would leave to live with her new husband."

Theo bristled inside at the very idea of Vivian marrying, and he realized that he had to stop believing that what he felt for her would ever have any substance. He also felt displeased to hear of Estelle's hope for Vivian to live here as part of the family. He didn't want to see Vivian every day, multiple times a day. He couldn't see it boding well given their contentious relationship, not to mention that seeing her every day would not help his desire to be free of the strange affection he felt for her that hovered inside him despite everything else that had happened. Perhaps her distrust and anger toward him were more hurtful *because* he felt such a distinct affection for her. But oh, how he wished he did not! This situation was plenty complicated without *that* thrown into the mixture. In truth, he was glad to recall Vivian's declaration to him earlier that she had no intention of living here with her grandfather. Despite knowing it would surely be difficult for her to be separated from Samuel, he felt certain that such a decision would be best for everyone involved.

Estelle went on. "I believe Vivian is very reluctant to live here and be a part of the family." This came as no surprise to Theo until Estelle explained her reasons. "She believes that the rest of the staff would see her as being given unfair advantages, and she would feel uncomfortable having them waiting on her and taking care of her, words to that effect, anyway. That's the general idea of what she told me . . . before we were interrupted."

Theo knew he had been the interruption, but his own relief over not having Vivian live under the same roof turned to a sudden sadness on Vivian's behalf as the entire picture became clearer—and he had certainly not helped the situation in any way. Vivian's grandfather was moving in with Estelle following their marriage, and Vivian had the quandary before her of facing some potentially enormous changes in her life while the people she had become comfortable working with would be watching her every move—and likely gossiping about her. Theo had absolutely no idea how the servants might feel about such a thing, but it didn't take much thought to try and put himself in Vivian's position and know that he would likely feel *extremely uncomfortable*. And now he had made the situation worse. He personally *didn't* want her around all the time and becoming a part of the family, but he didn't at all like her reasons for believing she shouldn't make the choice to be a part of her grandfather's new life.

Theo heard the maid coming with the tea tray and hurried to make an appropriate response. He simply said, "This must all be very difficult for her."

Estelle looked surprised by his comment, and he wondered if sounding compassionate was so unusual for him; it probably was, which made him feel like he really needed to consider being more conscious of his behavior. "Yes, it must be," Estelle added, and their tea was set out on the little table between them. Thankfully, the conversation between him and Estelle turned to more trivial matters. Nothing at all was said about the forthcoming wedding or the drama that had occurred between the two families—both today with Vivian, and years ago with his father and hers. Theo loved and admired Estelle so greatly that he felt deeply thankful to know her marriage would not take her away from him and they would remain close, despite her having a new husband in her life. He only wished that the same could be true for Vivian.

Chapter Eight
LETTING GO

Vivian was so lost in her dismal thoughts that she was startled by her grandfather sitting down in his usual chair near her side. She offered him a genuine smile, since it was always good to see him, but she couldn't think of a thing to say.

Samuel took hold of Vivian's hand before he spoke in a voice that was especially soft and gentle. "You came home from work early . . . and went to sleep. Are you not well?"

"Just . . . very tired," she said, wishing that would be sufficient to avoid telling him the real reasons Estelle had instructed Mrs. Thatcher to send her home.

"I see," Samuel said, acknowledging what she'd said but clearly knowing there was a great deal more she hadn't told him.

"And who was it that came to the shop?" he asked. "Someone you wanted to speak with privately; that much I know for sure."

Vivian decided to just answer the question directly and see how the conversation evolved from there. "It was Theo. He came to apologize for . . . a rather ugly exchange we'd had earlier in the day." Samuel's eyes widened and his eyebrows raised into high arches that deepened the wrinkles in his brow, but he said nothing; he was obviously waiting for Vivian to explain, and she had no choice but to do so.

"As soon as I arrived at work, I was told Estelle wanted to speak with me in her sitting room. We were discussing whether I should live there with you after you're married, and I suppose you could say we were contending with our difference of opinion on the matter." Vivian sensed her grandfather's curiosity rising over what she'd said, but she chose to look at the fire instead of directly at him while she hurried to get the most difficult aspects of this conversation out into the open.

"Theo came into the room without knocking and interrupted us; he was furious, and—"

"About the marriage?" Samuel interrupted, his concern evident.

"Yes, although in the end he was very much reassured by your insistence to legally make certain that Estelle's wealth will not be transferred to you." Vivian looked at him. "I've never understood such things very well; I don't suppose there was any reason to, given the life we've lived. But I have to say that I'm awfully glad you are doing this. I do not want *anyone*—whether it's Estelle's family or any member of the staff in the house—to believe for a moment that you are marrying Estelle for financial gain. This will put any potential gossip or rumors to rest."

"That was my thinking, exactly," Samuel said. "And we would have told you that yesterday if you hadn't left so abruptly."

"I apologize for that," Vivian said and squeezed her grandfather's hand tightly. "I admit to being . . . surprised . . . and it will certainly bring some enormous changes into our lives. I want you to know that my own . . . shock over the matter . . . and the potential changes for *me* do not in any way diminish my happiness on your behalf. I don't question for a moment that this is the right path for you and Estelle, and I'm overjoyed that you're both willing to take this step at your time of life when many people would be too settled in their old habits to have the courage to start over. I love you, Grandpapa, and more than anything else, I just want you to be happy."

"I thank you for that, my dear," he said. "Your support means more than I can say, and I apologize if our announcement was put to you too abruptly. But let me say that I love *you*, my dear girl, and more than anything else, I want *you* to be happy. If my marrying Estelle is going to bring difficulties into your life, I'm not certain I could—"

"No!" Vivian interrupted. "You mustn't think that way. This can never be about choosing between me and Estelle; you have no reason to think that you won't always have me in your life simply because you will be moving into a new home. I will visit often. I can sneak up the back stairs and meet you regularly for visits after my work is done and—"

"What are you saying?" he asked, so astonished that Vivian was struck temporarily dumb. "You cannot believe that we would allow you to keep working—in the very house where you should be living—after Estelle and I are married! You're my family; my only family."

Vivian cleared her throat and looked away. "Estelle will be your family, and her family will become yours. You and I will *always* be family, Grandpapa."

She looked up at him. "But I cannot live under the same roof; I simply cannot live there. I cannot!"

"Why?" he asked, and with that one word the disappointment and confusion on his face pushed Vivian close to the point of tears. But she choked them back, cleared her throat, and pressed forward into the dreaded territory that Theo had brought to light, although she decided to ease into it with the hesitancy she had already been feeling before these new revelations had destroyed any possible chance of Vivian even thinking she could become a part of her grandfather's new family.

Vivian cleared her throat again. "I work in that house, Grandpapa. I enjoy my work there, not necessarily because the work is enjoyable, but it's fulfilling. And I enjoy it mostly because I've come to very much like the people I work with. There are a few who keep to themselves, so I don't know them; and there are some who don't engage in conversation much and so I do not know them well, and yet they are still kind to me. And there are others who have become friends. There is a trust among the staff that is difficult to explain, a mutual affection and respect. I've grown to care for these people and they for me. If I were to suddenly become a member of the family, how could I expect these people to wait on me . . . and take care of my needs . . . when I did nothing to deserve such advancement over them? The awkwardness of such a situation is something I cannot even comprehend. I don't know how to explain it any more than that, Grandpapa; I can only tell you that's how I feel."

"I see," he said, but she knew he wasn't at all pleased with her reasoning. "Does Betsy's experience have anything to do with your concerns?"

Vivian could never refute the truth in his question, but she simply clarified, "I can't possibly deny that her experience has contributed to my concerns. We both know that what she endured was horrifying, and if I allow myself to think about it . . . well . . . it's frightening. But the situation is far more complicated than that. I don't know how to explain it any better than what I've already said," she repeated.

"I see," Samuel said again. "And?" he added.

"And what?"

"There's something else," he said. "Why did Theo come to apologize? You haven't told me about that yet."

Vivian drew in a long, sustaining breath and forced herself to just say it. "Theo interrupted my conversation with Estelle . . . furious over the news of the marriage . . . which he'd heard from his valet because Estelle had not spoken to him about it yet. And . . . he said that . . . my father and his father were involved in some kind of . . . unethical . . . scheme." Vivian heard Samuel let out a weighted sigh, but she ignored him and pressed on or she would never be able to finish. "He said that it was my father who had lured his father into these dealings; that it was my father's fault; that they wouldn't have died if they'd not been crossing the channel with intentions that had to do with the hope of . . . I think he said something about . . . trying to swindle money from . . . my mother's wealthy parents . . . who lived in France."

Vivian summoned courage and looked at Samuel as all her unanswered questions came rushing forward. "I know my mother's parents lived in France before they passed; that's all I know. I never received so much as a letter from them."

"They never approved of the marriage between your parents," Samuel said. "You know that."

"Yes, I know that," Vivian admitted. "My mother came from a wealthy family, and my father was a cobbler." Considering what Vivian now knew about her grandfather's life, a new idea occurred to her and she added, "That must have seemed strange to you after your past experience with Estelle."

"It did indeed," he said. "Your grandmother and I talked about it at the time. I experienced some uncomfortable emotions, but my sweet Edna helped me contend with them. And of course, we were incredibly happy, so I had no regrets. And your grandmother and I were thrilled with the marriage of your parents; they loved each other very much, and their social differences didn't matter to them—or to us."

Samuel sighed and tightened his hold on Vivian's hand. "Now that this information has come to you, allow me to say that I had hoped you would never find out that your father was involved in some unsavory dealings. We were concerned for him. Your grandmother and I had many conversations with him, trying to understand his motives, trying to set him straight. Your mother did the same; she was extremely concerned. But I can tell you in all honesty that none of us knew any details regarding what exactly was taking place. I know that it was a chance meeting at a pub that brought your father and Theo's father together. Apparently, Theo's father had known about the situation between Estelle and me, and so the name Peyton caught his attention and they both soon realized the connection. Beyond that, I sincerely know *nothing*, my dear. Your father told me that he and your mother were traveling to France to visit your grandparents. Until I heard what you just told me, I had no idea that there might have been any malicious intentions related to their journey. We all know how your parents died, and until Estelle and I discussed the situation very recently I hadn't known that Theo's father had died at the same time—when the ship encountered a storm and sank. Estelle and I both knew that my son and her brother were well acquainted and shared some questionable endeavors. But neither of us have any knowledge of the details of the situation—details that have gone with them to their watery graves; details we will never know, and which we must put to rest."

"It's evident that Theo has not put them to rest," Vivian stated, getting to the heart of the problem. "He's still truly angry over his father's death, and he blames *my* father for being responsible. Even if I were not uncomfortable with living in the home where I have been working for many months now, how could I *ever* live under the same roof with Theo, knowing he feels that way? He apologized to me for the way he handled the conversation earlier today, but I believe he did so more because Estelle insisted rather than from any genuine remorse on his part. I believe he dislikes me because I am the daughter of the man he blames for his father's death, and I have difficulty believing he will ever be able to let go of that. He's accepting you based on Estelle's love for you, and he would never do anything to disrespect her; I do know for a fact that he loves and admires her very much. But it's not the same for me, Grandpapa; it's so terribly complicated and messy. I simply cannot live there. And I can only hope that you will understand, and that you will forgive me. Everything will work out . . . it will be all right . . . I promise. It's just not going to be the way we might have wished."

Samuel sighed in a way that seemed to move through his entire body before he once again said, "I see." He sighed again, looking at the floor in front of him. "I would never want you to feel uncomfortable for any reason, my dear. A part of me wants to keep our lives just the way they are now, but . . . I cannot deny myself the opportunity to share the life with Estelle that we had hoped to share decades ago."

"And I would never want you to!"

"It has always been my hope that you would eventually find love and marry, and in that case, you would have left this home anyway, but . . ." He looked up at her with sad eyes. "This is still difficult."

"Yes, but we will adjust," she insisted, attempting to convince herself as much as him.

"Do you plan to just stay here?" he asked. "I'm assuming you're not comfortable with living in the servants' quarters at the house or—"

"No, I'm not," Vivian said, "even if it's difficult for me to explain the reasons."

Vivian went on to tell him her plan to try and find a room at a boardinghouse that might be closer to the Weatherby house so that she wouldn't have so far to walk. She talked of the way that Mrs. O'Neill and Mrs. Thatcher were always so kind in making certain she had plenty to eat on the days she worked, and how a large reduction in the rent she was now paying would allow her extra money to purchase food at pubs or from vendors on the days she didn't work, and her every need would be met. Samuel kept nodding his head as if to indicate that he was listening and that he understood, and that he was glad to know she had a plan. But Vivian absolutely knew he didn't like it one bit. He wanted her to live with him at the Weatherby house, and she knew that even though her reasons for not doing so were valid, her grandfather was still deeply disappointed. Deep down, Vivian was disappointed too. She couldn't acknowledge—even to herself—the part of her that couldn't help but long for the life of luxury and comfort that would be available to her. And even more inviting was the prospect of spending time each day with her grandfather and Estelle, sharing meals and enjoyable conversation. The very idea felt heavenly, almost idyllic—until she thought of the fact that Theo would always be there as well, and so would the staff who would serve her meals and clean her room and launder her clothing. She just couldn't do it.

Vivian went to her room, claiming the need for more rest. Once it was evident that neither she nor her grandfather had anything else to say, sitting together just felt awkward—an experience that was completely unfamiliar with this man who had helped raise her, and with whom she had always felt entirely comfortable.

Even though Vivian was unable to fall asleep, she remained in her bed with her eyes closed, at least hoping to get some rest, wishing her mind would let go of the overwhelming enormity of thoughts that just kept spinning around and around.

When Vivian knew it was nearing time for supper, she got up and went to the kitchen to heat up some of the ample amount of food Mrs. O'Neill had sent home with her. Vivian felt grateful as always for this wonderful benefit of working in the Weatherby house, and she was also grateful to have her grandfather come to the table to eat, behaving as if nothing were out of the ordinary. Vivian just wanted to spend time with him and enjoy that time while it lasted; she didn't want to talk about the questionable ethics of her father or the upcoming wedding and how both matters had turned Vivian's world upside down so quickly that she almost felt as if she might not be able to walk without getting dizzy. Thankfully, the sensation was more emotional than physical, and she managed well enough to behave normally. Still, she couldn't deny feeling legitimately exhausted, and her gratitude increased for Estelle's insight into her needing some time to adjust to all that was happening without having to work. It seemed that the emotional impact of all the drama was physically draining, and Estelle was insightful enough to know that—likely from personal experience. She'd certainly lived through more than one traumatic experience; she'd been forced away from the man she loved when she'd been a young woman, and she'd tragically lost her brother when Theo had been in his youth. Given what little Vivian knew of Theo's mother and sister, she felt certain that Estelle had mostly taken on the role of raising Theo. But it was readily evident that Estelle had no control over many of Theo's attitudes and behaviors—the same way that Samuel had not been able to influence Vivian's father against becoming involved in unsavory schemes. Vivian wished that Theo could see in his own father the same character flaw over which he was so angry regarding her father.

Once supper was over and she had put the kitchen in order, Vivian told her grandfather she needed to go to bed early and that she wouldn't be going in to work the following day. He didn't ask any questions, but simply wished her a good night and kissed her brow in his familiar way. Vivian hated the feeling that he surely had to be thrilled over the prospect of marrying his beloved Estelle, but that at the same time he likely felt a terrible sorrow over how that would impact Vivian. She wished she could make all this easier for him by simply agreeing to his desires, but she felt certain that doing so would cause such distress for her that she would end up making Samuel even more unhappy as a result.

Vivian woke to the light of dawn peering through the window of her room, glad to realize she'd fallen asleep quickly even though she'd gone to bed early, and that she'd slept well. She lay in bed for a long while contemplating all the difficult conversations that had taken place during the last couple of days. Weary of attempting to analyze all her complicated emotions and the potential results of her decisions, Vivian just put the entire matter away for now, firmly resolving to find a room at a boardinghouse as soon as possible, continue working at the Weatherby house just as she was doing, and do her best to keep her connection to Estelle's fiancé from becoming known throughout the household. And above all else, she wished to avoid Theo completely. If she never saw him again it would suit her just fine.

With this decision set firmly in her mind, Vivian got out of bed and hurried to light a fire in her room so she could get cleaned up and dressed without being cold. Normally at this time of year she would just hurry to get ready for the day and get warm in the parlor, but she was hoping to spend most of the day resting in her room—and perhaps reading—and therefore she wanted the room to be warm.

Before Vivian had finished dressing, she could hear her grandfather working in the kitchen, presumably heating up some porridge left over from the previous day's breakfast. Knowing that he liked to feel useful, Vivian didn't make any effort to hurry; she was only too glad to not have to make breakfast. Despite a good night's sleep, she still felt tired. And somewhere between putting on her dress and her stockings it occurred to her that this simple experience of being in this room and hearing her grandfather in the kitchen was something she would not be able to enjoy much longer. In less than a month Samuel would be married and living with Estelle, and the cobbler's shop would return to the control of the landlord who would rent it out to someone else as quickly as possible. Vivian sat on the edge of her bed and wept, keeping her hand over her mouth to muffle any sound. This was the only home she'd ever known; the only home *Samuel* had ever known. Three generations of Peytons before her had lived and worked here, and now all that was coming to an end. For Samuel, it was a happy beginning elsewhere; for Vivian, it was simply a matter of change that she needed to accept.

"Breakfast is on, my dear," Vivian heard Samuel call, and she hurried to wipe her tears before glancing in the mirror to make certain she could convince her grandfather that everything was fine. On her way to the kitchen, she recalled the moment she'd made the decision to seek out Estelle Weatherby on her grandfather's behalf. Estelle had blessed both of their lives immensely, and Vivian could never regret that decision. Still, she never could have imagined that such dramatic changes would come into their lives because of Vivian's decision. And now she just had to learn to live with it and find a way to be happy despite all that was about to change.

Vivian was surprised at how much she was able to sleep throughout the day, deeply grateful that she had this time to rest when she'd not anticipated how thoroughly exhausted she would be. She was also grateful for Mrs. O'Neill's food that could easily be heated up, and for the way her grandfather took charge of doing so. Vivian only ate and slept and considered it a miracle that all her sleeping throughout the day didn't at all hinder her ability to sleep that night. When she awoke at the usual time, knowing she had to get up and go to the Weatherby house as usual to put in a day's work, she felt more prepared to return to life as it normally unfolded, and to simply set aside all the things that troubled her, things that she could do nothing to change.

Nothing notably unusual happened throughout the day, and Vivian didn't sense any difference in the attitudes toward her from any other members of the staff. This came as a great relief to her, since she took it as an indication that no one had heard any gossip that might connect her to Estelle's fiancé. There was certainly talk of Miss Weatherby's forthcoming marriage and some speculation over what her new husband would be like and how his living in the house might change some things. But for the most part, everyone seemed nothing but happy for Miss Weatherby, and they were excited to be hosting a wedding celebration in her honor here at the house following the marriage at the church. They all admired and respected their employer greatly and saw her wedding as something joyful and worth celebrating, even though it meant more work for all of them. Vivian was glad to just be able to sit among her fellow workers and listen to their conversations as if nothing in the world was wrong, as if this wedding they were talking about wasn't changing her life in nearly every way.

On Vivian's day off she did some searching for a suitable room at a boardinghouse where she might rent a room. The first four places she visited that were within a comfortable walking distance from the Weatherby house proved to be uninhabitable in Vivian's opinion. They were either excessively noisy from drunk tenants or the crying of neglected children, or they were severely lacking in cleanliness or basic repairs. When her fifth attempt turned out to be a room with a cracked window and paint peeling off the walls, Vivian began to fear she wasn't going to be able to find what she was hoping for.

Vivian stopped her search long enough to enjoy a late lunch at a nearby pub and was glad to find a place to sit in a dimly lit corner where she could have some privacy that would allow her to examine her thoughts. She turned her mind to silent prayer, knowing that she *had* to find a place to live that met the minimum requirements of peace, cleanliness, and safety. If not, she would be forced to live at the Weatherby house for reasons she could never explain. But she believed that God understood the deepest thoughts and feelings of His children when they sought His guidance in their lives.

After Vivian had finished her meal, she enjoyed one more cup of tea before heading out again on her search. While she cradled the warm cup in her hands, her mind went of its own volition to Theo. Her first thought was a perfect memory of how it had felt to have him kiss her. His approach had been completely inappropriate, and she still believed that he had warranted the slap she'd given him in return. Still, he had kissed her! And it may well have been the most thrilling and blissful moment of her life. Vivian had to remind herself that one blissful moment could never outweigh all his arrogance and lack of kindness toward her. He was a large part of the reason she could never live at the Weatherby house—not in the servants' dormitories, and certainly not as a member of the family. He wasn't the *only* reason, but he certainly hadn't made the situation any easier.

Vivian settled the bill for her meal and thanked the serving girl who had been so kind to her before she set out again, heading to a boardinghouse that this girl had recommended. Vivian held a prayer in her heart that this place might be different—more accurately, that this place might meet the minimum requirements in being somewhere she could live and be comfortable.

When Vivian arrived at the appointed place, she stood in front of the tall, narrow edifice and looked up, overcome with a good feeling that she hoped would prove to have merit. It appeared to have once been one of the many fine homes of wealthy families who lived in this area, but it had been modified into a boardinghouse to provide living quarters for individuals. From what Vivian could see, the structure was in good repair, and in fact it blended well into the many fine houses in this area.

Vivian went to the front door and struck the knocker against the door three times. She waited only a moment before the door came open and the tallest, plumpest woman she'd ever encountered stood before her, with cheeks as pink as a rose in full bloom, and a smile that lit up her round face. Her brown-and-gray-streaked hair looked as if it had been neatly pinned up earlier in the day, but it had fought its way out of any confinement to create a kind of fuzzy halo around her head.

"Hello, deary," the woman said, her accent thick with evidence that she'd likely grown up in the very northern part of England. "Might I help you?"

"I'm looking for a room to rent, and a kind serving girl at a nearby pub told me she knew that this place might suit my needs. Do you have any rooms available and—"

"Oh my, yes!" the woman said and opened the door wider, motioning for Vivian to enter.

Vivian stepped inside and heard the door close behind her. It took only a moment for her to recognize an entirely different ambience to this place in contrast to those she'd visited earlier in the day. Sunlight streamed through clean windows into the foyer in which they stood. The staircase in front of her was fine but not grand, and there was a quaint parlor to one side of the foyer where Vivian could imagine tenants being able to comfortably meet with visitors. While Vivian was taking in the inviting appeal of the parlor, her hostess directed her to a room on the opposite side of the foyer, which reminded Vivian of Mrs. Thatcher's office, except that it was much brighter due to the number of windows.

"Please sit down," the woman said, "and tell me about yourself." She plopped heavily into a large chair that was well acquainted with her. "You can call me Mel, which is short for a great deal of name which is just a nuisance." She laughed as if having gotten rid of the rest of her name had been a great relief and had also given her immense pleasure. "And you are?"

"My name is Vivian Peyton," she said. "I work at the Weatherby house but would prefer to not live in the dormitories there. My wages are ample to be able to afford to rent a room for myself, but I haven't been able to find a place where I would *dare* live even if I'd wanted to."

This made Mel laugh again. "Oh, I know just what you mean, deary. When I inherited this house from an uncle I didn't even know I had—but I didn't have enough money to afford keeping it up—I decided to use it to offer a proper place for fine young women like yourself to be able to live. No men live here, deary, so there's no need to be concerned about encountering a man when you need to leave your room to use the privy or for any other reason."

"Oh, that's very nice," Vivian said, not having even thought of the possibility of finding a place that was only for women; but she liked the idea very much indeed.

"I keep the doors locked but give each of my residents a key so you can come and go as you please, but we can all feel safe."

"Oh, *that* is very nice, as well."

"I require a certain respectability of my tenants," Mel went on, her voice completely serious but her face seeming to be unable to do anything but smile. "You are clearly a respectable young woman; polite and well-groomed and all that—or I wouldn't have let you in the door." Again, she laughed at herself before she became serious again. "I've found there's a great number of young women who are in similar situations as yourself in this part of the city, working at grand houses or pubs or the like, and they just need a safe place to live. And so, I've made myself a good living by providing such a place, and I very much enjoy the friends I've made among the people who've lived here; some of them have come to feel as good as family."

She went on to tell Vivian the standard price to rent one of her rooms and added—much to Vivian's surprise—that clean linens would be provided on a regular basis, and that the rent also included three meals a day.

"Oh, my!" Vivian said with pleasure; the rent was a little higher than the other places she'd visited, but still well within her budget and well worth it, considering everything she'd heard so far. "That's a nice surprise. I didn't at all expect that, but it's wonderful. At the house where I work . . . they are very generous with meals on the days that I work, but it's nice to know I won't have to go elsewhere to find a decent meal on my days off." She also wouldn't have to pay extra for meals elsewhere, which made the cost of the room even more appealing.

"Indeed, you won't," Mel said. "And I can adjust your monthly fee if you're only eating here part of the time." She stood up with a groan, leaning her hands on the desk to help get her overly large body out of the chair. "Would you like to see the two rooms we have available? And if living here is to your liking, you can choose which one you prefer."

"I'd like that very much," Vivian said, knowing she would never find a place better than this.

Vivian expected Mel to lead her out of the office, but instead she rang a little bell and a moment later a young woman with very blonde hair, a pretty face, and a slim figure appeared through a different door, holding a large basket against her hip.

"This is Sally Mae," Mel said. "I pay her to do all the things I'm just too old and fat to do myself." Again, she laughed at herself, and Vivian laughed with her, having become accustomed to the way that Mel seemed to just have a jolly attitude about everything, and an uncanny ability to find humor in her own eccentricities and even her own shortcomings. More seriously, Mel added, "I do all the cooking and seeing to business matters, so you put your rent directly into my hands before the first of each month. Sally Mae washes the linens and helps keep things clean. She's a fine girl!"

"Ah," Sally Mae said, making a self-deprecating gesture with her free hand and chuckling comfortably, "you say that every time we get a new one."

She set the basket down in an empty chair and held out a hand toward Mel as if she knew exactly what she needed to do. Mel put two sets of keys into her hand, and Vivian could see that each set of two keys was connected to a fob that was engraved with a number.

"Tell us your name again, deary," Mel said. "I'll remember it after I hear it a few times."

"Vivian Peyton," she said, returning Mel's infectious smile.

"Good to meet you, miss," Sally Mae said to Vivian.

"And you, as well," Vivian said.

"Let's go look at the rooms, shall we?" Sally Mae said, heading through the door that went back into the foyer. "Mel's not been up the stairs for years. For all she knows, it's nothing but bats and ghosts up there."

This made Mel laugh boisterously. "I do think someone would've complained if that were the case."

"Maybe," Sally Mae said mischievously and led the way up the stairs.

On the landing, they turned and went down a hall where Sally Mae turned a key in the lock. The number four on the door coordinated with the same number on the fob attached to the keys. The maid opened the door and motioned for Vivian to enter ahead of her.

Vivian gasped pleasantly to see a truly fine room. The decor was simple and anything but lavish, but the furnishings were more than adequate; the bed looked comfortable, and everything was clean and in good repair. "Oh, it's lovely!" she said and crossed the room to look out the window where she could see the street below; it was evident this room was at the front of the house.

"Glad you like it," Sally Mae said, "but let's have a look at the other empty room to see which one you might prefer."

"Of course," Vivian said and followed Sally Mae out of the room and up another flight of stairs to the door marked with the number nine. While she unlocked the door, Sally Mae pointed out that each floor had a water closet located at the end of the hall; she pointed toward it before opening the door of room number nine. This room was nearly identical in the way it was furnished, but the view out the window was of the outside wall of the neighboring house, and Vivian immediately decided that it would be far more practical to only have to walk up and down *one* flight of stairs instead of two. But before she made a final decision, she had one question for Sally Mae.

"Is there anything in your opinion that might make the location of one room better than the other? Are any of the other tenants more prone to be noisy or—"

"Oh, Mel don't allow any noise that would disturb others after supper's over in the evening, or before breakfast in the morning. But I will say that during the days, there can be some giggling coming from *that* room." She pointed to number seven across the hall.

"That settles it," Vivian said. "I was leaning toward number four anyway. I'll take it."

"Very good!" Sally Mae said with an enthusiasm that implied she had already grown to like Vivian, but then Vivian had already grown to like Sally Mae *and* Mel. And she felt as if her every prayer had been answered more abundantly than she ever could have hoped. Now that she had found such a fine place to live, her decision to *not* live at the Weatherby house settled in with more peace.

Sally Mae led Vivian back to the office where Mel was sitting at her desk. She gave both sets of keys back to Mel before she picked up her basket, exchanged some friendly words with Vivian, and returned to whatever she had been doing before she'd been summoned.

Mel informed Vivian of all the rules of her household—rules which Vivian liked very much because it meant that others in the house would not be allowed to disturb her or cause any trouble. Mel also showed Vivian the simple contract she needed to sign, which obligated her to comply with all these rules and to pay her rent on time. If and when Vivian decided to move out, she needed to give Mel a month's notice, and if she rented the room for part of a month, the rent would be adjusted. Mel expected a month's rent in advance before the deal was complete, but Vivian had expected this and had the money in the small satchel she'd kept close all day.

Once their business transaction was complete, Mel handed Vivian the set of two keys attached to the fob. "The smaller key is for your room, and the larger one is for the front door of the house. Keep them safe; I can have more made if you lose them, but it will cost you more than you'd want to pay."

"I understand," Vivian said, and they parted cordially. Even though Vivian wouldn't be moving in for a few weeks—a fact of which she had informed Mel during their conversation—Vivian felt a great burden lifted to know that she had a safe and comfortable place to live once her grandfather was married. She could now officially inform the landlord of their current home that they would be moving out in less than a month's time, which just so happened to be when the rent she had paid would run out.

Vivian stood in front of her new home for a minute or more and just looked around to acquaint herself with its location. She was glad to note that the walk to and from here to the Weatherby house was less than half the distance it had been from the cobbler's shop. She would appreciate that, especially on cold and stormy days.

Satisfied and deeply grateful, Vivian headed home, stopping at a few shops on the way to purchase some bread and scones from a bakery, some fresh butter, and a few vegetables, and even the rare treat of some sweets that she and her grandfather could enjoy together. She knew he preferred that she live at the Weatherby house, but she also knew he respected her choices, and he would be glad to know that she'd found someplace safe and fine to live. It was certainly cause for celebration.

Vivian was pleased to have days pass into weeks without any undue drama in her life. When she'd told her grandfather about the lovely boardinghouse in which she'd rented a room, he'd expressed his pleasure that she would be safe and comfortable, and he said nothing more. She knew he wanted to convince her to move into the Weatherby house instead, but he was respecting her decision and she appreciated it more than she could say—but she tried anyway and told him how grateful she felt that he would be so supportive of her choices. He only hugged her tightly and told her that she had been supportive of *his* choices, and he was counting on her coming to visit him frequently.

Estelle made one more attempt to talk Vivian into living in her home and making herself a part of the family, but Vivian only thanked Estelle for her kindness and politely declined, offering her a brief explanation of her new home, and reinforcing her desire for her connection to Samuel to remain unknown among the rest of the staff.

"I can't make any promises about what they may or may not figure out," Estelle said, "but I promise you that I won't say anything to anyone."

"Thank you," Vivian said. "And thank you for making him so happy. He hasn't been so full of life and energy since my grandmother died, and nothing could make *me* happier."

"Oh, it is I who am perfectly happy," Estelle told Vivian before she made promises that they would find ways to discreetly visit, and that everything would surely work out well.

Estelle also offered to get Vivian a new dress for the wedding, but Vivian graciously declined, assuring her that her Sunday dress would do. She said nothing about how she felt torn regarding whether she should even attend the wedding. She knew that neither Estelle nor her grandfather would understand her emotional dilemma; it was certainly a big day in Samuel's life, and by every measure of logic, Vivian knew she should attend. She'd mentally tallied a great many excuses for not going, but in the deepest part of her heart she knew that the most valid reason was her fear of making a fool of herself by crying like a baby. She was doing her best to accept these changes graciously and with dignity, but in reality, she hated it—a fact which she could never admit aloud, simply because it sounded so selfish. No matter how difficult this was for her, she needed to express nothing to Estelle or Samuel except her happiness on their behalf, and she wasn't certain she could attend the wedding and maintain that façade.

Vivian didn't see Theo at all—much to her relief—and the days passed in a way that made it easy to ignore the fact that everything was about to change.

A few days before the wedding, Vivian moved into the boardinghouse. She had the day off work, which gave her plenty of time to make certain the house behind the cobbler's shop was in perfect order, and to pack up everything that belonged to her—all of which she was able to fit into a portmanteau that had belonged to Edna and a large satchel of her own. Beyond her clothes and personal items, Vivian had little of value. At her grandfather's insistence, she took the three novels that Edna had owned—books that Vivian had read many times and that had become precious to her. Samuel reminded Vivian that he would have access to the library in his new home, which housed an endless number of books. She also took a few small personal possessions that had belonged to Edna and her parents, simply for their sentimental value. Beyond that, there was nothing she wished to keep.

A couple of weeks earlier, Vivian and Samuel had begun working together to go through everything in the house, separating their personal belongings from those that had come with the house and belonged to the landlord. It was strange for them both to realize that all their furnishings and some of the basic items in the kitchen they'd been using for their entire lives had never actually belonged to them. They carefully sorted through the things that *were* theirs and donated most of them to the poor. Samuel had never wanted to get rid of Edna's clothes and other belongings, but as he prepared to step into this new chapter of his life, it was easier for him to realize that Edna's things could benefit those in need, and he would always have his tender memories of her. Both Vivian and Samuel believed that Edna would be pleased with Samuel finding love again, and Samuel was content to keep a brooch and a hair comb that had belonged to his late wife as reminders of her. He let everything else go, and slowly packed his belongings into a small trunk that had remained unused in his room for a great many years. He'd inherited it from his father, but he'd never had cause to travel, and now he would use it to transport his very minimal belongings the short distance to the Weatherby house. He told Vivian that Estelle had already taken him to be fitted for new clothes—including a fine suit he would wear to the wedding—so he wouldn't be needing his old clothes for much longer. Apparently, their excursion to order Samuel a new wardrobe had taken place while Vivian had been working, and Samuel had forgotten to mention it. She felt a little hurt for a moment, then reminded herself that their paths were separating, and it was the natural order of things. She needed to let go of her desire to take care of her grandfather and move forward with her own life.

"What will *you* wear to the wedding?" Samuel asked Vivian the evening before the wedding while they were walking slowly together through the shop and house to make certain they hadn't missed anything. Vivian had already moved into the boardinghouse but had come back each evening to bring supper from the big house that she could share with Samuel, and to help him finish up the little details of moving and cleaning.

Vivian felt stabbed by guilt as she considered the fact that Samuel was getting married tomorrow, and she had said nothing to him about her feelings on the matter. She took a deep breath and just forced the words out. "My Sunday dress will do fine," she began with trepidation, "although I'm not entirely certain I'll be able to be there."

"What are you saying?" he bellowed, which was understandable, but Vivian still felt unprepared for how upset he was. "Why would you not be there for my wedding?"

"I have to work, Grandpapa," she said, clearing their supper dishes from the table while she avoided looking at him.

"You work for the woman I'm marrying," he insisted as if she might not have already known. "You and I both know that she would not expect you to work, and she would certainly allow you the day off and do so discreetly if that's what you prefer."

"I know," Vivian said, then felt horrified when a torrent of tears rushed out of her. Before she could say anything else, Samuel had come to his feet and wrapped her tightly in his arms.

"What is this?" he asked gently.

"I'm so happy for you, Grandpapa," she murmured through her ongoing tears. "It's just . . . well . . . the changes are . . . difficult and . . . I don't know if I can be there and . . ."

He held her and let her cry while Vivian tried to accept that this was truly their last time together in the house where they'd always lived. But they had to let go of the past—and of each other. They would always be a part of each other's lives, but nothing would ever be the same.

After Vivian had calmed down, Samuel said nothing more about her coming to the wedding, and they worked together to tidy up the kitchen, and Vivian put the clean dishes that belonged at the Weatherby house into the canvas bag she carried back and forth.

At the door they exchanged loving good-byes, and Vivian concluded by simply saying, "I'll see you soon." She still hadn't decided whether attending her grandfather's wedding was a good idea; she preferred to just spend the day as if it were any other and simply focus on her work and remain invisible.

Chapter Nine
DECADES LATE

VIVIAN ARRIVED AT HER NEW home and used her key to go in the front door, which she locked behind her as she realized that Mel and Sally Mae and a couple of other women who lived there were visiting in the parlor. Mel called a greeting to Vivian and invited her to join them, and she decided that it might be a nice distraction from the difficult transition taking place in her life. She sat and visited, thoroughly enjoying the conversation and laughter of this colorful variety of women. When Mel announced that she needed to get some sleep, Vivian too excused herself, explaining that she needed to be awake early to get to work on time.

When Vivian was finally in her new bed—which she found incredibly comfortable compared to the one she'd slept on all her life—she couldn't hold back a few more stray tears. But she wiped them away with the sheet, forced her mind elsewhere, and thankfully fell asleep before she had time to allow herself to consider the situation any further.

Vivian arrived at the Weatherby house a few minutes early, and before she'd hung up her coat, she was keenly aware that the house was filled with a great deal of excitement and bustle. Until that moment, she'd not considered the fact that Estelle's wedding dinner and celebration would be held here after the marriage took place at the church. She'd known this when the wedding had initially been discussed, but she had honestly forgotten. Over the past week or so, she'd been assigned extra cleaning duties in rooms that were rarely used since they were built to accommodate large numbers of guests. Of course, Vivian should have logically figured out the reason, but perhaps she'd put those thoughts away with everything else related to this wedding that she didn't want to think about.

Vivian could hear Mrs. O'Neill shouting orders in the kitchen as she walked toward the roster hanging on the wall to see what tasks had been assigned to her today. She was certainly glad to not be among the group of maids that were assigned to help serve the food and drinks for the wedding guests. At the same moment when she realized her name wasn't on the roster, Mrs. Thatcher approached her and leaned close to her ear, saying softly, "Get your coat and come to my office."

Mrs. Thatcher moved away before Vivian could question her reasons for such an odd request. But she did as she was told and retrieved her coat before she went to the housekeeper's office where Mrs. Thatcher was waiting near the door, which she closed as soon as Vivian entered.

Motioning toward her sitting room, Mrs. Thatcher said, "There is a dress Miss Weatherby had made for you; she consulted me a couple of weeks ago, and I assured her I knew your size because I provided your uniforms. You need to change and put your coat on if you don't wish anyone to see what you're wearing. I'll help get you out to the carriage and—"

"I don't understand," Vivian said, feeling panicked.

"Well, we're going to your grandfather's wedding, my dear," Mrs. Thatcher said as if it were obvious. "As close as I've worked with Miss Weatherby all these years, she's invited me to attend, and she asked me to make certain that you attend as well."

"How long have you known?" Vivian asked, trying to recall any incidents between herself and Mrs. Thatcher where the housekeeper's behavior toward her might have changed.

"Known what? That your grandfather is the man Miss Weatherby was visiting? Had loved decades ago and loves him still? Why, I've known all along, my dear." She took Vivian's hand. "There's no need to be concerned, Vivian. I realize this must be a strange situation for you, but no one—especially not me—is going to begrudge your being related to the new master of the house."

"But . . ." Vivian muttered and couldn't find a single word to follow that might express her astonishment. "Now, listen carefully, young one," Mrs. Thatcher said as if she were speaking to a child, but not in a way that was at all condescending. Mrs. Thatcher took hold of both of Vivian's shoulders and spoke in a soft, motherly voice, "Miss Weatherby has always entrusted me with any and all information that she considers pertinent in this household, and I have done the same in return. We are as close to friends as women can be who live such different lives—which is why she invited me to attend the wedding. But as usual, we try to keep our friendship discreet. She told me your reasons for not wanting others to know your situation, and believe it or not, I understand—likely more than Miss Weatherby could ever comprehend. I will not tell a soul, Vivian; nevertheless, I must warn you that while everyone you work with calls you by your given name, I can't say for certain that no one knows your surname, and someone might very well connect it to that of the man Miss Weatherby is marrying. If that happens, we will take the matter on together, and everything will be all right. Do you understand?"

Vivian nodded to indicate that she did, but she could never admit aloud just how deeply such an idea terrified her. Her mind quickly considered the few members of the staff—all men—with whom she'd never shared any conversation. How could she possibly know their attitude about something like this? Thoughts of Betsy's assault tempted her to feel sick, but she quickly forced her mind entirely to the present. Thankfully, Mrs. Thatcher continued to speak. "Whatever the circumstances, neither Miss Weatherby nor I believe it's right for you to miss your grandfather's wedding. We both fear that you would come to regret such a decision, and there's no doubting that the wedding will not feel right to your grandfather if you are not there. Now, I have a perfectly good explanation to get us out of the house. All you need to do is change into that new dress, and feel free to use my comb and hairpins if you have the need. Although we should leave in about half an hour."

"Oh, thank you!" Vivian said, throwing her arms around Mrs. Thatcher with no thought over whether doing so would be appropriate. Vivian realized in that moment how much her own fears and concerns had falsely affected her perspective of the situation, and she *did* need to be at the wedding. Her grandfather would be brokenhearted if she weren't there; how could she have been so selfish as to not consider such a thing? And Mrs. Thatcher's kindness and insight had just lifted her spirits immensely. She felt relieved to know that the housekeeper was aware of the situation; from here on she would have an ally in being able to discreetly visit her grandfather and Estelle, and she felt confident that Mrs. Thatcher would always respect her wishes concerning the situation. She could only hope that no one else in the household figured out her connection to Estelle's new husband.

"One more thing," Mrs. Thatcher said before letting go of Vivian's shoulders, "forgive me for being repetitive, my dear, but I know this is a sensitive matter for you and I want to be perfectly clear, so I'm going to say it again. As of now I don't believe anyone else in the household knows of your connection to the man Miss Weatherby is about to marry, but she is very soon to become Mrs. Peyton. Most of those you work with only know you as Vivian, but there's no telling when someone might figure out the connection, and I think you should be prepared for that possibility. But listen to me, my dear; I don't think that they will be nearly as uncomfortable with it as you might believe they will. Whatever happens—whenever it happens—I will do all I can to help manage the situation, so please . . . please . . . don't let it upset you or make you afraid."

"Thank you," Vivian said again, trying to suppress her fears as she let out a sigh of relief that seemed to settle from the top of her head all the way to the floor. She was glad for the housekeeper's efforts to clarify this possibility and offer Vivian reassurance, because she *did* feel less afraid, given this kind woman's support and encouragement; surely this woman knew the character of those who worked under her supervision. Still, Vivian hoped and prayed it would never come to that.

"Now run along and get yourself ready," Mrs. Thatcher said. "I'm going upstairs to my room to change into a nicer dress. Stay in my sitting room and keep the door closed. I won't be long."

Vivian nodded, suddenly unable to speak for fear of crying—but for the first time in weeks, her threat of tears was founded in happiness rather than sorrow, and she felt excited to be able to surprise her grandfather. Or perhaps Estelle had told him to expect her. Either way, this day was going to be much, much better than she had anticipated.

In the housekeeper's sitting room, Vivian found a dress finer than anything she had ever worn. It was not so fancy that it would look out of place for attending church on any given Sunday, but the pale-blue fabric adorned with white lace at the collar and cuffs was so lovely it took Vivian's breath away. She changed into the new dress and realized she would need Mrs. Thatcher to fasten the buttons down the back of the dress; but as far as she could tell the fit was almost perfect. She also found a lovely lace handkerchief and appreciated this thoughtful detail. Ever since Estelle had provided her with a handkerchief when she'd been so upset, Vivian had taken up the habit of keeping one in her apron pocket. But her own were not nearly as soft and fine as this, and she was glad to tuck it beneath the cuff of her dress, certain she would not get through the wedding without some tears.

Vivian removed her maid's cap and smoothed her hair, redoing a few of the pins so that it looked suitable. She couldn't help admiring her reflection in the mirror on the wall, even though it only showed an image from about her waist up. Still, she very much liked what she saw and doubted that she had ever felt so beautiful.

Mrs. Thatcher knocked at the door, saying, "It's just me." Vivian opened the door and Mrs. Thatcher expressed enthusiastic approval over Vivian's appearance as she began fastening the buttons. She paused, then surprised Vivian with a small, slender box.

"What is this?" Vivian asked, taking it from her as if it might break.

"A little gift from the bride and groom," Mrs. Thatcher said, which let Vivian know that her grandfather was likely in on this surprise. "You should open it so we can be on our way."

"Of course," Vivian said and opened the lid to reveal a fine silver chain with a tiny heart hanging from it. "Oh, it's beautiful!" Vivian declared. "I've never had anything so fine—except perhaps this dress."

Mrs. Thatcher let out a delighted laugh and helped fasten the necklace around Vivian's throat, followed by the rest of the buttons down her back. She then turned her around and said, "You look absolutely lovely, my dear. Now put your coat on—as I will do myself—so that we can get out of the house without looking too suspicious."

Once out of the housekeeper's office, Vivian was glad to see that no one was in the hallway between where they stood and the door where they needed to exit. "Go on out," Mrs. Thatcher whispered. "Twig and Cooper will be waiting with the carriage. They'll keep our secret."

Vivian had come to know these men during the many meals they'd shared, and she liked them very much. She also knew there were others who often drove Estelle when she had the desire to go anywhere, and they had surely already left with Estelle to take her to the church.

"Don't you look lovely, Miss," Twig said even though most of her dress was covered by her coat.

"Thank you," she said, and to reassure herself added, "I understand we are engaged in a secretive outing."

"Our lips are sealed upon pain of death," Cooper said, then added, "and we delivered the groom to the church only minutes ago, after we waited for his new valet to help him get ready."

"Oh, I see," Vivian said, wondering how Samuel Peyton would feel about having a valet.

Vivian was helped into the carriage only a moment before Mrs. Thatcher appeared and sat down across from her. "There now," she said triumphantly. "I told Mrs. O'Neill that I had some errands to take care of and you would be busy with a special assignment I'd given you. She assured me that everything is under control for the wedding festivities, and she didn't even seem nearly as anxious as I might have expected with such a large feast to prepare." Vivian smiled at the housekeeper and thought about who would be present at this wedding feast. She knew from the servants gossiping about the wedding for the last couple of weeks that the groom had no guests who would be attending, but the bride had many friends with whom she wanted him to become acquainted. Vivian felt a tiny twinge of sadness that she wouldn't be at the feast, but she quickly pushed that concern away. She would be able to attend the wedding, and no one would be any the wiser. To her, nothing else mattered right now, and she was once again grateful for Estelle's insight and her grandfather's support. And she was newly grateful to know that Mrs. Thatcher was aware of her situation and would help her with whatever might come up regarding it in the future. She was pleasantly surprised to realize how such knowledge eased a great deal of her anxiety.

The drive to the church took only a few minutes, but of course there were churches scattered all over this enormous city, and the one Estelle attended would not be far from her home. Cooper helped Vivian and Mrs. Thatcher step down and promised they would be waiting to take them home when the time came. Just inside the church there was a room for hanging coats; the two women did just that and then surveyed each other's appearance approvingly before they stepped into the chapel where several guests were seated, listening to the organ music, and waiting for the grand event to begin.

Vivian immediately saw her grandfather standing at the head of the chapel with the vicar and was glad when he saw her as she moved discreetly up the aisle with Mrs. Thatcher to find a seat. Vivian waved at him and saw the hint of moisture glisten in his eyes while he smiled with perfect joy. He also nodded in a way that she knew was his silent way of saying he thought she looked beautiful. She couldn't help but notice how finely he was dressed in a fashionable suit, complete with a silk cravat surrounding the high collar of his brilliantly white shirt. Not only did he look very handsome, but Vivian also believed he looked many years younger than he'd looked ever since he'd lost Edna.

Vivian and Mrs. Thatcher sat down on a pew that was not close enough to the front to be easily noticed, but not so far back that they didn't have a perfect view of where the marriage ceremony would take place. Vivian was surprised when Mrs. Thatcher whispered, "I see Mrs. Weatherby and Miss Lilith." She nodded forward and to her left and Vivian looked in that direction while it took her a moment to realize she meant Theo's mother and sister. "I daresay this is one of the few times they've been out of the house in years."

"Oh, my," Vivian whispered in reply, her curiosity aroused, but she had no idea exactly which ladies Mrs. Thatcher's nod was meant to indicate.

Vivian was glad when Mrs. Thatcher clarified her comments with a description of their hats, which then made their location obvious, except that Vivian couldn't see them at all due to the size and adornment of those hats and the angle at which the ladies were sitting.

While she was hoping for even a glimpse of these mysterious Weatherby women, the organist changed the melody, and the vicar motioned with his hands for everyone to stand. Vivian noticed that many of the guests consisted of elegantly dressed women and very few men; if Vivian were to make a guess, she could easily imagine that most of Estelle's friends were also unmarried women, but a few of them had husbands. Maybe some of these women were widows. Perhaps these men were brothers of the women with whom they were attending, or perhaps they were simply unattached; however, Vivian decided she shouldn't make assumptions. Nevertheless, she was glad that the number of guests was minimal, which for some reason helped her feel more comfortable and less conspicuous.

As everyone turned to look toward the back of the chapel, Vivian did the same and caught her breath to see Estelle beginning her trek down the aisle. She looked radiantly happy and beautiful. She too looked years younger than her actual age, and Vivian was warmed by the idea that finding real love could have such a positive physical impact on a person.

Vivian was so focused on looking at Estelle that it took her a moment to realize that Estelle was being escorted by Theo, who looked so handsome that she caught her breath again, but this time she found it more difficult to let it go, and for a moment she felt mildly dizzy and took hold of the pew in front of her until her head felt steadier. And just when she felt confident about her equilibrium, Theo's eyes came to rest on her, and he showed a faint smile that was enhanced by a distinct sparkle in his eyes. She wanted to convince herself that his reaction meant nothing, but she could feel the truth as surely as if he'd spoken it loudly enough for all to hear. He was glad to see her! And surprisingly enough, she was glad to see him. And so extremely glad to see him smile at her that way. In that moment, she realized that she had genuinely forgiven him for his bad behavior toward her, for which he'd sincerely apologized. She thought about how she'd told him she couldn't trust him, and she couldn't deny that this was still the case. Still, she could never convince herself that she didn't feel something for him that was far beyond anything she *should* feel, given their obvious differences. She wanted to believe that at the core he was a good man;

it was difficult to imagine—especially seeing him now, escorting the bride—that Estelle would be so close to him if he weren't inherently good.

As Estelle and Theo passed by and moved on toward the front of the chapel, it occurred to Vivian that perhaps the feelings Theo had clumsily attempted to express that day in the library had been sincere and it was his method of communication that had been a problem. They'd had many tempestuous encounters since then, and she'd seen him incredibly angry. But could it be possible that his opinions regarding what he believed about her father—and his concerns about his aunt's marriage—truly had nothing to do with his feelings for her, whatever they might entail? Vivian knew that any presumptions would be ridiculous for more reasons than she could count, but that didn't prevent her stomach from fluttering and her heart from beating more quickly. She tried to credit her response to the wonder of seeing Estelle and her grandfather join hands to be wed, but watching Theo move to a seat at the front of the chapel, she couldn't lie to herself enough to be convinced that seeing him didn't have something to do with how she was feeling. Nevertheless, such a response was in no way an indication that she could or should trust him, and she needed to remember that.

Vivian forced herself to focus on the marriage taking place and her gratitude for being present for this event. The ceremony was simple but beautiful, and she had to take advantage of her handkerchief to dab away a few tears as she considered the miracle of these two wonderful people coming together again after all these years to find a happiness they would share for the remainder of their lives. The changes in Vivian's life because of this union fell into perspective as she took in the perfect joy on the faces of the bride and groom, and she impulsively reached over and took Mrs. Thatcher's hand, squeezing it in a silent gesture of appreciation. As they shared a quick glance and a smile, Vivian knew that she understood, and she could also see evidence that this woman was equally touched by seeing her friend and employer of many years finally being able to join her life with the man she'd loved all those years ago, and whom she had grown to love again. Vivian didn't believe that anyone involved regretted how their lives had turned out. Estelle always spoke of Edna with great respect and admiration; Vivian would not be who she was if her grandfather's life had turned out differently. But their coming back together now felt perfectly right. It might have been decades later than they had originally planned, but as they exchanged a tender kiss to seal their marriage, Vivian felt nothing but happiness on their behalf.

The moment the ceremony was over, Vivian's warmth and gratitude turned to a desire to leave the chapel before any of the other guests had the chance to even see her and question who she might be and her connection to the bride and groom. As if Mrs. Thatcher had read her mind, she whispered, "Let's hurry out. We can offer our private congratulations to them at another time. They know we were here and that's what matters."

"Yes, thank you," Vivian said, and they hurried out of the chapel before Estelle and Samuel could even notice, caught up in each other as they were while at the same time receiving warm wishes from the vicar. Only then did it occur to Vivian that she'd been hoping to get a better look at Dorothea and Lilith Weatherby, but it was too late for that now.

The two women were quick to grab their coats and put them on as they exited the church. Twig and Cooper were waiting with the carriage and helped them step inside. Vivian was barely seated before the carriage began to move, and she felt as if she and Mrs. Thatcher were a couple of naughty children who had sneaked away from their studies to indulge in a bit of mischief. But the feeling was delightful, and Vivian let out a small laugh.

Mrs. Thatcher observed, "You look much happier than when you arrived at the house this morning."

"Oh, I am!" Vivian said. "I cannot thank you enough! I'm so glad I was able to be there!"

"It was my pleasure, to be sure," Mrs. Thatcher said, "although it's Miss Weatherby that you need to . . . oh, my." Mrs. Thatcher giggled. "It's Mrs. Peyton now." She giggled again as if the joy of the wedding had left her almost giddy. "That will take some getting used to."

"For both of us," Vivian said, "and with any luck my fellow workers will continue to only know me as Vivian." She didn't voice the thought that she honestly couldn't recall if she'd ever been introduced to anyone in the house with the inclusion of her surname. If that had occurred, she hoped it had been forgotten. But she wasn't going to worry about that now. She'd been blessed with the opportunity to attend her grandfather's wedding; she didn't have to worry about him being disappointed over her absence, and she wouldn't have to live with the regret of having missed such an important event in Samuel's life. But recalling the beauty of the wedding faded into thoughts of seeing Theo, and her heart and stomach responded as if Theo had somehow become literally connected to these physical reactions. She sighed and looked out the carriage window through the remainder of their brief drive back to the house, choosing not to think about the reality that nothing more could ever exist between her and Theo than what they had already shared—and that was mostly a great deal of arguing. She turned her attention toward returning to work with the hope that no one would have noticed her absence. For all any of her fellow workers knew, she had just been alone cleaning somewhere in the house all this time.

Once back at the house, Mrs. Thatcher made certain no one was in the hallway before Vivian hurried into the house and directly through the housekeeper's office and into her sitting room. Mrs. Thatcher followed to help Vivian with the buttons down the back of her dress, then she left her alone to change and went to her own room to do the same.

At Mrs. Thatcher's suggestion, Vivian went to the kitchen to ask Mrs. O'Neill what she might do to help. The focus now was serving a wedding luncheon for the bride and groom and their guests, all of whom would be arriving soon. Vivian hummed as she worked, not caring in the least that she wouldn't be a part of this meal with all its fancy trappings and toasts offered up with expensive champagne. She felt content with all she'd been blessed with so far this day, and confident that both she and her grandfather could settle into their new lives easily enough.

As Theo observed his aunt exchanging vows with Samuel, he was surprised to feel a distinct warmth in his heart. In the weeks since he'd first learned of her intentions to marry, he had become brutally aware of his own tendency to be selfish in his thinking, and of just how quick he had always been to become angry and speak without first considering the potential impact of his words on other people. Estelle had been offering gentle guidance regarding his faults for many years, but he'd been too foolish to pay attention enough to have a sincere desire to change. He knew now that it was the way he had hurt and disappointed Vivian that had sparked in him a sincere aspiration to become a better man—even if his desire to change had come decades later than it should have. He'd thought of her often in the weeks since he'd last seen her, and he'd been haunted by her justified disdain toward him, but he'd also been caught up with a strange fascination with her that bordered on obsession. He had hoped to see her at the wedding, but he hadn't been prepared for how thoroughly disarmed he would feel when he'd seen her looking so perfectly lovely. The serenity in her expression had soothed an ache in his spirit, and he believed that he could be sustained through every difficulty life might throw his way if he could only see Vivian Peyton look at him that way each and every day.

The moment the ceremony ended, Theo stood and turned around with the hope of seeing Vivian again—and perhaps even being able to speak with her. He wanted her to know that he was trying to become a better man; in fact, he was surprised by how badly he wished for her to be aware of the changes taking place within himself. But he only caught a glimpse of her as she hurried toward the door to leave. He knew she likely didn't want to be seen or recognized, even if he still didn't fully understand the reasons. But he couldn't deny his own disappointment in not being able to see her again. He wondered for only a moment if she would be attending the wedding celebration at the house; he loved the idea of sitting with her to share a fine meal. But he absolutely knew she wouldn't be there. He tried to focus on the happiness of Estelle and Samuel, glad to feel sincerely happy on their behalf. But his thoughts were drawn to Vivian, and he wished that she could have been there by his side for this celebration. In fact, he wished she could be by his side for every aspect of his life. The more time that passed, the more he had come to feel that way. He just didn't know what to do about it.

Vivian settled comfortably into her new life at the boardinghouse, and she enjoyed the company of Mel, Sally Mae, and most of the other nine women who lived there. A few of them were so dramatically different from Vivian that she found their company unpleasant if not annoying. But thankfully these women worked evenings at pubs and slept late in the mornings; therefore, they rarely shared a meal or crossed paths in any other way.

During the first month or so of the Weatherby household adjusting to calling their employer Mrs. Peyton, Vivian was pleased to note that nothing at all had changed with her own life regarding her employment. There had been talk about how the name of the house would never change because it was the family name, and eventually Theo would inherit the house. But no one except Mrs. Thatcher seemed to have any idea of the connection Vivian shared with Estelle's new husband. There was talk among the servants about how happy the new Mrs. Peyton seemed, and about how kind and humble Mr. Peyton was, and what a joy it was to serve him. A few of the staff had even told stories of how Samuel Peyton had taken the time to ask them a little about themselves, wanting to get to know the people who worked in the house, and overall, everyone was impressed with him and liked him. None of this was a surprise to Vivian, but she was pleased and secretly proud of this man who had given her so much.

Mrs. Thatcher quickly established a pattern of secretly slipping notes to Vivian about when and where she could visit privately with her grandfather following her day's work and before she left to go home. Vivian became particularly good at sneaking up the back stairs without anyone noticing, since she used a narrow staircase that was rarely used by others; it was awkwardly located in its distance from the kitchen and laundry; therefore, it was more likely to gather dust than serve any purpose in contributing to the functions of the house. But it provided the perfect way for Vivian to slip upstairs where she could see down two hallways that met at the top of the stairs to be certain no one was there before she walked the short distance to the sitting room next to the enormous bedroom that Samuel and Estelle now shared. Sometimes she visited with her grandfather privately, and sometimes Estelle joined them. Either way, their visits were enjoyable, and Vivian was grateful—as she knew Samuel to be—for this opportunity to continue their comfortable relationships without compromising her need for privacy regarding her connection to Samuel Peyton.

Vivian quickly figured out how long she could visit before she needed to leave to arrive at the boarding house in time to share supper with those who weren't working during that hour. Not wanting to alert anyone at the Weatherby house regarding the change in her circumstances, Vivian had thought it best to eat supper at the boardinghouse, and Mrs. Thatcher had given Mrs. O'Neill a brief and practical reason as to why Vivian would no longer need to be taking food home with her in the evenings. The housekeeper had reported to Vivian that Mrs. O'Neill had asked no questions—because she was anything but curious—and no one else would notice. Vivian still loved having lunch with the household staff on the days that she worked, but she also enjoyed having breakfast and supper with the women at the boardinghouse, and there was always a great deal of delightful conversation and laughter. She even enjoyed helping—as everyone did—to clear the table, clean the dishes, and put the kitchen in order. This was not something that Mel required of her tenants, but most of the women seemed to want to help simply to ease Mel's workload, which made it possible for her to spend more time relaxing in the evenings. On some evenings Vivian joined a few of the other women in the parlor to visit, and on others she preferred the privacy of her room where she could read or just relax on her own.

As winter settled in with harsh weather, Vivian was glad for the shorter distance she had to walk to get to work. She was also glad to take inventory of her life and realize that what had once seemed devastating had now become comfortable and easy, and she felt genuinely happy. Knowing firsthand of the happiness that Samuel and Estelle shared certainly contributed to her own sense of peace over the present state of her life. She only felt unsettled about one thing—and that was the way she so often thought about Theodore Weatherby and wondered what he might be doing at any given moment. And she recalled far too frequently how it had felt to have him kiss her, so much so that she began to regret having slapped him in response to such a pleasant experience. Thinking about him always provoked a strange warmth that seemed contradictory to the anger and frustration she had felt toward him regarding most of their encounters. At best, she felt confused over her fascination with this man, and knew it was good that she rarely if ever saw him—in fact, she'd not once caught a glimpse of him since the wedding, which she felt certain was for the best.

At the end of a typical workday, Vivian sat visiting with Estelle and her grandfather in the sitting room as was the case practically every day that she worked. When someone knocked at the door Vivian felt panicked. There was no reason for a servant to come here at this time of the evening unless something was amiss, but Vivian didn't want to be discovered here like this. She was considering how she might hide behind the draperies when the door came open before anyone had called out with permission to enter. Vivian breathed a sigh of relief to see Theo enter the room and close the door behind him, but her relief turned to something entirely different when her heartbeat quickened and her stomach fluttered as if they were required to do so in his presence—or even at the thought of him. Vivian had been completely unsuccessful at banishing him from her mind, and she couldn't avoid looking at him now that he was here in the same room. She'd not seen him since the wedding and wondered what he might think of her being here secretly visiting with Estelle and Samuel.

"May I come in?" he asked, leaning back against the door. He'd entered without permission, but it was evident he wouldn't intrude upon their conversation without Estelle's approval. "I don't want to interrupt anything important."

"We're just visiting," Estelle said. "Of course, you're welcome to join us."

"Thank you," he said and sat in a chair that directly faced the one where Vivian was sitting. She was startled when he smiled and winked at her, saying with a hint of mischief in his voice, "You're a sneaky little thing. I suspected you would find some secretive way to spend time with your grandfather—as you should—but I wasn't certain how you might be managing in a house where everyone generally knows everyone else's business."

"And if I told you, it would no longer be a secret," Vivian said to him, returning his smile while at the same time recalling that she didn't necessarily trust him.

"Touché," he said, his smile widening, which increased the fluttering in Vivian's stomach. Why did he have to be so remarkably handsome? If he were hideous to look at, perhaps her memories of his kiss and the times when their conversations had been pleasant might have been easier to block out of her mind. Although she corrected her thinking with the reminder that she was not someone who judged a person by their appearance. Still, Theo was incredibly attractive; it was a fact, and she couldn't help but enjoy just looking at him, sitting there as casually as if he'd been there for hours. And he was being so kind! How could she not be warmly affected when he was putting forth his best self?

"Well, I'm glad you've found a way to visit," Theo said and seemed to mean it. "As you should. I know you don't want others in the household to be aware of the connection, although in my opinion it shouldn't matter. But I respect your wishes and . . . well . . . again . . . I'm glad you're spending time together."

"As am I!" Samuel said with enthusiasm. "Needless to say, I'm so happy to be here with Estelle, and everyone in the house has been so kind. But I'd miss my sweet Vivian if I didn't get to see her."

"I would as well," Estelle said with a warm smile directed at Vivian. "I've grown to love this girl. She's truly precious."

"Indeed, she is," Theo said, much to Vivian's surprise. But she was downright alarmed when she saw that Samuel and Estelle were both looking at Theo as if they expected an explanation for such a comment. In response to their silent inquisition, Theo added, "I've grown quite fond of Vivian. Who wouldn't?" He turned to look at her and Vivian felt both thrilled and wary. Was his kindness genuine, or was he simply assuming a façade to please his aunt? "I've very much enjoyed my conversations with her—most of them anyway—although I'm hoping that she's forgiven me for the times when I spoke harshly or out of line." An earnestness pervaded his gaze, as if what he intended to say to her next should be taken very seriously. "If I'm being entirely honest, I must admit that I'm trying to be a better man . . . to be more kind and less . . ."

"Arrogant?" Estelle provided in a light tone that didn't diminish the fact that she was completely serious.

"Thank you, Aunt," Theo said facetiously. "Your straightforward manner is always appreciated . . . even if it stings with truth."

Vivian watched them exchange a smile that held an underlying mutual respect. She recounted the words that had just been said and what it meant regarding Theo's character. It couldn't have been easy for a man to say such things about himself, especially in Vivian's presence when she would have thought he'd prefer to keep his own vulnerability from showing. But he turned directly toward her once again and said, "And I do hope you'll eventually forgive me for the times I've behaved badly. Perhaps you'll even allow me to prove that I mean what I'm saying."

Vivian saw an unfamiliar intensity in his eyes, sparking something in her that was both frightening and thrilling. She rummaged through her own confusion for the right words, while at the same time putting herself on alert as to whether he was being sincere. Still, it was easy to say, "Of course I forgive you. I've not always behaved well, myself. If you—"

"I'm absolutely certain," Theo continued, "that anything you said or did in my presence that might be considered less than kind was absolutely warranted as a response to *my* . . ." he turned to look at his aunt and gave her a crooked smile, ". . . arrogance." He turned back to Vivian and added, "Perhaps we can begin our friendship anew . . . now that we are as good as family."

"Of course," Vivian said, even though the implication made her nervous for reasons she couldn't define when she had no idea what *his* definition of a friendship between them might entail. She was pleased with his kindness and his desire to prove that he had expended some effort to become a better person. But she also reminded herself once again that one favorable conversation didn't mean she could truly trust him. It would take time for her to be convinced that he sincerely meant everything he was saying, and that this wasn't simply a way for him to attempt to make peace within the family. Or perhaps he was simply attempting to impress his aunt and her new husband—and Vivian as well. She needed time to be certain, but she was willing to keep an open mind and allow him the opportunity to prove himself.

"I wonder," Theo said, still speaking to Vivian as if no one else was in the room observing their conversation, "if you might consider taking a little stroll with me." Before Vivian could ask exactly how that might be accomplished when she had no desire for anyone else in the house to ever see them together, he added, "There are endless hallways in this house where no one would ever go—especially at this time of day." He stood and offered his arm to Vivian as if he meant to accompany her to a grand social event. "Would you walk with me, Miss Peyton?" he asked. "Although . . ." he looked mildly alarmed, "the halls are chilly so perhaps—"

"No need to worry about that," Estelle said and jumped out of her chair like a woman half her age. She disappeared into her bedroom and returned a moment later with a large, heavy shawl that she handed to Vivian. "This should keep you from being *too* chilly."

"Thank you," Vivian said, quickly taking in the thoroughly pleased expressions of Estelle and her grandfather—and Theo. She felt a little as if she were the subject of a conspiracy on their part, except she had no reason to believe that Samuel or Estelle had known that Theo would intrude upon their conversation and invite Vivian to join him for a stroll. Unexpected as it might have been, they both looked excessively pleased, and she wondered if having Theo and herself on good terms with each other meant so much to them. And despite their negative encounters in the past, she had to ask herself what kind of woman she would be if she didn't at least attempt to give him another chance to prove himself to be a man of integrity.

Vivian kissed both her grandfather and Estelle, reminding them that they would see each other the day after tomorrow, since she wouldn't be working the following day and therefore wouldn't be in the house.

With Estelle's shawl wrapped tightly around her, Vivian took hold of Theo's arm, since ignoring his silent invitation to do so would have been awkward. But just touching him ignited feelings she'd been trying to suppress. The thought occurred to her that being Theo's friend might be easier said than done when she couldn't help being preoccupied with memories of his kiss. And she caught herself wondering what would have happened if she'd listened to what he'd been trying to tell her about his own feelings instead of reacting so badly by slapping him.

Once they reached the hallway, Theo picked up one of many lamps that had been left on tables along the walls of the corridor, and which were kept lit until everyone had gone to bed. They walked in silence for a minute or two while Vivian quickly lost track of where they were after he'd turned more than one corner, going in a direction she had rarely—if ever—gone. She wondered if this was where she'd gone that day when she'd been searching out a place to hide so that she could cry without being discovered. But she allowed Theo to navigate and found that it took all her mental energy just to be in his presence like this while being careful about what she said and how she said it—and not to react badly to anything he might say. She could feel her lack of trust hovering just beneath the surface and had to remind herself that she could still be amiable even if she didn't trust him.

Vivian was relieved when Theo finally spoke, and she was pleasantly surprised by his genuine kindness, which helped her believe that his declarations about trying to be a better man might be sincere—even though she was still determined to give the matter some time to arrive at a more accurate judgment.

"How are you doing with all of the changes in your life?" he asked. "I've wondered. It can't have been easy . . . to leave your home, and . . . well, everything."

"I'm doing better than I expected, to be truthful," she said, marveling that she felt so comfortable admitting such feelings to him. "I like where I'm living, and I like my work here. Being able to see my grandfather and Estelle regularly has helped immensely. I had wondered if that would be possible."

"If you ever come up against any challenges in that regard," he said, "please let me know and I'll do what I can to help you."

"Thank you," she said. "That's very kind."

"If I may go back a little to something you just said . . ." He stopped walking and turned to face her, which made her hand naturally fall away from his arm. It seemed that he had something particularly important to say, which made Vivian nervous. "You *like* your work? Truly?"

"What are saying, Theo?" she asked in a snappy voice. "Is it impossible for someone of your station to comprehend that actually doing work might be . . . fulfilling . . . gratifying?"

"That's not what I meant," he countered, sounding a little snappy himself. Then he looked down, and she heard him take a deep breath before he looked up again. "Forgive me." He cleared his throat. "I'm trying awfully hard to be more . . . empathetic toward others, although I cannot deny that I have some extremely poor habits in that regard. I ask for your patience."

Vivian appreciated his apology and sensed that it was genuine. She motioned with her hand and said, "Of course. Go on."

"I have a deep regard for any person who works for their living, Vivian. I have some responsibilities here in overseeing the finances and such of the household, but . . . sometimes I think that being raised without my needing to work is likely a disservice. But I'm getting off the path here. I must know. You *enjoy* cleaning out fireplaces and scrubbing pots and pans, and other such tasks? You *like* your work? It's not my wish to offend you. I'm simply curious about your perspective."

"I like to feel useful," she clarified. "I like being able to accomplish tasks efficiently and confidently, and to know that my work is appreciated. I like being able to earn a wage that makes it possible to meet my own needs. There is satisfaction in that."

"You are a remarkable woman, Vivian Peyton," he said, surprising her. Such a compliment from Theodore Weatherby warmed her deeply, but she sincerely hadn't spent enough time with him to know how to tell for certain if it was genuine. She decided to take him at his word but to remain cautious and not get too caught up in her attraction to him.

"Am I?" she countered, trying not to become distracted by his eyes in the glow of the lamp. "I don't think I'm any different from any number of other women who work to provide for themselves—whether it's service in a house such as this, or as a seamstress, or serving meals and drinks at a pub, or . . . well, anything really. People like you *and* people like me all depend upon the services that other people provide through the work they do."

"That is absolutely true," he said, still facing her with no apparent intention to keep walking. "Although . . . more and more I find myself thinking about . . . well . . . why are there *people like me and people like you*? I believe Estelle's teachings about life have finally begun to sink in of late. I didn't do anything special to merit such a privileged life, and you certainly didn't do anything wrong to end up needing to work so hard for your living."

"I've had a good life," she clarified. "I've never gone without, and I've never felt like my lifestyle is a result of having done something wrong."

"I'm extremely glad to hear it," he said, "but you and your family have always had to work hard to meet your basic needs."

"And none of us have ever minded that fact," Vivian said. "I was raised to appreciate doing my part to contribute to our household by helping with whatever needed to be done. May I ask what has prompted such deep thoughts in you?" She hoped that the more they talked the more she might be able to determine his sincerity—or lack thereof.

"I'm not sure; a lot of it likely has to do with Estelle marrying your grandfather. Samuel has worked extremely hard all his life, and I have come to believe that he is a far better man for it than I could ever be—simply for the fact that I've never had to work hard at anything."

Vivian felt more relaxed as the conversation unfolded; his openness warmed her and helped her feel more comfortable talking with him. "I don't believe your circumstances are anything to be ashamed of, Theo. I don't believe it's a person's financial situation that determines their character; it's how a person treats other people. It's a person's level of integrity and kindness."

"You make a fair point," he said thoughtfully. "I believe I've always had integrity—or at least I've tried, although I'm certain there's room for improvement. But I can see that I've struggled with being kind." He chuckled uncomfortably. "I don't suppose I need to tell *you* that. Nevertheless, I am beginning to understand just how important kindness and respect are in the way we live our lives. Estelle has always been a shining example of that. But I think perhaps I've been lacking in that respect because I've not had a male adult in my life who could offer me an example in such matters."

Vivian thought of his father, and how Theo had only been a youth when the man died. She wanted to ask what kind of example he'd been when he was alive, but she wouldn't dare dive into any kind of conversation about their fathers.

"I can understand why that would be difficult," Vivian said, knowing that she too needed to strive to be empathetic. "Do you believe Estelle has tried to compensate for that?"

"Oh, absolutely!" Theo said.

"And what of your mother?" Vivian asked. "Does she—"

"My mother is a kind woman, but she's very . . . disconnected from the particulars of my life; she always has been, in truth. And my sister is very much like her."

"It feels a little strange to hear you talk about them; funny that I've never encountered either of them."

"And how could you when they hardly leave their rooms? They *were* at the wedding, but you wouldn't have had any way of recognizing them among the other guests for the brief time that you were there."

Vivian almost told him that she had seen the very impressive hats they'd been wearing—thanks to Mrs. Thatcher pointing them out—but she didn't know how to say it without sounding silly.

"I think that's the first time they've ventured out of the house in years," he added, which was exactly what Mrs. Thatcher had said. "I believe my mother was always fragile, and my sister has become the same—both because of my mother's example and her temperamental health. But after my father's death, my mother became more reclusive and uninvolved in my life—not that she was terribly involved to begin with. I can't judge her for being the way she is because I sincerely don't understand. And that's all right." He sighed, then chuckled. "I seem to be rambling now, but . . . I'm trying to say . . . if I daresay it . . . Vivian, your example . . . your presence in our lives . . . has made me stop and look at myself with more serious introspection than ever before."

"Me?" she asked, genuinely astonished. "Why?"

"Because you've never been afraid to tell me exactly what I needed to hear; you've never let my bad behavior go unchecked—and I found myself wondering if you were right. And you were. You are wise and insightful, Vivian—and courageous. Which I suppose is why I would like to ask your advice; I've admitted things to you that I never thought I'd share with anyone. But I trust you. And I admire you. And I wonder if you have any insight as to how I might . . . do better; to use what I've been blessed with to become a better man."

Vivian was so astounded that she found herself unable to move, let alone speak, while she closely examined his expression—and especially his eyes—in the lamplight. And the sincerity she saw there surprised her. She swallowed hard and considered his request carefully before she finally said, "That's easy. I told you that I've never gone without, that I've had a good life. But there are so many people in this city, Theo, who—through no fault of their own—are literally living on the streets, who don't have enough to eat. I believe most people of your social status are not even aware of such situations, because you simply don't go into those parts of the city. But it would take so little money to make an enormous difference in the lives of such people." She sighed and attempted to look away from his eyes but couldn't. It occurred to her that his response to her suggestions might go a long way in helping her determine whether his motives were sincere. "That's what comes to my mind in response to your question. If that's not the kind of answer you're looking for, it's completely—"

"No, it's a wonderful idea, Vivian," he said, sounding excited. "And I wonder if you might be willing to help me."

"Help you how?" she asked, thrilled at the prospect, but wondering how they could possibly take on such an endeavor without having people know that they were spending time together.

"You said earlier that you don't work tomorrow."

"That's right," she said, feeling leery.

"I wonder if you could show me these parts of the city you're talking about."

"And how would we do that?" she asked.

"Cooper and Twig know the truth about your connection to Samuel, do they not?"

"Yes," Vivian drawled.

"Then I will have them take me out in the carriage to meet you at a place of your choosing, and we can go together from there. Once we are away from the part of the city where we live, we shouldn't have any concern about being observed together . . . although it's my opinion that you really shouldn't worry about that."

"I accept your opinion," she said, "but I wholeheartedly disagree. You changed the subject before I had any opportunity to respond to your request."

"So I did," he said sheepishly. "My apologies. And what is your response to my request?"

Vivian felt nothing but delighted at the prospect of being able to help some people who were struggling and suffering—and if helping Theo take on such a project was a possibility, she would never turn down such an offer. And her confidence was growing over the possibility of this being an opportunity to determine his level of trustworthiness. Adding to that the possibility of simply spending time with Theo—especially now that she was seeing the best of him in a way she'd never imagined possible—she could feel nothing but excited about his proposition.

"I would love to, Mr. Weatherby," she said. "There's nothing I planned to do tomorrow that can't wait."

"Excellent!" he said triumphantly. "I will very much look forward to it." He began to walk again, and Vivian matched his leisurely gait in order to walk beside him, almost feeling as if she were in a dream and any moment she would wake up and find out that Theodore Weatherby was still an arrogant and distasteful man.

Chapter Ten

THE TRANSFORMATION

FOLLOWING A STRETCH OF COMFORTABLE silence, Theo said, "I feel as if I've been searching for an elusive idea of how I could make a positive contribution to the world, and now I feel much better." He let out a small laugh. "I should have known you would have the answer. Next to Estelle, I think you are the most wise and insightful woman I've ever had the privilege to know."

"I will take that as the highest of compliments," she said, flattered but still feeling cautious regarding his sincerity. "I admire Estelle very much; being compared to her in any way is high praise indeed."

"And well deserved," Theo said, holding out his arm again with the silent implication that she should take hold of it. Vivian did so, loving not only the feel of his fine coat beneath her fingers, but the simple physical connection she was sharing with him. In fact, she was loving everything about this secretive excursion, and she wondered what miracle had taken place to cause such a glorious change of heart in Theo. Perhaps his heart had always been good, and he'd simply had trouble expressing himself appropriately. Or perhaps this was all a charade to keep favor with his aunt. Whatever the case, she felt nothing but thrilled to be with him now and to know that they would be spending time together the following day. If she kept her head about her and was careful not to allow her enjoyment to overpower her judgment, she didn't see any harm in spending time with Theo this way.

"Tell me more about yourself, Vivian," he said as they strolled along the dark hallway, using the lamp he carried to light the way.

"There's little to tell," she said. "I've lived a simple life."

"But a good one, as you told me," he pointed out. "You lost your parents when you were very young, and yet you speak of your life as if it were practically idyllic."

"I can't deny that their deaths were very difficult for all of us," she admitted, hoping they wouldn't tread into the territory of Theo's belief that *her* father had been responsible for the death of *his* father. "Nevertheless, there was a strong bond between me and my grandparents, and I always felt like we shared our grief, and therefore we were never alone in our feelings. It's strange that I don't remember my parents very well, but I vividly recall the grief of losing them; perhaps that's because it took years to come to terms with it. I remember always feeling like it was all right to cry as much as I needed, or to say anything I needed to say—even if that meant I sometimes felt angry over what had happened. And I certainly had some emotional outbursts. But I watched my grandparents experience outbursts of grief as well. They took good care of me, and I always felt safe and loved. So yes, I had a good life."

"Much of that sounds like the things Estelle tried to teach me, but I'm afraid I wasn't a particularly good student. I see more and more evidence that Samuel and Estelle are very much alike. Perhaps we have them to thank for whatever is good in us—or rather, I should say that I believe Estelle was able to see whatever is good in *me* and nurture it. I think you are likely one of those people who is just naturally good, and you don't have to work at it."

Vivian laughed softly. "My grandfather might disagree. I had my difficult stages . . . throughout my childhood and youth. But my grandparents guided me well through those times; their boundaries were firm, but so was their love. Eventually I figured that out and I remember a time when it seemed that we all found a distinct peace with the tragedy that had taken my parents away, and we were able to move forward and be happy."

"How long did *that* take?" he asked. "I don't know if I've found peace over my father's death yet."

"Well, it was years," she said. "I don't recall exactly."

Vivian's mind went to what Theo had once said in anger about the connections between their fathers and she wanted very much to bring up the matter and clarify some of the things he'd implied. But she didn't want to mar the pleasant mood between them. She was surprised when he once again stopped walking, and again her hand fell away from his arm as they turned to face each other.

"Vivian, I need to apologize very specifically about the things I said . . . concerning your father. Estelle was right regarding the fact that we know precious little about what happened, and I was wrong to allow my anger to overtake me like that. I think that was one of the moments that made me realize that I need to change . . . I need to find peace . . . to come to terms with what happened . . .

because to be completely truthful, I'm thoroughly embarrassed over the way I behaved that day, and I very much want to put that kind of behavior behind me. It's so many years in the past, and yet in some ways I've felt like the angry young man who lost his father was still brewing inside of me. When I realized that you had lost *both* of your parents and you were *not* angry—combined with some firm admonitions from my aunt—I realized that I had not handled myself very well at all."

"Your apology is much appreciated," Vivian said, deeply relieved to have him address the very thoughts that she'd been wanting to be able to talk about with him. "I can't deny it was dreadfully upsetting; I'd never heard anything derogatory about my father . . . but that doesn't mean there might not be truth in what you said."

"As Estelle pointed out," Theo said, "the past is in the past . . . and we will never know exactly what happened. If you would be willing to forgive me for anything and everything I've said that was so inappropriate and hurtful, I'm hoping to be able to just . . . put all the past behind me and begin again."

"Of course, I forgive you, Theo," she said immediately.

"Truly?" he asked, the lamp illuminating the genuine surprise in his face. "So easily?"

"If you'll recall, I told you when you came to the shop to apologize that I forgave you."

"Ah," he drawled after thinking about that for a long moment as if he needed to summon the memory, "so you did. I also recall that you told me that didn't necessarily mean you could ever trust me."

Vivian looked down, not wanting to look at him but knowing she had to be honest. "I can't deny that's true." She summoned courage and looked up at him again. "I'm extremely glad to see evidence of your efforts to change, Theo; nevertheless, I have to clarify that you have done and said some things that were very hurtful, and . . . well . . . simply put . . . I feel that I must give myself time to know for certain if I can trust you . . . to know if the changes in you are real. I hope you can understand what I'm attempting to explain."

"I'm trying to," he said, his brow furrowing.

"Forgiveness is not the same as trust, Theo. I forgave you long ago." She recalled how the last time she'd told him she'd forgiven him, she'd known that it would take time for her to fully make peace with the things he'd said. But time had passed, and she *had* forgiven him—fully and completely. And she wanted him to know that she meant was she was saying. "I was extremely upset, and I needed some time to . . . well, to come to terms with it, I suppose. But I'm not one to hold grudges, Theo. And I can understand why you would have felt angry."

"No matter how understandable my anger might have been, my behavior toward you was *not*."

"Nevertheless, all is forgiven. I have no desire to carry the burden of anger toward you or anyone else. Life can be challenging enough without choosing to hold onto such feelings."

Theo looked down thoughtfully. "I never considered it that way before," he said, looking at her again before they began walking once more. "And I never considered that trust and forgiveness are entirely separate matters." He sighed deeply. "Do you think you will ever be able to trust me? Do you believe it's possible for you to know that I am being sincere . . . that I'm telling you the truth?"

"Right now, I'm willing to give you the benefit of the doubt and believe it *is* possible, Theo . . . but I need time."

He thought about that and nodded, but she wasn't certain he completely understood. However, as she'd just told him, they needed time. Surely time would prove to her whether he could be trusted, and perhaps time would teach him exactly what that meant regarding the changes he was trying to make in his life.

Minutes passed in silence beyond the soft sounds of their footsteps landing in perfect synchronization. Vivian sensed that Theo was descending deeper and deeper into his thoughts regarding all they'd said to each other in this conversation—things she *never* would have expected either of them to say. Considering the possibility that while remaining cautious it still would bode well to offer Theo some encouragement, Vivian concluded that she should still give him cause to *want* to be trustworthy. When the silence between them began to feel strained, Vivian said, "You should know I'm a firm believer that it's never too late for people to change."

"That's very good to know," he said, tossing a quick smile in her direction.

"Nevertheless," she added more lightly, "I hope you don't change *too* much."

"How is that?" he asked, turning his head to smile at her more directly while they kept walking.

"Looking back, I can't deny there were always things I liked about you. Besides, Estelle has told me you're a good man, and if I can't trust Estelle to be completely truthful, who could I *possibly* trust?"

"You make a fair point there," Theo said. "She liked *you* before she even met you."

“How is that possible?” Vivian asked, surprised.

“When I first met you at the gate that day . . . and you made me promise to give Estelle your message, she had been sitting in the upstairs hall with a perfect view of where we were standing. She told me then that you seemed sweet.”

Vivian laughed softly. “How could she have possibly known anything about me?”

“Good instincts, perhaps,” Theo said. “I’m sure you wouldn’t be surprised that I argued with her about her intentions to visit your grandfather, and of course she set me straight.”

“I’m only surprised that you’d admit to it,” Vivian said lightly but had to add, “however, given all else that you’ve admitted to now, I suppose I shouldn’t be.”

They both realized in the same moment that they had come back to the place where their stroll had begun, and Vivian was struck by a strange sensation of having completely lost track of the time. “Oh, my,” she said, “I really need to get back to the boardinghouse before supper is completely over and cleaned up.”

“I’m certain Mrs. O’Neill would be happy to—”

“Oh, no,” Vivian said, hating the way she’d been abruptly returned to the reality of her life and the fear she had of anyone discovering the truth. “I don’t want her to go to any trouble.” She smiled up at Theo. “Thank you. I enjoyed our stroll very much . . . and especially our conversation.”

“As did I,” he said. “I’ll see you tomorrow?” he asked as if he’d be utterly devastated if she’d changed her mind.

“Of course,” she said, and they decided on an exact place and time to meet before Vivian bade him good evening and hurried to get her coat and be on her way home. She realized she still had Estelle’s shawl, but she folded it neatly and put it into her canvas bag, knowing she could return it the next time she saw her.

Vivian awoke the following morning and immediately felt excited over the prospect of going on an excursion with Theodore Weatherby. She wasn’t necessarily pleased with the nature of their outing; it was always difficult to be confronted with stark evidence of poverty and suffering. But she felt deeply warmed with Theo’s desire to expand his perspective of the world around him with the intention of using his resources to make a positive difference to people who lacked the common necessities of life. How could Vivian not be pleased about that? And the very idea of spending time with Theo made her downright giddy. She had to work ridiculously hard to not show too much excitement at breakfast because she didn't want the other women asking questions about her reasons for being in such a thoroughly positive mood.

Before heading out, Vivian bundled up to protect herself from the winter air. The skies were heavy with clouds and there was an extra bite to the hefty breeze winding through the city streets. As Vivian walked the short distance to meet Theo where he promised the carriage would be waiting, she felt freshly amazed at the changes that had taken place in him—and even more so at the changes evolving between *them*. He'd transformed from a man she wished to avoid into someone she might sincerely consider a dear friend, and she prayed that he *would* prove trustworthy when all was said and done. Given all the changes that had taken place in her life, such a friend would be a great blessing. She liked Mel and Sally Mae and most of the other women at the boardinghouse, but she couldn't imagine unburdening herself with very personal feelings to any of them. But strangely enough, Theo had become such a person in her life. She believed she could tell him anything and he would be compassionate and understanding. Or at least she hoped that was the case and that she wasn't being naive to believe such a thing, given all that had happened between them. She simply had to maintain a balance of allowing Theo the opportunity to prove that he had truly become a better man, while at the same time remaining cautious and discerning in her observations of his behavior. She could hardly believe he was the same man who had been so rude to her when they'd met at the gate of the Weatherby house, and she couldn't help but be excited to see him. The secrecy of their meeting—as well as the purpose of their excursion—added a childlike thrill over the prospect of what this day might bring.

Vivian's heart quickened when she saw the familiar carriage right where she'd expected it to be. Even from a distance, she could see Twig and Cooper—also dressed to protect themselves from the cold—leaning against the carriage wheels and chatting like the good friends she had found them to be. They noticed her approaching and both smiled in a way that made her feel more at ease.

"Good morning, Miss," Cooper said.

"I hope you're not too chilly," Twig added. "Winter is sure enough in the air today."

"It is indeed," Vivian said, "but I'm well enough. And you?"

"No such thing as weather too cold," Twig said with a chuckle and a wink, "only clothes that don't keep you warm. And we're blessed with plenty to keep us warm."

"What an excellent way of looking at it," Vivian said. "I shall have to remember it."

Cooper opened the carriage door and offered his hand to help Vivian step inside. She focused on making certain she didn't trip as she placed herself on the empty seat, then she looked up to see Theo sitting across from her, a smile lighting his eyes as well as his face.

"Good morning to you," he said. "Punctual, as always."

"Of course," she said. "Good morning to *you*."

Vivian realized then that the carriage door was still open, with Cooper standing in its frame. "I'll be needing directions, Miss," he said. "Where is it that you want to go?"

Vivian told him the area of the city she wished to see, and he scowled slightly. "You're certain?" he asked.

"Yes," she said. "We won't need to stop or get out of the carriage; we just need a brief tour of the area. If you could just drive through the streets there for a short while, that will be sufficient."

Cooper glanced at Theo as if for approval, and Theo said, "I've already told you the purpose of our excursion. Just do as the lady says."

"As you wish, sir," Cooper said and closed the carriage door.

Vivian felt the carriage rock slightly as Cooper stepped up onto the driver's seat. As the wheels began to roll forward, Vivian couldn't resist saying, "You just called me a lady. You and I both know very well that with my upbringing and the life I live, I could never fall into that category."

"I've come to disagree with that theory," he said. "Would you like to know why?"

"I would," Vivian said, "although I suspect you would tell me anyway."

"Most likely," he said with a chuckle. "It's very good to see you, by the way."

She let out a small laugh. "You saw me not long before you would have gone to bed last night."

"I'm well aware," he said. "It's still very nice to see you."

"It's nice to see you, too," she said and meant it. "Now tell me why you called me a lady."

"You know, of course, that our family has no titles; there's no noble bloodline that we've inherited. I honestly have no idea how my ancestors acquired such a ridiculous amount of wealth, but I've been raised to understand that money very often makes some of the most snobbish of people willing to overlook the lack of title when it comes to socializing and even marriage. In these social circles, a lady is refined and graceful and has a certain decorum about her. I confess that when I first met you, I only saw evidence of our vastly different monetary situations. Now that I've gotten to know you, I see all too well that you are more of a lady than many very wealthy women I've associated with throughout my lifetime. And you will not be surprised to learn that Estelle taught me this principle—that it's the way a woman carries herself and lives her life that makes her worthy to be called a lady. Therefore, you are *certainly* a lady by every standard I can think of."

Vivian felt more than a little stunned as she attempted to take in everything he'd just said. She finally managed to utter, "I think that's one of the most astonishing things anyone has ever said to me."

Theo smiled. "You would do well to become accustomed to such astonishing compliments, my dear Vivian, because you are not only a lady, but you are also a rather remarkable one, and I can't foresee any reason why I should ever stop wanting to tell you so. In the same vein, I'd like to point out that I know a great many very wealthy men—even titled men—whose behavior is atrocious, and I have come to find that I would never think of them as proper gentlemen, even though they are considered as such by every social standard. On that point, you will easily recall several times when I behaved in a manner that was anything *but* gentleman-like. I've already apologized for that, but allow me to say that I will strive to be a more proper gentleman; I find that easier when I see your example of being such a fine lady."

"You make some excellent points, Theo," she said, still overcome with such a concept—and that he would relate it to her with such sincerity. "I'm still not certain I can see myself as a lady. I work as a maid if you recall."

"And that has nothing to do with what I just explained," Theo countered. "Speaking of which," he added, turning his head to look at her sideways, almost as if he feared she wouldn't like what he had to say, "I've given it a great deal of thought and I do wish you'd reconsider the wishes of Estelle and your grandfather to just move into the house and be a part of the family."

Vivian bristled and felt her every muscle tighten as she looked away from him, wishing he hadn't said something to dampen the bright mood she'd been enjoying. She knew he sensed her displeasure when he hurried to add, "I'm well aware of your reasons for wanting to remain anonymous in the household; I don't know that I necessarily understand, but that doesn't mean your feelings about the matter aren't valid, and I respect that."

"Thank you," she said, a little more relaxed and certainly appreciative of his clarification, but still not liking this turn of the conversation.

"Nevertheless, it's my opinion from what I know of the staff that they might not be nearly as disapproving as you might think."

"Well," Vivian unconsciously brushed her hands down over the front of her coat as if that might shield her from the discomfort of what Theo had just said, "we will never know, because no one is going to find out."

"Those who *do* know are nothing but happy about the connection," Theo pointed out.

"And they are likely the only people who work for your family who are not prone to idle gossip," Vivian countered, looking at him again.

"*Our* family," Theo corrected. "Do you think that the closeness I share with Estelle—both in our familial connection and in our relationship—is any different than what you share with your grandfather?"

"As you well know, I'm still remarkably close to my grandfather *and* Estelle. Everything is fine just the way it is, and I'd be grateful if we left it that way. I'd also be grateful to not have this conversation again."

She became aware of him gazing at her intently, as if he were trying to see past the words she had spoken and attempt to find the true meaning behind them. Vivian tried to ignore his gaze, feeling highly uncomfortable, but her discomfort deepened when he asked, "Is there some particular reason I'm not aware of that has made you so stubbornly determined to remain anonymous? Have you experienced something negative because of prejudice against—"

"I really do not want to talk about this, Theo," she said, not caring that she sounded terribly defensive. She hoped her tone of voice would make him less likely to bring it up again, because she certainly didn't trust him enough to tell him Betsy's story and how it had played a part in making her decisions.

Theo put his gloved hands up in surrender, but he looked both concerned and curious. "Very well," he said. "Forgive me. It was not my intention to upset you; I only know how Samuel and Estelle feel about the matter—and I agree with them. I felt that I had to at least try once more to convince you that—"

"And you've spoken your piece," Vivian said. "Enough said."

"Enough said," he echoed, once again putting his hands up before he abruptly changed the subject of their conversation. "Tell me how it is that you're aware of the situation in the area we are going to see."

Vivian blew out a long, slow breath to calm herself while she mentally put away the tension of their previous topic of conversation. She was relieved to talk about something else. "Before my grandmother's death, we walked together once a week to this area with baskets of scones to pass out to those who were living on the streets and clearly starving. We had little to share, but my grandmother was adamant that we share what we *did* have. I continued her tradition until my grandfather's health suddenly declined, and I'm ashamed to say that I've not resumed doing so even though our circumstances are much better now. Truthfully, I've been thinking about this very thing—about taking up the habit again—and our conversation last night connected with that thought, I suppose."

"This seems like a very long walk from the cobbler's shop," Theo said.

"It was significant, although the carriage is moving very slowly as they do through the crowded, narrow streets through which we've been traveling. We've not gone terribly far."

Vivian was surprised when Theo knocked on the top of the carriage, which she knew was the signal for the driver to stop. She felt the rocking motion of someone climbing down, and it was Twig who peered through the window.

"Is there a problem, sir?"

"Not at all," Theo said, "but . . . are there any bakeries nearby? Do you know?"

Twig glanced around as if he might see one magically appear. "We will find one," he said. "They're common enough everywhere in the city. It shouldn't be too hard."

"Thank you," Theo said, and Twig got back up onto the driver's seat and they were moving again.

"Do you have a sudden craving for fresh baked goods?" Vivian asked.

"Something like that," he said with an almost mischievous sparkle in his eyes, and she wondered if her suspicions about his purpose might be correct.

They found a bakery within just a few minutes. The carriage stopped and Theo helped Vivian step out. They went inside together where the warmth of the ovens and the aroma of warm bread assailed Vivian's senses.

"Might I help you, sir?" a young woman asked from behind a counter where baskets of a variety of baked goods were displayed and available for purchase.

"I would like to buy *everything*," Theo said, and Vivian gasped.

"Everything, sir?" the young woman repeated, understandably surprised.

"Yes," Theo said. "I would like to purchase everything you have for sale that is edible, and if you have . . . baskets . . . or bags . . . that we could either purchase . . . or borrow for a while . . . to transport them . . . I would like those, as well."

"Perhaps," Vivian pointed out, "we should leave something here for customers who will need to purchase bread and—"

"Oh, we've got the ovens full," the young woman said, "and we can make more, easily enough. I'm pleased as could be to sell you what we've got. And if you promise to bring the baskets back say . . . in the next hour or so . . . I'd trust you to borrow them."

"I promise," Theo said. "And thank you."

"And I'll send some towels to cover the goods to keep them clean and fresh," their eager proprietor offered.

"Excellent; thank you," Theo said with enthusiasm.

Cooper and Twig were called upon to assist in carrying baskets of a variety of baked goods to the carriage, but all four of them had to go in and out of the shop more than twice, and the seats and floor of the carriage were so filled with baskets that it was tricky for Vivian and Theo to wriggle their way in and sit down.

Not many minutes later Vivian found herself moving among the poorest of the poor, passing out bread and scones and rolls to eager hands in exchange for expressions of gratitude and sometimes tears. She and her companions moved slowly through an area that was well known as a gathering place for people who had nowhere to go and no way to earn a living. She remained discreetly aware of Theo's reaction to what he was seeing, certain he'd never encountered anything like this in his life. Twig and Cooper didn't seem at all surprised, but certainly disheartened. Still, being able to offer food to so many made the experience a bit more positive in contrast to feeling completely helpless.

Vivian was surprised to realize that while Theo was offering bread to the hungry who were eager to take it, he was asking them questions and listening attentively to what they had to say. She wished that she were nearer to him so she could hear what was being said, but she felt the need to pass out her offerings by moving in a different direction. She glanced toward Theo frequently, struck by how her admiration and respect were rapidly growing. She saw nothing but complete sincerity and genuine compassion in him at this moment.

When there were no more baked goods to give away, they took the borrowed baskets and towels back to the bakery. Then the carriage moved slowly back toward their own neighborhood.

"I have never even imagined such . . . desperation," Theo said gravely, looking out the window with glazed eyes. "Of course, I've heard all my life that there is poverty in the city, that some people live very rough, but . . ." He didn't finish but shook his head, then looked at Vivian. "Do wealthy people protect their children by never allowing them to see such things?" he asked as if she might have the answer to every question in the universe.

"I don't know, Theo," she said gently, feeling compassion as well as empathy for his present state of shock. "I remember well the first time my grandmother took me there. I remember feeling almost guilty for the hearty supper I had that evening."

"And you were just a child?" he asked.

"It was after my parents died," she said.

Theo turned again to look out the window, and there was silence between them for less than a minute before he leaned his head closer to the window and asked, "What is that?"

"What?" Vivian asked, leaning in the same direction to try to see. What she saw appeared to be an incredibly old building that had once been a hotel but was now abandoned. "I should think the answer to that question is obvious," Vivian said.

"Yes, but . . . I want to look at it."

They went through the ritual again of stopping the carriage, and Theo helped Vivian step out so they could get a better look at the old, empty building, but they could do little more than just stand there because all the doorways and windows on the ground floor had been boarded up and there was no way to even look inside.

Theo stood there thoughtfully for a few minutes, and Vivian just stood beside him, wondering what on earth he was thinking. The only thing he said before they got back into the carriage was, "I need to speak with my solicitor."

"About what?" she asked.

"I think I want to buy that building . . . and have everything repaired and put in good order."

"You do?" she asked, confused.

"Just imagine how many beds could fit into such a building," he said, his eyes bright. "And if it was once a hotel . . . there would be a large kitchen . . . and dining areas. Think of all the people who could be fed from there. With my own personal funds, I can certainly afford to maintain such a place for the rest of my life and not cast a bit of a shadow on meeting my own needs or cause any difficulty for my family; in fact, I could stipulate in my will that even after I die the money that I've inherited will go toward maintaining this place . . . to help the poor. I can provide employment for those who are willing to cook and clean and manage and . . ." He seemed to be so brimming with ideas that he couldn't form the words he wanted to speak. He then suddenly looked right at her and asked, "What do you think, Vivian? Is it a crazy idea?"

Vivian's first thought was that Theo seemed by all accounts to be completely genuine, and she could find no reason to believe otherwise. His enthusiasm and determination touched her deeply, but a seed of suspicion unexpectedly leapt through her lips. "Please tell me you're not doing this simply to try and impress me . . . or to convince me that you've changed."

Theo looked so disarmed—even hurt—that she immediately wished she hadn't said it, although a part of her was glad she had. She needed to follow her instincts, and she couldn't just instantly dismiss his past arrogance and lack of kindness.

"Vivian," he said, sounding as if he were trying extremely hard to suppress his anger, "I realize that I've been less than . . . respectable in the past, but . . . do you honestly believe I would . . . *pretend* . . . to embrace such an idea for . . . what? To play out some charade with the hope of impressing you?"

The hurt in his eyes deepened before he looked away abruptly and Vivian could almost believe he was trying extremely hard to suppress his tears. She hurried to examine her instincts over what he'd just said and realized that she could find no evidence of a lack of sincerity. She felt confident in being able to say, "Forgive me. It's only that . . . the changes I've seen in you are rather drastic, and . . . I suppose I just need to become accustomed to the man you're becoming."

"As opposed to the man I have been in the past," he said, sounding as if he understood, rather than being defensive or angry—which he very well could have been.

"Yes," she admitted and quickly filled the ensuing silence by answering his original question. "I think anything you choose to do that can help those in need is anything but crazy." She laughed softly as she felt the tension between them disappear; the very fact that he'd so quickly let go of his anger over her questioning his motives seemed further evidence of the changes in him. "I actually think it's marvelous! Although . . . I do agree that you should consult your solicitor, and you should consult with experts regarding everything so that you don't encounter problems, but . . . you have my endorsement; not that you need it."

"I very much value your opinion, Vivian," he said as if their momentary disagreement had not even occurred. "And I'm so glad you took me there today. Your insight truly is remarkable. This is exactly what I needed."

"I'm pleased as well," Vivian said, both stunned and excited by his ideas and his enthusiasm. And the prospect of feeding and sheltering so many desperate people certainly warmed her heart.

As the carriage came to a halt, Vivian glanced out the window and realized they were not at the location where she and Theo had met earlier. In fact, she had no idea where they were.

"It's getting on lunch time," Theo said, noting her confusion. "If it's all right with you, I thought we could have lunch at one of my favorite pubs. You know, of course, that there's always an abundance of wonderful meals at the house, but sometimes I just feel the need to get out of the house and be on my own—and this is one of the places where I go. It's finer than most pubs and the food is excellent. Would you do me the pleasure of joining me for lunch, Miss Peyton? And I'll make certain Twig and Cooper are properly fed, as well."

"I will join you as long as Twig and Cooper are seated at the same table with us."

"Very well," he said.

"It's more proper that way," she explained before he had a chance to question her reasoning. "Besides, I think it would do you good to get better acquainted with the people who work for you. That *does* fit in with your plan to become a better person, does it not?"

"You are absolutely right, Miss Peyton," he said, his expression showing enlightenment just before he stepped out of the carriage and helped her down.

Lunch proved to be especially enjoyable. The food was indeed particularly good, and Vivian thoroughly enjoyed observing Theo as he made an effort to ask Twig and Cooper questions about their lives apart from working for his family. The two men were good friends, and both had a marvelous sense of humor. The result was a great deal of laughter while Vivian felt as if she were witnessing a transformation taking place right before her eyes. Before they had finished their meal, it was evident that Theo had stopped seeing these men as merely employees with whom he had always been on friendly terms, and Twig and Cooper had come to see Theo as simply a man, not so different from themselves. They were extremely interested and impressed with Theo's idea about purchasing the old hotel and having it renovated and turned into a place that could help the kind of people to whom they'd been distributing bread earlier. Vivian hoped that Theo had noticed the change of perspective he'd just been given, and that he might continue to make a similar effort with others who worked at the Weatherby house.

"Now," Theo declared when they were ready to leave, "I suddenly feel very anxious to share my plans with my aunt." He turned to Vivian and said, "Won't you come with me? Surely, we can sneak you into the house and up the stairs without anyone noticing if that's what you prefer. I do so want you there when we talk to Estelle, and your grandfather too, of course."

Vivian thought about it only long enough to realize that her desire to be a part of this conversation far outweighed her concerns. She too felt confident that she could get into the house and upstairs without being seen, especially if Theo helped make certain the path was clear before she even ventured inside.

"I would like that very much," she said. "As long as you help me, I'm confident all will be well."

"Excellent!" Theo declared with enthusiasm as he stood, and they all left the pub to begin the brief journey to the Weatherby house.

The carriage stopped directly behind the door that the servants most often used at the back of the house. Theo stepped out and went inside to see if anyone was in the short length of hallway between the door and the stairs. He motioned with his arm, and Twig helped Vivian step down from the carriage. She whispered a quick "thank you" and hurried through the door and to the stairs with Theo right behind her.

Just as she did every time she went up these stairs to visit with her grandfather and Estelle, Vivian hurried as quickly as possible, not wanting to be seen. She could hear Theo matching her pace as he ascended behind her, then they moved at an equally fast pace to the sitting room that was their standard meeting place. Of course, Estelle and Samuel wouldn't be expecting her at this time of day, and it occurred to her that they might be elsewhere.

Vivian paused not far from the sitting room and said quietly to Theo, "If they aren't there, I'm going to wait and let you go find them."

He nodded his understanding and stepped past her to knock at the sitting room door, but then typically entered without waiting for any response, and Vivian followed right behind him, closing the door as she did.

"What a nice surprise," Estelle said with a glowing smile and an expression of curiosity that Vivian and Theo were there together—on Vivian's day off work.

"Indeed, it is," Samuel added, looking completely comfortable in these new surroundings—and perfectly happy—which warmed Vivian deeply. But he too looked curious, and perhaps a little confused.

"I confess I'm very excited about something," Theo said, looking mostly at his aunt as both he and Vivian were seated on the same sofa. "As a direct result of Vivian's marvelous insight, I've become aware of some terrible challenges that afflict a great many people, and I want to use some of my own financial resources to make a positive difference in helping these people."

"Oh, this sounds wonderful!" Estelle said, and both she and Samuel became eagerly attentive.

Vivian just listened as Theo related the entire experience of their excursion, beginning with his sincere declaration that he'd been trying awfully hard to become a better man and to find ways to make his life more meaningful. Estelle nodded, but didn't seem surprised, and Vivian felt certain they had already been talking about his desire for change. This added weight to Vivian's hope that she would be able to trust that Theo's motivation to change was sincere. When he finished his story with the announcement that he wanted to purchase a dilapidated hotel and arrange for all the necessary work to be done to have it fully restored and functional as a place where many people without homes could find refuge and work, Estelle was so visibly filled with glee that it couldn't help but make Vivian want to laugh with delight—but she didn't want to interrupt Theo's momentum. Samuel was also clearly pleased, and they continued to listen as Theo went on to talk about his ideas for hiring people to manage this new institution of his, and the employees he would need to hire to clean and cook and serve meals. It was also his idea that the people who stayed there—at least those who were physically capable of working—would contribute to the work in order to feel useful and to earn their keep as much as possible. He also talked about the possibility of having an employee there who was qualified in helping people find work so they could move toward becoming independent. Vivian hadn't yet heard that idea, but she liked it very much and told him so. He concluded by saying that of course he would need to speak with his solicitor first thing to make certain that everything was done properly; but he was eager to get started on this grand project right away.

Once Theo had finished sharing all the ideas that had been circling in his mind, Estelle and Samuel both expressed sincere and enthusiastic approval over such a plan. Estelle added with pride aimed toward her nephew, "I think it's wonderful! Just wonderful! I want to hear every detail of your progress, and I look forward to the day when it's ready to begin functioning."

"As do I," Theo said. "Until that time, I want to make arrangements for baked goods to be delivered each day to those who are living on the streets. It was so deeply gratifying to help in this small way that meant so much to these people; I had difficulty not getting all weepy."

"Weepy?" Vivian echoed in a teasing voice. "You?"

"Yes, me," Theo countered, also teasing. "Perhaps I'm not as hardhearted as you might have believed."

"Perhaps you're not," Vivian replied, still holding out on whether she could completely trust him, but very much liking the progress she was witnessing. Whatever his motives for this project, it would bring about a great deal of good and she was thrilled to see Theo using his wealth to benefit those who were suffering.

"As I was saying," Theo continued, "I want to make arrangements with more than one bakery for large orders every day—although they would be closed on Sundays, which might mean acquiring a much larger order on Saturdays."

"People are certainly every bit as hungry on the Sabbath as any other day," Samuel said, "even if the bakeries are closed."

"Exactly my thoughts," Theo said. "Cooper and Twig seemed to very much enjoy our excursion, and I do believe they would be willing to take charge of such an endeavor. And I don't see why a few maids or groomsmen—perhaps the assignment can be rotated—couldn't go with them to assist. On some days I would like to go myself."

"On the days I don't work I would like to go with you," Vivian said enthusiastically, and Theo seemed pleased.

"I would certainly like to go at least once or twice a week," Samuel declared. "My Edna was diligent in doing this very thing."

"She is the reason I came up with this idea," Theo said, and Samuel looked surprised. "Vivian told me how Edna would take her to pass out scones among the poor; that even though your family had little extra to give, Edna was determined to share anything extra that you had. I was very touched by such a principle."

"She was a good woman," Estelle said with a smile toward Samuel as she reached out to squeeze his hand. She then turned to Theo and added, "I too would like to help with this aspect of your project. Samuel and I will plan on going out with Cooper and Twig at least twice a week."

"Excellent!" Theo said. "I will make the arrangements!" He let out a gratified sigh and took a long, deep breath, as if he could now breathe normally again after having shared his flurry of ideas.

"Oh!" Theo added. "One more thing. I should like to call the home when it's completed—because it will indeed be a home for those who need one—The Edna Peyton Memorial Home, in her honor. What do you think?"

Vivian was immediately moved to tears and didn't even have enough warning to keep them from trickling down her face. But a quick glance showed her that both Estelle and her grandfather had tears running down their cheeks.

The room became suddenly still as they mutually shared the tender emotion evoked by Theo's idea. Theo showed no sign of tears, but he was clearly moved by the response to his idea. While the others were wiping their faces with handkerchiefs, Theo said in a teasing voice, "Well, if my idea is so upsetting to all of you, then perhaps . . ." This immediately turned the tears to laughter before everyone told him the name was perfect and they were all thrilled with his ideas and were looking forward to being involved with regular assistance to the hungry, as well as observing the progress of the home that would be named in Edna's honor. Vivian truly hoped this was coming genuinely from Theo's heart, and that he wasn't simply trying to impress his aunt—or her—despite how vehemently he had denied such a possibility. She decided to simply enjoy being a part of his plans and reserve judgment regarding his motives.

Chapter Eleven
CONSORTING

THEO WAS DELIGHTFULLY SURPRISED—ALTHOUGH he believed that he likely shouldn't have been—to find himself feeling happier than he ever had as he embarked upon overseeing his new projects and being directly involved as much as possible. Every member of the household staff had been enthusiastic about helping Cooper and Twig with the daily distribution of baked goods among the poor, and Theo arranged with three different bakeries to help supply an even larger amount than he had purchased impulsively that first time. The owners of the bakeries were pleased to have the extra business, and he realized that he had inadvertently been given the opportunity to help them as well. Deep down, he felt a warm and soothing kind of pride; a humble pride in doing something that really mattered. He didn't want to tell anyone how he felt; he simply wanted to keep moving forward with being able to help people in ways that he anticipated would continue long after he was dead and gone. He would make certain of that.

Theo thoroughly enjoyed telling his mother and sister every detail of his recent experiences, his desire to change, and the projects he'd initiated. Each day when he spent time with them, he always had more news to share, and they were both eagerly enthused about every facet of the situation. Dorothea told him more than once how immensely proud she was of him, and Theo couldn't help but feel warmed by such a sentiment from his mother.

With the assistance of his solicitor—a fine man who was not only qualified in handling complicated projects but had many good connections—Theo was able to quickly purchase the old hotel and hire some well-recommended people to begin the massive renovations. And Theo's solicitor also made certain that all legalities were taken care of and that everything was seen to properly.

Within just a few weeks, both of Theo's projects were settling in smoothly, and he enjoyed occasionally visiting the hotel to see the progress being made.

Most of all, he enjoyed the days when he went with Twig and Cooper to personally pass out food to the hungry on the streets. He always did so on days when he knew that Vivian was not working, and she would be able to join him. Not only did he love participating in such a wonderful endeavor with Vivian near his side, but he also enjoyed being able to share lunch with her and the carriage drivers at a pub afterward, since it had quickly become a habit.

The more Theo got to know Vivian, the more he absolutely adored everything about her. In fact, a day came when he simply had to admit to himself that he had genuinely fallen in love with her and wanted to share *every* aspect of his life with her for the remainder of his life. But memories of how badly he'd treated her haunted him, and he believed he had a long way to go to prove himself to her. He found it sickeningly ironic to recall that on their first meeting he had felt so justified in considering himself far above her in every way, and now he felt entirely unworthy of her. She was good to the core in every way. Her integrity was solid, and she knew how to work hard to provide for herself in a way that he had never experienced. She carried on her grandmother's legacy of compassion and dignity in a way that left him in awe. He had never known Edna Peyton, but he'd now heard a great many stories about her, and he felt increasingly confident that naming his grand project in her honor was the best possible choice. Estelle also admired Edna deeply, even though she only knew Samuel's first wife from his stories of her. But Theo loved to sit with them and listen to those stories, and he was in awe of the way that Samuel and Estelle could share stories about the lives they'd lived during their decades apart and do it with such mutual respect and genuine interest. In fact, the love that glowed in Samuel and Estelle's faces every time they looked at each other was something that Theo wanted desperately in his own life, and he found himself praying often that such a love might be possible between him and Vivian, although he knew he had a long way to go in proving himself worthy of her.

As winter eased toward spring, Theo was pleased to know that the daily distribution of bread among the poor had become a comfortable part of the routine in the Weatherby household. The servants who were involved enjoyed their opportunity to help on the days when it was their turn, and it became a coveted task among those who had eagerly agreed to be a part of the project when it had first been presented to them. Theo was also pleased with the progress of putting the hotel in good repair. There had been setbacks when it was discovered that the building was in far worse condition than they had initially realized, but Theo was grateful to have the financial resources to hire the people who could solve those problems. And progress continued.

On the first truly warm day of spring, Theo took Estelle, Samuel, and Vivian with him to see the progress that had been made, and he loved the way they were all so immensely pleased as he gave them a brief tour of the building, taking care to stay away from the areas where the ongoing construction might prove hazardous. The only thing that bothered Theo about their excursion was the fact that Vivian still insisted on meeting the carriage some distance from the house so that no one would find out that she was socializing with the Weatherby family. For the same reasons, she also continued to sneak in and out to visit with the family. Theo had made himself a part of those visits and had enjoyed becoming better acquainted with both Vivian and her grandfather. He'd also enjoyed an occasional evening stroll with Vivian through the hallways of the house. They'd shared a great deal of stimulating conversation, but he was relatively certain she still wasn't sure whether she could trust him. He wondered if her distrust of him had anything to do with her hesitancy about moving into the house, but he had no idea how he might convince her that he had changed. And as far as her reasons for not wanting any of the staff to know about her connection to Samuel, Theo wished he could convince Vivian that her fears were not valid. If there was any judgment or ridicule toward her from anyone on the staff, Theo felt certain it would be short-lived and a new life for Vivian would quickly settle into place. In his heart he wanted to be able to officially court her, but he could hardly even consider such a step when she was determined to work as a maid in the house where he lived and to keep secret what she had come to call *consorting* with the family, as if they were some kind of criminals. He knew her intention in saying such things was all in jest, but he doubted she had any idea how he really felt about her, and how his feelings made such comments sting—much the way the sting of her slapping him still haunted him rather frequently.

For all that Theo disagreed with Vivian's decision on how to manage the situation, he knew it was vital to respect her choices without question. He would certainly never be able to win over a lady like Vivian by telling her he believed she was wrong, especially when they'd already talked about it more than once and she'd made her stand noticeably clear. All Theo could do was hope and pray that eventually she would come to see that she didn't need to keep living this way, and that making herself a part of her grandfather's new family was not only all right, but it would also surely bring many blessings into her life that she richly deserved.

Vivian awoke on a rainy spring morning to the crack of thunder and looked at the clock to realize she still had a while before she needed to get out of bed and get ready for work. As she lay in the warm comfort of her bed, listening to the rain and the occasional rumbling thunder, her mind went—as it often did—to Theodore Weatherby and how she was growing to admire him more and more. For many weeks now, she'd been observing him closely and analyzing practically everything he said and the way he said it. Any suspicion she'd had that his projects to aid the poor were motivated in attempting to impress her or his aunt had been completely abolished. His sincerity had become increasingly evident, and she loved hearing him talk enthusiastically about the progress of the hotel almost as much as she loved the days when she was able to go with him to pass out bread among the poor who were living on the streets. Together they'd become acquainted with many of these people, and Vivian loved their excitement when the carriage appeared and Theo's little team was able to help ease their suffering momentarily, and to visit with them and gradually learn more about their lives and the hard times that had come upon them, rarely through any fault of their own.

Vivian also thoroughly enjoyed the fact that Theo was nearly always present when she sneaked upstairs to visit with Estelle and her grandfather. As the four of them talked and laughed and shared stories with each other, she came to see more and more that Theo was indeed a good man. He'd admitted more than once that he had some difficult character traits that he'd been working on improving, and Estelle had said multiple times that she could see the positive changes in him, and she was proud of him—even though she'd always known that at the core he *was* a good man. Vivian liked the way they could all talk so comfortably about such things, and she was able to share some feelings about how grateful she'd become for the changes in her own life that had initially been so frightening and overwhelming. Her grandfather expressed how proud he was of *her*, and that she'd always been a light in his life.

Mingled throughout all the time Vivian spent with Theo, she had gradually become accustomed to the way she would often find him just watching her with a sparkle in his eyes that implied he was still a victim of the feelings he'd once confessed to before he'd kissed her. The timing and his behavior had been all wrong that day, but a great deal had changed since then, and time had also given them both the opportunity to get to know each other much better. Perhaps more unnerving than Theo's meaningful gaze was the way that Vivian had, little by little, found it increasingly impossible to look away, despite the way she would inevitably be overtaken by an intense tingling that felt as if stardust were falling over her like magical snow.

While the rain and thunder continued to accompany Vivian's mental review of all that was good in her life, and the changes that had taken place between her and Theo, it occurred to her quite suddenly that she had fallen in love with him. She gasped aloud when the idea first materialized, but as it settled in, she was overcome with a warmth that permeated from the center of her chest, and the familiar tingling that consumed every part of her. Their ugly encounters from the past briefly intruded on her thoughts, but she pushed them away, reminding herself that he deserved the right to change and to prove himself a different man—and he had certainly done well in *that*. Nevertheless, she was still a maid working in his home. For all that they were a part of the same family in a strange way due to the marriage of her grandfather and his aunt, they were still from completely different worlds. Of course, the example of Estelle and Samuel's relationship was proof that love could successfully transcend such social boundaries, but Vivian wondered if such could be the case for her and Theo. They had become friends, and she treasured their friendship, but that didn't mean anything more would ever come of it—even if she had come to realize that what she felt for him was very real and undeniable. She thought of the way she often caught him gazing at her and wondered if he truly might have the same kind of feelings for her that she had for him. The very idea made her tremble with a combination of excitement and trepidation.

Another glance at the clock showed Vivian that she needed to get up and face her day. Walking to work in the rain was never pleasant, but thankfully there was no wind, and she was able to get to the Weatherby house without being too adversely affected by the wet weather.

Vivian's morning proceeded as usual while her thoughts were drawn to Theo more than ever. She felt a tender warmth while thinking of the love she felt for him and considering how her admiration had grown. But at the same time, she was overcome with frustration when considering all that stood between the possibility of anything evolving between them that went beyond the friendship they already shared.

Just a few minutes before lunch, Vivian was busy scrubbing pots in the kitchen when one of the maids told her that Mrs. Thatcher wanted to speak with her. Vivian hurried to finish cleaning the pot she was working on before she dried her hands and went to Mrs. Thatcher's office. It wasn't at all unusual for the housekeeper to send any one of the maids to take care of an extra task that had come to her attention; therefore, Vivian wasn't the least bit concerned until she entered the open door of the office to see the housekeeper look up from the work on her desk with a somber expression, saying softly, "Please close the door and sit down, Vivian. We must talk."

"What's happened?" Vivian asked, showing great restraint when she instinctively wanted to give in to the sudden terror she was feeling and react with an unrestrained emotional outburst.

Mrs. Thatcher clasped her hands on her desk and looked directly at Vivian with unmistakable compassion. "I'll come straight to the point," she began, and Vivian was glad for that; she didn't think she could bear dragging out this conversation while she wondered if her worst fears had come to pass.

"Last evening," Mrs. Thatcher went on, "I entered the servants' dining hall for supper, and when I realized the nature of the conversation taking place I held back and listened instead of making myself known right away. Vivian, my dear, it became immediately evident to me that every member of the staff has known about your connection to Samuel Peyton since before the wedding."

Vivian gasped and put a hand over her mouth to prevent herself from making any further unsavory sounds in response to this horrible news.

"I'm not certain," the housekeeper continued, "how it was initially discovered, or by whom, but many of them *did* know right from the start that your surname is Peyton. And gossip spreads in a house like this; that's just the nature of so many people working closely together and always wanting to have something to talk about. But before you go and get all upset, I need to make it perfectly clear that the things they're saying about you are in no way malicious or rooted in negativity. My dear Vivian, they are *happy* for you and your grandfather. What I overheard was a conversation about their confusion as to why you would be trying to keep your identity a secret and continue working in service when you could be enjoying a new life with the man who raised you."

Vivian was deeply surprised to hear this but not quite willing to believe it. When she could think of nothing to say, Mrs. Thatcher filled the silence.

"When I'd heard enough to be certain of the nature of their attitudes, and to know that what they were saying was genuine—because they didn't realize I was listening, and they had no reason to try and simply say what they believed I would consider appropriate—I made myself known and joined them for supper as usual. I purposely encouraged the conversation to continue by asking some questions about their feelings, and many spoke up eagerly. They truly are happy for you! I didn't sense even a pinch of resentment from anyone, and if it were put to a vote, I believe they would all want you to take your rightful place among the family and stop working when there's no need for you to do so. I'm aware of your concerns, Vivian, and I'm telling you that in this case—in this house—they are entirely unfounded. It's my opinion as someone who has come to know you well, that you should reconsider your situation."

More silence ensued, but this time Mrs. Thatcher *didn't* say anything to try and fill it; she was clearly waiting for Vivian to speak. But everything Vivian had just heard felt so shocking and disconcerting that she was entirely at a loss for words.

When the silence became noticeably uncomfortable, she finally managed to speak. "I . . . don't even know what to say . . . what to think. I confess that I feared this might happen, but . . . well . . . perhaps I should have prepared myself with a plan for what to do if it happened. Perhaps I should find work elsewhere, or—"

"No, no, no, my dear," Mrs. Thatcher said emphatically. "If I may speak candidly, and I will. I *am* the housekeeper here, after all, and you *do* work for me, so I want you to really listen to what I have to say. I'm not certain regarding the basis of all your fears and concerns, but I've done my best to respect them anyway. And now I'm telling you that there is no need to be concerned any further. Perhaps it might have been different if you'd been working in a different household. But Mrs. Peyton's kindness and generosity have created a general attitude in this house where all who work for her are impacted by it and follow her example. I can tell you that when employees have been cynical or lacking in respect for others, their employment here has not lasted long. You are working with genuinely good people. Why would you believe they might harbor such ill feelings toward you?"

Vivian took in all that she was hearing, glad to note that the beating of her heart was slowing down somewhat. Had she truly allowed her knowledge of Betsy's terrible experience to impact her own beliefs so deeply? It seemed so. Her difficult encounters with Theo had certainly contributed to her convictions about not integrating herself into the family, but he had genuinely changed, and she could say in all sincerity that this was no longer an issue. Had she been so unnecessarily stubborn over something that could have been alleviated by more honest and open communication? She needed to consider such questions more carefully, but she suspected the answers would make her feel like an absolute fool.

Vivian was startled from her thoughts when Mrs. Thatcher stood up, prompting Vivian to do the same. "We're going in to lunch now—together—and we are going to address this situation once and for all." Vivian felt a new terror engulf her, but Mrs. Thatcher was entirely in housekeeper mode now, stating an order that she expected to be followed. "No more secrets, no more hiding. Whatever you choose to do after lunch and from here forward is up to you, but I'll not have this brewing in my household any longer." With more softness and compassion, she added, "I will do the talking, and I'll be right beside you. There's nothing to worry about."

Vivian managed to nod in response, but she heartily disagreed. She felt utterly terrified and found it difficult to even make her feet move to follow the housekeeper to the dining hall. When they entered, Vivian was glad to see that no food had been served yet so that it wouldn't be growing cold while Mrs. Thatcher said whatever it was she intended to say. Then Vivian noticed that Mrs. O'Neill and those who assisted her in the kitchen were already seated, which was something they never did until all the food had been brought in from the kitchen. They had all known Mrs. Thatcher would be speaking to Vivian and addressing this issue while the entire staff was gathered—but before they began their meal. Vivian just wanted to melt into the floor and disappear.

"Thank you all for waiting to begin," Mrs. Thatcher said. "I've spoken with Vivian, and now we all know the truth and there's no need for secrets." She turned to look at Vivian and said with kindness, "It is entirely up to you, my dear, if you choose to continue to work, or if you do as Mrs. Peyton and your grandfather have wished from the beginning—and that is to officially become a part of the family in this household. If there's anything you'd like to say, now would be a good time."

"Um . . ." Vivian managed then cleared her throat; she hadn't expected to be saying anything and felt entirely unprepared. But her most prominent thought came easily to mind; it had been the basis of her concerns from the beginning, and she forced herself to speak. "I . . . well . . . after having worked with all of you . . . I would feel so terribly uncomfortable to have any of you waiting on me . . . and helping see to my needs; it just doesn't seem right. I haven't done anything to deserve such treatment. Why should I be elevated to such a position any more than any of the rest of you? It's just a matter of . . . luck; of a strange and unexpected connection." In her mind she knew there was a deeper fear related to this concept, and that was the possibility of others being so offended by such a discrepancy that they might punish her for it, or even hurt her—the same way that it had happened to Betsy. But she'd clearly not allowed herself to consider the alternate possibility of all that Mrs. Thatcher had already explained to her. "I grew up working," Vivian continued, "and that's who I am; I find fulfillment in the work, and—"

"Oh, honey," a maid said and came to her feet, walking around the table to stand directly in front of Vivian. Her name was Abigail, and Vivian knew her well and had always been comfortable with her, even though their conversations had never been deep or personal. "Now you listen to me." Abigail took hold of Vivian's shoulders and looked at her firmly. "I believe I can speak for everyone here, and if anyone disagrees, they are welcome to say so when I'm finished. You are one of the kindest, most sincere and hard-working women that any of us have ever known. There's not one of us who has ever heard a complaint or a cross word from you, even when you've had to do the worst of jobs in the house, and even when you had every right or reason to be frustrated because the rest of us are not always as kind and respectful as you are. We've all grown to love you, Vivian, and we *want* this for you! Don't you see? If someone who is one of us can be blessed with a happily-ever-after, it makes the rest of us all feel like we have a little part of it. And that will make us happy! You must believe us."

Vivian could hardly comprehend what she was hearing, and while she was trying to convince herself that surely not everyone could agree with Abigail's attitude, she heard a chorus of '*hear hears*' and '*amens*' resounding throughout the room.

"Besides," a man's voice said, and Vivian recognized it as belonging to Twig even before she looked past Abigail's shoulder to see him leaning back in his chair, "you have already been doing so much good in helping Mr. Weatherby with his projects—things that every one of us is proud of; proud to be part of a household where such things spring from. And I daresay you'll keep helping him. And I wouldn't be surprised if you become even more involved in this hotel project he's so keen about, because none of us can imagine you being content with sitting still for long. You deserve the chance to have a comfortable life, Miss, but consider this: consider all the good that someone like you—someone who grew up poor and working like the rest of us—could do by living on the other side. You've been a good influence on Mr. Weatherby; we all know it."

Vivian was disarmed to hear *that*; she wondered what else they all knew and felt suddenly foolish for having believed that she could truly keep secret all the things that could likely never go unnoticed in such a house.

"I . . . I don't know what to say," Vivian declared quite honestly; she felt too overcome to be able to coherently put words together.

"You don't have to say nothing," Cooper chimed in. "We all just want you to know that there's no need to pretend with us, and not one of us is anything but happy for you. You should be living in one of the fine bedrooms in this house and enjoying life with your grandfather and Mrs. Peyton. You're family!

Mr. Peyton is a good man, to be sure, and we all know this would make him and Mrs. Peyton so incredibly happy. We work for good people. Why would we not want them to be happy? Why would we not want *you* to be happy?"

His questions were left hanging in silence until Mrs. Thatcher said, "Is there anything that anyone else wants to say?" More silence followed, implying that the message they'd wanted Vivian to receive had been well stated. The housekeeper then asked, "Is there anyone who would have any difficult feelings about Vivian making these changes in the ways she's living?" Vivian held her breath, certain that even one disgruntled naysayer could entirely taint all the good she'd just heard. Mrs. Thatcher added a clear disclaimer, "No one will be looked down upon for expressing an honest opinion. I do believe Vivian wants to know exactly how you all feel."

"Yes, I do," Vivian declared firmly.

More silence ensued before Abigail again spoke. "I think it's evident how everyone feels." She turned toward the large group seated around the long table and asked, "How many of you are pleased for Vivian and wish for her to become someone we all have the privilege to work for?"

The chorus of vocal agreements and the resounding applause threatened to bring down the ceiling. Vivian had to wipe a sudden rush of tears from her cheeks, and the moment the noise settled, she simply said, "I thank you all for your kindness and support. It means more than I can say. I . . . I . . . need to think about it. This is all very new . . . and strange . . . for me. Still, I thank you. And I am glad I don't have to feel the need to keep secrets any longer. Thank you."

Having run out of things to say, Vivian looked helplessly toward Mrs. Thatcher who saved her by saying, "Now that we've cleared that up, let's eat. I think we're all very hungry."

"Indeed," Mrs. O'Neill said before she bustled off to the kitchen with a handful of other people following her. Vivian reluctantly sat down with the others, glad that conversations were taking place all around her that had nothing to do with the unexpected meeting they'd just endured that had been all about Vivian and her bizarre situation. Vivian had to force back that growing sense of feeling overwhelmed as everything that had been said circled around in her mind. Right now, she just wanted to get through lunch with the hope that she would be able to work alone this afternoon. And tonight, when she was back at the boardinghouse, she would hopefully be able to think clearly enough to make the best decision for her future, given the dramatic changes she had just been made aware of. Right now, she could barely force herself to eat even though she was hungry. But she knew she needed a full stomach to give her the strength to get through the remainder of the day, even while she couldn't even yet imagine what tomorrow might be like.

After lunch, Vivian returned to work as usual even though others on the staff expressed confusion over why she would do so. The only answer she could give was that she just felt the need to work.

When the day was done, Vivian slipped discreetly out of the house after asking Mrs. Thatcher if she would let her grandfather and Estelle know that she wouldn't be visiting this evening.

"I just need some time to think," Vivian told her.

Mrs. Thatcher understood and promised to deliver the message before she asked, "And what will you do tomorrow, my dear? It's your day off. Will Mr. Weatherby be expecting you to meet him to—"

"Oh, my!" Vivian said, so disoriented by the dramatic change that had taken place she almost felt dizzy. "I need to let him know that—"

"You need some time; I know," Mrs. Thatcher said. "I will give him the message to not expect you. Is there anything else I can do?"

"Not at the moment," Vivian said. "But thank you . . . for everything." She then left the house, feeling like a different woman than the one who had arrived that morning.

Vivian had trouble sleeping that night as she attempted to put all the pieces of her life together in her mind and have them make sense considering where she had come. There were things she'd deeply believed that she now knew were simply not true, and she wondered if that meant there were truths she'd been unwilling to fully acknowledge.

When morning came, she was glad to have the day off and to know that Theo wouldn't be expecting her. She decided to just stay at the boardinghouse and relax, hoping to rejuvenate herself for whatever she might have to face once she pulled herself out of this strange limbo where she felt completely caught in a sort of void between two worlds. She took time to soak in the warm spring sun streaming through the windows, which offered a strange kind of comfort. After breakfast was over and she had helped clean up, Vivian went to the parlor to read but couldn't focus on her book for more than a moment at a time. She was glad when Mel and Sally Mae joined her to take a break from their work, but was surprised when Mel asked boldly, "What is it that's bothering you, deary?"

"What do you mean?" Vivian countered.

"No point trying to pretend," Mel went on. "It's as plain as that cute little nose in the middle of your face. Something's weighing heavily on you—ever since you came home last evening—and maybe you need to talk about it."

Vivian couldn't deny feeling some relief at being able to talk about it with women she could trust; women she didn't work with and who were not involved in the situation. Once she got started with telling her story, she found it surprisingly easy to tell them almost everything. Even though she told them how Theo's difficult behavior had contributed to her decisions, she didn't offer even a hint of her true feelings for him, and she made it clear that he had changed for the better and she had come to enjoy the comfortable friendship between them.

When Vivian finished by declaring the quandary before her, Sally Mae said firmly, "I don't understand why there's any question about what you should do."

"I'd have to agree," Mel said.

"What do you mean?" Vivian asked, uncertain about which path they thought she should take.

"I mean," Sally Mae said, "that you belong with your grandfather; he's family. That's the way family works, and if you're blessed enough to share your life with family of any kind—especially people so good—you should thank God and enjoy every minute."

"Amen!" Mel said. "I'd say you get yourself up to your room, put on that pretty dress you were given for your grandfather's wedding, and go be a part of your family. I won't be needing any notice from you for moving out. You shouldn't be living here, but we'd love to have you come visit. You're a one in a million, you are."

"Amen," Sally Mae said just as Mel had said it a moment ago.

"Truly?" Vivian asked, surprised at how comfortably the idea was settling in. After stewing all night over her choice between two lives, it seemed that all she'd needed was a little nudge from these two women she'd grown to care for.

"Truly!" they both said at the same time.

"But . . ." Vivian said, "I can't possibly wear that dress. It's far too fancy for—"

"Is it fancier than what your new grandmama would be wearing?" Sally Mae asked.

Vivian thought about it. "A little, maybe, but . . ."

"Just wear it!" Mel said.

"And go!" Sally Mae ordered as if she were a military general.

Vivian took a deep breath and felt surprisingly calm and at peace. She stood and bent over to hug Mel and Sally Mae while they remained seated. "Thank you! You're both so dear! I will come to visit; I promise."

"You'd better," Mel said, then laughed as Vivian rushed up the stairs. She hurried to change her clothes, although in examining her options she didn't feel comfortable with the idea of wearing a dress that had been made for an elegant occasion, simply to show up at her grandfather's new home to announce that she'd changed her mind about how to go forward. Wearing her Sunday dress—however lacking it might be in quality and comeliness—felt far more appropriate. It didn't take her long to pack what little she owned, and as she did so, her inner peace grew and radiated throughout her entire spirit. She now knew this was right; she had absolutely no doubt about it. She knew it would take some adjustment on her part, but when she thought of how happy her new family would be with her choice, she had trouble not laughing out loud.

Arriving at the Weatherby house, Vivian became suddenly nervous. The very thought of entering without being dressed in her maid's uniform left her decidedly uncomfortable. But she took a deep breath and went inside carrying her luggage, which she set down in the place where coats and umbrellas would be left on cold or stormy days. Glad that the hall was devoid of any people, Vivian hurried to Mrs. Thatcher's office, hoping the housekeeper wouldn't be elsewhere seeing to her many duties. She nearly bumped into Mrs. Thatcher who was about to leave the office, and they both laughed a little over the near mishap before the older woman took in Vivian's apparel and said, "Oh, my! I take it you've had a change of heart."

"I have," Vivian said, "although . . . I'm not exactly certain what happens next . . . or what I should do . . . or—"

"Come sit down," Mrs. Thatcher said and motioned her into the room before she closed the door. Once the two women were seated, the housekeeper said, "As I see it, my dear, what happens next is perfectly simple. You just need to get settled into your new room; I've had in mind the perfect room for you ever since I became aware of the truth. It's just down the hall and around the corner from Mr. and Mrs. Peyton's room." Hearing this increased Vivian's discomfort, but she wondered what she might have expected. Of course, she would need a room, and of course Mrs. Thatcher would think of everything.

"Now," she went on, "your grandfather and Mrs. Peyton are not in the house at present." Vivian felt a rush of panic, certain she needed them to help her take this step, and she couldn't imagine being able to do anything except rush up to their sitting room and hear them reassure her that she was doing the right thing. "They've gone to visit a friend for lunch, and I was assured they would return before tea. In the meantime, why don't you have lunch with your friends?"

Vivian's discomfort was soothed slightly by the word *friends*. Was it truly possible that the people she'd worked with would remain her friends despite the changes in her life? She felt intrigued with the idea of finding out, and what better way than to share lunch with them while what she was wearing made it evident she hadn't come to the house to work.

"And after lunch," Mrs. Thatcher continued, "we'll get you all settled in, and then you can go to the sitting room where you always gather to visit with your family and wait there until they return. I'm certain they will be pleased beyond measure to find you there!"

"I do hope so," Vivian said, then admitted. "I feel terribly nervous despite having come to believe that this is the right course for me."

"Everything will settle into place," Mrs. Thatcher reassured her as she stood and moved toward the door. "You'll see; all will be well."

As Vivian entered the servants' dining hall at Mrs. Thatcher's side, she was greeted with enthusiasm and warmth, which helped dispel her anxiety immensely. Sitting here and sharing a meal with these people helped her realize that Mrs. Thatcher had been right. They *were* her friends—at least in varying degrees—and there wasn't a soul there who seemed the least bit put off by Vivian's change in station within the household. Many of them asked her questions about how she was feeling, and she was able to answer them honestly, which in turn brought on a great deal of reassurance and happiness on her behalf.

When lunch was over and the staff all dispersed to see to their work, Vivian retrieved her luggage, and Mrs. Thatcher herself led the way up the back stairs to show Vivian the room that would now be hers. Vivian felt as if she'd been transported to some extraordinary dimension where time and space were altered, and the girl who had grown up in the cobbler's shop had mysteriously ended up embarking on the kind of life she'd never even dreamed of living.

Vivian had worked in the house long enough that she wasn't surprised by the beauty and fineness of the room; she was only surprised to realize that it would now be hers, and she knew it would take some time to adjust to this fact. Still, her decision felt right, and despite the feeling of unfamiliarity still hovering inside her, there was a deep underlying peace that kept her steady. The room was decorated in varying shades of pink and cream, and all the furnishings and decor were as fine as any other room in the house.

"Oh, it's lovely!" Vivian said to Mrs. Thatcher. "I can hardly believe that—"

"You'll adjust quickly enough," Mrs. Thatcher interrupted, "and I know you'll be happy here. I just know it!"

"Thank you for everything!" Vivian said and impulsively hugged the housekeeper, which she felt certain wouldn't be considered appropriate, but Mrs. Thatcher let out a surprised laugh and returned the brief embrace.

"You're a sweet thing," Mrs. Thatcher said. "Now, you get settled in. I'll have some fresh water brought up for you, and you can share tea with your family. You can either wait here or in their sitting room." She laughed softly. "Well, it's your home now; you know where everything is. It's not for me to tell you what to do."

"You've been so very kind," Vivian said and thanked her once more before she left.

Vivian examined the room more closely, just soaking in its beauty and attempting to accept that it was hers. She then noticed an open door on the wall adjacent to where they'd entered from the hallway and she went through it to discover a sitting room so lovely and comfortable looking that it made her gasp. Of course, she knew that every bedroom in the house had an accompanying sitting room, but again it felt so strange to think of having such luxury and privilege for herself.

Vivian hurried to put her belongings away, and the promised fresh water arrived while she was doing so. She exchanged a bit of comfortable conversation with the footman who had brought it before he left her to continue settling in. When there was nothing more to be done, she freshened up and examined her reflection in the long mirror in one corner of her bedroom. Not wearing a maid's uniform had made her feel out of place among the servants, but the dress she was wearing certainly made her feel out of place to think of socializing—and especially going out into public—with her grandfather and Estelle. She had been saving all her wages that she hadn't needed for living expenses, and she was now determined that at the first opportunity, she would use what she had saved to get herself at least one dress that was more appropriate for her new life; with any luck she would have enough money for two dresses.

Unable to do anything about that today, Vivian went to the sitting room where she always visited with her grandfather and Estelle, wishing that the usual time when tea would be served wasn't so far off. She felt out of sorts and longed for the comfort and reassurance that she knew they would give her.

Vivian had only been sitting there for a few minutes when she heard footsteps in the hallway through the open door—and she knew that it was Theo. Her heart quickened as it occurred to her that she'd been so overwhelmed with today's transition in her life that she'd been forcing herself to not even think about how this might affect her relationship with Theo. She had no reason to believe he wouldn't be pleased by her decision, but she wasn't naive enough to think that the reality would necessarily be what either of them might have expected—whatever that might be.

Vivian didn't even have time to consider what she might say to Theo before he appeared in the doorway and saw her sitting there. She wished it were possible to quell the way her heart quickened just seeing him, but all she could do was try and pretend that her feelings for him were simply based in friendship.

"Oh, hello," he said. "I was hoping to speak with Estelle, but this is a pleasant surprise, and . . ."

When he stopped talking abruptly, Vivian knew he'd suddenly noticed the obvious.

"What?" she asked when he seemed momentarily frozen.

"Well . . . you're . . . here in the middle of the day, and yesterday was your day off and . . . you're not wearing a . . ."

Vivian stopped his stammering by declaring in a light voice that she hoped might ease any potential awkwardness, "You're very perceptive, Theo. Something has obviously changed."

"Indeed," he said, then motioned toward the sofa where she was sitting. "May I?" he asked.

She would have preferred that he sit elsewhere, but she simply said, "I'm just waiting for Estelle and my grandfather to return home. You're far more welcome to sit in this room than I am."

"Now that's not true," Theo said, sitting on the same sofa but at the other end, maintaining a respectable distance between them. She wanted to protest against what he'd just said, but he added quickly, "You changed your mind. You've finally decided to stop working here."

"Yes," she said.

"And dare I ask if you've decided to actually live here?"

"Yes, I have," she added, looking at her hands that were folded in her lap. "Mrs. Thatcher has already made certain I'm settled into my new rooms."

"Excellent!" Theo said with enthusiasm.

"I suppose we'll see," Vivian said with a bit less enthusiasm.

"May I ask what precipitated this change of heart?" Theo asked, and Vivian was grateful for the opportunity to explain. She told him everything that had happened regarding the situation since she had last seen him, and the many paths her thoughts had taken to bring her to this decision. He listened attentively and expressed his pleasure and approval, which helped Vivian feel a little better—especially when she considered the fact that Theo had once been one of the biggest reasons she hadn't wanted to live in this house. They had come a long way, to be sure. She also told him about her friend Betsy, and how Betsy's terrible experience—and the way it had ended with Vivian losing a dear friend—had contributed a great deal to her thinking. She was surprised to hear Theo say with compassion, "It's not difficult to understand why that would influence your feelings about your own situation." He went on to express sincere compassion regarding Betsy and how horrible it must have been for her, and subsequently horrible for Vivian, given how close they had been and how Vivian had cared for Betsy following her assault. Vivian was pleasantly amazed by the depth of Theo's empathy and kindness, and the way his understanding helped her believe that her feelings had been valid, even if she might have taken them to extremes in the way she'd allowed them to influence her decisions.

Vivian continued, "Maybe I should have made this choice a long time ago, but then . . . maybe I wasn't ready. Looking back, I'm not entirely certain why I was so stubborn about all of this. I do think Betsy's experience was more traumatic for me than I'd realized; I loved her dearly and I lost her because of what happened; I also saw firsthand how brutally she'd been treated. But now I can also see that I allowed it to taint the situation here, which is nothing the same."

"I believe the same was very much true for myself," Theo said. "Looking back through my adult life I can see that I was very stubborn about my attitudes regarding certain things. I can now see that perhaps I just needed a new perspective at a time when I was ready to not only consider it but to really examine it." Vivian appreciated the sentiment and found her thoughts caught up in the changes she'd seen take place in him. She was surprised to hear him add, "And I'm absolutely certain that my behavior toward you did nothing to help you feel comfortable in this house; I apologize for that."

"You've apologized more than enough, Theo, and we've put all of that in the past." Trying to get back to the moment, Vivian hurried to add, "I feel at peace over my decision, although I still feel quite out of place."

"I'm certain that feeling will diminish with time," he said kindly. "And Estelle and your grandfather will be thrilled. They told me they didn't see you yesterday and they felt concerned. They will surely be pleased to find you here waiting for them."

"I'll be very glad to see *them*," she said.

"I'm very glad to see *you*." He smiled at her in a way that made it difficult to not let on to how his nearness—and his kindness and charm—affected her so deeply. She had to look away for fear of losing control of her senses. While she allowed herself to wonder how living in this house might impact her relationship with Theo, something warm and at the same time giddy consumed her, momentarily smothering any concern or reason for anxiety. In that moment she felt nothing but happiness knowing that she would now be living in the Weatherby house.

Chapter Twelve
UPSIDE DOWN AND BACKWARDS

Vivian became freshly seized by nervousness when she heard her grandfather and Estelle approaching. As if Theo sensed this, he said in a soft, calming voice, "There's no need to worry. They will be overjoyed about this."

Vivian nodded in response and prepared herself to face them, but they went to their bedroom instead and Vivian was left to wait longer. Of course, after having been out they both surely felt the need to freshen up, but Vivian hoped they would soon come to the sitting room rather than deciding to take a nap or something.

Thankfully, it was only a few minutes later that Estelle and Samuel came through the open door between the bedroom and sitting room only to stop abruptly as if they'd been struck by a freezing wind.

"Oh, my goodness!" Estelle finally said, moving toward Vivian, who stood to face her, with Theo standing by her side. "Does this mean what I hope it means?"

"I was hoping to have tea with you, if that's all right," Vivian said, and Estelle laughed before she engulfed Vivian in a tight hug while it was difficult to tell if she was laughing or crying. But Vivian noted from her view over Estelle's shoulder that her grandfather was dabbing his eyes with his handkerchief, and Theo put a comforting hand on Samuel's shoulder.

Estelle finally let go of Vivian who then hurried to receive her grandfather's warm hug, after which Estelle said, "Sit down and tell us everything. What has finally brought you to this decision?"

Before Vivian began, she turned to Theo and said, "There's no need for you to sit here and listen to the entire story again."

"I would *love* to hear the entire story again." He smiled and winked. "It's a very good story."

Vivian once again started at the beginning, telling them some things they already knew and others that they did not. She talked about Betsy's situation and how she'd allowed it to distort her perspective and create fear inside herself that wasn't warranted in her *own* situation. She was surprised when Theo admitted to them that he knew he had been less than kind to Vivian and this had surely contributed to her not wanting to live under the same roof, but she reassured him that such things were all in the past.

Vivian went on to tell her grandfather and his new wife about more recent events—beginning with Mrs. Thatcher informing her that the entire staff was already aware of the situation and ending with the decision she'd made just this morning that she was wasting precious time she could spend with her grandfather and Estelle, which made them both dab at their eyes with their handkerchiefs.

"So, Mrs. Thatcher already has me settled into a room down the hall and around the corner, and I think I might be the only person in the house who is struggling to adjust to such changes."

"All will be well quickly enough," Samuel said, "and I can never express how happy this makes me. I never wanted to force your hand . . . or have you making any decisions simply out of some distorted sense of duty or obligation. But oh! I'm so happy to have you here now! What fun we'll have!"

"Indeed, we will!" Estelle added.

Through a moment of silence that seemed much longer than it actually was, Vivian's mind went to the dress she was wearing, and she unconsciously pressed her hands over her skirt. "I have some money saved and I would like to get a new dress as soon as possible—maybe two—so that I won't stand out like a weed in a garden and—"

"There's no need to worry about *that*," Samuel was quick to say. "I'm certain not one of us cares what you wear, my dear."

"No, indeed," Estelle said firmly. "It simply doesn't matter."

"I agree," Theo said, much to Vivian's surprise, since he was always dressed so finely.

"Nevertheless," Samuel went on, "I've been given some ridiculous kind of allowance simply for having the good fortune of becoming Estelle's husband. I don't understand it, but apparently the solicitor insisted that this is how things are done. As you know, I've been able to get myself some fine new clothes, and I have more than enough to get you whatever you like, my dear."

Vivian was positively dumbstruck. She couldn't think of what to say in response to such an offer, and even if she'd been able to find the words, she doubted they would make it out of her mouth. She couldn't deny that being able to wear suitable clothing for her new life would help her feel more comfortable. Wearing a maid's uniform had helped her feel like she belonged among the serving staff when they all wore uniforms as well. The clothing she'd worn when she wasn't working had been perfectly adequate because she'd been living a simple life, mingling with the women at the boardinghouse and sneaking in to visit Samuel and Estelle. When she'd gone out with Theo it had been to distribute food to the poor and eat at a pub. No one had expected her to be anything more or less than a former cobbler's daughter who had then found work as a maid. But if she were to daily socialize with her new family—including attending church and going out for other reasons that she couldn't even comprehend in that moment—she didn't want to feel out of place. And even more so, she didn't want her grandfather or Estelle to feel embarrassed by her appearance. She believed them when they said that it didn't matter, but she also had the good sense to know that it would be better if she were able to dress appropriately.

"We'll go shopping tomorrow, my dear," Estelle said. "Just us ladies. And we'll have lunch together at my favorite tea shop."

The very idea felt dreamlike and exquisitely wonderful to Vivian, so much so that she had to fight to keep from getting teary. When she had first met Estelle and had been taken in by her genuine kindness and sincerity, she never would have dreamed of the two of them taking such an excursion. She suddenly felt incredibly happy—not because she was able to live in a grand house with her own beautiful rooms, and not because she would be getting a new wardrobe suitable to her new station, but because she felt so much love and joy from Estelle and her grandfather. Her decision to share their lives here in this home had made them so genuinely happy that their delight just seemed to spill over and fill the room. She even believed that Theo was genuinely happy about her decision. She never would have believed that she'd come to care what he thought one way or the other, but she'd come to care very much—more than she dared admit. All things considered, she felt the underlying peace that had been accompanying her throughout this day suddenly blossom and fill every part of her being. For the first time since her grandfather and Estelle had told her about their decision to marry, Vivian felt truly at peace.

Within a few days, Vivian felt so comfortable in her new circumstances that it was difficult to remember why she had been so resistant. Her shopping excursion with Estelle had been delightful, and they were both looking forward to many more such adventures. Under Estelle's guidance, an entirely new wardrobe was ordered for Vivian. It would take time for most of it to be made and delivered; however, it was fortuitous that the dressmaker had a couple of ready-made dresses which fit Vivian fairly well so that she wouldn't feel out of place in the meantime—especially since they would be attending church the following day.

Going to church with her grandfather, Estelle, and Theo turned out to be a far more pleasant experience than Vivian had expected. She enjoyed listening to the sermon and singing hymns—just as she always did at church—but she also enjoyed feeling like part of a family. Even long before Estelle had come into their lives, her grandfather had stopped attending church due to his health, and he'd never gotten back into the habit until after he'd married Estelle. She loved sitting at his side, and she enjoyed the way Estelle so kindly and proudly introduced her to several of her friends after the service was over. Vivian was keenly aware that Theo was never far away—which had become the case with their sharing meals and tea each day with Estelle and Samuel—but having him around more frequently had only made Vivian even more aware of the warm affinity she felt toward him, even if she doubted that she could ever admit to such feelings aloud.

As a new week began, Vivian embarked on establishing her own routine within the household. Whenever Theo went out to help distribute bread to the poor, she went with him. And if he went to personally check on the progress of the construction at the hotel, she enjoyed being a part of that as well. She loved the way they could discuss their strong feelings about being able to make a positive contribution to assisting those in need. And quite simply, she just loved spending time with him. He seemed to enjoy her company as well, and Vivian couldn't deny her pleasure in that. Despite how much joy she found in spending time with him, Vivian found it difficult to acknowledge her deeper feelings. She could never admit to the fact that he was in her thoughts almost constantly, and every time he smiled at her or touched her hand to help her step into or out of a carriage, her heart always quickened with a secret thrill. Since she'd come to live at the Weatherby house, their familial connection—with her grandfather being married to his aunt—had made her almost feel as if she and Theo had become cousins, which strengthened their friendship but made the possibility of anything else ever evolving between them feel highly improbable. She found it ironic that she had come to fully trust him, and she knew beyond any doubt that he *had* changed. She'd come to spend a great deal of time with him on a regular basis, and she never saw any evidence of arrogance or anger toward anyone he encountered; in fact, he went out of his way to be kind and respectful to others, no matter their station in life. As a result of these changes, Vivian also observed that he seemed much happier and less tense. She was bold enough to mention her observations to him, and he just smiled as he said, "Yes, I feel much happier."

Vivian enjoyed being able to have private conversations with her grandfather as well as with Estelle. And sometimes they visited together. And at other times Theo joined them. The four of them often shared meals and tea, where they never ran out of things to talk about. Nevertheless, Vivian had made a habit of going to the servants' dining hall after her own lunch was over so she could sit with her friends and visit while they ate. She was relieved that they didn't treat her any differently, and many of them seemed pleased that she still considered them her friends—some came right out and said so.

Vivian enjoyed exploring the library and finding new things to read. She spent time every day finding different beautiful places in the house where she could lose herself in a book, and she also enjoyed the remarkably beautiful gardens behind the house where she loved to wander and take in the glory of spring coming forth and filling the bushes and trees with vibrant color. Exploring the gardens was an activity she relished in solitude, since Estelle and Samuel were in the habit of taking a walk together at a different time of day. But on the days when the weather permitted, Vivian loved being able to immerse herself in nature and just ponder her life and how very blessed she was. If she focused carefully on the sounds of the birds singing from where they were perched in the trees, she could manage to completely ignore the noises coming from the busy London street at the front of the house. And the deeper she went into the gardens, the less she could hear anything except the sounds of nature.

Vivian was surprised one morning after breakfast was over to have Theo ask her quietly if he might join her for a stroll in the garden. "If you prefer to be alone," he said, "I completely understand, but—"

"No, it's fine," she replied in earnest. "I'd love to have you join me."

A short while later they met at the beautiful glass doors that exited the house from one of the parlors onto a lovely patio, which merged into the lawn that formed the perimeter of the complex and delightful gardens. As soon as they were outside, Vivian was surprised when Theo offered his arm, but she put her hand there, reminded of the long strolls they'd once taken through the darkened hallways of the house. A great deal in both of their lives had changed since then. He truly had become a more kind and compassionate person, and she had gotten past her own stubbornness and fear regarding the changes in her life. But it wasn't necessary for them to talk about such things any further; in fact, they had talked about all that a great deal—often with Samuel and Estelle involved in the conversation—and more and more they were able to simply accept that the past had been left in the past.

"Thank you for letting me join you," Theo began as they strolled at an easy pace toward a long corridor of flowering shrubs. "I've noticed you usually come out here about this time of day when the weather is fair, and I've been hoping to speak with you privately. But . . . it's been difficult to know . . . what to say . . . and how to say it, and . . ."

Vivian realized he was sounding nervous, which made *her* nervous. Trying to put him at ease while she attempted to ignore the secret truth of her own feelings, Vivian said, "I hope you know you can tell me anything, Theo. You can trust me."

"I do know that," he said. "In fact, you and I have shared a long journey toward the trust we now share, and I'm grateful for that."

"As am I," she said, proud of herself for keeping a steady voice.

When he descended into silence while they eased farther away from the house, Vivian gathered all her strength to keep her true feelings from showing while she both hoped and feared that he might be trying to admit to similar feelings for her. He'd declared his attraction to her that day in the library when he'd kissed her—an event that now felt like a lifetime ago. But Vivian wondered how his feelings had evolved in the time since. Had he come to realize that what he'd felt had been nothing more than a passing fancy? A brief infatuation? Or was there something deeper he was trying to confess? Or perhaps what he wanted to talk about had nothing at all to do with the relationship they shared. Still, his nervousness and hesitancy to keep talking led her to believe that such a topic was likely on his mind. She couldn't think of anything else that might make him so anxious. She only wished that she weren't feeling so anxious herself.

"Shall we sit down?" he asked, motioning toward a bench beneath an incredibly old, large tree with leafy branches that stretched over them like an umbrella.

Vivian nodded and they sat side-by-side, although Theo turned to face her as much as it was possible.

"I want you to meet my mother and sister," he said, surprising her; this was not what she'd expected him to say. "It's strange that we've come to know each other well—and your grandfather is married to my aunt—and you've not yet even encountered them."

"As a maid in this house, I had strict instructions to avoid them," Vivian reminded him. "I was told they only allowed a few designated maids into their rooms; women they knew well and with whom they are comfortable."

"Yes, that's true," Theo said. "But you now live in this house, and you are now a part of Estelle's family. It only seems right for you to meet them. I will talk to them about it so they're prepared and it won't be upsetting for them. I just . . . want you to meet them. And in truth I think they will like you very much."

"If you want me to—and you go with me—then I'd be delighted to meet them—as long as you're certain it won't upset them."

"I'll talk to them and make arrangements," Theo said with a smile. "I'm certain it will be fine."

Once the matter of his desire for her to meet Dorothea and Lilith had been concluded, he seemed to be collecting himself enough to know what to say next. Vivian just waited patiently, enjoying the ambience and serenity of the gardens in which they were sitting.

"Vivian," he finally said and surprised her by taking her hand. The gesture, combined with the deep intensity she saw in his eyes, provoked her heart to begin pounding as she tried to recall any hints she might have seen regarding Theo's feelings toward her. Then she realized that she needed to focus on the present moment and just hear what he had to say rather than trying to assemble the complicated puzzle that had been pieced together little by little ever since they'd first met at the front gate of the house. "I realize that everything started out between us very badly, and that's entirely my fault."

"We've come far beyond that, Theo. There's no need to bring it up again."

"Please hear me out, Vivian. I *do* need to address it because . . . well . . . I especially need to say once again how deeply sorry I am for the way I behaved that day in the library."

The memory made Vivian's face go hot and she looked down, hoping he wouldn't notice. She'd come to see that encounter very differently in retrospect than she had when she experienced it. Regardless, she still couldn't think about him kissing her without feeling as if she might melt.

"The thing that I need to say," he went on, "is that . . . I handled everything all wrong that day. We hadn't known each other long enough for me to be saying such things to you . . . and kissing you like that . . . and I regret it deeply, except . . . even though I went about expressing my feelings for you in all the wrong ways, you need to know that the feelings I had then have only grown deeper and more sincere with time."

Vivian looked up to check the sincerity in his countenance, not surprised but suddenly elated to see that he meant what he was saying. She felt herself growing more flushed but found it impossible to break away from his gaze as he continued, tightening his hold on her hand. "I've wanted to tell you how I feel for a long time now . . . or rather to clarify how I feel . . . but I didn't want you to think that I was saying such things simply to try and influence you to move into the house—or perhaps I was more afraid that if I told you how I feel, you might *never* move into the house."

He chuckled nervously and looked down for just a moment before his eyes connected with hers again. "But now that you're here . . . and we've come this far . . . I can't hold all this inside any longer." He took a deep breath and drew back his shoulders. "I love you, Vivian. I do. And I hope you can believe that I'm telling you the truth . . . for all the right reasons. I hope you know that you can trust me."

Vivian was finding it so difficult to breathe that she found it impossible to respond, even though she could see vulnerability rising in his expression now that he'd opened his heart to her. He looked down and said somewhat sheepishly, "I want to clarify something . . . even if you might think that we've already talked about it enough, but . . . when I kissed you, my feelings for you were right, but the way I expressed them was all wrong. A kiss shouldn't be so . . . impulsive and . . . well, unexpected. It was entirely unfair to you. A kiss should be . . . tender and . . . the result of mutual respect and affection . . . and much conversation, and . . ." He looked up again and seemed to be summarizing what had apparently weighed on his mind a great deal. "Again, I'm so sorry."

As Vivian looked into his eyes, quickly reviewing everything he'd just said—as well as the evolution of their relationship—she became overcome with tingling, combined with a fluttering in her stomach, combined with the pounding of her heart. In an instant she knew what to do, and what to say, and she didn't care whether it might be considered socially conventional; she only wanted to let Theo know exactly how she felt and where she stood.

Without further analyzing or pondering, Vivian simply reached up with her free hand and touched the side of his face. Only then did she realize just how long she'd wanted to do that. He gasped softly but with relief as his eyes widened expectantly.

"So," she said, feeling mildly mischievous, "as you described it . . . a kiss should be more like . . . this."

Vivian heard him gasp again just before she closed her eyes and gently touched her lips to his, aware of all the tenderness and mutual respect and affection that he had declared should accompany a kiss. She felt *his* hand on *her* face, and his lips softening against hers before she drew back to look into his eyes if only to further gauge his reaction. Given everything he'd said, and what she'd felt in his response, she expected him to appear pleased—which he did—but she wasn't at all prepared to see the sparkle of tears in his eyes. It was much easier than she'd ever anticipated it might be to say to him, "I love you as well, Theodore Weatherby." His eyes widened, and she noticed the slightest quivering of his chin. "I have for so long, but . . . the very idea of encouraging such feelings has just felt . . . ludicrous."

"No, not ludicrous," he replied, a slight tremor in his voice before he kissed her again. He let out a small but delighted laugh as he drew back to look at her, pressing his hand more ardently against her face. She heard him take another deep breath, then he said with firm resolve, "I want to ask your grandfather's permission to court you officially . . . if that's all right with you." He chuckled and added before she could respond, "Samuel and Estelle of all people could never have any concern over what the world might view as differences between us."

Vivian felt herself smile—a smile that felt as if it had overtaken every part of herself. "Yes," she said with ease, "it's perfectly all right with me . . . although I believe you're going to have to help guide me in being able to do what's proper . . . if I'm going to become more a part of your world."

"You are a remarkable lady, Vivian . . . so overflowing with grace and dignity. There's nothing you can learn from me that will make you any more of a lady." He kissed her once more, quickly, then said, "Shall we speak with them now? Your grandfather and my aunt?"

"In a few minutes," she said. "I'd like to just . . . sit here with you a little longer."

"Of course," he said and let go of her hand to put his arm around her shoulders as she relaxed her head against his side. "With any luck," he said, sounding happier than she'd ever heard him sound, "I will be able to convince you to become my wife, and . . ." Vivian lifted her head to look at him, surprised but wondering why she should have been; they'd agreed to court officially, and that was always considered a declaration of intention toward the hope of marriage. Still, to hear him actually tell her he wanted her to be his wife was something she could hardly comprehend. "If I *can* convince you," he went on, "it will be terribly convenient for both of us. Once we're married you won't have to move far—just to the opposite side of the house."

"That *is* convenient," she said, still overcome with an inability to stop smiling, "but why don't we just focus on courting for now. Perhaps as you spend more time with me, you'll decide marriage is not as right for us as we might want to believe."

"Oh, I'm not worried about that," he said and pressed a kiss into her hair from which ripples of tingling spread over her head and down her back. "I don't think there's anything in the world you could say or do that would change my mind."

"I do hope that's the case," she said, resuming her comfortable position, leaning against him, loving the feel of his strong, supporting arm around her, "because I don't believe there's anything that could change *my* mind either."

"About what?"

"About how much I love you," she said, and he tightened his arm around her.

Vivian closed her eyes to listen to the sweet sounds of the birds in the trees and to take in every facet of this experience of sitting here with Theo—and all that had been said between them. It was as if the world had turned upside down and she'd ended up sitting on the very top of it. She'd never been so happy in all her life.

Vivian and Theo talked for a long while about their feelings for each other and their mutual relief to finally have those feelings out in the open so that they could both stop trying to hide them. They talked about their desires for the future and what was tremendously important to each of them in the way they hoped to live their lives—just to be certain that those desires were compatible. And neither were surprised to find that they both very much wanted to have a family, live indefinitely at the Weatherby house, and continue to be involved in helping those less fortunate as much as possible.

They finally returned to the house and went up the back stairs, giggling like children over the prospect of telling Estelle and Samuel about the change in their relationship—although they agreed that his aunt and her grandfather were both very perceptive people, and they wouldn't be at all surprised to hear that their secret feelings had not been nearly as big a secret as they might have believed. Still, Theo was determined to officially seek Samuel's permission to court Vivian, and Vivian felt certain that her grandfather would be nothing but thrilled. He and Theo had grown to care for each other very much, and the situation surely couldn't be more ideal. In fact, Vivian felt such a deep relief to have her feelings in the open—and to know that Theo shared them—that she wished they had been able to talk about this a long time ago. But then, it likely wouldn't have been the right time. She concluded that the steps they'd both taken in their lives since they'd first met had been necessary to prepare them for this moment when they were both finally ready to move forward together.

As they approached the sitting room where Estelle and Samuel were most often found, Vivian felt giddy with excitement. But the peace and joy consuming her slipped away as they entered the open doorway. She immediately felt a hot tension in the room that was completely unfamiliar, and she knew Theo had felt it too since he seemed as frozen at her side as she had become. Estelle and Samuel were seated side-by-side on their favorite sofa as they often were, but Estelle was crying with a handkerchief pressed over her mouth—and from the redness around her eyes it was evident she'd been crying a great deal. Samuel just looked upset; *terribly upset.*

"What's wrong?" Theo demanded just before Vivian managed to ask that exact question.

Estelle only shook her head and pressed the handkerchief more tightly over her mouth, as if to declare that she couldn't speak. Samuel spoke for her, but his voice betrayed a husky tremor. "Theo, your . . . father . . ."

"My father?" Theo asked, understandably confused. Vivian couldn't imagine what about his father might have upset Estelle and Samuel so greatly when the man had been dead for so many years.

Samuel nodded toward the other side of the room. Theo and Vivian both turned in that direction at the same moment to see what Samuel wanted them to see. Vivian saw an impeccably dressed man with graying dark hair and handsome features standing there. She was startled to realize that someone else had been in the room when they'd entered and neither of them had noticed. But it wasn't until she heard Theo gasping for breath that she began to consider the presence of this man as the reason Estelle and Samuel were so upset. Theo sank onto one of the other sofas and Vivian instinctively sat beside him, fearing from his present behavior that he might lose his ability to breathe.

"That's . . . impossible . . ." Theo managed to mutter between heaving breaths.

Only then did Vivian manage to connect everything in her mind that had occurred in the seconds since they had entered the room, and one point stood out strongly. Her grandfather's words echoed over and over through her mind as if that might help her understand. *Your father.*

Theo finally got hold of his senses enough to look at this man directly, muttering in a tone that was both confused and angry, "You're supposed to be dead." The anger in Theo became dominant as he shot to his feet and moved toward the man who was supposedly his long-deceased father, and the man stepped backward, looking as if he feared Theo might do him harm. In truth, Vivian shared this man's concern. But Theo only stood face-to-face with this man, snarling quietly with controlled fury, "How can you have supposedly been dead for half of my life and yet you are suddenly *here*?"

"That's what I asked him," Estelle said, gaining control of her weeping in a way that implied having Theo here to speak on her behalf made it easier to handle the situation. Vivian was simply so shocked by what she was hearing she could only sit silently and observe; she sensed the same was true of her grandfather. But then, this situation had nothing to do with them directly; they were only here to support the people they loved. For a moment Vivian recalled that she and Theo had come here with the intention of declaring their intention to begin courting, but all of that was lost for the moment—and given the enormity of such a thing as a man returning from the dead this way, Vivian wondered how much time might pass before the love that she and Theo had declared for each other could even be acknowledged to their loved ones.

"And?" Theo snapped at his father, motioning abruptly toward Estelle as if to reiterate his need for her support of the all-encompassing question that hovered in the room.

"I was attempting to explain all of that," Theo's father said in a snide voice that irked Vivian on behalf of Theo and Estelle, "when my sister became too upset to hear what I had to say." There was a mildly accusing manner in his words, as if Estelle's emotion had been nothing but an annoyance when she'd just been confronted with her brother coming back from the dead. Vivian found his attitude strange to say the least. A man who had been believed dead for so long would surely return with contrition and humility in his explanations and some compassion for the impact of such a revelation. But there was no hint of any such thing from this man.

"So, explain it *now*!" Theo barked. "We're all listening." Vivian found it ironic that she considered Theo's anger in this situation to be entirely valid, as opposed to times in the past—before he'd put so much effort into changing—when he would become angry over inconsequential things.

Vivian expected this man whom she was trying to accept as Theo's father to embark on the necessary explanation, but he immediately attempted to deflect the attention away from himself by gazing past Theo to look directly at Vivian, saying as if they were at a friendly social event, "And who is this lovely young lady? Will you not introduce us?" Vivian felt a shudder go through her, almost as if this man's attention toward her was accompanied by unsavory intentions. She was glad to have Theo here for a great many reasons.

"She's Samuel's granddaughter," Theo said and motioned toward her with terse impatience. "Vivian Peyton, this is my father, David Weatherby." Theo then turned toward his father with a threatening stance. "Now why don't you sit down and start talking! I think you have a great deal to explain."

David took a seat and crossed his legs with a nonchalance that seemed to silently declare that he had no idea why everyone was so upset—as if his appearance after having been believed dead all these years was a normal occurrence. This was verified when he said, sounding a little miffed, "I thought you'd all be glad to see me."

Theo sat back down next to Vivian, almost collapsing onto the sofa as if he were finding it difficult to maintain his strength, although his voice betrayed no weakness when he said to his father, "I suppose that all depends on the reasons for your absence—and your reasons for coming back now. As I said, you have a great deal to explain."

"Indeed, I do," David said.

"Have you seen Mother and Lilith yet?" Theo asked.

"Oh, goodness no!" David said as if the very idea were terrifying. Vivian could understand his hesitancy—given what she knew of Dorothea and Lilith. But then he said something that made Vivian gasp. "Since I won't be staying long, I didn't see any need to upset them." He sighed as if he were trying extremely hard to remain patient, and Vivian was astonished at how oblivious he was to his own deplorable attitudes. "I sneaked up the back stairs, and I doubt anyone beyond us knows I'm here; it might be better if we kept it that way."

"So . . ." Theo drawled, and Vivian could hear the anger simmering in his voice, "you just appear after all these years like some kind of . . . magician . . . but your intention is to *disappear* just as quickly?"

"I simply felt the need to let you and my sister know that I'm alive and well," David said as if his explanation made perfect sense. "I don't see the need to cause any kind of stir."

"Cause a stir?" Estelle echoed. "Do you think walking into my sitting room after more than fifteen years hasn't caused a stir? You left two children to contend with your untimely death, and a wife who has barely managed to function. And you left *me*! Your *sister*! For all our differences, you should have known how dear you always were to me. How could you just . . . disappear like that . . . for so many years . . . and never even send a letter or—"

"Have you been in prison?" Theo demanded, as if he'd been desperately trying to think of possible reasons for this incomprehensible situation, and that was likely the only thing he'd been able to come up with. "Is that the reason you—"

"No," David chuckled with that same nonchalance that was becoming increasingly annoying. "No, no, no. I haven't been in prison."

"Then what?" Estelle demanded. "I think you'd do well to start at the beginning."

"Very well," David said. "I suppose you all know that my good friend Richard Peyton and I had plans to travel to France to visit with his father-in-law." He chuckled. "Ironic, isn't it?" He motioned toward Estelle and Samuel. "That my sister would end up married to Richard's father." He then motioned to Vivian, "And you must be his daughter, you sweet thing." Again, something about the way he looked at Vivian made her shudder, but she said nothing. "It was our hope to be able to acquire a loan from the man in order to fund a venture we were planning and—"

"A loan?" Samuel questioned, sounding every bit as angry as Theo. "It was my impression from things my daughter-in-law told me that your intentions were far less ethical than asking for a loan. Swindling the man out of a great deal of his fortune was her fear. And just how much did my son approve of this venture?"

"Well, he's dead and gone now," David said as if that fact meant nothing, and Vivian wanted to leap across the room and do him harm. She was grateful for the discreet way that Theo put his hand over hers where it was clutching the edge of the sofa cushion. His touch had a soothing effect, even though she could sense his growing anger as clearly as if she might have known it was going to rain because she heard thunder rumbling outside. "And his wife along with him, may they rest in peace." Vivian squeezed Theo's hand, glad to realize no one had noticed. "Therefore, I suppose that what dear Richard did or didn't do hardly matters anymore."

"It matters to *me*!" Samuel declared with heightened anger.

"No need to get upset, old man," David said with absolutely no respect. "Richard was . . . shall we say . . . easily influenced, and . . . somewhat reluctant about our planned endeavors. But that doesn't mean he wasn't willing to go along."

Vivian heard her grandfather let out a long sigh which she understood completely. Despite learning that her father may have been involved in David's unsavory schemes, just hearing that he was reluctant and easily influenced made his role easier to accept. The outcome was the same, but for some reason just hearing that much information helped Vivian feel better, and she felt certain her grandfather did, as well.

Vivian was relieved to have the attention diverted away from her father when Theo said to David, "We're still waiting to hear some kind of explanation over your supposed death . . . and why you would allow your family to believe you were dead all these years."

"Well, it's really quite simple, my boy," David said as if Theo were a child. "I had originally paid for passage on the same ship to cross the channel with Richard and his wife, but then another matter of business in France came up and I decided to leave earlier. I had already been in France for days when the unfortunate sinking of that ship occurred; lucky for me." He chuckled in a way that completely disregarded the deaths of Vivian's parents, and she had to hold Theo's hand even more tightly to prevent herself from saying or doing something that she would surely regret.

"Yes," Theo said with stark sarcasm, "lucky for you. Not so lucky for your friend and his wife. Bear in mind there are people in this room who loved them; people who have been greatly affected by their absence."

"Oh, yes," David said as if he had truly forgotten. "My condolences." The two words came out as an obligatory comment that held no sincerity whatsoever, and Vivian found it impossible to believe that Theo and Estelle were related to this man. She found it *easier* to understand why Dorothea lived her life as if she'd been perpetually traumatized. If she'd had to endure years of marriage to David Weatherby, it wasn't difficult to have compassion for her. And Lilith had no doubt been traumatized by her father's bad behavior as well. Vivian also wondered if this man was the greatest source of the negative character traits in Theo that he'd worked so hard to overcome. Obviously, there was much that was good in the family. Theo had proven that by the changes he'd made, and Estelle was *nothing* like her brother. Praise heaven!

"So . . ." Theo drawled once again, motioning with his hand in a way that made it clear there were many missing elements to this story. "You made it to France safely . . . and we've not heard a word from you since? Not a single indication that you were alive all this time?"

David sighed and looked toward the window as if he found all this terribly annoying, perhaps even boring, instead of having the slightest inkling how difficult this was for his son and for his sister. "I know it may sound strange to you, and you might not understand, but . . . I'd just become so weary of life here. Dorothea complaining and nagging incessantly. And I'm not ashamed to admit that fatherhood did not suit me well."

"We can agree on that count," Theo said brashly, but Vivian was appalled that a man would admit such a thing—especially to his son.

David ignored his son's comment and continued, "When I realized that my name had been published in the newspapers as one of those who had died when that ship sank, I saw it as an opportunity for a fresh start. After all, my father had already written me out of his will and given everything to my . . ." he motioned toward Estelle and gave her an angry glare, ". . . sister. What kind of a man disowns his own son in that way?"

Vivian was proud of Estelle for the way she stated firmly, "For all his faults, our father had the good sense to see that you would very quickly squander the entire family fortune, and there was only one way to protect it."

"Think what you want, Sister," David said with a cruel smirk, "but the man was an odious cretin. I hated being a part of this family, and I was only too glad to be given such a grand opportunity to create a new life; a life that was much more to my liking. I had the good fortune of making myself useful to a great many affluent people along the way, all of whom were very generous in allowing me to stay in their homes. All in all, it's been a good life."

"And that's it," Theo said, clearly appalled. "You left a wife and children and your sister to believe you were dead . . . to cope with the belief of your death . . . because you found your life here . . . *distasteful*? And I suspect what you really mean by saying that affluent people were generous in allowing you to stay in their homes is that you've been taking advantage of people and manipulating them into providing every possible luxury for you. So that's all you have to say?"

"I suppose that would fairly sum up the situation," David said with a smile that was entirely out of place for the conversation, and appalling given what he'd just admitted to with no apparent remorse whatsoever.

"I see," Theo said, and Vivian could tell that he was fuming inside but trying hard to maintain his composure. "And why . . . now . . . all of a sudden . . . have you come back to grace us with your presence and to finally tell us the truth?"

"I just . . . thought you should know," David said as if boredom might have been his greatest motivation for reconnecting with his family.

"You just thought we should know," Theo repeated. "Well, now that we know, I think you should just sneak right back out of this house, and with any luck we will all be able to forget very quickly the appalling tale you have just told us."

David's casual attitude suddenly disappeared in a way that made Vivian believe his true reasons for coming back—whatever they might be—were being threatened with the prospect of having his son send him away.

"You cannot just kick me out of my own home," David insisted angrily. "And I—"

"This house belongs to Estelle," Theo said. "My grandfather left nothing to you for reasons that are obvious; what makes you think that might have changed?"

David's countenance shifted abruptly into one of contrition as he looked at his sister and said, "Estelle, dearest, I'm certain you can understand that I deserve at least something of all that Father left to you. I—"

"You came back here for money!" Theo declared with angry astonishment. He chuckled with disgust and no trace of humor. "Dare I guess that all of your *friendships* with affluent people have now diminished? Did they all finally figure out that you were nothing but a leech? So now you've come back to your *distasteful* home because you have nowhere else to go? No money to your name? You selfish, despicable—"

Estelle held up a hand toward Theo to stop him as she said to her brother, "Your coming back here now has done nothing but validate the evidence that our father made the right decision. Theo is right. You need to leave. Now."

David's expression then became duplicitous; it was as if he were a human chameleon, capable of immediately changing his attitude to suit his needs. "I could be persuaded to leave quietly with a little incentive. If you don't want my presence here to upset Dorothea and Lilith, perhaps we should simply come to an agreement and—"

"You cannot be serious!" Theo interrupted his father. "Are you truly trying to—"

"Come now, Sister," David continued, interrupting Theo, and remaining focused on his sister, as if he believed Estelle might be more likely to give in to his pleadings. "You have been given such an enormous fortune that you would hardly notice what little I would need to be able to—"

"To what?" Estelle countered. "Keep up a lavish lifestyle that you never earned? You couldn't even maintain any kind of decency and integrity enough to be worthy of an inheritance."

"And that is where you and I disagree," David said with a malicious confidence that left Vivian feeling as if they were all hanging at the edge of a dangerous precipice. She didn't know what this man might be capable of doing to hurt the family she'd come to love—the family she'd come to be a part of. This unexpected appearance from the ghost of David Weatherby had turned everything upside down and backwards, and she felt certain that everyone in the room was at least as confused and concerned as she was. And worst of all, she sensed that for all of David's outward bravado and calculated nonchalance, he was in truth masking desperation. And when a man had such a complete lack of any ethical compass, such desperation made her fear that this was far from over.

Chapter Thirteen
DEAD AGAIN

"I'll come straight to the point," David said.

"I do wish you would," Theo countered with barely controlled anger.

David then looked directly at his sister and said in a voice that was laced with the hint of a threat. "I've spoken with a reputable solicitor and he has assured me that if the case of our father's will were to be taken before a judge, our father's decision would be considered by the law to be something that could have only been made as the result of insanity. He believes that the validity of the will can be overturned easily enough, and our father's inheritance would come to me—as it should have to begin with."

Vivian expected Theo to boldly argue with him, to get hotly angry again. Instead, she felt him squeeze her hand as if it were intended as a signal to remain calm; and at the same time, she saw him nod very discreetly toward Samuel and Estelle who were looking at Theo as if he *should* be the one to speak for them and to solve this problem.

Theo sounded surprisingly calm as he said to his father, "Then I suppose we should all sit down and speak with your solicitor."

"I suppose we should," David said, seeming pleasantly surprised that Theo was being cooperative. Vivian suspected that David believed this was some indication of his threat being taken seriously. But Vivian had a sense that it was more likely that Theo had an idea that had made his father's threats less valid.

"However," Theo said, "from what I know of the judicial system in this city, it could take an exceptionally long time for such a matter to even come before a judge, and then the case could be dragged out for an exceedingly long time."

"I suppose that all depends on the people you know," David said with a smirk and a wink, and Vivian experienced another of those shudders that rushed through her, making her dislike this man more intensely by the minute.

Vivian was surprised when Theo stood up and said, "You can't remain here in the house under the circumstances. I'll call for a carriage and escort you to a fine hotel and make certain you have everything you need, then I'll come for you in the morning, and we can go meet with your solicitor. You let me know the time and I'll be there."

"That sounds reasonable," David said and stood as well. The others remained frozen where they sat, too overcome by all of this to even move. The way that David so easily accepted Theo's offer to provide a hotel room and all that he needed added validity to the fact that he likely had little if any money left to his name and he truly had come here out of desperation. She was also glad—as she believed Estelle and Samuel were—that Theo was insisting that David spend the night elsewhere. The very idea of having him in the house—especially when he couldn't be guarded every minute—was unnerving to say the least.

David said his farewells to Vivian, Estelle, and Samuel as if they'd just enjoyed a pleasant social visit, then Theo escorted him from the room, saying before he left, "I will see all of you very soon. Keep the tea warm." He winked and smiled as if nothing in the world was wrong, and since David had already exited the room, Theo's positive attitude was obviously not meant for his father.

After the two men had left, Vivian heard Estelle beginning to cry again, and she hurried to close the door before she sat next to Estelle on the opposite side from where Samuel was sitting.

Vivian sought to reassure them by saying, "I believe it's evident that Theo feels very calm about what he said at the end of the conversation. We all know he's remarkably clever, and we also know he would do anything to defend what's right and best for this family. I believe we should just do our best to remain calm and let Theo take care of the matter for now."

"I'm certain you're right," Estelle said, "it's all just so . . . upsetting."

"It is indeed!" Vivian said. "I can't even imagine how you must be feeling to see your brother come back from the dead like that!"

"And the way he showed no remorse whatsoever!" Samuel said, clearly angry. "You told me he'd been a difficult man," he added, looking at Estelle, "but I never could have imagined such callousness and arrogance."

"He was always that way for reasons I'll never understand," Estelle said. "People are certainly born with their personalities intact, I suppose. But the man we just spoke to is far worse—and far less subtle—than I ever knew my brother to be. It's evident his years away have only enhanced the worst in him." She then had to wipe away fresh tears.

They talked for a while longer about their feelings on the matter, and Vivian felt certain that just being able to express their emotions over this shocking occurrence was helping them feel calmer; thankfully, it was not having the opposite effect, which was likely because Estelle and Samuel were both rational people, and they *did* trust Theo to know what to do.

When a maid brought tea into the room, Vivian was glad to see that Estelle and Samuel were both able to eat something and enjoy the soothing warm tea, even if their appetites were understandably less than normal. When they had finished, Vivian recalled Theo telling them to keep the tea warm, which was an indication that he should be returning soon. Since the teapot was covered, there was nothing more to be done to keep it warm, although she suspected his request was more about soothing their anxiety rather than his concern about the temperature of his tea.

Vivian was caught up in wondering when he *would* return, when at that very moment he entered the room, and they all breathed a unified sigh of relief.

"Are you all right?" Estelle asked Theo as he closed the door and plopped down on a sofa.

"As well as could be expected," he said, "after having faced my father's ghost."

"Doing so might not have been so difficult," Vivian said, "if his behavior had not been so deplorable."

"Hear, hear," Samuel said with chagrin.

"He's settled for the night, and the servants have instructions to keep the doors locked and monitored; I told Mrs. Thatcher there had been word of some thefts in the area, and we should take some extra precautions. She heartily agreed and told me she would take care of it. Allow me to simply say that I don't believe his threats have nearly as much weight as he thinks they do, and I will take care of the matter in the morning. With any luck, it will all be resolved by tomorrow at this time."

"How is that possible?" Estelle asked, sounding mildly panicked.

"Just . . . let me see what I can do, and we'll decide whether it's necessary to take any further action that's more aggressive. I want to speak with his solicitor and hear his opinion on the matter before giving too much credence to what my father believes to be the case." Theo smiled as if everything were fine, and Vivian wondered if it was sincere or an effort to calm the others. But he declared that he was hungry and helped himself to the food remaining on the tea tray.

When Theo poured himself a cup of tea, Vivian said, "We tried to keep it warm."

"It's perfect," he said, winking at her. "Thank you." He then turned to look at Samuel and surprised Vivian by saying to her grandfather, "There's something I want to talk to you about. Indeed, it was our purpose for coming to find you earlier, and I've decided that I'm not going to let my father's foul behavior intrude upon my own happiness. There's nothing more that can be done about him today, so I think we should just set all of that aside for now and enjoy the remainder of the day as if he'd never been here."

"That might be easier said than done," Estelle said, still clearly unhappy about the appearance of her brother and his atrocious demands.

"If you'll allow me to finish what I have to say," Theo said, winking at Vivian in a way that made her stomach flutter; she knew his intentions now, and she couldn't help being pleased, "then perhaps we all might feel a little more cheerful."

"Very well," Samuel said, now looking at Theo intently, "go on then, son."

Theo took a deep breath, chuckled softly, then sighed before he said to Samuel, "I would like to formally ask your permission for the privilege of courting your granddaughter."

Samuel's eyes widened. Estelle gasped in a way that conveyed nothing but pleasant surprise. Samuel looked at Vivian as if to assess her feelings on the matter, and she could do nothing but smile.

"I knew the two of you had become friends," Samuel said, "and Estelle and I have been nothing but pleased by that fact. But I had no idea that . . ." He looked at his wife. "Did you know that . . ." He didn't finish his sentence, perhaps because what he wanted to ask was so obvious.

"I didn't!" Estelle said and laughed. "And here I've always prided myself on being so perceptive."

"Well, if it's any consolation," Theo said, "I believe that both of us have been trying ridiculously hard to not allow our feelings for each other to show. The truth is that we've both felt . . . drawn to each other for a long time, but . . . I had a great deal of growing up to do to be worthy of such a fine lady, and of course . . . the circumstances have been somewhat strange. We've both made progress, and we've talked about it and agree that this is the proper step to take next." He turned to smile at Vivian and at the same time took hold of her hand. "It's my hope that I can convince her to marry me, but we've agreed to give the matter some time and get to know each other better in order to determine whether that is indeed the right course for both of us."

"Oh my!" Estelle said with a quiver in her voice that indicated she was feeling emotional over this announcement. "Short of marrying Samuel, I don't think anything could make me happier than seeing the two of you together." She pointed a finger at Theo and added, "She is by far the best thing that has ever happened to you, and if you *don't* prove yourself worthy of her, I shall be very cross with you."

"I agree completely, Aunt," he said, "and if I were fool enough to do or say anything unworthy of such a precious lady," he pressed his lips to Vivian's hand while keeping his eyes connected to hers, "then you would be entirely justified in being very cross with me."

"I'm not worried about that," Vivian said, trying not to reveal the tingling effect of his kiss. "Theo has proven time and time again that he has become the finest of men." Vivian stopped herself from adding, *'Unlike his father.'* She didn't want to dampen the mood, especially when everyone now seemed so happy.

"Of course, you have my permission," Samuel said to Theo, "and my blessing. You *are* a fine young man, and I do believe you would do everything in your power to make my dear Vivian happy."

"I will," Theo said with deep sincerity. "Nothing means more to me than Vivian's happiness, I can assure you."

"Well, this is wonderful news," Estelle said, seeming to have completely forgotten about her brother's upsetting visit. She then began to ask Theo and Vivian questions about how their feelings for each other had evolved. They took turns telling pieces of the story, leaving out the episode in the library when he had kissed her and she'd slapped him in return. But they all laughed many times as certain episodes were repeated in detail of how they'd met at the gate of the house, and the many arguments they'd had along the way. And then everything between them had begun to change, and Samuel and Estelle both looked as if they were children listening to a fairy tale as Vivian and Theo talked about how they'd come to enjoy their time together assisting the poor, and the many conversations they'd shared that had led them both to believe they had far more in common than either of them might have once thought.

Their conversation came to a halt when Theo announced that he needed to go speak with Dorothea and Lilith to tell them the good news, and to see when they might be up to meeting Vivian. The idea made Vivian a little nervous, but more than that she genuinely wanted to meet his mother and sister. She wanted to understand their challenges and be a part of their lives. And now that she'd met David Weatherby, she certainly had a great deal more understanding and even compassion regarding those challenges.

Vivian remained in the sitting room to continue her visit with Estelle and Samuel, and Theo returned much more quickly than any of them had expected.

He simply held out a hand toward Vivian and said, "Come along. They would love to meet you and are quite anxious to do so. Now is as good a time as any."

"Very well," Vivian said as she stood and slipped her hand into Theo's, then together they walked out of the room.

Vivian heard Estelle wishing them luck as they hurried away, and a moment later Theo said to her, "I should have done this a long time ago."

"For what purpose?" Vivian asked with a small laugh. "To introduce them to one of the maids?"

"Nothing wrong with that," he said firmly, "considering you were the maid who was also the granddaughter of Estelle's new husband. They've not visited with your grandfather very much, but they've told me they like him and they're happy for Estelle. Why would they not want to know his granddaughter?"

"But now everything has changed," Vivian said, suddenly overcome with nervousness. "Do you think they will like me? Do you think they will be pleased that—"

"Everything will be fine," Theo assured her with a warm chuckle, and the remainder of their brief trek through the house passed in silence.

Vivian took in a deep, sustaining breath when Theo stopped at a door and knocked lightly, after which a woman's voice immediately called for them to come in. Entering the especially lavish sitting room, Vivian wasn't certain what she had expected, but it took only a couple of seconds to absorb the unusual nature of the room and the two ladies seated there. The room itself was tidy but especially cluttered. There were a great many knickknacks and books and trinkets that seemed to fill every available space, as if all the things they loved had been crammed into this room where they spent most of their time, since they rarely left the room to enjoy anything elsewhere.

Dorothea and Lilith themselves were a surprise to Vivian. Dorothea's subtly lined face and the hints of gray in her brown hair were the only indications that she was the older of the two women. Lilith's face was thinner and paler, but beyond that they could almost have been identical twins except for the age difference. They both had delicate, lovely faces with rounded cheeks and perfectly shaped noses and chins. And Vivian could also see a resemblance to Theo. His own attractive face was very much a male version of the beauty of his mother and sister.

Since Vivian understood that these ladies rarely left their rooms—and this sitting room was obviously where they spent most of their time—she might have expected them to be wearing fine dressing gowns, but they were each dressed as if they were about to receive guests in the drawing room, and a skilled lady's maid had clearly styled their hair to perfection earlier in the day.

While Vivian continued to quietly observe this scenario, Theo made introductions, and Vivian was pleased to see both Dorothea and Lilith smiling toward her.

"Do come and sit down," Dorothea said, motioning toward an empty sofa. Looking directly at Vivian, she added, "You must be a fine young lady, indeed, Miss Peyton; Theodore has never brought a lady to meet us before."

"I was beginning to wonder if he ever would," Lilith said, winking at her brother.

As they chatted comfortably, Vivian was fascinated to see evidence of the close relationship Theo shared with his mother and sister, and she was pleasantly surprised by just how kind and amiable they both were. A variety of rumors circulated through the house about these two women, likely because their seclusive nature was great fodder for mystery. But now that Vivian had met them, she knew for herself that they were both the kind of women that Vivian would like to get to know much better, and she felt almost giddy to think that she might very well end up marrying Theo, and Dorothea and Lilith would become family to her.

When Theo stood and announced that they needed to leave so they could get ready for dinner, Dorothea held out a hand toward Vivian as she stood beside him. Vivian stepped forward and took the outstretched hand as Theo's mother said, "Do come and visit often, my dear. You are a precious thing."

"I like her very much, Theo," Lilith said with a genuine smile.

"Well, I like the both of you very much," Vivian said, "and I *will* visit often. I promise. I very much look forward to many grand conversations."

"Excellent," Dorothea said before they all exchanged appropriate farewells and Theo guided Vivian out of the room.

"They're delightful," Vivian said as soon as he'd closed the door.

"Yes, they are," Theo said as they began to walk with some haste so they wouldn't be late in meeting Samuel and Estelle for dinner.

"I've heard many theories about their remaining mostly secluded," Vivian said, "but . . . what is your belief?"

"I believe my mother has a sensitive spirit and she had a difficult upbringing, which was surely damaging. I had always wondered if the way my father treated her only enhanced that problem, and now I know that to be true. I hope and pray my mother and sister never find out he's alive and—"

"Let's not talk about him right now," Vivian said as they continued to walk.

"Therefore, my mother just feels more comfortable and . . . perhaps safe . . . by staying in. Although she goes out more than people realize. They both enjoy an excursion to town now and then, even though they rarely get out of the carriage. It doesn't happen very often, but still . . . more than people are aware because they're careful about going in and out of the house discreetly."

"And Lilith?" Vivian asked. "What is the situation with her?"

"It's true that her health has always been fragile, and when she exerts the energy to go out, she's especially tired for days afterward. The cause is a mystery, but we've all become accustomed to the fact that she will not likely live a long life, although she's happy and content."

"I like them very much," Vivian said, saddened to hear this fact about Lilith.

"And it's evident they like you," Theo said, smiling toward her. "With any luck we'll all be family . . . the sooner the better, in my opinion."

"With any luck," Vivian said and laughed.

They went their separate ways to freshen up before meeting again in the dining room where Samuel and Estelle had just arrived. Vivian was pleased and relieved that the conversation during their meal was relaxed and comfortable—as it always was—and that if any of them were thinking about the unexpected appearance of David Weatherby, they weren't willing to talk about it and dampen the mood. Whatever his despicable actions might bring about had yet to be seen, but for now, they were all content to just be together as a family, and Vivian was surprisingly comfortable with the idea of living in this house as Theo's wife. In fact, she couldn't think of anything that would make her happier. Not only would she become the wife of a wonderful man, but she would also gain a grandmother, a mother, and a sister. The very idea of becoming part of this family left her practically giddy.

Later that evening, Theo walked Vivian to her room and took hold of both of her hands after he'd set down the lamp he'd been carrying. She was glad to be able to see his face in the glow of the lamp, especially when the love he felt for her was so evident.

"I don't want to even bring it up," Theo said, "given that we have so much to be happy about, but . . . I was hoping you would go with me in the morning. I don't want Samuel and Estelle to come; they don't need to see him again, and I can handle this situation, but . . . I just think I will feel more . . . confident . . .

if you're with me. Nevertheless, if you don't *want* to go, I wouldn't blame you, and—"

"Of course, I'll come with you," she interrupted in a firm voice. "If you want me there or . . . need me there . . . or both . . . you need only ask. I'll be there by your side." She gave a quick nod to add emphasis to her promise. Besides, being able to go with him would spare him from having to tell her everything that happened. She couldn't help being curious over how all this would unfold.

"Thank you," he said, then chuckled. "Perhaps I need you there to make certain I don't do something deplorable like . . . break his nose or . . ."

"I seriously doubt you would descend to such behavior," Vivian said, "although I can't blame you for wanting to. Still, I'll be certain to keep a close eye on you and make certain you behave yourself." She said the last in a teasing tone and he let out a small laugh before he kissed her. Vivian was surprised by how quickly his kiss had come to feel so natural and comfortable, but she was also surprised by how it was every bit as exciting as it had been when he'd kissed her earlier in the gardens.

"I should say goodnight," he whispered close to her lips, "but I don't want to."

"Nor do I," she said, and he kissed her again. "Nevertheless, I know well enough that you are a gentleman and therefore . . ."

"I will say goodnight." He laughed softly once more, kissed her quickly, and hurried away, saying over his shoulder. "I will meet you in the foyer as soon as we've finished breakfast."

"I'll be there," she promised and watched him disappear, marveling at how this day had brought about such dramatic changes in their lives. Their declarations of love had made her happier than she'd believed possible. And meeting his mother and sister had added to her happiness. The appearance of his supposedly dead father made her almost seethe with anger just to think of it. She knew her emotions were shared by the only other three people who were aware of both situations. She only hoped that tomorrow would bring about some hope that they could find a way around David's threats, and that he wouldn't become a persistent thorn in all their sides.

Vivian met Theo in the foyer at the appointed time, so glad to see him she found it difficult to not shout for joy—something that would surely cause a stir in the household. They had all eaten breakfast in their respective sitting rooms, so Vivian hadn't yet seen Theo today, but she was glad that neither of them had seen her grandfather and Estelle, certain they would both be concerned and likely full of questions that Theo couldn't yet answer. It was better that she and Theo could sneak away. They could all talk later—hopefully after progress had been made, or at the very least after they'd gathered some information on the situation that might help them be better prepared to contend with David's deplorable motives.

"Shall we?" he asked with a smile while holding out his arm for her to take. She credited the smile to his pleasure at seeing her, which warmed her heart; she couldn't think of any reason why he would be in a good mood regarding the situation they were about to face with his father.

After they were comfortable in the carriage, sitting side by side, Theo surprised Vivian with a tender kiss. "I've been thinking about this moment since I woke up this morning," he said, "when we could be alone without anyone observing." He kissed her again, then eased away and took hold of her hand.

"I thought you would be a great deal more . . . nervous . . . or upset," Vivian pointed out at the risk of souring the mood between them.

"I confess that I have a bit of a plan that I believe will allow us to be rid of my father for good," he said, "and I made some arrangements late last evening. With any luck, it will all come together in the way I'm hoping."

"Will you let me in on your secret?" she asked.

"I would be happy to," he said as the carriage rolled to a stop, "but we're here."

Vivian glanced out the window and stated the obvious, "This is not a hotel, Theo. I thought we were meeting your father and—"

"We *will* collect my father from the hotel soon enough, but I allowed plenty of time to first collect my solicitor. I would never be foolish enough to meet with anyone over any legal matter without having my solicitor there to represent my best interests and those of my family." Theo stepped out of the carriage, then held out his hand to help Vivian step down. "There is one brief matter of business we need to take care of here, and I want you to not only be aware of it but to witness it."

"Very well," she said, both intrigued and somewhat anxious as she went with him into an office with a bell above the door that reminded her of the cobbler's shop. The room in which they stood was tidy but so filled with stacks of papers that Vivian couldn't imagine how anyone could ever keep track of what was where.

A man appeared through the door from another room and greeted them with a quick smile. He was a silver-haired gentleman of average build who wore spectacles through which he seemed to be trying to avoid looking directly at Vivian.

Theo motioned toward this man and said, "Mr. Barder, allow me to introduce Miss Vivian Peyton. Miss Peyton, this is the solicitor who has assisted my family for a great many years, Mr. Barder."

"A pleasure to meet you," Vivian said.

"And you," the man replied, still not looking at her directly in a way that let Vivian know he was terribly shy. "You're the granddaughter of Samuel Peyton," he said with a confidence that seemed a contradiction to his difficulty in interacting with her.

"Yes, I am," Vivian said.

"A fine man," Mr. Barder said. "Do you have the papers?" he then asked Theo with a self-assurance that belied his apparent shyness; but then he knew Theo well since they worked together regularly.

"I do," Theo said, and only then did Vivian notice that Theo had been carrying a leather bag which he now set on the desk and from which he drew out a couple of sheets of paper.

"Very good," Mr. Barder said and laid the papers down to examine them carefully, adjusting his spectacles as he did so. "It appears that everything is in order to proceed."

"What is happening?" Vivian asked Theo quietly.

"May I?" Theo asked Mr. Barder, who nodded.

Theo picked up a piece of paper and showed it to Vivian while he explained, "Mr. Barder came to our home at my request late last night and we spoke with Estelle and your grandfather. Samuel was hesitant to go along with my plan, but Estelle and I were eventually able to convince him that it was not only necessary, but it was also the right thing to do. This," Theo held the paper closer to Vivian's face, "is a document that is signed and witnessed, stating that your grandfather's earlier decision to waive his rights to Estelle's fortune are now null and void."

"What?" Vivian asked, sounding as astonished as she felt. "Was this your idea, Theo?"

"It was, indeed, Miss," Mr. Barder said, "and an excellent idea at that. Your grandfather is a good man, and this will protect the family's assets."

"And now that we have both copies of the original document here," Theo went on, motioning toward two identical papers on the desk which Vivian now realized were the documents her grandfather had signed to relinquish all his legal rights to Estelle's fortune, "we can do away with them and no one will be the wiser. The document your grandfather signed to undo what was done is simply a formality for Mr. Barder to know that he is taking this action legally, and it will no longer be needed. Whatever anyone may or may not have known will have no proof with the absence of the documents. And my father will have absolutely no rights to anything."

"Shall we?" Mr. Barder asked, mildly impatient. "We mustn't be late."

"Of course," Theo said while Vivian was filled with questions but realizing they would have to wait. She then gasped when Mr. Barder tossed all three documents into the fire, which she had just now noticed was burning in a heating stove in the corner of the room.

"Oh my!" Vivian said, watching them disintegrate into ashes. A moment later they were all walking back to the carriage while Vivian tried to comprehend what this meant. She knew the money meant nothing to her grandfather, and she also knew that Estelle trusted him completely; and gradually Theo had come to trust him. If Vivian had felt any reason to doubt being able to trust Theo, it had all vanished when those documents had been tossed into the fire.

Once in the carriage, with Theo and Vivian sitting across from Mr. Barder, a stark silence descended, but that only gave Vivian time to contemplate this strange situation. There were many questions she wanted to ask, but before Vivian could think of anything else to say, the carriage halted again, and Vivian had to remind herself that the distance between locations in this part of the city were minimal when walking was not required.

"I will get my father and be right back," Theo informed Vivian; Mr. Barder already seemed to know what was taking place. It was then she noticed that the solicitor was holding tightly to a leather bag as if it contained great valuables.

Vivian made a couple of attempts at conversation with the solicitor, then gave up when he barely answered her questions and seemed uncomfortable doing so. They waited together in the carriage in tense silence far longer than she would have liked, even though she suspected it wasn't as long as it felt.

When Theo stepped into the carriage, Vivian was relieved to have him sit beside her, especially knowing that his father would be joining them, and she certainly didn't want to sit next to *him*. When David stepped into the carriage, he immediately looked surprised by the presence of another man he didn't recognize.

"And who is this?" David asked, sitting down reluctantly next to Mr. Barder.

"Our solicitor," Theo stated. "Did you really believe we would conduct such a meeting regarding the family's financial situation without having legal representation?"

David didn't answer the question, but he was clearly displeased by it. As the carriage moved forward again, Vivian felt David's eyes on her and decided she absolutely hated the way he looked at her, even if she couldn't exactly define what his gaze might be implying. As if they were lifelong friends, he said, "Good morning, my dear. How lovely you look!"

"Please do not refer to me as *my dear*," she stated firmly but without any of the petulance she felt. "There is no source of endearment between us, Mr. Weatherby, I can assure you. If you must address me, Miss Peyton is sufficient."

David looked at his son and said with subtle snideness, "She's a little too impudent and should mind her place, don't you think? Especially given the fact that's she's nothing more than a cobbler's daughter."

Vivian bristled from the sting of his words but fought to keep her expression steady. She was deeply grateful for Theo's response when he said with a tinge of anger in his voice, "Her impudence is exactly perfect when addressing someone who has shown no respect whatsoever to her or the people she loves. And whatever her origins might have been, she is the finest lady I have ever known, and you will address her properly or not at all. If you had any idea whatsoever of how sincerely kind and gracious Miss Peyton is, you would realize how deeply she dislikes you. But then, I dislike you as well."

David shifted in his seat and folded his arms tightly over his chest as if they might protect him from Theo's sizzling words. "Lucky for you, as soon as our business is concluded, I will be gone, and we won't be required to engage in such unpleasant conversation."

"Is your plan not to take over the entire estate?" Theo asked, feigning ignorance. "If that is the case, will you not be staying? Becoming a part of the family again?" He paused long enough for David to respond but he didn't, so Theo continued. "But of course . . . your plan is to get as much money as you possibly can so you will be able to disappear from our lives once again; dead again to us, no matter how that might affect anyone else."

Still David didn't speak, but Vivian could see from his expressions that this was *exactly* what he intended to do. Vivian hoped to never see this man again, and she felt certain Theo—and Estelle and Samuel too—felt the same way. Still, it had to be heartbreaking at some level for Theo to realize that his father would put his own selfish interests above wanting to be a part of the family.

The carriage stopped, and Theo announced, "We have arrived at your solicitor's office according to your instructions."

"Excellent," David said and was the first one to step out of the carriage once it had stopped and the door was opened.

Theo stepped out and helped Vivian do the same, with Mr. Barder following directly behind them as they all entered the office of David's solicitor. Vivian immediately noticed a dramatic difference between this office and that of Mr. Barder. There was no order whatsoever; it was anything but tidy, and in fact it was rather dusty and had a strange odor as if many meals had been eaten in this room but never quite cleaned up properly.

David introduced them to the very bald and very rotund Mr. Jenk who occupied the office, and Vivian did her best to remain mostly behind Theo while this exchange took place. She was glad that Theo had asked her to come along; she was glad to know what was taking place. But she didn't like the way Mr. Jenk looked at her any more than she liked the way David did. She would be glad to have all this over and done with and be away from these despicable men.

Theo and Mr. Barder remained completely silent while Mr. Jenk sat behind his desk and gave a long and odious speech about the rights that David had to his father's fortune, and how the will could easily enough be disputed because as Mr. Jenk put it, "No woman is considered worthy enough to inherit such a fortune when there is a living male relative; it's simply not done." This bristled Vivian even further, but she bit her lip to remain silent, only too glad to let Theo handle all of this, and so grateful to know that he was a good man who could be trusted.

Mr. Jenk rambled on for several more minutes, often repeating himself as if doing so might help drive home the point that David Weatherby should be entitled to *everything* his father had left behind, the implication being that the remainder of the family would be reduced to abject poverty.

When Mr. Jenk *finally* stopped talking, Mr. Barder spoke in a voice that completely dispelled any prior evidence of shyness; it became evident to Vivian that the solicitor was brimming with confidence when it came to matters of business. "Are you finished, Mr. Jenk?"

"For the moment," Mr. Jenk said, as if he wanted to make certain an opening was left for him to speak again should he feel the need.

"There is a legal element in place here," Mr. Barder began, "which I believe you have both completely overlooked. Estelle Weatherby is no longer in possession of anything that she inherited from her father, simply because she is no longer Estelle Weatherby. Mrs. *Peyton* relinquished her every financial asset to her husband when they were married—according to the law."

Vivian noticed that David looked disarmed just before he glared at Mr. Jenk as if the solicitor should have known this—which he certainly *should* have. Or perhaps David had failed to tell his solicitor that Estelle had gained a husband.

"It doesn't matter!" David insisted. "My sister inherited everything many years ago and—"

"I'm afraid it *does* matter," Mr. Jenk said to his client with an expression that betrayed his own dislike of David Weatherby. "I agreed to take on a complicated and risky case with some reluctance, and now it has become even more complicated. The time I would have to devote to this case—the court appearances and the paperwork—are simply not practical for me. And I know well enough you do not have the money to pay me. Our agreement was that I would take a percentage of your inheritance for my efforts, but that clearly is not going to happen."

David leaned over Mr. Jenk's desk and snarled, "You agreed to represent me. You cannot just—"

"Perhaps," Mr. Barder said, "we have a solution to the problem that will be beneficial to all of us."

"I would very much like to hear that," Mr. Jenk said.

"I have here," Mr. Barder said, reaching into his leather bag to pull out a couple of pieces of paper as if he were a magician, and he set one of them down on the desk in front of Mr. Jenk, "a banknote for an exceptionally large sum that Mr. Peyton has authorized to pay Mr. David Weatherby as a gesture of good faith. The amount has been determined in relation to the standard allowance that has been paid to other family members in the past, and estimated over the years of Mr. Weatherby's absence, and allowing for some years into the future."

Vivian noticed David staring at the banknote as if it were a great feast and he was starving; she could practically see him salivating. But his expression darkened as Mr. Barder went on.

"We will gladly give Mr. David Weatherby this banknote on the condition that he sign *this* document, which will be witnessed and made legal and binding."

"What is *this*?" David demanded and grabbed it before Mr. Barder could place it on the desk.

"You're welcome to read it before you sign it," Mr. Barder said, remaining completely calm, "nevertheless, allow me to explain. It states that upon your acceptance of the money, you will not contact any member of the family ever again. If you make yourself known to any one of them, you will be in violation of our agreement. You will not be allowed to step foot in the house or even upon the grounds. Given our knowledge of your past indiscretions with the law, I believe your adherence to this agreement would be in your best interest."

"In other words, Father," Theo said, "you made the decision years ago to make yourself dead to this family, and you will remain that way. You have been dead to us for years, and you will now be dead again. You will disappear and never be heard of again by any of us. And if you do *anything* to compromise this agreement, you will sorely regret it. Legal action will be taken against you, and all your past crimes will come to light in a very public manner."

"Your son is correct," Mr. Barder said. "If you do anything to go against what you are agreeing to in order to receive this generous gift from your brother-in-law, I will use every legal connection I have in this city to bring down the full measure of the law for any and every crime you have ever committed. And trust me when I tell you that I have *many* connections, and you would not do well with the results."

"You're threatening me!" David said, as if he were somehow being victimized.

"Yes, I am," Mr. Barder said without flinching. Mr. Jenk offered David a glare much like Mr. Barder's; without saying anything, it seemed he had changed his allegiance and would now stand behind Mr. Barder's threat.

"I advise you to sign the document and take the money," Mr. Jenk said, setting his hands complacently on top of his rounded belly. "You will never get any better outcome than this under the circumstances, and I will expect a reasonable fee for my efforts on your behalf."

David made a harsh growling noise before he cursed and grabbed the paper, signing it with petulance oozing from his aura. He grabbed the banknote from Mr. Barder's hand and attempted to leave the office, but Mr. Jenk grabbed the banknote and held it out of David's reach. "Come back in an hour and we will go to the bank together so that I can collect my fee." David grumbled under his breath again and left the office as if a wild beast might be trying to devour him.

"Well," Mr. Barder said, "there's all that taken care of."

"It shouldn't have been that easy," Vivian said, overcome with disbelief.

"Oh," Mr. Jenk drawled, "when it comes to dealing with a certain sort, you just have to know how to get them out the door. I commend you for your excellent plan, gentlemen." He nodded toward Theo and Mr. Barder. Then he nodded politely toward Vivian. "A pleasure, Miss. And I wish you all a good day."

"And to you," Mr. Barder said at the same time that Theo said, "Thank you," and they all hurried out of Mr. Jenk's office and into the waiting carriage.

"Is there anything else I can do for you, Mr. Weatherby?" Mr. Barder asked while the carriage moved toward the solicitor's office. Vivian noticed him tucking into his case the newly signed document that was a great threat to David Weatherby, and she felt certain he would keep it safe.

"Not at the moment," Theo said. "I thank you for your extra efforts with this, and for your excellent advice."

"Glad to be of assistance, as always," Mr. Barder said, smiling at Theo just before the carriage halted and the solicitor exited after polite farewells were exchanged.

"Well," Theo drawled and exhaled a long, loud sigh, "there's all that taken care of."

It took Vivian a moment to realize he was imitating Mr. Jenk, then they both laughed and shared an awkward embrace sitting next to each other in the carriage.

"Do you think he's really gone for good?" Vivian asked.

"I really do," Theo said. "Mr. Barder was not making idle threats, and I believe my father is likely guilty of far more criminal activity than we could ever imagine." Theo shook his head with disbelief, and Vivian could sense his sorrow and disappointment. "Now we only need to try and forget any of this ever happened and go forward with our lives. He's been dead to us for years; the adjustment shouldn't be too difficult."

When they returned to the house and went straight to the sitting room where they commonly found Samuel and Estelle, their bright moods reiterated what Theo had said. They had already known about the plan to make certain David never bothered anyone in the family ever again, and they were nothing but glad to hear how well it had gone. There was a moment of sadness as they discussed the sorrow David had brought into both of their families, and Theo profusely apologized for anything he'd said in the past to put the blame on Vivian's father for all that had happened.

"Clearly I was very wrong in my thinking," Theo said, "and even though I'd accepted that we simply didn't know what had happened and it didn't matter, now we *do* know, and I feel like such a fool to think of what I'd believed and how I behaved."

"It's all in the past," Samuel assured him with compassion. "You were young and what happened was difficult."

"I'm simply glad that it's over and behind us—for good this time." Estelle's positive attitude was infectious, and they were soon visiting comfortably about delightfully trivial things, which made the events regarding Theo's father feel like nothing more than a bad dream. But Vivian put all of that out of her head and reminded herself that she'd also been blessed with an incredibly good dream that she'd hardly had a chance to enjoy. She and Theo were officially courting and they both felt confident that marriage was inevitable. Nothing could be more wonderful than the prospect of sharing her life with him, especially when they would both be able to share their lives with Samuel and Estelle, as well as Dorothea and Lilith. The laughter that suddenly filled the room only accentuated her happiness, and she felt certain all would be well.

Epilogue

Vivian shared lunch with the staff in the servants' hall as she did two or three times a week. She enjoyed the conversation and laughter and this group of friends who always made her feel as if she belonged and that they genuinely cared about her; and there was absolutely no sense of feeling that she was caught between two worlds. In fact, over time, she'd been able to fit perfectly into every facet of living at the Weatherby house.

After lunch, Vivian took advantage of a perfectly lovely summer day to walk a short distance to where a cluster of shops were located so she could simply enjoy looking over the wares available, visit with the proprietors, and purchase a few little things. As she walked at a leisurely pace toward home, her mind took her back to when she had been living with her grandfather in the little house behind the cobbler's shop, and how happy they had been together. In fact, she'd always been happy there—although there was no denying the strain that had weighed upon them when Samuel's health had failed and subsequently their financial situation had become difficult. Vivian felt deeply blessed to know that her grandfather's health was as good as it could possibly be for a man his age; and in fact, sometimes she found it difficult to keep up with him. She was also grateful for the embrace of generosity Estelle had provided, which had eliminated their financial woes. Vivian understood that most people were not so fortunate, but she and Theo were spending many hours every week doing all they could to help such people. Not only was she glad to not feel idle in how she spent her time, but the gratification of being able to make a difference—and to share the experience with Theo—made her genuinely happy.

As Vivian approached the grand Weatherby house that had comfortably become her home, she saw a man approaching from the opposite direction and smiled when she realized it was Theo. They shared a loving gaze as they approached each other slowly, meeting directly in front of the gate.

"Well, hello, Mr. Weatherby," Vivian said with a small laugh. "How lovely to see you."

"Good afternoon, Mrs. Weatherby," he replied and laughed as well, as if he found joy in simply being able to call her that, even though they'd been married for several months. "Did you enjoy your little excursion?"

"Very much, thank you," she said with a mock formality that made him laugh again. "And you?"

"Yes, indeed," he replied. "There's nothing like a brisk walk."

"So you tell me," she said, "although we've established that you enjoy walking a little too briskly for me. I prefer an unhurried stroll."

"How very incompatible we are," he said with light sarcasm and a teasing wink.

"Only when it comes to how we enjoy our walks," she declared. "I daresay we could make a very long list of activities in which we *are* compatible."

"Indeed, we could," he said with a hint of mischief that made her laugh.

"So," she drawled while she looked around herself, then back at him, "this is the exact spot where we first met."

"I was just thinking the same thing," Theo said. "Our conversation that day was not nearly so cordial."

"Only because you were rude and dismissive," she stated.

"So I was," he agreed and chuckled. More seriously he added as he took her hand into his, "What would we have thought then if we could have looked into the future to see ourselves now?"

"Neither of us would have believed it to be possible," she observed.

"Well, then," he said and bent over to kiss her quickly, "it's a good thing that we both believe nothing is impossible if you work hard enough at it."

"How very compatible we are on that count," she replied, and he smiled just before he placed his hand over her well-rounded belly; the baby was due to arrive in the early autumn. After he kissed her again while keeping his hand on her belly, Vivian said with mild scolding, "We mustn't do such things out here on the street where everyone can see. It's scandalous."

"My dear Mrs. Weatherby," he said, "I'm absolutely certain that everyone who knows us—or even those who do not—are well aware from simply looking at us that the relationship we share is definitely scandalous." He kissed her again and added, "Oh, but wait. We're married, so it's not, is it!"

"Well said." She smiled up at him. "But why don't we go inside anyway. After my walk I am thinking that I need you to rub my feet. That *is* an obligation you agreed to in order to help me get through this pregnancy."

"I did, indeed," he said as if nothing in the world would give him more pleasure than easing the ache in her feet. "After you, my lady," he said, opening the gate, and together they went into the house.

About the Author

Anita Stansfield has more than seventy published books and is the recipient of many awards, including two Lifetime Achievement Awards. Her books go far beyond being enjoyable, memorable stories. Anita resonates particularly well with a broad range of devoted readers because of her sensitive and insightful examination of contemporary issues that are faced by many of those readers, even when her venue is a historical romance. Readers come away from her compelling stories equipped with new ideas about how to enrich their own lives, regardless of their circumstances.

Anita was born and raised in Provo, Utah. She is the mother of five and has a growing number of grandchildren. She also writes for the general trade market under the name Elizabeth D. Michaels.

For more information and a complete list of her publications, go to anitastansfield.blogspot.com or anitastansfield.com. You can also follow her on Facebook, Instagram, and Twitter.